The Forever Pact

Jaimie Casey

To my mum in heaven, I miss you.

Blurb

The Forever Pact

A Sweet Romantic Comedy

Welcome to Paradise Valley, Montana
Population ~~500~~ 501

Blurb

What's that saying? What can go wrong will go wrong?
I think that should be the saying for my life.

I'm Pippa Chase. I was about to become Pippa Snothead, but then my fiancé cheated on me, and I called off the wedding... I'm heartbroken, but at least I avoided a horrible last name.

And now, I'm on my way to Paradise Valley, Montana, to lick my wounds and figure out what's next in my life. I'm going to live with my childhood best friend, TJ Wyatt, on a ranch he bought. Ever since we were young, we had a pact that if one of us needed the other, we would be there for each other.

Granted, TJ and I haven't seen each other since we were thirteen, and we stopped our barrage of letters and emails when we were eighteen. However, we still send Christmas cards yearly, and in one of them, he did say, "If you're ever in this part of the country, drop in." I don't think he meant it as literally as I took it.

So, that's how I ended up living on a remote ranch, in a log cabin with a man who didn't seem quite as happy to see me as I thought he would be. But maybe it didn't help that I showed up in my wedding dress, and everyone in town thought I was his new bride. Oops!

This may not have been my best decision, but I'm hoping that Paradise Valley can help to mend my broken heart.

Prologue

Pippa

"We're going to go to Shakespeare in the Park tomorrow night, right?" I prodded my best friend, Emma, as she looked around the room for something to eat. "They're going to perform *Hamlet*." I sipped on my bubbly glass of champagne as I stood there, feeling dreadfully out of place at Emma's work event.

"Yeah, I'll come." Emma nodded, her light-blue eyes thoughtful as she gazed at me. "It's just going to be us, right?" She gave me her innocent "this question doesn't mean anything" look, but we both knew her question was loaded. If I told her Stephan, my fiancé, was coming, I knew she'd drop out of the event faster than a cat drops out of a dog race.

"Yes, but would it really be so bad if—"

"This is a perk of my job that I don't hate." Emma changed the subject quickly as she grabbed a handful of salmon and caviar blinis from a passing waiter. She held up her small white real-china plate to me, and I shook my head, declining her offer to share the expensive appetizer. I wasn't into caviar, and even though I did like to think I appreciated the finer things in life, I couldn't get past knowing where it came from. My mom would be ashamed of me if she knew I was passing up anything that expensive that was free.

"Hmm." The groan coming from Emma's mouth was loud and inappropriate to be heard in company. I suppressed a giggle as I noticed two younger, nerdy-looking guys next to us watching her in befuddled amazement as she took her first blissful bite. "This tastes like heaven on earth," she exclaimed, happy for a few moments.

"Aren't you supposed to be overseeing the event instead of eating?" I teased her as I gazed around the crowded room. We were in a large conference room at the Hilton in Midtown. There were large red-and-blue signs saying, "Do You Live To Code or Code To Live?" everywhere on the crisp white walls, and I'd never felt more out of place.

We were surrounded by hundreds of tech nerds, most male, younger than me, and wearing cartoonish T-shirts. "Why didn't you tell me everyone would be dressed so casually?" I asked her, frowning as I gazed down at my black designer dress pants and cream silk shirt. My long dark hair hung straight down my back due to the two hours I'd spent blow-drying and flat-ironing out my curls. I stared at my reflection in the glass champagne flute, my brown eyes staring back at me in bemusement. I noted that my eye makeup was still on point. The green glitter eyeshadow matched the green necklace I was wearing. And my red lipstick made my entire face pop. I knew that my presentation was pretty hot and sophisticated (save for the lemon-lime earrings I'd bought on a whim).

All in all, I was dressed to impress, even though it wasn't like I was trying to impress anyone. I wasn't interested in finding a job in tech (not that they would want me; I knew zero code), and I was semi happily engaged, so I wasn't searching for a man. I also hadn't realized that I was going to end up resembling a strict teacher in a class full of first-year students. I was starting to wish I'd told Emma I wasn't going to be able to attend the event.

"Only the software engineers dress like bums." Emma looked around distastefully. "The execs dress up. And, of course, I have to dress up as well." She bit down into her second blini and licked her lips to ensure she didn't waste any of the expensive black unfertilized eggs (the way I thought of the expensive treat). Her face was almost child-like as she concentrated on the food and not her job.

I'd only attended the event because Emma had asked me. I'd wanted to go and check out an off-Broadway show that a former classmate had written called *Lemon Meringue Pie For Dinner*. It didn't sound like the sort of show I would love, but I was pleased that my friend had been able to put on her own show. Something I could only dream about.

"I still don't feel like I fit in here," Emma whispered, and I could hear the nervousness in her tone. Emma was normally confident about her job, but she felt like the men didn't take her seriously in this role. She'd even changed her hairstyle into a blunt blond bob because it made her look stricter and meaner than she was.

I thought she resembled a middle-aged librarian giving you a stink eye and relishing telling you to be quiet. Emma stated that was the persona she needed to make it in corporate America. As the pretty marketing VP for a tech company full of men, she said she needed to exude power and strength. I didn't think the bob was doing any of that for her, but I knew better than to tell her what I thought of the hairstyle. That didn't mean I wouldn't support her at a work event. At least for a few hours, then I was going to surprise Stephan.

Stephan would be pleased to see me dressed so professionally. He complained that I dressed like a hippie flower child with my long skirts and colorful tops.

Normally, I portrayed a very different image to the world with my wild, long, dark-brown hair that even hair stylists found hard to tame. The sprinkling of freckles across my nose and cheeks and wide brown eyes made me look much younger than I was and full of mischief, which I didn't mind, seeing as I loved to have new adventures; I was goofy as a teen, and I was pretty sure my mom was even more thankful that I grew out of that stage.

Many people were surprised that Emma and I were best friends, seeing as we appeared to be such opposites, but we balanced each other well.

"I have to leave in an hour." I glanced down at the time on my phone to make sure I wouldn't be late. "It's the anniversary of my and Stephan's first date, and I'm going to pick up a pizza and surprise him with it."

"Lucky him." Emma took another long gulp of her champagne to stop herself from saying anything else. Which I was grateful for. Emma hated Stephan and had almost started crying when I'd told her about our engagement nine months ago. "Hopefully, he has a present waiting for you as well." She gave me one of her "we both know he doesn't" glances and I ignored her. I'd made the mistake of telling her that he hadn't ever gotten me a birthday present, and he didn't believe in Christmas gifts, so nothing ever came then, either. It was disappointing, seeing as I loved presents, but he said that wasn't his love language.

Emma and I had been best friends and roommates since freshman year at college, and while I wished she got on with Stephan, I understood why he wasn't her favorite person. He was one of those men who initially rubbed people the wrong way with his upper-middle-class, private and Ivy League–educated upbringing. However, I felt that he was much easier to love when you got to know him—most of the time.

I stared at the sparkling two-carat diamond engagement ring on my hand and reminded myself that I was excited about marrying him. My mom loved him. In fact, sometimes I thought she adored him as more than just the man in my life. She certainly seemed to like him more than she did me. I ignored the gnawing feeling at the pit of my stomach as I imagined spending the rest of my life with him.

"Is there anything you need to do?" I asked, surveying the room of men. "Do you need to actively recruit any of them to the company?" I wasn't exactly sure what Emma was supposed to do in her role, only that I was there to support her. "Or do you see anyone you want to date?"

"Not interested in dating any tech bros, thank you very much," she said in a low voice. "Just like I'm not interested in dating anyone that works in banking." That was a low blow! She knew Stephan worked on Wall Street. I was going to say that everyone who worked in finance wasn't horrible, but when I thought about Stephan's work friends and how they thought they owned the world, I decided to keep quiet.

"But you are interested in dating someone?" I asked

gleefully. Emma's last relationship had ended badly, and she hadn't gone on a date in over a year.

"Maybe." She wrinkled her nose and fluffed her blond bob. Her blue eyes crinkled in the corners as she took in my eager face. "Do not try setting me up with any of Stephan's friends. Or signing me up for a dating app."

"Would I do such a thing?" I pouted and took another sip of my champagne. "I fully trust that Mr. Right will come along when it's the right time," I added so she wouldn't feel discouraged.

"Yeah, I feel the same way for you," she said softly, and I ignored her dig. "Ugh, my boss is calling me to come over." She nodded to the corner of the room, and my eyes widened as I saw a guy who looked like he was twenty-two signaling to her.

"Wait, what?" I frowned. "That's your boss?"

"Yup," she said through gritted teeth as she plastered on a fake smile. "I need to get out of this world."

"What, New York?" I shuddered. "Or this job?"

"This job, goof." She laughed. "We would never leave New York."

"Never ever." I grinned as I searched for another waiter to grab a new flute of champagne. "This is the best city in the world."

"It truly is." She took a deep breath and nodded at me. "Though sometimes, I think we both need to go on an adventure." She sounded wistful as she stared at me, and I watched her shoulders stiffen as someone cleared their throat next to us.

"Ms. Young." Her boss stepped toward us with a puppy-dog expression on his face. It was hard for me to take him seriously, as he was wearing a Rick and Morty lime-green T-shirt. "Can we talk?"

"Yes, Luther," she said quickly, then mouthed to me. "Wish me luck. I'll be back."

"Good luck." I watched her walk away and pulled out my phone to see if Stephan had messaged me. He hadn't. Was he even excited about this wedding? Was I?

"I am getting married in a week," I mumbled, realizing I wasn't the least bit excited. I knew it was likely nerves, but then I thought about how Stephan had laughed derisively when I'd invited him to attend the Shakespeare in the Park event with me.

"Not to be." He'd snorted like he couldn't believe my request was serious. It was almost as if he didn't know how much I loved Shakespeare and theater. Or maybe it was that he didn't care. The gnawing feeling in the pit of my stomach was there again. I had to put my fears behind me. I'd thought up until a week ago that once I was married, everything would feel right.

* * *

The smell of pepperoni on the sizzling large pizza wafted through the box as I made my way toward Stephan's apartment. I couldn't wait to sink my teeth into the gooey cheese and crusty dough. I licked my lips happily as I stopped outside Stephan's door. I hoped he wouldn't be too mad that I'd opted for pizza and not a tofu dish. I didn't want him to make a comment about me fitting into my dress or looking good in a bikini in our honeymoon photos. I wasn't sure why I felt guilty. It didn't matter anymore. I checked my handbag to make sure that the card and envelope were still there.

I debated knocking or letting myself in. He didn't like me showing up unannounced, but this was a special surprise. I reached for my key in the forest-green Kate Spade bag Emma had gotten me for my birthday five years ago and unlocked the front door.

I felt surprisingly nervous as I stepped inside. Stephan's apartment was functional, expensive, and reminded me of a show home. It didn't look lived in, even though he'd lived there for years. He hated clutter, color, and anything cute, which was apparent by the stark black leather chaise that sat opposite a humongous TV that hung on the dark-gray wall. The TV was on, so I knew he was home. I placed the pizza box on the black marble countertop and looked around the apartment. The smell of roses in the air made me pause. It was a strong odor, too strong to be an actual bouquet. It was more like a perfume.

"That's weird," I mumbled as I headed down the short corridor toward his bedroom. That's when I saw the heap of clothes. I frowned slightly, confused as to why there was a bright-pink bra on the floor next to his pants. I didn't own a bright-pink anything.

"That tickles," a female voice announced, and my body froze. I stood in the hallway, shocked, as I tiptoed to the open doorway. I stared into the bedroom from my position against the wall. Stephan was there with his neighbor, and they weren't playing chess. I knew I should have screamed or run into the bedroom shouting, but instead, I backed away and went to the front door. I was about to leave when I quickly returned to the kitchen, grabbed the pizza box, and left. Tears streamed down my face as I entered the elevator and grabbed a slice of pizza.

Stephan was cheating on me.

The man I was supposed to marry in a week was in bed with another woman.

I couldn't believe it. This was not supposed to happen to me. This was not the life plan my mom had outlined for me. Or that I'd envisioned for myself either.

I debated going back up to the apartment and leaving the card and letter on the countertop but decided against it. I didn't want to feel even more pitiful than I already was.

As I exited the building and joined the crowds of people walking the streets of Manhattan, I almost felt a sense of relief. Though I attributed that to shock.

"What am I going to do now?" I mumbled to myself as I sobbed, stuffing my face with pizza. I didn't know where to go or what to do. I was too embarrassed to tell Emma what had happened. I knew she'd be at her work event for a few more hours.

I wanted to go home and put on my wedding dress. I loved that wedding dress. *Maybe more than you loved Stephan*, a voice whispered in my head, but I ignored it.

I would try on the dress one more time to see how beautifully it fit me. Then, I would cut it into pieces and throw it in the trash. What a waste of money. However, it was too late to think about that now. Or my mother's reaction when I told her the wedding was off.

I was no longer going to become Mrs. Snothead.

"Thank God for that." I giggled through my tears as I wiped tomato sauce from my chin. I would go home, cry my eyes out, think back to my childhood, and remember my life when it had been so much simpler. The thought of my future fiancé cheating on me had never crossed my mind as a kid who'd been in love with love.

I'd thought I'd have the job of my dreams, live in a brownstone with a cute yard, my gorgeous loving husband, and our pet dog, Zippy. I'd pictured myself eating Magnolia

Bakery cupcakes all day. Now, I couldn't even glance at a cupcake without gaining five pounds.

Adulthood was definitely not all it was cracked up to be.

Chapter One

P ippa

Hi TJ,

It's me, Pippa, your best friend. I'm so sad that you moved and that you're not going back to camp this summer. However, I'm super happy you said yes to sending letters. This way, our parents can't read what's in our emails. I might try out for the tennis team or maybe the swim team in the fall. Are you still thinking of baseball? My mom is really getting on my nerves. She keeps yelling at me to tidy my room. I'm like, what do you care? It's my room! She didn't like that. Hope your mom is not as annoying as mine.

Remember when we made s'mores at the campfire, and you used three pieces of choco-late, and Noah didn't get any and cried? Big baby, haha. You were so sweet to give him the candy bar you brought from home; it made Noah's entire evening.

That was a fun night. It was so cool we got to swim in the lake and stare at the stars. I'm glad we made that pact. You're my best friend. Am I still yours? Just checking.

Write me back soon,

Pippa

P.S. You just drove away from your house with your mom, but I want you to remember me always.

P.P.S. I will always remember that my 13th year was the year my life changed forever.

"Where are you, TJ?" I mumbled to absolutely no one as I sat there feeling like I'd yet again made another mistake in my life.

My wedding dress was covered in chocolate ice cream. And so was my face. My face was also covered in dried tears and smeared red lipstick. My long dark hair was a frizzy mess, and I wondered if birds flying by had to double-check to make sure I wasn't a scarecrow.

I knew I looked a mess. I wasn't the sort of woman who shimmered like a beautiful swan with red eyes and blotchy cheeks. No matter how many makeup tutorials I watched on YouTube.

In fact, some may even say I looked a "hot mess." Cue every trashy reality TV show on Bravo. Not that I watched any of them.

I'm too classy. Far too classy. Okay, so I sometimes watch *Vanderpump Rules*, but who doesn't?

I knew my best friend and roommate, Emma, would say that I could have appeared way worse. She's the sort of best friend that makes it worth having friends. She always tries to make me feel better about myself, even when I'm an absolute idiot.

My mom would say I resemble something the cat dragged in. I knew if I glanced in the mirror, I would be a sight to behold. She'd lecture me on always ensuring I took care of my appearance because you never knew who was observing you. I was glad she couldn't see me now.

Frankly, I didn't even care how bad my appearance was. My Vera Wang dress was ruined, the cowboy boots I'd bought on a whim at the airport this morning felt too tight, and the bale of hay I was seated on made my behind numb. I was uncomfortable, broke, and heartbroken.

I stared at the phone on my lap and debated calling Emma, but I didn't want to talk to her right then. I didn't want to hear her talk about knowing that Stephan was a jerk from the very beginning. Because then I'd have to acknowledge that I ignored all the flashing warning signs that had been apparent from the first moment I'd looked into his baby-blue eyes.

"Here comes the bride, all dressed in white..." I sang in an out-of-tune voice as I scrutinized the unfamiliar surroundings. "And brown now," I sang as I inspected the smeared melted chocolate on the expensive material.

"What have I done?" Reality slapped me in the face as I took a deep breath and studied my foreign environment. The red barn behind me was more rusted than red, but it stood out against the miles and miles of green grass. I had really left New York. I pinched myself to ensure I wasn't dreaming.

I had no idea what I was doing here in the country. I was a city girl through and through. I was used to skyscrapers standing tall and menacing in an overcast gray sky, not stretches of open blue sky and grazing cows. As one of the cows headed in my direction, I moved my face slightly to the right. I didn't want to make eye contact with any of them or make them feel like I wanted to be friends.

"Welcome to the other side of the world," I whispered. The other side of the world, as in the middle of nowhere, Montana. Well, that wasn't true. This town had a name. Paradise Valley, to be precise. It was about an hour from Yellowstone National Park, and even I had to admit that it was beautiful.

It was all lush green, with rivers, wildflowers, and mountains in the distance. A far cry from the concrete jungle of New York City, where I lived. I'd only been here for an hour, but I already felt calmer, even though the nerves in my stomach were dancing a never-ending waltz.

The fresh air filled my lungs in a pleasant way, but I had to remind myself that I was not here for a vacation or to enjoy the mountains.

I was here because I needed to get away from the city. Fast.

Speedy Gonzales, fast.

Seeing your fiancé in bed with his neighbor and supposed nemesis will make you run like you're competing for a spot on the Olympic track team. Seeing that betrayal and going home to stuff my face with pizza wasn't the best idea I'd ever made. Then, drinking a bottle of cabernet by myself and trying on my wedding dress before I debated ripping it to pieces were the next in a line of bad decisions.

Then came the watching of *The Notebook*, a love story far from mine. But it had made me go to my small cedar box and pull out a stack of letters. Letters that I'd received over a span of five years.

And before I could think anything through with a clear head, I was in a taxi on the way to the airport, looking like a crazy woman. And now here I was in Montana. All because Stephan had cheated.

The thought of the day before made me feel nauseous. However, I was unsure if my stomach rumbling was from thinking about my ex, Stephan Dmitry Snothead, or because I overate chocolate ice cream. Not that it stopped me from purchasing another tub before I got there.

Or maybe I was having second thoughts about jumping on a plane and going out to a random ranch in Montana to visit my childhood best friend—a man who had no idea I was there. A man I wasn't sure even remembered me, as we hadn't been in contact since we were eighteen, and ten years had been a long time.

Two striking monarch butterflies chasing each other across the field made me stand up to peek at their colorful wings. My legs shook from being numb and tired, and I needed to stretch them. I decided to walk aimlessly around the property while I waited for TJ to get home.

My eyes followed the butterflies as they flittered from wildflower to wildflower and I took everything in with wide eyes. I'd never expected TJ to end up in a place like this.

My phone beeped, and I saw that Emma had texted me. She was going to kill me when she found out I'd left New

York without letting her know. I made my way back to the barn and hay bales and responded.

Emma: Pippa, where are you?

Pippa: Somewhere on the Earth.

Emma: Seriously?

Pippa: I'm in Montana.

Emma: Is that a new bar?

Pippa: The state.

Emma: What? Call me now.

Pippa: You told me to do it.

Emma: To do what?

Pippa: Go on an adventure.

Emma: Pippa, are you out of your mind?

Pippa: No...maybe...who knows?

Emma: What about your job?

Pippa: Alistair is back in England for the next two weeks. I can work from home.

Emma: But you're not home.

Pippa: You know what I mean.

Emma: Girl...your wedding is next week.

Pippa: The wedding is off. Stephan can go and take a long walk off a short cliff. He cheated on me. And I saw.

Emma: Oh, Pips, I'm so sorry. :(

> Pippa: So yeah, that's over. I'm not getting married, and I'm taking some time away from the city. I'm a country girl now. Well, for a week or so anyway.

> Emma: Pippa, please come back to New York. You cannot just up and leave. When I said you needed an adventure in your life, this is not what I meant.

> Pippa: I need a break right now. I'll be back soon.

A car door slamming made me pause and look around nervously. I wasn't sure why I felt so apprehensive. This was TJ, my best friend, from the age of three until we were eighteen. He knew me better than anyone. Well, aside from Emma. But that didn't count because she had only come into my life in college.

"I have three steeds that should be able to..." The husky voice behind me made me jump high off of the hay bale. I watched in dismay as my ice cream tub fell to the ground in front of the three men, who were all standing there with incredulous expressions on their faces. They all looked as equally shocked to see me as I was to see them. One of the men was older, and the two other guys appeared to be brothers around the same age. Though, if I had the right ranch, they couldn't be brothers. TJ was an only child.

"Who are you?" the husky voice spoke again, and the man rubbed his forehead. He was handsome, in a Henry Cavill meets Kevin Costner way. "And why are you sitting on my hay bale?" he asked before I could answer. That wasn't TJ, was it? It couldn't be. TJ was overweight with pimples and blond hair. At least he had been as a child and teenager. This man was hotness personified.

"Can you talk?" he asked again, stepping forward. I just stared at him, unable to answer.

This was not going as planned. The three men were all staring at me with aghast expressions that would have been comical if I didn't already feel so out of place. Which one of them was TJ?

The oldest man, who had on a tan cowboy hat and held a coil of rope in his hands, almost had his jaw on the ground. Did I resemble an alien from outer space or something? Or maybe they didn't see a crazy, wild-haired woman in a wedding dress hanging out, eating ice cream on their farm every day?

"I'm...um...here to see TJ," I stammered as the old man started grinning and showed off a missing tooth. His eyes held merriment as he winked.

"Well, I never..." He stepped forward, removed his cowboy hat, and lowered it before him. "Howdy, ma'am."

"TJ?" My voice sounded nervous and shocked. For a split second, I wondered if this was TJ, all weathered and toothless. But then common sense slapped me in the face, and I chastised myself. It wasn't possible that buying a ranch had aged him sixty-plus years. No matter how hard those years had been.

"TJ? Me?" the old man guffawed and slapped his mud-encrusted palm against his thigh. "Who's asking?"

"It's me..." I took a deep breath and focused on the two younger men standing behind him. One of them had to be TJ. "Pippa..." I swallowed hard. TJ and I hadn't corresponded regularly in about ten years. Not since we'd both gone off to college and life got in the way of our best-friends-forever pact.

We'd both sworn that we'd remain best friends when his parents had divorced and his mom had moved him down to Florida to live with his grandparents. In the beginning, we'd written weekly, then monthly, and that had whittled down to yearly Christmas cards once we'd started college.

I still included long letters in my cards, but all he included was his name, and he never answered my letters. I wasn't sure why.

However, I felt like he should still remember me.

Shouldn't he?

"Pippa." The older man took a couple more steps closer to me. "Of course, Pippa, the bride..." He peered back at the other two men and started humming. "That should be a song. Maybe I'll grab my guitar. Pippa the bride, Pippa the bride..." he sang in a low country voice that sounded surprisingly close to Garth Brooks. He bowed and held his hand out to me, and I didn't know if he wanted to pull me into his arms or dance.

However, I was not interested in either one of those options. This was not going as planned. Why didn't one of the younger men step forward?

Which one was TJ?

I glanced down at the dark-brown cowboy boots I'd bought on a whim at the airport when I'd arrived. They were too tight, but would they allow me to outrun this man?

I wondered if I'd gotten the address wrong. I felt like I'd made an impetuous mistake. After seeing Stephan cheating, I didn't know what to do. All I'd known was that I wanted to escape. I didn't know where I wanted to go, but then I remembered TJ and the pact we'd made as kids.

We'd sworn we would always be there for each other. I'd been a little drunk when I took the taxi to the airport and may have paid too much money for the first flight to Montana.

But I had to flee the city.

I'd slept some on the flight to Montana, then I rented a car and drove to the address on TJ's last Christmas card, stopping at a local convenience store for some much-needed water and ice cream.

But now that I was here and no longer acting out of shock, I wondered if I'd made a huge mistake.

Would TJ even remember the forever pact we'd made as kids?

"TJ is here, right?" I asked, taking a deep breath. Had I taken a flight to an alternate reality? Or was this all a dream? That was it. This was a dream. Stephan hadn't cheated, and I wasn't in Montana. I closed my eyes and tried to think of a way to wake myself up. "Come on, sheep," I muttered, but then groaned as I recalled that was a way to fall asleep. Not to wake up.

"Oh, dear, is she crazy?" The older man stepped forward, his hand down, his face worried. "Is everything all right?"

My eyes slowly opened, and I peeked at him. He had a kind face, even if he did look completely opposite to the men I was used to seeing on the streets of Manhattan. I gazed past him to the other two men. The one talking about horses looked like he was bemused, and the other man, who I noticed was also very handsome, was straight-up laughing. His head was cocked back, and his hand hit his thigh in merriment.

I wasn't sure why he was acting like he was at a Dave Chappelle comedy show. This situation wasn't that funny.

"You here from Russia?" The older man cocked his head to the side and narrowed his eyes. "You that mail-order bride TJ ordered?" He grinned, and this caused the hot blond guy to laugh even harder.

"I'm American." I cleared my throat as my voice sounded high and agitated. "And no, I'm not—"

"Rob, stop teasing the poor girl." The first man stepped forward, shaking his head. He frowned as he headed toward me. "Pippa..." He paused as if he didn't know what to say. His blue eyes surveyed my face, then my wedding dress, and he frowned, his eyebrows creasing in a familiar way that made my heart thud. "Pippa Chase..." His eyes widened. "From Brooklyn?"

So the Henry Cavill look-alike was TJ? My jaw dropped. How had TJ gotten so hot?

"It's me," I said, nodding, waiting for him to give me a huge grin and a hug. TJ had grown up, and I wasn't mad about how gorgeous he now appeared to be. "Your best fr—your childhood best friend," I corrected myself. I could hardly consider myself his best friend when we hadn't spoken in a decade.

"What are you doing here?" he asked, a slightly perplexed expression on his face as he stood still.

This was not the reaction I'd hoped for or wanted. He didn't seem pleased to see me at all. All of a sudden, I wanted to melt into the ground. Coming to Montana had been a mistake. I wondered if I clicked my cowboy boots three times if they'd take me back to the city and allow me to forget the last twenty-four hours.

Chapter Two

T^J

Pippa Pippy Pipsqueak,

How's it going? Miss camp already. And you. How rad was it when we grabbed all the toilet paper from the counselor's cabins and threw it in the trash? I can still see Jimmy running around shouting with his pants down... I swear I saw sh...doo, whatever is polite to say to a girl on his ass. Highlarious!

Sorry your mom is being annoying. Last night, my mom was like, TJ, you gotta start taking out the trash more and vacuuming, and I was like, I'm not a girl, Mom. Didn't make her happy. She told me I was acting more and more like Dad, and then I laughed, and she just shook her head. I kinda felt bad then, so I took the trash out. I told Mom to get a robot vacuum cleaner, seeing as neither of us like to do it. And she said we can't expect Gramps and Gramma to do it as they're old now and letting us stay for free.

Do you think you'll ever visit Florida? Also, yes, you're my bff 4 eva as you like to say. The pact is for life. If we ever, EVER, need the other person, no questions asked, we will be there for them. Anywho, got to go, Brady (my new neighbor) is here, and we're going to play Bball.

Write back soon.

TJ

Pippa's cheeks were a deep red, her long black hair hung in curls down her back, and she wore a *wedding dress*.

A long white (well, it was stained now) wedding dress. Had she lost her mind? What was she doing on my ranch in a wedding dress?

I knew I was being rude, but I was gobsmacked for what may have been the first or maybe the second time in my life. What was Pippa Chase doing standing here on my ranch looking like the star of a love story gone wrong movie? I could see Old Man Roberts and Jack Marley, my best friend, staring at her and then at me and wondering what on God's green earth was going on.

The fact that she'd wondered if Old Man Roberts was me, for even the briefest of seconds, told me she was in a weird state of mind. Or she'd grown up to be a bit dense.

Neither one of those options boded well for her common sense or eyesight. But then the Pippa I'd known as a child had always had her head in the clouds. She'd been a creative dreamer and made my childhood the stuff of something in books. The good kind of books.

I rubbed my forehead as I stared at her, all big brown beguiling eyes and trembling lips. Was this a scene from a play she'd written?

I couldn't believe that my old friend was here in Montana *in a wedding dress*. Her eyes appeared wide and frightened and the expression on her face made it appear as if a raccoon had done her eye makeup.

"Are you going to answer me?" I prodded Pippa into a response. I wasn't sure if my words had been too harsh because she looked like she was about to cry. And the last thing I needed was a crying woman on my ranch.

"Is everything okay?" Jack stepped forward and offered her his handkerchief. He was always a gentleman. Well, that wasn't particularly true, but he tried his best. She stared up at him with big, rapidly blinking eyes and shook her head slightly. Her lower lip jutted out, and she took a deep breath as if trying to stay strong.

The small movement pierced a forgotten memory in my brain from my childhood. A memory from our past, when she'd wanted to play flag football with the neighborhood boys and me, and I'd told her no, and she'd gotten all upset. A smile crossed my face at the memory. I wondered if she was still as obstinate as she'd been as a child.

"Not really." She shook her head and attempted to smooth her wedding dress down. I had no idea why she was wearing a wedding dress. "It's been a long twenty-four hours." She bit down on her lip, and I could see they were quivering. Her eyes were sad, and it seemed like she was barely holding herself together. I prayed that she wasn't about to cry. I had no idea what to do with a crying woman. We hadn't been friends for years now. I didn't know if it was appropriate to hug her or not.

"You getting married?" Old Man Roberts asked, moving back next to Jack. Whatever she was doing here, it was clear she wasn't getting married. And everyone here knew it.

I could see Old Man Roberts's eyes gleaming, and I knew that his wife, Annie, would be hearing all about this encounter within the next few hours. Which meant that everyone in Paradise Valley would know by tomorrow morning. Sigh.

I loved Old Man Roberts and his wife, but she was part of an elderly group of local gossips who hung around the coffee shop every single day and acted like the town telephone system. Somehow, they knew everything going on in town and spread it around, whether it was true or not. And I was of the mind that Old Man Roberts was their number one informant.

"Not anymore." Her lips trembled, and she looked at me again.

"TJ turn you down?" Old Man Roberts frowned and gave me a look. I kept my mouth shut so I wouldn't say anything rude. The man was like a father to me. I didn't want to be disrespectful, but he was being deliberately ignorant. But then again, he loved to stir up the drama. That was just his personality. His parents must have loved the drama themselves because they named him Robert Roberts.

"Huh?" She rubbed her forehead and smeared a line of dirt across her cheek.

"Don't mind him, Pippa," I said softly, stepping forward.

"Oh, TJ," she exclaimed before running toward me, her hair flying in the wind as she got closer and closer. It felt like I was in a movie, only I was not supposed to be in the movie. Certainly not a movie like this.

Jack and Old Man Roberts resembled circus clowns, their mouths so wide as she ran toward me.

Time seemed to stop still as she tripped on a rake and went flying into my arms. I opened them automatically and stepped forward to catch her so she didn't fall. She was breathing hard as I caught her, and she pressed her head into my shoulder, sobbing.

"Everything has gone drastically wrong," she screeched dramatically as I patted her shoulder, not knowing what else to do.

"We should go." Jack poked Old Man Roberts in the shoulder and signaled back to his dark-gray Chevy pickup truck. "I'll give you a ride home."

"You guys don't have to leave," I said hurriedly, not wanting them to get the short end of the stick, but I feared it was already too late. The two men gave each other a knowing look that meant they thought that Pippa was here because of me.

"We'll try not to tell Mindy anything." Jack winked at me as he jumped into the truck, and I growled at his comment without responding. Pippa continued to sob into my shoulder as the two men got into the truck and drove off. I heaved out a huge sigh, and then the gravity of the moment hit me.

Pippa Chase was here.

On my ranch.

In a wedding dress.

Crying.

The Pippa Chase.

My childhood best friend. My heart thudded, even as a mixture of anxiety and anger filled me.

What was going on?

"Hey, Pippa..." I slowly pushed her back and looked down into her face. She looked back up at me with beguiling brown eyes and wiped her tears away as she stepped back, her eyebrows twisting together angrily.

"TJ Wyatt, what was that greeting?" She pushed me slightly, her brows still furrowed, as she folded her arms and stomped her cowboy boots. Since when did Pippa wear cowboy boots?

"Huh? What?" She was angry at me? I was the one that had every right to be angry with her.

"You acted like you didn't even know me." I didn't want to tell her that I'd had no clue who the crazy woman in the wedding dress was when I pulled up. I didn't think it was smart to tell her I'd debated calling the police.

"Um, I acted like I didn't know you? I haven't seen you in over a decade." I shook my head. "You can't talk, Pippa. You thought I was Old Man Roberts." I gave her a pointed look. "Let's not talk about people not knowing who was who."

"I didn't really think he was you." She giggled, her brown eyes crinkling at the side in a familiar way that took me back to my teenage years in New York. "I was just slightly taken aback."

"By what?"

"Well, you lost your acne and..." She paused and looked down at her feet, a wash of red covering her face as if she were embarrassed to continue.

"And my childhood fat?" I finished the sentence for her and laughed. I'd been slightly overweight as a kid, not that that had stopped our friendship. I wasn't going to tell her that she looked different as well. I'd found out the hard way that women didn't want to know when they looked a bit of a mess, even when they asked.

"Well, you know." She shrugged, but there was a wide smile on her face now. "You look different."

"Good different?" I asked her, and she blushed. The color lit up her face, and I realized she was even more beautiful than she'd been as a teen girl. Not that she'd ever known that I'd thought she was beautiful or cute. I'd never told her about my crush. I had always just been her friend. "I'm guessing no answer is a yes." I grinned at her, and she rolled her eyes. I was grateful for the fact that she was no longer crying. "So, Pippa, what are you doing here? In a wedding dress, to boot."

"You stopped writing to me." She jutted her chin out in that obstinate way that she did when she was annoyed at me. "I wrote you letters from college and you never responded. Only sent cards."

"I'm sorry." I didn't know what to say. I didn't want to get into it.

"Did you get the letters?" There was a hopeful tone to her voice, and I knew what she wanted me to say. She'd made me watch *The Notebook* at least ten times. I knew she wanted me to say I hadn't gotten them. That they'd been kept from me. And I wanted to say that. I wanted to say that so badly, but that wasn't the truth. And I didn't abide lies.

"Yes." I nodded slowly, and I watched as her face fell. A look of uncertainty crossed her features, and I could see that she looked unsure of herself. "Why are you here, Pippa? We haven't spoken in years."

There was a poignant silence between us as we sized each other up. We both knew that I was the reason why we hadn't spoken in years. Yet, she didn't know the reason why. A dull knife blade twisted in my heart as I recalled the past.

"We made a pact, remember?" she asked me slowly, her eyes searching my face, and I nodded. I wasn't surprised she hadn't mentioned my silence. Pippa had a way of not wanting to acknowledge the uncomfortable.

"I remember the pact." Funny how it only seemed to go one way.

"What happened though?"

I didn't get why she was here. "But why are you here... in that dress?" I pointed at the now extremely dirty gown.

"I was supposed to get married." She shrugged, squaring her shoulders in defiance. "I caught him cheating." Her voice cracked. "I needed to get away." Her words were stilted as she threw her hands up and spun around. She attempted to offer me a semblance of a smile, the twist of her lips not quite reaching high enough to be believable.

"I feel like I'm in *The Sound of Music*, surrounded by all these green hills and mountains."

"I'm sorry your fiancé cheated." I processed what she'd just told me. She'd been engaged? "I assume you're no longer getting married to him?"

"Yes. That's why I'm here. It's over between us." She gulped as if processing that fact for the first time. "Stephan was his name."

"The name alone sounds like he's a dork," I said, and a

warm feeling filled me as she giggled. She ran her fingers back through her long, dark hair and attempted to put it up in a bun before giving up the task as thick tendrils escaped her grip.

"He was a dork and a really horrible man." She growled as she rubbed her eyes and yawned.

"If he cheated on you, I'm sure he was." I stared at her, wondering why she'd come to Montana. I didn't want to make her cry again, so I had to tread carefully. "So you called off the wedding?"

"Kinda." She wrinkled her nose. "It is definitely off, but..."

"But what?"

"Only you and I know, so far...aside from Emma." She licked her lips nervously. "I literally caught a plane and came here when I found out. I needed to get out of New York City. I needed to be out of my apartment. I didn't want to talk to anyone. I was too—" She stopped talking as her phone started ringing. I watched as she riffled through her handbag and looked at the screen. "It's Emma," she mumbled.

"And who is Emma? The woman he cheated on you with?"

"Emma's my best friend," she said, shaking her head at me. I had to admit that it would be weird if Emma had been the one her fiancé was cheating with. "She always disliked Stephan."

"Oh." Why did women never listen to their friends? I'd had several female friends who had dated the worst men. And even though they were warned, as soon as they started dating, that they were bad news, they ignored every flashing red light telling them to stop.

"I should answer." She sighed, looking at the phone, hoping it would stop before she had to answer it. "I have a feeling she's worried about me."

"Because you're upset, and she thinks tha..." My voice trailed off. This was an odd situation, and I wasn't sure what to do or say. I also wasn't sure how I felt about seeing Pippa again after all these years.

"Because about ten minutes ago, I told her I was in Montana and my wedding was supposed to be next week." She grimaced and then gave me a wry smile. "And nobody knows that I won't be there."

"Oh, boy." I wasn't sure what to do with that information. "Your fiancé doesn't know?"

"No." She pressed her lips together. "Not yet."

"I see." I folded my arms and tried to think of something to say to comfort her when her phone started ringing again. "Emma?" I guessed as she looked at the screen and then nodded. "Answer it, Pippa."

"Fine," she said, reluctantly pressing her finger down on the screen. "Hey, Ems."

"Pippa, where are you?" a loud voice screeched through the speaker. "Please tell me you were joking when you said you were in cowboy land, Montana? Where is that on the map anyways?"

"Cowboy land?" I laughed as I gazed at Pippa. "Is that what you called my home?"

"No," she said, rolling her eyes. "I never called it cowboy land. Emma is just extra."

"Who is that?" Emma screeched. "Are you with a man?"

"I'm at TJ's ranch."

"TJ?" Emma sounded shocked. I was glad to hear that

someone else was taken aback by the fact that Pippa was with me on my ranch. "Your childhood best friend that ghosted you?"

"That would be me," I spoke up, feeling guilty. Was that what Pippa thought? That I'd ghosted her? Technically, that was true, but I'd had my reasons. The ironic part was that I'd gone cold to keep my distance from her, but now here she was, on my ranch.

"Pippa, take me off of speaker now," Emma shouted. "What is going on?"

"It's fine, Ems. I'm fine. I'm here with TJ and I'm just going to lie low for a few—"

"Your wedding is next week." Emma sounded frustrated and slightly snarky, though that may have been her nerves.

"Stephan cheated on me, Ems. I'm not marrying him."

"But you have to let people know. People are flying in for the wedding."

"I will send out an email tonight, okay?" Pippa looked up at me from under her long lashes. There were remnants of black mascara smudged beneath her eyes that made her resemble the raccoon that loved trying to get into my trash can. She was even giving me the same nervous look he gave me when I shooed him away. I looked away from her to stop my lips from twitching at the comparison. "You have internet, right? And a laptop."

"I do." I nodded and frowned. "You're staying here?"

"Where else would I stay?" She blinked, looking confused. "That's why I came here."

"You'd stay at a hotel," Emma responded to Pippa. "You can't stay with a strange man," she shouted. "Pippa, life isn't a Hallmark movie. You don't leave the city to go and find yourself in some small town. Especially not with some strange man."

"Hey, I'm not strange," I protested, even though I thought Pippa had been foolhardy to just up and fly out here. I didn't want her to stay with me. I had no space for her.

Pippa giggled at my protest, and her hair went flying as she shook her head. I noticed her hair had grown much longer since I'd last seen her. It also looked extremely frizzy and unkempt, but then again, her entire look had seen better days. If she'd shown up at the wedding looking like that, the groom would have been the one leaving.

"He's not strange. He's TJ." She looked over at me and smiled, a warm, enveloping smile. It made me uncomfortable and also surprisingly satisfied. "He's my childhood best friend. And we promised each other that if we ever needed each other, we'd be there for one another..." Her voice trailed off. "And I need him and a place to stay. Plus, you know I don't have much money. My credit cards are basically at their limit. I can't afford to stay in a hotel."

"You could have come to me." Emma sounded sad. "You know I would have had your back if he came to the door."

"I know, but I needed to get out of the city. I needed to run away." Pippa sighed. "I'll be back in a few weeks."

"A few weeks?" Emma and I exclaimed simultaneously, and Pippa smiled.

"See, you guys are thinking alike already." Pippa's voice was excited, and I could hear Emma sighing loudly. "You don't mind me staying here, do you, TJ?" she asked me in the sweetest voice I'd heard in a while, and my heart flipped. So, she still had a way of playing with my emotions. I wasn't sure how I felt about that.

"I mean, I don't have..." My voice trailed off as a bright-red Ford pickup truck came speeding up the road toward the ranch. "Oh shoot," I mumbled under my breath. This was the absolute last thing that I needed. My eyes followed the truck as it came barreling toward us.

"What's going on?" Pippa frowned as she turned to look at what had caught my attention. "Who's that?" Her eyes narrowed as she gazed over her shoulder.

"What's going on?" Emma asked, her voice high and anxious. "Pippa, what's going on?"

"I don't know. Someone just showed up." Pippa seemed far too surprised that I'd have a guest than I thought she should be. The Ford screeched to a stop, and a car door slammed shut.

Pippa looked over at me, a question in her eyes as curvy and crazy Mindy Messina came marching over in her skintight jeans, white top, and long dark hair. "TJ." Her voice sounded garbled as she looked at me accusingly, hands on her hips. "Who is that?"

"Um..." I stared at her wild eyes. The last thing I needed was Mindy Messina in my business.

"Are you getting married?" she asked as she glanced at an equally shocked-looking Pippa.

I took a deep breath and uttered the only words I could think of to say at that moment. "It's complicated." Oh shoots, why had I said that? Now she was going to think that I had something to do with this debacle.

"Travis James," she shouted as she stepped in front of Pippa and me. "You're getting married and I don't even know who she is." She glared at me. "Don't you think this is something you should have told me?"

I could see Pippa's jaw dropping as she stared at the two of us, and I knew I had a long night ahead of me.

To think, this morning, I'd woken up and had not a care in the world, aside from raising money to expand and build on to my ranch.

Now, here I was, with not one but two crazy women by my side and a whole lot of explaining to do. Why did life always have a way of turning upside down, no matter what you did?

Chapter Three

P ippa

Hi TJ,

Today is the first day of camp. I can't believe you're not here. It's not the same without you. All the other boys are so goofy. Or they want to kiss. As if I want to kiss any of them. I'm holding out for Brad Pitt. I don't care if he's older or not.

What are you doing this summer? We're going to go swimming in the lake tomorrow. Did I tell you I'm trying out for the swim team in the fall? I think I have a shot of making it for freestyle and/or backstroke. We'll see.

What are you doing right now? Maybe I'll try and call you next week. Ashley is here and *was asking about you as well. We might go to the MOMA and make fun of the artwork.*

I miss you my friend,
Pippa
Your Bff 4 eva

If my jaw were any closer to the ground, ants would crawl inside. I stared at TJ, and I stared at the woman who had just shown up, and then I stared at TJ again. Nothing about my spur-of-the-moment trip to Montana was going as planned.

To say I was shocked at that moment would be an understatement. The woman standing in front of me looked like a more glamorous version of me, with her perfectly straight, long black hair and big brown eyes highlighted by sparkly green and gold eyeshadow that made them pop in a way I'd only seen in magazines. She, unlike me, looked gorgeous. I patted my frizzy hair back self-consciously as I stared at her and waited for TJ to introduce us.

"Hi, I'm Mindy," she said, holding her hand out. "Mindy Messina." She said it in a way that made me think I should know who she was. Was she famous, and I somehow hadn't realized it? She kind of resembled the actress Salma Hayek from her younger days, but I didn't want to ask if they were related.

"Uh, hi," I said weakly, shaking her hand. "I'm Pippa. Pippa Chase."

"Means nothing to me." She looked over at TJ as if he'd forgotten to tell her a vital piece of information. Who was this girl? The sinking feeling in my stomach told me I had a good guess.

Was she his girlfriend?

No wonder he'd looked so nervous when he'd seen me. No man wanted a strange woman showing up to stay with them without running it past their girlfriend first. All of a sudden, I felt guilty.

"Mindy, this is Pippa. She's my childhood best friend from when I lived in Brooklyn," TJ explained patiently and smiled awkwardly. "Pippa, this is Mindy Messina. She owns Mindy's Cupcakes and Coffee, the local coffee shop," he said as if that gave me all the information I wanted or needed. I wanted to ask if she was his girlfriend, but I didn't know how to ask without being nosy.

"Is that his girlfriend?" shouted Emma from the speakerphone that I'd forgotten to hang up. I blushed at her words, though inside, I was grateful for the fact that Emma always had to know everything about everyone, whether or not she knew them well.

"No way." Mindy made a face and shuddered as if someone had just asked her if she'd like to eat spinach for every meal for the rest of her life. "I'm TJ's friend, one of his good friends, I thought. When Old Man Roberts told me that TJ had a mail-order bride show up at the ranch, I had to come down and see what was going on."

"I'm not a mail-order bride," I said quickly, ignoring the relief that washed through me at her words. So, Mindy wasn't dating him and didn't appear to want to date him either. That didn't mean he was single, of course, but it wasn't like I cared about his relationship status. I didn't want to make my staying on his ranch awkward.

"She's not a mail-order bride, Mindy, so you can go back

and report to everyone that she's my childhood friend who's come to visit."

"Come to visit in her wedding dress?" Mindy looked me up and down. "Where are you staying?" she asked, tapping her fingers against her thigh.

"Here," I said hopefully, looking over at TJ.

"But where?" Her eyes widened, and she looked slightly scandalized. I frowned. What was the deal? I knew this was a small town, but friends didn't have friends stay?

"I only have a log cabin right now." He stared at me for a few seconds. "It's just one big room and a bathroom."

"One big room?" I blinked at him. "What?"

"He only has one bed," Mindy stated, pressing her lips together.

"And a couch," he added and sighed. "I guess if you really want to stay, I can sleep on the couch."

"If you wouldn't mind," I said, smiling at him widely. It wasn't like I had many options. It would also allow us to catch up and maybe rekindle our friendship. It had haunted me for ten years that we were no longer as close.

"Pippa," Emma screeched through the phone. "That is not a good—"

"I'll call you back later, Emma," I said, hanging up quickly before letting out a long and deep yawn. I was tired. The adrenaline rush that had carried me through the flight and car ride had disappeared, and I needed a nap. "Fancy showing me to that bed now, please, TJ?" I asked him in my sweetest tone. "I really need to get some sleep."

"Okay." He nodded slowly and then looked back over at Mindy. "Please don't let the rumor mill go out of control," he pleaded with her.

She laughed as she shook her head and sashayed back to her truck. "This is Paradise Valley, TJ. You know that's not possible. The rumor mill is already churning out stories." She opened her truck door and offered me a small wave. "Nice to meet you, Pippa. Y'all come to the coffee shop tomorrow morning, and I'll make you some breakfast sandwiches." She jumped into her truck and sped off as if a tornado followed her. I stood there wondering what had just happened.

"She seems nice," I said as I looked at TJ.

"Everyone in Paradise Valley is nice," he said slowly. "But they also love to talk. I have a feeling that we're going to be a very juicy topic of conversation tonight down at Montana Knights, the local bar." He sighed and tapped his foot against the dirt. His eyes looked me over for a few seconds like he was thinking hard about what to do next. "Come on, follow me. Let me show you to the cabin. You can get some sleep, and then tomorrow morning, we can talk and figure out exactly what's going on here."

Chapter Four

T J

Dear Pippa,

Florida is so hot and humid. My gramps took me to a local park today, and we saw a gator. A real live alligator. I was shocked. Gramps said that people forget Florida is swampland cause they're so focused on the mouse! And by the mouse, he means Mickey and Disney.

Do you remember when we were ten, and you said you wanted to have your birthday party at Disney, and your parents took us to Coney Island instead! That was cool. I miss living next door to you. And your mom's cook-

ing, Gramma makes a lot of meatloaf, and it seems to get worse every week. But Mom and I pretend we love it cause we don't wanna make Gramma sad.

I haven't heard from my dad in a couple of months now. It's weird. I don't know if he's upset we left Brooklyn or what. Have you seen him?

Miss you,
TJ
P.S. Did you make the swim team?

Pippa looked ridiculous, trudging through the field in her wedding dress. She was also walking funny, and I wondered if she'd twisted her ankle when she'd tripped over the rake.

"You okay?" I asked reluctantly as I waited for her to catch up with me. Was I going to have to carry her to the cabin? That would be awkward.

"I'm fine." She nodded, pressing her lips together. "You don't have to keep asking me that. To be quite honest, I was having doubts about Stephan anyway."

"No," I said, shaking my head as I looked at her, limping toward me. "I don't mean emotionally. You're walking funny." I hoped she wasn't going to tell me that she was doing some fancy New York catwalk move. I knew she was all about city life. It was funny to me that I used to be a city boy. That life was so behind me now, Brooklyn a mere memory in the cobwebs of my mind.

"Walking funny?" She glared at me. Her eyes crinkled thoughtfully before she burst out laughing, the sound carrying through the fields to the horses. "It's the boots," she admitted, looking down, a pinched expression on her face. "They're too tight and my feet are killing me. Each step I take is like torture."

"Oh no." I stared at her fancy boots. "Are they new? You need to break them in." I laughed as she made a face. "It can take from several days to weeks to get the made-for-you fit." She groaned. "Can you make it another couple hundred feet?" I pointed to the log cabin to the right. "If not, you can take them off and walk in your socks, or I can carry you."

"I think I'll take them off," she said quickly with a nod and bent down to pull the boots off. She stood there barefoot and looked up at me, looking very much like a damsel in distress. It was only then that I realized that I didn't see a suitcase in her hands. Or a duffel bag. She had nothing but a small black handbag on her shoulder.

"Where's your suitcase?" I asked, looking back at the rental car parked on the grass next to my tractor. "Is it in your car? Do you want me to go and get it?"

"I didn't bring a suitcase." She rubbed her forehead. "That would have been a good idea though."

"You don't have any other clothes?" Had she gotten on the plane in her wedding dress? I wondered what everyone must have thought? I wondered if she'd been sobbing. I felt sorry for her but also very curious about the spectacle she must have made.

"I didn't think this through, okay?" She shrugged and sighed. "Which is most probably my biggest issue in life. I keep making decisions, and then they go bad, and I end up feeling like a fool and wondering where I went wrong." Her voice wobbled, and I was nervous she would start crying again.

"It's okay," I said, looping my arm through hers. "It's going to be okay, Pippa. I promise." She smiled at me warmly as we continued walking. "You can wear some of my clothes tonight, and then tomorrow we'll go into town and you can pick up some pieces for your stay." I wanted to ask her how long she planned on staying. It couldn't be more than a few days, could it?

A week, max, I was sure. Pippa was a city girl. Had always wanted to be a city girl. I didn't think she'd last long in Montana, even in Paradise Valley.

"Thanks, TJ," she said, her voice low and tired. "Sorry for just showing up, but I didn't know where else to go. In fact, there was nowhere else I wanted to go." She looked up at me. "I've missed you, TJ. Growing up and living next door to you were the best years of my life. We had such a great childhood. I wanted to relive that. Even if just for a little bit." She beamed at me, and I could see she was reliving our happy memories.

She was willing me to acknowledge our bond and how close we'd been. And for the most part, she was right. We'd had an idyllic childhood. Our friendship had been the best part of my youth, but as I'd come to find out, the rest of it had been a lie.

I'd been running from that lie for the last ten years. I'd distanced myself from Pippa because I'd wanted to start afresh. Now, here she was, back in my life, bringing up all the old memories again. Just when I'd thought I was finally on the other side of all that trauma, she was here to bring it all back again. And I couldn't have that. I was going to have to get her out of my cabin, off my ranch, and out of Montana as soon as possible.

Chapter Five

P ippa

Dear TJ,

Ashley and I went to Bloomingdale's yesterday and then to Greenwich Village. Remember how we couldn't wait for the days our parents would let us take the train into the city by ourselves? Well, that day was yesterday. And it was awesome. We even went and got cupcakes from Magnolia Bakery. Delicious. Remember when we made those cupcakes and ate all the batter before we baked any?

I would love to go to Disney. Don't know if my parents are interested, though. You know *how they feel about vacations having an educational purpose. Boring.*

I did see your dad a few days ago. He was with a lady (don't tell your mom). I waved at him, but he didn't see me. He was laughing loudly at something the lady was saying. Did you ever find out why your parents divorced? Do you want me to investigate?

Your Bff 4eva,
Pippa

My legs were tired when we finally reached the log cabin. The reality of the situation didn't hit me until we were right outside the front door. It was small. Much smaller than I'd thought. I held my breath as he pushed the door open and we stepped inside. It was bright and warm. Immediately to the right was a small brown leather couch with a coffee table made from natural wood in front of it. Directly opposite the couch was a TV on the wall, and to the right of the couch and TV was a large window with sheer white curtains. There was a rawhide skin of some kind on the floor under the coffee table, and I wondered if TJ had killed the animal.

I looked up to the ceiling and admired the high exposed wooden beams. The cabin's height made it feel much larger than it was, and I continued looking around. To the left of the door was a small seating area with a fireplace and a bookshelf full of books and board games. Right next to that was an island countertop with three stools that looked into a spacious kitchen. The countertops were clean and white, and I smiled at the stack of baseball cards sitting on the island. So, he was still into baseball then. On the far right-hand side was a full-size bed with an ugly gray duvet. Opposite was a door, which I assumed led to the bathroom.

"It's really nice." I glanced at TJ, who was staring at me as I explored. "So cozy."

"I know it's small." He looked around, almost as if he were self-conscious about the place. He was still very distant, which hurt, but I supposed he was still shocked to see me. "And very masculine."

"It is masculine." I tittered, attempting to lighten the mood. "But it's not that small. You forget I'm from New York."

"But you always wanted to live in a penthouse," he said, smirking as he recalled my childhood dreams. "Overlooking Central Park."

"You remember that?" I asked, surprised. I'd been so naive when I was younger. I'd thought living in a large home equaled warmth and happiness, but Stephan's place had been over two thousand square feet and the coldest place I'd ever been in. I was supremely grateful that I would no longer have to move in there. I hadn't been looking forward to it at all. That should have been another sign.

"How could I not?" He chuckled as he walked toward the fridge. "You talked about it all the time. Your rich husband with the job on Wall Street and your fancy driver and housekeeper." He stared back at me. "And all the shopping you'd do on Fifth Avenue."

"I guess I did talk about it a lot," I admitted as I headed over to the couch and had a seat. I was too tired to stand any longer. "I guess I—"

"Want a beer or a drink or anything?" He cut me off, his voice tight as he pulled out two cans of beer and held them up. "I have wine and lemonade, as well. No Capri Sun though."

I laughed at his comment. I'd lived on strawberry kiwi Capri Suns when we were younger. "Some water, please." My voice was fraught with uncertainty as I sank back into his couch. I was just about to ask him why he'd moved to Montana when a small dog jumped off the bed and ran into the kitchen. "Oh," I exclaimed, surprised, as the dog darted back and forth.

"That's Apple." He observed my delighted face with a small smile. "She's a deep sleeper." Apple must have been wondering who he was talking to because she came running out of the kitchen toward me in the living room. She was small and plump, with a lot of golden-blond curls covering her cute little face.

"Hi, Apple." I smiled at the dog, who surveyed me curiously. "She's cute. What breed is she?"

"She's a mini golden doodle." He turned the faucet on and ran water into a glass for me. "Normally, she's very alert, but we had a late night last night, so she must have been catching up on sleep."

"Late night?" I asked, curious about what had kept them up all night.

"We went camping, and we had a visitor." He brought the glass of water over to me. He knelt and rubbed Apple on her belly as he passed her. She immediately rolled onto her back and looked up at him adoringly.

"A visitor?" I took the glass from him and nodded my thanks. "Who? Not Mindy again?"

"No." He chuckled. "It was Big Benjy. A black bear."

"A bear?" My jaw dropped, and I swallowed hard. My

heart raced as it struck me that there were many wild animals I might come into contact with. "Oh my God, I would have died if I'd seen a bear."

"Big Benjy is known around these parts. He won't harm folks. We just ignore him and stay out of his way." He shrugged. "It's the tourists that get themselves in trouble trying to take selfies and all that."

I pressed my lips together, grateful I hadn't asked him if he had any photos with the bear like I'd wanted. "So what kept you up all night then?"

"Apple loves making friends." Her ears perked up at the sound of her name. "And unfortunately, she kept trying to get out of the tent to make friends. And I had to keep her occupied until she finally quieted down and that took half the night." He smiled. "Hence, she was exhausted today."

"Aw." I sipped on my water and stared at them both. TJ looked so opposite to Apple. Him, being so tall and muscular, and her being so tiny and wiggly. "Do you go camping a lot, then?"

"Every couple of weeks." He nodded. "I love being down by the water. Sometimes, I think if I didn't live here, I'd live on a boat."

"I can't wait to see more." I wasn't sure if I saw disappointment or impatience on his face, but it made my stomach churn. "I mean, if you have time."

"I'll have to show you around tomorrow. Let you see the sights of Paradise Valley. It's gorgeous here."

"Oh, are there a lot of sights to see?" I asked eagerly, wondering if there was a shopping mall with a lot of designer stores. I didn't have much money to spend, but I figured the prices had to be much cheaper in Montana. Maybe I'd even find a discount Chanel handbag, though I thought that was highly unrealistic. Plus, my credit card would hate me if I tried to get a handbag.

"Not the sort of sights you're thinking of, Pips." He laughed and walked over to the back wall of the cabin. He stopped next to a chest of drawers and opened it, pulling out a T-shirt, a pair of shorts, and a towel. "Here you go, champ." He threw them to me as if he were throwing a football. "In case you wanted to have a shower before you took your nap."

"Oh, thanks." The items fell to the ground, and I picked them up quickly. I headed toward the door and stopped. "This is the bathroom, right?"

"Yes, ma'am." He grinned. "I'm going to go outside and tend to some of my veggies. Feel free to help yourself to anything in the kitchen. And settle down on the bed. Don't be scared if Apple joins you. She loves to snuggle."

"Sounds good. And thanks, TJ. I really appreciate it," I said, stifling another yawn. "I guess I'll have a quick shower and then head to bed."

"Sounds like a plan. I'll try and stay quiet." He nodded his head and headed back toward the front door. "Sleep well."

Chapter Six

T^J

Dear Pippa,

My mom and I went to Siesta Key Beach last weekend. It's in Sarasota. It was kinda cool. The sand was really white. Much nicer than Coney Island. The water was warm as well. But I missed the rides and hanging out with you. We didn't get hot dogs either. Mom brought sandwiches from home that Gramma made so we could save money.

Your last letter made me laugh. You need to stop thinking you're Harriet The Spy. You could go to jail for some of the things you've been doing. Thanks for the friendship bracelet.

I will try to make you one as well. Okay, that's a lie. Most probably not. Wanna chat on the phone next weekend? Haven't made many new friends here yet.

Your friend,

TJ

"Come on, Apple," I called to my little dog. She was digging in the mud, getting herself all dirty as she searched for a bone she'd buried. I'd thought she would stay in the cabin with Pippa, but she'd run outside with me as soon as I left. "There's no need to be scared of Pips. She won't hurt you." I rubbed between her ears as she jumped up on my legs. "She'll be gone soon and then everything will go back to normal." I looked around the ranch and took a couple of deep breaths. "There's no shopping here that will keep her occupied." I laughed as we walked over to one of the fields, where two of my horses, Stella and Nightstar, were grazing.

Stella looked up at me hopefully as I opened the gate. Every time she saw me, she hoped for some carrots, and I just shook my head. She looked at me for a few moments with her large, brown, expressive eyes and then moved her head back down to continue eating grass.

Apple ran up to Nightstar and tried to play, but Nightstar just neighed and kept grazing. I laughed as Apple ran circles around the two chestnut thoroughbreds, who completely ignored her.

"Don't take it personally, Apple." I surveyed my land

and stared at the mountain range in the distance. It was a beautiful evening; the sun was setting, and half of the mountains were shrouded in shadows while bright light shone on the other mountain peaks. The lush green grass beckoned to be rolled in, and the clear, cerulean-blue sky was picture perfect. The ten acres I owned in Paradise Valley were my pride and joy, and I had plans to build a larger house and some cabins down by the river on the far periphery of the property. I didn't have the funds to build my dream yet.

"Come on, Apple. Let's go tend to the veggies," I called to the dog as I made my way to my vegetable and herb plot. Normally, I would have ridden one of the horses, but tonight, I wanted to walk and think. I was still in shock that Pippa Chase was here. I was still processing how I felt about that. I was trying to accept the fact that she'd been engaged. She hadn't told me. But then why would she have? We only sent Christmas cards. Well, I only sent signed cards. She still sent letters. I just never responded to any of the questions she asked in hers.

Our friendship had become a distant acquaintanceship in my eyes. I'd once been close with her, but she was a part of my past. I'd never considered that she would feel differently. Or she'd arrive at my sacred space and expect to stay by bringing up a pact we'd made before we'd even hit puberty.

I grabbed the hose, turned it on, and walked over to my heads of lettuce. I had so much lettuce that I was going to look like a rabbit if I ate it all. I considered what Mindy had mentioned a few weeks before when I'd been complaining about my harvest being too fruitful.

"Go to the farmers' market," she'd said as she poured me some coffee. "Sell it there."

"But everyone grows veggies in Paradise Valley," I'd protested, and she'd laughed.

"I don't. Tourists don't. Lots of people don't. It's a way for you to make more money to save to expand your property. You really need to consider this option if you're serious about setting about your eco-tourist cabins down by the river." She'd shrugged and then walked away to serve another customer. We hadn't spoken about it again, but the thought had remained in the back of my mind. I looked over my land. I had plenty of lettuce, arugula, tomatoes, peppers, cucumbers, zucchini, onions, winter squash, beets, carrots, and kale. I could only make so many salads and stir-fry.

"What do you think, Apple?" I asked the dog, who was now sniffing the lettuce, in the hopes that it had turned into a juicy steak overnight. She looked up at me hopefully. "Do you want to spend your weekend mornings at the farmers' market with me?" Apple wagged her tail in response, and I reached down to pick her up and cuddle her in my arms. "You are just the cutest dog, aren't you?" She licked my nose in response, and I put her wiggling body back on the ground. "I can't believe I'm talking to you as if you could respond." Apple looked at me and then ran, stretching her little legs as she greeted her best friend, Donkey, who just happened to be a goat.

Donkey had been given to me as a gift from Jack when I'd moved to Paradise Valley and bought the land. He was gray, only slightly fluffy, and very grumpy. Jack had laughed and said that Donkey was like me in goat form. I didn't know whether to laugh or cry at his comment.

I knew Jack wasn't trying to offend me, though. In fact, Jack had helped me build my cabin. If I were honest, I would say Jack built my cabin, and I assisted him, but then he had all sorts of skills, having grown up in the area.

Jack Marley was a cowboy through and through. One of the best men I'd ever met in my life. I was proud to call him my best friend. We'd met in Colorado on a hiking trail and then gone climbing in Wyoming, Washington State, and California. I'd been a nomad at the time, having made money in the stock market (risking everything I had on a stock that had gone through the roof) and trying to figure out my life. He'd convinced me to visit him in Montana, and I'd fallen in love with the state. The rest, as they say, was history. It almost seemed like a weird kind of fate to find out that my father was somewhere in the area as well.

Donkey and Apple chased each other back and forth as I watered the veggies. I had a sprinkler system, but sometimes, I liked to use my own personal touch in the garden. I hadn't grown up with a green thumb, but the fact that I could grow my own food never ceased to amaze me. I loved my piece of heaven. I'd spent almost every penny I'd had on this land. Land that came with water was expensive, but I didn't regret it. I fished weekly, kayaked, swam, and enjoyed the best of life. This was my piece of nature, and I enjoyed my solitude.

Apple's excited barking made me look up to ensure she wasn't getting herself in trouble. My eyes searched the fields to see where she was, and I paused as I watched an angelic figure moving through the grass toward me. Pippa was wearing my blue shirt, and it was so long that it fell to her knees and completely covered the gym shorts I'd lent her. Her hair was long and flowing behind her back. Her long legs moved gracefully, and I saw she had no shoes on. I'd have to take her first thing in the morning to grab some things. There was a broad smile on her fresh and now clean face as she moved closer to me. I stilled as I noticed her natural and radiant beauty, the dimples in her cheeks that

I'd forgotten about. The way she constantly wiggled her eyebrows when she was nervous.

"Hey," she said as she bent down and ran her fingers across the pink and cornflower-blue wildflowers. "I couldn't sleep," she offered as an explanation as she looked up at me. "I thought I'd come and see if you needed any help."

"I'm good." I shook my head, annoyance carrying in the wind and across the mountains. "Do you know much about gardening?" I attempted to soften my tone. I knew my words were a bit blunt, but I was perplexed and taken aback.

The truth of the matter was that I was annoyed by her being here. Annoyed by her not going to sleep and giving me time to think. Annoyed by the fact that I wasn't as annoyed to see her as I wanted to be. Annoyed that she'd grown into a beautiful woman who caused my insides to react in a way I didn't like.

"No," she said as she looked down at my pepper plants, trying to stifle a giggle. Her eyes flashed at me with a look of nervousness, and I realized she was giggling because she was uncomfortable, not because she thought it was funny. "I had a monstera once that lasted for over a year, but then it died." She winced. "I guess you can say I have the opposite of a green thumb."

"Aw, that's a pity," I said, trying to ignore the urge to put her at ease as she moved closer to me. "Did you call your friend or fiancé?" I asked abruptly as I took a deep breath. The smell of gardenias floated in a mist past my nose. Pippa literally exuded flowery sweetness, and I would not allow that to invade my mind.

"I didn't call Emma or Stephan." She sighed deeply, "And interestingly enough, Stephan hasn't called me either. I bet he doesn't even realize that I'm not in town."

"He sounds like a winner." I turned to look at her, unable to stop my commentary on the man she was going to marry. Not one thing she'd said about him had been complimentary. "What were his good qualities?" I asked her curiously because nothing she had told me about the man she'd intended to marry was positive, nothing at all.

"He was handsome. And he had a good job." She wrinkled her nose. "And he liked to take me shopping. Wow, that makes me sound really superficial, doesn't it?"

"I'm not sure if you want to hear this, but...kinda, yeah." I shrugged, surprised at her self-awareness. She burst out laughing and pushed me on the shoulder. The touch of her hand against my shirt was warm and soft, and a tingling sensation filled me.

"You're not supposed to say that, TJ." She stared into my eyes, her brown irises iridescent in the dimming light. "We can't all be salt of the earth people."

"I never said I was a salt of the earth person." I laughed at the thought. "But then again, I was never into material things."

"What about your baseball card collection?"

"Hey, those are for my kids and grandkids one day," I murmured. If I one day had them. "I'm providing generational wealth to my future family."

"With baseball cards?" She giggled. "I could say the same thing about Chanel handbags. Did you know they keep their value and it oftentimes goes up as they become vintage?"

"Vintage as in old?" I winked at her. "Well, I'm glad to hear getting older increases your value in some regards."

"Getting older is great," she said, looking me up and down. "I have to say that you certainly benefited from it."

"Oh?" I asked her, raising an eyebrow as I looked at her

beautiful face. Her lips were slightly parted, and I watched them curve into a familiar smile. It struck me that Pippa was always happy and quick to smile. Even now, while she was in a state of shock, she could still smile and make jokes.

I remembered how she'd always made me laugh as a kid. No matter what was going on. When my parents argued, she'd invite me over (that was the thing with thin walls in Brooklyn apartments; you could hear everything), and when my parents stayed out late and never came home, she'd invite me to sleep over. She had a bunk bed, and she'd always let me sleep on the top bunk while we chatted all night long about what we were going to do at camp or where we'd go when we were older.

At those moments, I'd forgotten about the stress at home. She'd taken me to other worlds when she talked about books she'd read or ideas for the future. She'd make us act out different scenes for plays she was writing and clap with glee when something had gone particularly well.

She'd always been there for me. The sudden realization of how I'd treated her arrival, given how she'd always been there for me when we were younger, made me feel guilty.

"Hey, if there's anything I can do for you…" I shrugged and looked around. It was hard getting words out that made you feel conflicted. "To help you feel better or whatever…" I issued her a wry smile. I knew I sounded awkward, but I didn't have a way with words like she did. "Well, you just let me know."

"Aw, thanks, TJ." She beamed warmly at me. "I thought that you didn't want me here." She ran her fingers through her hair, rushed over to me, and hugged me. The feel of her arms around me melted my icy heart for a few moments.

"I've missed you, TJ." She gave me a quick kiss on the

cheek and stepped back. "I'm so happy we can rekindle our friendship."

"Yeah," I muttered as I turned back to watering my plants. "I'm glad to help." Slight lie. "But I do think we should put some rules in place." I looked at her through narrowed eyes. "This is a small town, and I don't want anyone talking about us and suggesting any impropriety."

"What?" Her jaw dropped, and I could see that she thought I was joking. "Um, what do you mean?"

"I mean..." I took a deep breath, dropped the hose head to the ground, and turned to face her again. I crossed my arms and thought about all the things she represented that I'd run away from. I had to stop remembering who she was as a teen. I had to stop remembering where and who she came from.

Pippa was a grown woman now. An attractive, overly effusive, and superficial woman. She'd basically admitted it. She cared more about shopping and makeup than about stargazing, foraging, and being there for others. "I don't know if it's a good idea that you stay here. But we can figure something out in the morning."

Disappointment crossed her face, and she nodded slowly. She bit down on her trembling bottom lip, turned away from me, and faced the mountains. "It sure is a beautiful evening," she said as she gazed at the lowering sun.

"It sure is," I said as I stared at her profile. She looked sad, and guilt flooded through me. This was Pippa. My Pippa. The girl who had made me laugh almost every day when we were younger. I wanted to take it back. I wanted to tell her she was welcome as long as she wanted to stay. I wanted to tell her that I'd missed her as well. But the words wouldn't come. My lips were obstinate to the mutterings of my heart.

There was no way I could have her staying here with me. I didn't want her bringing up past emotions in me or making me become too attached to her again. Especially as she'd be going back to the city faster than I could race Apple back to the cabin.

Chapter Seven

Pippa

Dear TJ,

Do you know what I was thinking about last night? I was thinking about when we dared each other to stay up all night, and you said I couldn't stay up past 2 a.m., and we bet $5. Do you remember that? I think we both fell asleep at 4 a.m. My dad found us fast asleep on the couch with cookies in our laps. That was so much fun.

My mom said she wants me to go to finishing school in Switzerland. She says I have no manners. I complained to Dad, and he *burst out laughing. He said that Mom thinks that she's royalty, that he's made of money, and that the only other schooling I need is to learn how to shoot a gun. I had to laugh. Never has it been more apparent that Mom is from England and Dad is from the South.*

One of these days, I'm going to ask how they ended up in Brooklyn.

How's it going in Florida? Did the mosquitoes suck away all your blood yet?

Your BFF4EVA,

Pippa

I felt like I had a large bushy tail between my legs, metaphorically speaking, of course, as I walked back to the cabin behind TJ. My face was burning, and I was annoyed. TJ was being so cold to me. I could tell he wasn't happy I was there and wasn't sure why. Granted, we hadn't seen each other in years, but friendships were meant to be like riding a bike. No matter how much time apart you had, you were still meant to be able to catch up as if there had never been any break.

I was upset at his coldness. Especially seeing as he was the one that had just stopped writing to me. I was the one that should be upset. I was the one that should be cold to him.

"You head inside," he pointed to something on the right, "I gotta take care of something. I'll be in later."

"Okay."

The cabin door squeaked as I opened it and stepped inside. The room was warm, and there was a musky, masculine smell that I hadn't noticed before. Even though the decor was reminiscent of a bachelor pad, TJ had made his cabin a home. I grabbed my phone as I made my way to the bed and called Emma back. I knew she'd be mad at me, but we were such good friends that I knew she'd forgive me. The phone rang three times before she answered, and I sank back into the plush pillows while I waited for her to chew me out.

"Is that you, Pippa, or did your—"

"It's me." I rubbed my forehead and closed my eyes. "I'm sorry that I hung up earlier. It's all been a bit crazy."

"Crazy is an understatement." Emma let out a deep sigh. "I'm worried about you, Pippa. What's going on? Are you okay?"

"I'm fine." I turned onto my side and snuggled into the bed. "Stephan cheating on me with Yoga Queen Kendra makes me feel like a winner in life." I knew I was being sarcastic, and I paused. "Sorry. Look, I came to Montana to get away. I needed to just run away, and I thought to myself, why don't I visit my childhood best friend?" I lowered my voice. "And guess what, he's as happy to see me as a kid is to see broccoli on his plate for dinner."

"I love broccoli."

"Because you're a weirdo." I laughed. "But the best kind of weirdo," I added quickly.

"Nice save, goof. So what's this you're saying about TJ? He's not happy to see you?" Emma sounded affronted for me. "What's his problem? Do you want me to come down there and beat him up?"

"I'd love for you to come to Montana but not to beat him up." I rolled onto my back and sighed. "He has way too many animals that will come to his defense."

"Animals plural?" Emma said. "Like cats and dogs?"

"He has a dog, horses, a goat, cows, and I think I even saw some sheep." I laughed. "He's a real farmer now...or cowboy...or cowboy farmer." I paused. "I know this is going to sound ignorant, but are cowboys farmers?"

"I think cowboys that raise beef cattle are called ranchers." Emma giggled. "Ask me how I know that?"

"*Yellowstone*," I said without even thinking for a second. For a city girl, Emma loved the show *Yellowstone* and all of its iterations more than I would have thought possible. "Talking of *Yellowstone*, did I tell you that TJ is kinda looking like Kevin Costner and Henry Cavill if they were somehow brothers and hot?"

"He is?" Emma sounded shocked. "Your childhood friend that you said—"

"We don't need to recall what I said." I cut her off. "TJ has grown up in all the right ways. He's superhot now. Being a rancher or farmer or whatever agrees with him."

"Let's just call him a cowboy and forget about the technicalities," Emma said. "Also, can you sneak a photo of him and send it to me? I want to see this Kevin Costner look-alike."

"Kevin Costner and Henry Cavill." I giggled. "He's got the grumpy persona to go with it as well."

"What's got him so grumpy?" she asked, and I frowned at her question. That was exactly what I wanted to know as well. Had I done something to him and didn't remember?

"I'm not sure, but it makes me sad. I need to figure out what's going on and I need to make him want me back in his life." I paused. "Maybe I'll make him breakfast in the morning, really bright and early, and coffee." I frowned as I remembered what Mindy had said. "Though maybe he wouldn't want that because that girl Mindy said that he was to bring me with him in the morning when he went to get his coffee."

"Is that his girlfriend?"

"No...it's his friend." I stared at the ceiling and then looked out the window. "Unless they were both lying. Which I don't think they were. I didn't get the sense they had a history. Not that I care, of course. All I want is to be friends with him again."

"You looking to replace me or something?" A twinge of jealousy in Emma's voice made me smile. We'd become fast friends the first week of college, and she'd confided in me that I was the first real best friend she'd ever had. For all her bravado and talk, Emma was sensitive and needed me as much as I needed her.

"Of course not. You're irreplaceable. You're my best friend. No matter if TJ and I become best friends again, no one will replace you. You know that. TJ is not going to eat ice cream with me at midnight or go to five karaoke bars in one night and pretend to be members of a famous European pop band."

"That was hilarious." Emma laughed. "Princess Philippa of Monaco-adjacent."

"Which would be France." I giggled. "Not that anyone seemed to get that, Queen Emmaline."

"Remember the song we sang all night?" she asked softly.

"'I Will Survive,'" we said in unison and burst out laughing.

"I miss you, Emma. I'm sorry I didn't tell you I was leaving the city." I knew I'd hurt her. I knew I'd acted impetuously. That was one of my negative attributes. Sometimes, I didn't want to face reality. Sometimes, I just ran away. It was a problem that I needed to face at some point. "You'd love it here though."

"When are you coming home?" Emma asked. "And when are you calling Stephan?"

"Do I really have to call him?" The thought of calling him made me feel sick. "I just don't..." My voice trailed off as the door opened and Apple came bounding in. She barked happily, ran toward the bed, and jumped up. She looked at me for a few seconds, then jumped on top of me and licked my face. "Apple!" I reprimanded as I rubbed her belly. I looked over at TJ as he closed the front door and waved a hand at me. "Hey, Em, TJ just got back," I whispered into the phone. "I'll call you tomorrow."

"Night, Pippa," Emma said and hung up. I sat up in the bed and continued rubbing Apple's soft golden fur as TJ headed into the kitchen.

"Still can't sleep?" he asked, poking his head around the corner and gazing at me.

"I guess my brain is thinking too hard," I said with a smile. "Maybe I'm related to Einstein and didn't know it."

"If you were related to Einstein, your mom would have told the world." He winked as he walked over to the couch and sat down. "How is she, by the way?"

"My mom?" I asked in surprise, and then my face paled, and I shrieked so loudly that TJ jumped off the couch and ran over to the bed.

"What is it?" he asked, looking around furtively. "A spider?"

"A spider? Where?" I jumped off the bed in fright. "I hate spiders. Where's the spray?"

"What spray?" He looked confused. "Why did you

scream?" He looked down at me, his blue eyes crinkled in the corner. His face was close to mine, and I was able to appreciate just how handsome he'd grown to be. His blond hair was dark now, but he still had some golden highlights. He had grown into a gorgeous man. I felt weird noticing that his arms were muscular and tan, the hairs on his skin like golden yarn.

"You made me think of my mom and I just realized that I haven't called her to tell her where I am or what's going on." I exhaled. I didn't want to deal with the real world. I didn't want to have the hard conversations with anyone. I just wanted to pretend that none of it had happened.

"Sounds like you've got a lot of calls to make tomorrow." TJ offered me a warm smile. "You better get a good night's sleep."

"I'll try. Night, TJ."

"Night, Pips." He nodded his head and headed to the bathroom. "I'll try and stay as quiet as possible."

"It's your home," I said, shaking my head at him. "Be as loud as you want. But maybe not as loud as you were the night we had that impromptu midnight party at camp."

"When I stole the speaker and blasted it on high volume by mistake?" He chuckled. "I nearly got kicked out and sent home."

"I know. They nearly kicked me out too. We were terrors."

"We were just having fun. I promise I won't blast NSYNC at one a.m., though maybe you'd like that. I seem to remember you wanted to marry Justin Timberlake."

"I wrote him like ten fan letters begging him to marry me." I buried my face in my hands. "So cringe."

"I remember. I'm glad you got over your obsession."

"Me too." I sat back down on the bed and yawned

loudly. My eyes were barely able to stay open. "I think the sleep mites just hit me." I stretched my arms out before pulling the sheets back. "Night, TJ."

"Night, Pips," he said softly before switching off the light and enveloping me in darkness.

Chapter Eight

T^J

Dear Pippa,

Did you know that Florida has the best sunsets in the world? Like jaw-droppingly beautiful. My grandpa said that the sun shines its prettiest here on the SW coast. I wish you could see it. I bet you would love it. Did I tell you that Mom said I could get a dog? I think she feels bad that Dad hasn't called or seen me in six months now. I don't understand it, but I guess he's taking the divorce badly.

I kinda miss him. I never thought I'd say that. How do you miss your own dad?

But recently, it's felt like I don't even have one. I met a new kid at school who also just moved to Florida from Colorado, named Cody. He's super cool, and he talks about all these mountains he's climbed. I don't know if the stories are true or not, but it sounds cool. We don't have any mountains here in Florida, but I am going to try climbing at a gym if Mom lets me.

Talk soon.

TJ

The smell of burning oil woke me up three seconds before the smoke detector went off. I rubbed my eyes as I jumped off the couch, my back aching in places I hadn't known existed. The couch was not comfortable, and I was in a rotten mood.

"Stupid smoke." Pippa jumped up and down, waving her hands around aimlessly. Had she never seen a smoke detector before? Did she not know how they worked? I glided across the room so that I could turn it off.

Pippa mumbled something under her breath as she grabbed a dish towel and jumped up and down again, this time waving the towel in the air. Her hair flew from side to side as she tried to get rid of the hazy smoke. My lips trembled at the movement as I hurried over to the kitchen to help her.

"Oh no, you're awake," she wailed as she gazed at me. "I wanted to surprise you with breakfast."

"I'm surprised all right." I looked down at the stovetop. The pan was filled with oil and bacon that had been burned to crisp, black charcoal. "Take the pan off of the fire, Pippa." I reached up and pressed the reset button on the smoke detector. "And let's open some windows and air the place out." I watched as she moved the pan and bent down to pet Apple, who looked hopeful.

Apple certainly didn't care if the bacon was burned or not. She'd love every morsel.

"I'm sorry." Pippa sighed as she opened the window above the sink. I reached behind her and turned on the exhaust fan above the stove. The air cleared out, and I leaned back into the cupboards as she peeked into the pan. "I guess you don't want to eat this."

"No, I don't," I said abruptly and shook my head. I didn't want to be rude, but I also didn't want her to take out plates and expect me to eat any of it. "Thank you for the gesture, but..." I shrugged, opened the fridge, and took out the jug of orange juice. "Want some?" I asked her, holding it up.

"No thanks." She bit down on her lip as she looked around. "Do you want some pancakes? I promise I will try not to burn them." Her lips twisted up at the side, and she groaned. "I can't promise they will be amazing though. I'm the eggs-and-bacon queen, not the pancake queen."

"I don't really think you're the eggs-and-bacon queen, either, Pips." I couldn't stop myself from laughing as I poured half a cup of orange juice and drank it down. "Maybe you can be the cereal queen?" I winked at her, and she made a face at me. "Sleep well?" I asked as I massaged my lower back. My muscles were not happy with me. I'd have to grab a blow-up mattress in town, or maybe I'd go camping again. That would kill two birds with one stone.

"I did, thank you. Your bed is so comfortable." She yawned prettily, pulling her hair into a bun. I watched as it fell apart moments later and cascaded down her back. "I should have some coffee, though, or I'm likely to fall back asleep again." She looked around the sparse countertop and frowned. "Do you have a coffee maker?"

"I don't." I shook my head and laughed at her horrified expression. "It helps me to limit my intake. I found when I had a machine in the house, I would be drinking cups morning, noon, and night. Now I just have one coffee a day at Mindy's coffee shop." My stomach sank as I thought about Mindy and the rest of Paradise Valley. The locals had probably spent the night discussing what was going on between Pippa and me.

"I think your phone is ringing." Pippa interrupted my worried thoughts, and I nodded my thanks as I headed back to the living area and grabbed my phone. It was Jack.

"Hey, dude, what's up?" I asked him curiously. Jack was not one to call this early in the morning. "Everything okay?"

"I'm good, but I'm here at Mindy's coffee shop..." His voice trailed off, and my shoulders tensed.

"Yeah, continue."

"Charlotte is here, and I just overheard her talking with Annie Roberts, Ruthie Smith, and Katie Matthews." He paused, and I knew what was coming. Charlotte was Mindy's best friend and always seemed to be in everyone's business. It made sense that she organized the weekly trivia night at the local bar, Montana Knights. Annie was Robert's wife and was a member of the local neighborhood watch with Ruthie and Katie, two other octogenarians who always seemed to be in the coffee shop discussing the comings and goings of everyone in the town.

"What were they talking about?" I asked, looking over at Pippa, who had opened the fridge and was looking inside, searching desperately for something to make me for breakfast. Unfortunately for her, I hadn't collected any eggs yet this morning, and the fridge was pretty sparse.

"There's a rumor that you sent for a mail-order bride from Russia, but you got ripped off, and they sent an obstinate city girl instead." Jack's laughter was not amusing. "Ruthie's complaining about technology, and Katie's saying that it's all AI's fault."

"What does that even mean?" I asked incredulously. I knew the rumor mill would go into overtime, but I never thought it would be this bad. This was ridiculous. Far worse than I'd thought it would be.

"It means that everyone assumes that woman is your new blushing bride." Jack didn't sound like he'd been trying to dissuade them of that idea either. "Though I am also curious as to who your mystery lady is."

"She's a childhood friend going through a bad time." I lowered my voice. "I haven't even spoken to her in years. I have no idea why she came here."

"She's cute..." His voice trailed off. "Even if her face was a mess and she was in a wedding dress."

"She just called off her engagement, Jack," I hissed. "Do not make a move on her."

"I wasn't even thinking of making a move on her." Jack sounded far too innocent. "I was just noting that she was cute, as in, with a shower and some new attire, she could be quite pretty." The call went quiet before he added, "Don't you think?"

"I don't know," I growled, watching Pippa stare at me with a look of interest on her face. She was trying to pretend she was staring out the window, but it was clear that she was eavesdropping, which wasn't hard to do in a five-hundred-square-foot cabin. It was a good thing she didn't have hopes of being a spy.

"Sure you don't, old boy. You're not a monk." Jack laughed, and I could feel myself getting annoyed. "How's she looking this morning?"

"We'll be at the coffee shop in about thirty minutes." I wanted to cut off this line of conversation right away. "And I'll be addressing any rumors people want to come at me with."

"You know those ladies aren't going to tell you what they've been saying, but I'll see you all later. You still planning on going to the tack store later, or will you be otherwise occupied?"

"I have to take Pippa to the store to buy some clothes and shoes," I said as I looked down at her bare feet. She was now standing next to me, a question in her eyes, and I hoped she wasn't going to ask me to take her to the grocery store so she could make me dinner. I didn't want her burning my cabin down.

"Did you have work you needed to do?" she whispered up at me, her brown eyes soft as she spoke. "You don't have to take me shopping if you need to work."

"It's fine." I shook my head and stared at her. "The tack store is not going anywhere." *Though maybe you should soon.* I chastised myself for my thoughts. It wasn't that I didn't want her here. It was just that she had no right to look that pretty and happy in the morning. Especially seeing as our friendship had pretty much ended ten years ago. Which she didn't seem to be computing.

"But the halters won't be on sale tomorrow," Jack said in

my ear. "Didn't you say you wanted to get Stella and Night-star engraved twisted leather halters?"

"I'll figure it out," I said sharply. "I'll see you in a bit, Jack."

"See you and your new wife soon, Mr. Wyatt." He laughed like he'd just told the funniest joke on earth and hung up before I could respond to him. I loved Jack. He was more like a brother than a friend. But I knew he was likely stoking the fires of the gossipmongers at Mindy's.

Which was ironic because Jack was the most confirmed bachelor I knew. He rarely dated and never spoke about any women from his past. And I'd never asked. We teased each other, went out drinking, and flirted up a storm with different ladies, yet neither of us had been in a serious relationship since we'd lived here. And neither one of us talked about it.

"We don't have to go shopping," Pippa said nervously. "I don't really want to get in the way of your routine and—"

"Why are you walking on eggshells around me, Pips?" I stared at her and folded my arms. "You've never been this passive, apologetic person before and—"

"You want me to leave?" She pointed at me, a hurt expression on her face. "You don't want me here, and I just want you to know that I'm sorry about whatever I did to make you mad at me. And I'm sorry for just showing up. And I'm sorry if your friends—"

"Pippa." I shook my head, grabbed her hands, then dropped them quickly and pretended I hadn't grabbed them and continued. "I was just shocked to see you show up here. I'm not trying to be rude, but it's not like we've been in contact for years."

"I know, but I don't know why." She blinked, her eyes

surveying my face. "And I needed you, TJ. As soon as everything happened, all I could think of was the pact."

"The pact did say that we would always be there for each other when we needed the other person," I admitted, though there was hurt in my voice. Maybe even anger. Seemed like the pact only went one way; that was what I wanted to say, but I didn't.

"I can leave," she said, shuffling her feet, her face down. "I will go. You're obviously mad at me and—"

"I didn't say I wanted you to leave. And I'm not mad at you." That was a partial lie. "The reason I suggested we figure out another arrangement was for your benefit. Paradise Valley is a small town and the rumor mill is already at work. I just didn't want people talking or thinking negatively about you. That's all."

"Oh, I don't care what they say about me." She made a face. "It's not like they know me." She played with her hair and started braiding it. "Is that really the only reason why you wanted me to leave?"

"Of course," I lied. I was not getting into the real reason why I didn't want her here. There was no way on God's green earth that I was going to have a heart-to-heart with Pippa Chase or delve into all the reasons why her being here was not a good idea for either of us.

"Okay then, let them talk." Pippa's expression changed, and she beamed at me. "I don't care. Shoots, I can go to the coffee shop and introduce myself to all of them and make them talk." She winked at me, and I narrowed my eyes as I watched her return to the bed area. She walked with a pep in her step, grabbed the sheets, pulled them up, and then smoothed them out.

"You don't have to make the bed," I said as I surveyed the lumpy mess. She'd tried, but she certainly wasn't going to get a job in room service at a five-star hotel. "You want to get ready? We can grab breakfast and coffee at Mindy's."

"Sounds good." She grinned at me. "I'm so hungry right now." She sniffed and wrinkled her nose. There was still a distinct, subtle smell of burnt bacon in the cabin. "Sorry about my failed attempt at breakfast. I'd hoped to surprise you with something delicious."

"Well, the thought was nice." I surveyed the mess and withheld a sigh. "You wanna go and wash your face and stuff, and then I'll brush my teeth and get ready?"

"Sure." She nodded. "You can use the bathroom at the same time if you want. I don't mind if you take your shirt off in front of me."

"Nah, that's okay," I said quickly. I didn't want to take my shirt off in front of her. "You go ahead. I'm going to take Apple outside to pee and check and see if the chickens laid any eggs."

"Oh, okay, sure." She licked her lips and offered me another small smile. "You're so country now, TJ. I never would have believed it if I hadn't seen it with my own two eyes."

"I guess we all change," I said, staring at her. "Sometimes life has a way of taking us in directions we never saw coming."

"You can say that again." She nodded slowly and sighed. "I never thought I wasn't going to marry Stephan, but it looks like that's not in my future." She looked thoughtful for a few moments, and I thought she was about to cry again, but I was mistaken.

She smiled up at me and headed toward the bathroom before turning back to me and stating, "I think everything happens for a reason though. Every good thing and every bad thing. We're all on this path of life for a reason. And sometimes, we take the wrong path. I feel like it's okay to get turned around because our new destination is probably even better than the one we were headed toward in the first place."

"That's a great way to look at life," I said, nodding as I thought about her words. "I feel like none of us knows where the future will lead us."

"Well, I know that my future has pancakes and syrup in it." She giggled. "And some bacon and eggs. And maybe some hash browns." She rubbed her stomach. "I'm telling you from now on, so you won't judge me."

"I could never judge you, Pips. Now hurry up because you just made me really hungry." She hurried into the bathroom and closed the door at my words, and I stood there for a few moments, contemplating our conversation before heading outside.

The cool, fresh air hit me as I opened the door, and I took a couple of deep breaths. Apple ran ahead of me, searching for Donkey, and I decided to run as well. My legs were stiff as I moved, but I didn't mind. I made my way over to the chicken coop and surveyed my surroundings. The mountains looked ominous this morning, overcast in dark-gray clouds but still beautiful. I thought about Pippa's comments.

I'd grown up in a twelve-story apartment complex in Brooklyn, then moved to hot and humid Florida, and now here I was. On my own land. In Montana. I was a farmer. A rancher. A cowboy. I was someone I'd never conceived of being when I was a young boy obsessed with skateboarding, prank calls, practical jokes, and hanging out with Pippa.

I lifted my shirt, looked down at my chest, and touched my skin lightly. My heart raced as I stood there. Years ago, I'd been someone else. Done things I wouldn't do now.

Years ago, I'd been broken. I was someone different now. The land had saved me. Mother Nature had given me a purpose. And now, here was Pippa Chase, back in my life, beckoning me to be the old TJ Wyatt.

And there was no way I wanted to return to that place in my life, no way at all.

Chapter Nine

P ippa

Dear TJ,

There's a school dance coming up next month. Girls have to ask boys, and I am losing my mind. Who do I ask? How do I ask? Do we kiss at the end of the night? And if we do, do we use tongue (gross, by the way)? I don't know what to do? I don't even know if I want to go, but Ashley says that we have to go. That we might get boyfriends out of it.

I'm not ready for a boyfriend yet. Well, maybe I am. :)

It's just weird. Everything is so different

now. Do you have a dance at your new school?
Are you going? Are there any girls you like?
Do you remember when we were eight, we said
we'd be each other's first boyfriend and girlfriend? Guess that's not going to happen now.

Hope all is well.
Your BFF4EVA,
Pippa

Mindy's Cupcakes and Coffee was on Main Street,
which TJ told me was the busiest street in Paradise Valley.
Which wasn't saying much.

"Down the street is Sweet Eats." He pointed to the left
of us. "Folks around here tend to go there for lunch or
dinner. They have the best steaks."

"Oh, cool." I smiled, happy to hear more about the area.

"Next to Sweet Eats is Montana Knights; it's a bar. The
owner, Brandon, is cousins with Jack, my friend you met
yesterday."

"Aw, okay." The street was filled with a few people, all
walking leisurely. I watched as a group of boys headed
across the street to what looked like the town square. There
was a large fountain in the center and a bunch of benches.
It looked quaint, just like I'd imagined a small-town square
would appear. It reminded me a little of *Gilmore Girls*, and
I smiled nostalgically.

"They're most probably going to play some basketball."
TJ followed my line of sight. "There's a court next to the
town square. And next to that is the baseball field. We have
a local team that plays weekly."

"It sounds idyllic," I said honestly, as my eyes went to the store next to Mindy's. "Ooh, a bookstore?"

"Yes, kinda." TJ nodded. "It's owned by Vivian Donato, she's the mayor's wife, but she's always traveling and shopping, so it's barely ever open."

"Oh, that sucks. I love bookstores." I turned back to Mindy's Cupcakes and Coffee and studied the building. The storefront was cute, with stickers of cupcakes and flowers on the windowpanes and a huge pink store sign hung at the front. Planters outside of the door held monstera plants and red and yellow flowers. Main Street was a warm and welcoming place to be. "Shall we?" I asked TJ as my hunger got to me. He nodded and proceeded to walk inside. I followed behind TJ and wondered what awaited me.

The inside was just as cute as the outside, with a display case on the far left showcasing the most delicious-looking cookies and cupcakes I'd seen in ages. The smell of freshly brewed coffee tickled my nose, and I smiled at the heads that turned toward us as we passed the tables and made our way to the bar top.

"Morning, TJ." Mindy held up her hand in a wave as she welcomed him. She then turned toward me and grinned. "Nice to see you again, Pippa. Hope you slept well."

"I did, thank you." I smiled at her gratefully. "I love your store. It's so cute."

"Thanks." Mindy beamed. "I know it's not New York City, but I think it's pretty cute."

"It's adorable," I said and then rubbed my stomach. "Everything smells delicious."

"The food is great," TJ said as he looked back at me and then looked around. "Hey, Jack." He waved to the man I'd seen at the ranch yesterday. Jack stood up and headed toward us. His eyes took me in, and he beamed, a flirtatious look on his face as he looked me up and down.

"Howdy there, Pippa." He grinned. "You're looking mighty pretty this morning."

"Jack..." TJ gave his friend a warning look. I wondered what that was all about. It was uncanny how close they were. As both men looked at me, I noted that they had the same Roman noses and keen, thoughtful expressions on their faces. It made me feel like an exhibit at a museum.

"Y'all want to join me at my table?" Jack asked, a warm smile spreading across his face as he gestured at the empty seats.

"Sure," I responded before TJ could answer. "Sounds good to me."

"Y'all, I'll be with you in a few moments." Mindy smiled and waved from the counter. "TJ, grab a menu for Pippa and I'll be along to take your orders in a few."

"Yes, ma'am." TJ chuckled as he grabbed a few menus. We followed Jack back to his table and took a seat. That's when I noticed a group of older ladies staring at me from the corner of the restaurant with curious expressions. They looked like mother hens, and I almost wanted to laugh. "Oh, don't mind them," TJ said as he followed my gaze. "They think you're my mail-order bride."

"What?" I squeaked. "No way."

"Way." Jack laughed as he sipped on his coffee. "Everyone in town is talking about TJ's new bride showing up in her wedding dress."

"But I'm not his new bride." I looked him in the eye to make sure he knew that. I could tell from the smile on his face and the laughter in his eyes that he one-hundred-percent knew that that wasn't the case. "They don't really think I'm a sort of mail-order bride, do they?"

"They totally do." Jack grinned at me. "I don't know if they'd be more or less scandalized to know that you're a runaway bride."

"Runaway bride?" I groaned as I realized that his words were correct. How had this happened to me? I, Pippa Jane Chase, was not meant to be a runaway bride. I was supposed to be married with two kids by thirty, with the third coming along at thirty-two. I was supposed to have a four-bedroom apartment on the Upper East Side that over-looked Central Park. I was going to have two nannies who took care of the kids and the home but stayed in the back-ground enough for the kids to love me the most.

I was going to go shopping on Fifth Avenue weekly with Emma while lunching at every up-and-coming restaurant right before they made it big. I was meant to be married to a Wall Street banker who made more money than everyone in Paradise Valley, and as all those thoughts crashed down in my brain, I realized that none of those thoughts had been my dreams. The blood fled from my face as I realized I'd been living more than one lie.

"Oh, I'm just joking." Jack sounded panicked as he gazed at me. I blinked at him, realizing I'd just had a come-to-Jesus moment in the middle of this small-town coffee shop. "TJ, tell her I was joking."

"Pippa, he was just joking. You're not a runaway bride. You're a runaway fiancée," TJ said, and I just stared at him for a few seconds before laughing.

"That's the same thing, TJ."

"Huh." He cocked his head to the side and grinned. "I guess it is." He leaned forward and whispered, "Are you overwhelmed? Do you want to leave?"

It was my turn to say, "Huh," but then I realized they thought I'd spaced out because of Jack's runaway bride comment. Maybe they thought I was regretting my actions. But I'd never been more certain of something in my life. This had been a long time coming. "One second, please." I stood up and started to run outside, but then I almost tripped and slowed down. TJ had loaned me a pair of sneakers, which were way too big for me, and I had to be careful how quickly I walked. As soon as I stepped out of the coffee shop, I pulled out my phone and called Stephan. The phone rang several times before he answered.

"Pippa, doll, where are you?" He sounded preoccupied as he spoke. "Want to do dinner tonight?"

"Dinner?" My jaw dropped. "In New York City?"

"Well, I'm not surprising you with a trip to Paris, so yes, New York City." He chuckled. "How many times do I have to tell you that surprise trips to Paris are for cheesy romance movies on Lifetime?"

"You mean Hallmark," I said in an agitated voice. "Hallmark has the sweet movies, Lifetime has the suspenseful ones."

"Yeah, yeah," he muttered. "So, do you wanna do..." His voice trailed off, and I was almost positive I heard giggling in the background. My jaw dropped at the sound. Was he cheating on me as we spoke?

"Stephan, where are you?" I kept my voice even-keeled.

"In the office." He sighed. "Making money to pay for this wedding you wanted."

"You proposed to me." I ran my fingers through my hair. "So obviously, you wanted to get married as well."

"I wanted to get something." He laughed bitterly, and I froze. Had he proposed to me because I didn't believe in sex before marriage? I'd never considered that before, but then I'd been blind to his flaws for far too long.

"I'm not in New York..." I took a deep breath.

"What do you mean?" He had the gall to sound annoyed. "I just saw you last night."

"No, you did not just see me last night." My tone was angry now.

"Stop shouting, Pippa." He sighed. "Why do you always have to stress me out first thing in the morning? Don't you understand that I don't deal well with your drama?"

"My drama?" My voice was low now, and I didn't know whether to laugh or cry. "Well, guess what, Stephan?"

"What?" he asked, sounding bored.

"It's over," I said firmly.

"What's over?" He was distracted, and I could hear giggling again.

"We. Are. Over," I enunciated each word clearly. "There will be no wedding. We will not be getting married."

"Wait, what?" I had his attention now. "Are you okay? You sound like—"

"I am fine."

"Look, where are you? Let's get lunch."

"We cannot get lunch!" I shouted. "I am not in New York City. I am in Montana. MONTANA! On the other side of the country. We are over. You're a liar. A cheat. A scoundrel. You don't listen. You don't care. And the only person that's a bigger fool than you is me for putting up with you for so long."

"P-Pippa..." he sputtered. "Wha-what is—"

"Not listening. Have a nice life." I hung up before he could say anything else and stared at the screen. I'd done it. And I didn't feel sad. I felt nothing but relief. I couldn't believe it. The sound that burst out of me was maniacal, and I wasn't sure if I was about to break down in shock.

"You okay, Pips?" TJ's deep voice sounded from behind me, and I spun around in shock. His face had a look of admiration, and I wondered just how much of my conversation he'd heard.

"Yeah, just ended things with Stephan." I wrinkled my nose and rubbed my forehead. "It feels surreal."

"You're in shock." He stepped forward and opened his arms. "I don't think it's hit you."

"What do you mean?"

"That your relationship is over. The man you thought you were going to marry is no longer going to be in your life." He stared at me awkwardly, his arms still outstretched, waiting to see what I would do.

I stared at him for a few moments and took a step forward. He enveloped me in his arms, and I pressed my head against his shoulder. His words hit me. I was no longer engaged. I was no longer getting married. I no longer had to deal with Stephan. My life as I knew it was gone. The thought both scared and excited me. And then tears flowed from my eyes. It was like the plug had just been pulled from the drain.

I sobbed and heaved for a couple of minutes, TJ rubbing my back and murmuring that it was going to be okay. His chest was warm and comforting. And he smelled like a mix of apple cider and pinewood. I pulled back and looked up at his face. He gazed at me briefly, wiped the tears from my eyes, and then handed me a handkerchief from his back pocket to blow my nose.

"You okay?" he asked softly, and I nodded, offering him a small smile. I wanted him to know that I wasn't some broken girl. I wanted him to see I wasn't upset because

Stephan had cheated on me. I was hurt, yes, but I was more mad. Mad at myself for ignoring every sign that had flashed before my eyes since the first couple of weeks of our dating.

"I'm good." I grinned at him. "Can I have a little fun?"

"What do you mean?" He gave me a look. "What sort of fun?"

"With the women inside?"

"What are you going to do, Pips?" he asked me suspiciously, and I grinned wickedly at him. "Pips, tell me."

"Nothing awful." I laughed. "Nothing that will get you kicked out of Paradise Valley."

"Fine, but don't make me regret taking you in," he said, shaking his head and pointing at me. "Don't make me drive you straight to the airport."

"You wouldn't do that to me. I'm going to go inside now. Wait three minutes and then come in." I turned to walk back into the coffee shop when TJ stopped me.

"Pippa!" He stared at me. "Tell me what you're going to do."

"It's a surprise." I giggled. "Trust me."

"I trusted you when we were younger and you always got me into trouble. So much trouble."

"I didn't get you into that much trouble." I glared at him. "I mean, yes, sure, we almost got kicked out of camp twice and the police station did threaten to call our parents if we kept pranking 9-1-1, but we were nine at the time. I didn't even know that we were wasting their time by asking them if they knew the phone number to the Ghostbusters —"

"Because we've got some ghosts in the closet." He laughed as he finished my sentence. "I cannot believe we thought that was funny."

"It wasn't funny," I said seriously. "We were just two goofy kids."

"We were pretty cool," he said softly. "We had the best time. We shared everything."

"We were young." I nodded. "We didn't know we should keep things to ourselves."

"I guess those things are learned." He nodded and looked away for a few seconds. Then he looked back at me and studied my face for what felt like hours. I felt like I was an organism under a microscope, and he was the scientist studying me to see if I could be the cure he needed. My heart beat double time as he reached forward, moved some of my hair away from my face, and lightly touched the tip of my nose the way he'd done when we were kids, and he was really happy.

For a few moments, I felt like I'd gone back in time. I felt like we were those kids again, promising each other that we would always be best friends. I remembered going to the fried chicken place by the park and sharing a box of chicken and fries, both of us wanting the last piece of chicken. And then he'd handed it to me all seriously and said, "I love you enough to let you have the last piece of chicken." And I'd realized he was the best friend I'd ever have. Not that I would tell Emma that. She was just as close to me but in a different way.

"I won't do anything so bad that the police would want to talk to your parents," I reassured him, giggling slightly at the nervous expression on his face. "Eeezzz true. I vont do anytving too baaad," I said in my best Russian accent.

"What happened to your voice?" He touched my forehead, his palm cool against my skin. "Did you trip and bump your head and I didn't notice?"

"*Nein*." I laughed. "I'm Vussian today."

"Russian?" His lips trembled as he cocked his head to the side and sighed. "You do realize you sound like a cross between a German and a Frenchman? There is no Russian coming through in that accent."

"Ve shall see." I grinned at him, took a deep breath, and headed back into Mindy's. There was another girl behind the counter that I hadn't seen before, but I ignored her. Jack was still seated, staring at something on his phone, and the three older ladies in the corner were all sharing what appeared to be one biscuit with honey. I peered over my shoulder at TJ, who had followed me inside, winked, and then headed over to the table in the corner.

"Allo," I beamed at the three older women, whose eyes widened at my approach. "I vould like to intraduce me to you." I waved at them. "I am Pippa. I come to stay with TJ. The very nice man with the cabin in Paradise Valley. He very handsome, you think?" The older ladies looked at each other and then back at me. "I vink I make nice bride, no?"

"So you're here to marry him?" one of the ladies asked, looking shocked. I was surprised they were buying my bad act. I knew I wasn't that great an actress.

"Zee wedding is off. Off with their heads," I proclaimed and stifled a giggle as the lady closest to me sipped on her coffee with wide eyes. I noticed the other lady was texting something on her phone.

"Um, I'm Annie Roberts," the lady closest to me said, putting her cup on the table. "I'm Robert's wife. I believe you met him at TJ's ranch yesterday?" Wait, her husband, Old Man Roberts, was Robert Roberts. I didn't know what to make of that name yet.

Her blue eyes peered at me curiously. She had a kind face, with white-blond hair and rosy cheeks. She wore a red-and-white-plaid shirt and khaki pants, and I noticed a massive ring on her finger. She might have been country, but she still cared about her jewelry. I wondered how that worked when doing chores on a farm.

"Hi!" I spoke in my normal voice and laughed. "I'm Pippa. Sorry, I was just doing a bit because I thought it would be funny, but maybe it wasn't that funny."

"Oh, oh." Annie smiled widely. "You had us going." She shook her head. "You naughty girl."

"You had me going as well," the lady with the phone placed it on the table. "I'm Ruthie, Ruthie Smith." She held her hand out to me. "I used to teach at the elementary school. Retired now." She broke off a piece of biscuit and bit into it. Her dark-brown eyes were also warm and friendly. She had a tinge of an accent, but I didn't recognize it. "You from Hollywood?"

"No." I laughed. "I'm from New York. TJ and I were best friends as kids and I decided to come and visit him." I gave them the short version.

"TJ's a good man." The third woman nodded. "I'm Katie Matthews. Nice to make your acquaintance and welcome to Paradise Valley."

"Thanks. I'm enjoying my stay so far. I just wanted to introduce myself."

"Yes, yes." Annie beamed. "Robert did say you were a nice girl. Perhaps we will see you at trivia night tonight?"

"Trivia night?" I asked, not sure what they were talking about.

"Charlotte James runs it," Ruthie explained. "She always did love spelling and quizzes in school." She turned her head toward the display case up front, and her gaze landed on Mindy, helping some customers. "She's best friends with Mindy. You might see her in here later."

"Okay. Sounds fun."

"Oh, trivia night is the best night of the week in Paradise Valley," Katie said and then frowned. "Well, it used to be book club night, but we haven't had that in a while." She frowned. "I wish Vivian would stop gallivanting around the world."

"Getting plastic surgery," Annie added, looking scandalized. "What a thing." I bit down on my lower lip to stop from laughing. Was plastic surgery really that bad? Not that I'd had any, of course, but I already knew some women in the city who got Botox on a regular basis.

"Well, I miss the plays that we used to put on at the Playhouse," Ruthie said with a sigh. "Do you remember that year I was Lady Macbeth and Ethan put my photo on the first page of the Paradise Valley Gazette?" She paused and looked at me. "That's the local paper."

"Aw, I see," I said as if that hadn't been obvious. "There's a local playhouse?" I asked enthusiastically. "I love theater. I studied English and drama in college. It was my dream to write and direct plays." I ignored the dull throb in my head that asked me why I was working as an assistant to a man who produced horror movies instead of pursuing my real dream, but I ignored it.

"Not anymore." Annie shook her head. "The building is still there and the local schools have their graduations there, but there hasn't been a play in years."

"Seven years, to be exact." Ruthie's eyes expressed dismay. "Sadie Beltram and her husband both passed away and left the building to the city, but Sadie was the one that used to organize everything and I guess when she died, no one else wanted to take it on."

"You didn't want to?" I asked her curiously. She seemed like she missed the theater.

"Oh no, I'm an actress, but I'm not a director." She

made a dramatic face. "I would not want to be in charge of organizing all of those people. Nope. No, thank you. Not on your nelly."

"Not on your nelly?" I asked her, unsure of the expression.

"It's a British slang term," Annie answered for Ruthie. "Ruthie grew up in England before her parents moved to the States."

"My father was from Guyana, a British colony," she explained. "And my mother was an English rose. They moved over because my dad had a job opportunity." She smiled at the memory. "So I'm all American now, though I suppose I love Shakespeare so much because of my British heritage."

"And you love West Indian food because of your dad, right?" Katie added, and Ruthie laughed.

"The one thing my father missed the most was his Caribbean dishes," Ruthie explained. "You don't get many Caribbean restaurants around these parts, but he taught me how to make all his favorites, and I'll make them for Katie and Annie and other guests at my infamous dinner parties."

"Sounds fun," I said truthfully. "I'm from Brooklyn, so I actually had a lot of Guyanese friends growing up. My favorites were cook-up rice and chana."

"You know cook-up rice?" Ruthie sounded the most happy I'd heard anyone sound in years. "Oh, well, now we must be friends."

"I'd like that," I said and then realized that TJ was probably wondering what was going on. "But I should head back to my table. Sorry for disturbing you all."

"No worries, dear." Annie lightly patted my hand. "I'm sure we will be seeing a lot of you. Enjoy your breakfast."

"Thank you," I said as I headed back to my table, a small

smile on my face. Both TJ and Jack were staring at me with stunned and apprehensive expressions, and I knew they were dying to find out what had happened. An idea hit me, and an impish expression crossed my face. I wasn't done having fun this morning. Only this time, I was going to prank TJ and Jack. I just had to make sure I didn't burst out laughing before I got through saying what I was going to say.

Chapter Ten

T[J]

Dear Pippa,

If you could go anywhere in the world, where would you go? My grandma asked me this last night, and I had a really hard time answering. My mom said she would go to Italy so she could get real Italian leather goods and authentic Italian food. Gramps said he'd like to go to Australia to see kangaroos. And then I said I'd love to go to New York to see you again. Mom got all quiet, and I think she felt bad because she started wiping her eyes. She then said I could have some extra scoops of ice cream, so that was cool.

Gramps followed me into the kitchen and said maybe I shouldn't bring up New York for a bit cause of everything. So I'm curious, where would you go if you could go anywhere? Cause that will be my new answer. Just don't say Mississippi or something cause that's not the most exciting place to visit.

I had an idea. Let's plan on meeting some-where when we turn 18 and can go wherever we want. What about France? You could shop, and I could watch soccer. Talking of soccer, I have practice in 15 mins.

Til la8er.

TJ

Pippa sauntered over to the table with a wide grin and a bounce in her step that I hadn't seen since we were thirteen years old. She flounced over to us, her dark hair bouncing, her eyes gleaming, and I couldn't stop myself from smiling. It was nice having her here. I hadn't wanted to admit it, but it felt good seeing her again.

"What's got you smiling like that?" Jack was staring at my face. "Don't tell me you heard the pancake special today and got that excited?"

"Yeah, I'm really happy we can have pancakes with blueberries, chocolate chips, and real maple syrup." I nodded. "Mindy has outdone herself." He laughed at my sarcasm but then turned to stare at Pippa again. His glance was a bit too appreciative for my liking, but I knew I couldn't say anything.

"Darlink," Pippa skipped to the table, and I frowned at her weird accent. "I have told ze people our news," she said, wrapping her arms around my shoulders and kissing the side of my face. "It is good news. Everyvone tinks so."

"Why are you talking like that?" I narrowed my eyes as she took a seat next to me. I looked back at the three older ladies sitting in their booth, deliberately trying not to look over at us. "What's going on, Pippa?"

"I'd like to know as well," Jack asked. "Is that meant to be a French accent?"

"Russian!" Pippa exclaimed. "Are my acting skills seriously that bad?"

"Have they ever been good?" I asked her, thinking about the time she made me go with her to a local theater in Brooklyn so she could audition for *Annie*. She'd decided to create new lyrics to the titular song and performed "Yesterday" to a break dance movement she'd choreographed. Needless to say, she hadn't gotten the role of Annie and hadn't been invited to audition for any other roles either.

"Let me think...am I going to get an Oscar?" She paused and looked at me and then Jack. "Maybe not. Am I going to get a Golden Globe?" She looked at me, and I shook my head.

"Nope, you won't."

"Am I going to get a Tony?" She looked at Jack.

"I'm thinking that's a no."

"But would I qualify for a participation award?" She nodded enthusiastically. "Yes, yes, I would."

"Pippa, what are you talking about?" My stomach grumbled as Kaye headed toward our table with a notepad, and I could see her eyes on Jack, who was trying to avoid eye contact with her. Kaye's fiery red hair was piled on top of her head, and she had a pen between her lips.

"Nothing," Pippa said, glancing over to look at Kaye. "I was going to prank you, but..."

"Morning, cowboys." Kaye stopped at the table. "Y'all know what you want to order this morning?"

"I'll have the special," Jack said without looking at her. "And another black coffee."

"Nice seeing you, Jack." Kaye's voice softened. "I was just thinking about you the—"

"Have you met Pippa?" He cut her off and nodded to Pippa. Kaye sighed and looked over at Pippa.

"Hello," she said dutifully, but it was clear that she wasn't interested in getting to know her. "I'm Kaye, your waitress today. Do you know what you want to eat?"

"I'm still looking at the menu," Pippa said, shaking her head. "TJ, you go ahead and then I will choose something."

"Okay." I nodded. "I'll have a Denver omelet with hash browns, white toast, and a side of fruit. I'll take a black coffee as well." I handed Kaye my menu. "Oh, and go ahead and bring some butter and strawberry jam too. And some extra bacon on the side."

"I see you've still got the same appetite." Pippa looked up from her menu and smiled at me. "You're lucky all that food doesn't go to your hips."

"I guess I am." I winked at her. Kaye's eyes were darting back and forth now.

"You the bride?" she asked Pippa as she looked her up and down. I could see Pippa blushing at the interrogation.

"I am. Or rather was." Pippa frowned. "I'm not getting married anymore."

"So, you came to have some fun with TJ? What is he, your ex?"

"Kaye." I frowned at her. I didn't appreciate the way she

was talking. "Pippa is my childhood best friend. She's come to visit because she's suffering from a broken heart."

"Oh, I get it." Kaye glanced at Jack quickly, and he looked away. I wish I knew the whole story of their relationship. All I knew was that they'd dated in high school and then broken up. Honestly, I wasn't sure what Jack had seen in her. She was cute, but all she did was gossip and talk about people behind their backs. It seemed to me that she was bitter about life and didn't do much to hide it.

"How's Bobby?" I asked her quickly, and her face softened, thinking about her son. "Still playing baseball?"

"Yes, he's in Little League." She smiled. "He's getting so big now. He just turned nine."

"Wow, you have a nine-year-old?" Pippa asked in surprise. "You don't look old enough."

"Yeah, well." Kaye shrugged. "You know what you want?"

"I'll have the French toast with bacon please," Pippa said quickly. Kaye nodded and walked away slowly, stopping to say something to another table as she made her way back to the countertop. "Well, she's not the friendliest person I've ever met in my life." Pippa made a face. "And they say people in the city can be rude."

"Most people in Paradise Valley are nice," I said, wanting her to have a good impression of the small town, though I wasn't sure why. If she didn't like it here, she'd leave faster. "Don't you agree, Jack?"

"We're lovely," he said dutifully and leaned back. I could tell from the look on his face that he was going to go into classic Jack Marley mode. "And I'm the loveliest of them all."

"Oh, really?" Pippa tilted her head to the side and laughed. "Well, I'm glad to hear that TJ is keeping good company." She turned to me, her eyes teasing. "I was going to ask how you survived without me in your life all these years, but I suppose that Jack has been a good substitute for me."

"The best," I said, and I saw a flicker of regret and sadness in her eyes. Instantly, I regretted my flippant remark. I didn't want to hurt her. "Though no one is quite like you, Pippa," I added quickly. I'd forgotten how sensitive she could be as she masked her insecurities well. To the outside world, she presented a happy, confident, beautiful face, but she, like most of us, had insecurities. Hers stemmed from her mother, who was one of the most superficial women I'd ever met. Not that I'd understood when I was younger. But as I'd grown, I'd realized and hated it. I hated it because I could see her values reflected in Pippa's thoughts in the letters that she'd written.

"There's no one like you either," she shot back, and Jack groaned.

"There's no one like me either," he added, winking at her. "Shall we throw a party this weekend to celebrate that fact?"

"Very funny." I stared at him, my eyes telling him to back off with the flirting. I might not have wanted Pippa in town, but I certainly didn't want him making a move either.

The bell above the door chimed, and I looked over to see who was coming inside. Brandon, the owner of the bar; Aiden, the local vet; and Ethan, the editor of the newspaper, all walked inside with basketball shorts and oversized T-shirts. "Hey." I held my hand up and waved to them. "You guys been shooting some balls this morning?"

"Yup," Aiden answered as they walked over to the table, all of them eyeing Pippa. "I texted you to join us so we could have played two on two."

"I know. Sorry. I have a guest," I said, nodding over to Pippa, who was looking at the three men with an intrigued look on her face. I couldn't tell exactly what she was thinking, though I didn't love the wide, lazy, flirtatious smile on her face as she played with her hair. "This is Pippa, a friend of mine from New York." I nodded at her. "And Pippa, these are some of my friends, Aiden, Ethan, and Brandon."

Brandon stepped forward and introduced himself first. "Hey, I'm Brandon Knight. I'm the bartender and owner of Montana Knights, the local bar a few doors down." He held out his hand, his green eyes sparkling as he looked her over. His dark-golden-blond hair was cut close to his head, and I could see Pippa admiring his physique. Brandon was probably the buffest of all my friends, and he made sure he stayed that way by working out daily.

"Nice to meet you, Brandon," Pippa answered. "I heard you have a trivia night at your bar."

"We do." He grinned. "Charlotte runs it. You might see her around here somewhere. She's best friends with Mindy and is almost always here."

"Oh, awesome," Pippa said with a small smile. "Everyone really does know everyone, huh?"

"You could say that." I then introduced the other two men. Aiden was holding a newspaper in his hands, and I shook my head. "This is Aiden. He's the local vet. Also known as Don Juan. All the animals and ladies in town love him."

"I wouldn't say all." Aiden grinned as he held out his hand, his blue eyes laughing as he folded his paper on the table in front of him. "I'm still single, after all."

"Well, lucky girls then," Pippa said, and I rolled my eyes.

"And I'm Ethan." Ethan stepped forward and introduced himself before I could. "I run the Paradise Valley Gazette, the local newspaper. It's nice to make your acquaintance."

"Thanks, you too." Pippa gazed at him in awe. "Can I just say I love your curls? How do you keep them looking so beautiful?"

"I don't know." He laughed, shaking his head. "It must just be genetics."

"Oh?" Pippa looked him over. "Lucky."

"I'm Native American, White, and Black." He grinned. "I like to think I got the best of all worlds."

"You sure did." Pippa grinned, taking in his dark curly locks, hazel-green eyes, and dark skin. Ethan was the man that every woman in Paradise Valley initially wanted to date until they realized he was hyperfocused on the paper. Then they tried Aiden but soon realized he was all about animals. Then, they either tried to flirt with Jack, Brandon, or myself, but they soon realized that all of us were confirmed bachelors. I supposed it wasn't unusual for men in our age group to still be single, but I had a feeling that once one of us found ourselves in a serious relationship, we'd all follow suit pretty quickly. I didn't see that happening for a long time though.

"Morning, boys." Mindy sauntered over to the table with a tray full of cupcakes. "Try my new banana pudding cupcakes and tell me what you think."

"We haven't even had our breakfast yet, Mindy." Brandon shook his head and frowned. "Plus, you know I only do carbs once during the week."

"You're such a bore, Brandon Knight." Mindy rolled her eyes and placed the tray on the table. "Don't you let any of these men bother you, okay, Pippa?" She grinned conspiratorially at Pippa and glared at the other men before winking. "Because if you do, you'll have me to deal with."

"Oh, I'm so scared." Brandon pretended to shiver, and Jack laughed. I just shook my head at my friends' antics and pretended to look around the coffee shop while I gazed at Pippa to see if she was feeling overwhelmed by being around so many new people. I needn't have worried, as she was giggling and munching down on one of the cupcakes as if she didn't have a care in the world. Which was what I wanted her to feel. I didn't want her to be heartbroken over her cheating fiancé. He was lucky that I wasn't in town, or I would have had a serious talk with him. Maybe I'd even have offered him a talk with my fists to ensure he stayed out of her life because I had a feeling he wasn't going to take the breaking up of the relationship well.

I mean, who could ever really get over losing someone like her? She brought the sunshine to dark rooms on rainy days. She was the sort of person who radiated positivity and happiness. She could make even the most mundane of tasks interesting and fun. Shoots, she'd done that when we were kids. I'd even helped her do the dishes and laundry when we were younger, just because I enjoyed being around her so much.

I reached out and touched her on the shoulder. "Everything okay?" I asked, wanting to make sure that she wasn't in need of some time alone.

"I'm good. Thanks, TJ," she said with a soft smile that made my heart explode. "This is exactly what I needed."

Chapter Eleven

P ippa

Dear TJ,

I think Sadie Cohen has a crush on Tom Lindy. GROSS! Do you remember how she used to constantly talk about her ballet classes as if the whole world revolved around ballet? Booooring. Tom Lindy told Joe that he thinks I'm cute, but Sadie said she'd go to second base with him, so he's going to ask her out. Disgusting. I think she should have more respect for herself. Don't you?

How's Florida? Would you ever get a tattoo? Should we get best friend tattoos symbolizing our unbreakable bond? That would be so cool, huh? I think I will get one that says Pippa and TJ, Bffs 4eva and a day. What will you get? We'll have to wait until 18, of course. No way, my mom or dad will let me get one now. They are so boring.

    I've sent you some stickers. Do you like them? I think I might try to sell some to save money so I can buy these new designer jeans I saw in this boutique in the Village last week. Why can't I have been born into an oil family or something?

    Lots of love,
    Your BFF,
    Pippa

My stomach was full, and I was ready to go back to bed again. However, I wasn't going to tell TJ that. I didn't want him to think that I was lazy. The food had been amazing, and I would even go so far as to say that it was the best breakfast I'd ever had in my life.

"Your friends are really nice," I said as I got into the passenger side of TJ's white Ford pickup truck. He nodded, turned the radio on, and country music spilled through the speakers as he pulled off. "Are we going to go to trivia tonight?"

"Do you want to go to trivia tonight?" he asked, surprised as he looked at me. "I thought you'd want to chat on the phone with Emma or whatever and watch TV."

"I love chatting with Emma and I love TV, but I want to go out." I shrugged. "I want to get to know your friends and I'm pretty good at trivia, I'll have you know."

"You are?" He raised an eyebrow. "Since when?"

"Since they added celebrity gossip questions to the mix." I laughed, grinning at him. I looked out the window and admired the picturesque town square, basketball court, and baseball field next to it. "Where are we off to?" I asked him as he pulled out onto the main road.

"I figured I'd take you to the next town to get some clothes."

"You don't have to do that," I said, shaking my head. "I'm sure I can find some stuff here." I didn't think I'd find anything I loved, but I didn't think that was likely to happen in the next town either. TJ started to protest when my phone rang. I pulled it out of my handbag and sighed when I saw it was my mom.

"You can get it if you want," TJ said as he lowered the volume of the radio.

"Thanks," I said half-heartedly as I answered the phone. "Hey, Mom. How's it going?"

"What is going on, Pippa?" my mom screamed into the phone. "What's this that I hear?"

"I don't know, Mom." I held in a deep sigh. "What did you hear?" I pretended to be ignorant. Of course, I know why she's calling, but I want to delay the conversation for as long as possible. Even if it's only for twenty more seconds.

"Stephan called me in tears," she exclaimed, her voice shrill. "He said you've run off with some man you just met."

"What?" My jaw dropped. There was no way Stephan had been in tears. Absolutely no way. I knew him far too well, and I knew nothing I could say or do would make him cry. All he cared about was the stock market and the Dow. "That is not what happened, Mom."

"Where are you?"

"I'm in Montana."

"Montana," she said distastefully as if she couldn't believe what she was hearing. "What do you mean, Montana? Like on the other side of the country."

"Yes, Mom, the Montana on the West Coast, not the one next to New York."

"Don't you be smart with me, young lady," she snapped. "What are you doing in hillbilly land?"

"It's not hillbilly land, Mom." I could see TJ's lips twitch as I talked. "Everyone is really nice, and yes, many of them live on large plots of land in the country, but it's not like they're the Beverly Hillbillies."

"I wish I was one," TJ said with a chuckle. "I wouldn't mind finding oil and striking it rich."

"You seem like you're doing fine to me," I said to him, thinking of his wonderful tract of land. "You have your own river, for heaven's sake. And a pet goat."

"Pippa," my Mom cut me off. "Who are you talking to?"

"TJ, Mom."

"Is that the new man that—"

"TJ Wyatt, Mom. You remember TJ."

"TJ Wyatt?" She sounds shocked. "From next door?"

"Yes, Mom, that TJ."

"I didn't even know you kept in touch." She sounded disapproving. "I thought that friendship ended years ago. Especially after the scandal with his mom."

"Huh?" I blinked in confusion at her comment and snuck a look at TJ to see if he'd heard what she'd said. I could tell from the way his lips thinned as he glanced at me that he had. I wanted to ask my mom more about her comments, but I couldn't do that in front of TJ. Though I had no idea what she was talking about. What scandal?

"You must come home to your fiancé, darling. The wedding is next week. And just think of your honeymoon in the Maldives. Daddy and I spent a lot of money on that special gift for you. Over ten thousand dollars, darling. Daddy did have to dip into his Roth IRA and you know that he—"

"Mom, I didn't ask for that." I released a deep sigh. "Mom, Stephan cheated on me and I called the wedding off. I am not coming back to New York anytime soon. I am not going to the Maldives. I am not marrying him." I took a breath. "Frankly, I don't know if I ever wanted to marry him, Mom."

"But you loved him," she sputtered, shocked at my words. Even as she spoke, I knew what she said wasn't true. I was ashamed to admit it to myself, but I hadn't loved Stephan, not really. And I'd known it for a while and hadn't wanted to acknowledge it.

"I don't love him, Mom." I lowered my voice. "I think you did though."

"What are you saying, Pippa?"

"Not in that way," I said quickly. "But you loved him for me. For all the things you thought he could give me and bring to my life."

"Is that so wrong to want my daughter to be happy?"

"But I wasn't happy, Mom."

"But I suppose Montana makes you happy?" She sounded pissed. "What are you going to do now? Become some tree-hugging nut?"

"Mom, I've been here for twenty-four hours." I rolled my eyes. "I just needed to get away."

"We could have figured it out."

"Stephan is not an option for me, Mom. I'm not marrying him. I'm not going back to him."

"And what about your job? What does Montague have to say about you just up and leaving? It's totally irresponsible, Pippa. I didn't raise you to run away from your responsibilities."

"He's in London, Mom. I haven't run away from anything. I need to figure out what I want"—I paused—"in all areas of my life."

"What does that mean?"

"It means that I've been living your dream for me, Mom, and in twenty-four hours away from the city, I'm already starting to see things a bit differently."

"It's that TJ, isn't it? He always did fill your head with stupid thoughts and ideas."

"Mom, I'm going to go now," I said quickly. "I love you, and I'm fine, and I will speak to you soon." I hung up before she could protest. I squeezed my phone for a few seconds and looked out at the big blue Montana sky. "It really is beautiful here," I said after a few moments. "I understand why they call it the Big Sky now." I looked over at him. "Are you mad at me?"

"Why would I be mad at you?" he asked me softly, his eyes staring straight ahead. "You told your truth."

"But my mom was so rude and I know you could hear."

"That's your mom," he said with a shrug. "I guess I can understand why she's worried about you."

"She's not really," I said, feeling guilty for speaking negatively about my mom. "She's more upset that she can't tell her friends that her son-in-law is a hotshot trader on Wall Street making half a million a year."

TJ let out a low whistle. "That's a nice chunk of change."

"It is," I said, laughing. "But not worth marrying someone for."

TJ's expression changed as he gazed at me and nodded slowly. "You've matured."

"What does that mean?" I frowned, slightly upset at his comment. Did he think I was a gold digger?

"I seem to remember a time when money and fortune meant a lot to you." He shrugged.

"When I was young?" I glanced at him. "I don't feel like I ever said anything like that." I pressed my lips together, and he didn't respond.

"Did you mean what you said?" he asked finally as we pulled up to his ranch. I blinked in surprise that we'd come back home instead of shopping.

"About what?" I asked as he stopped the truck and jumped out. He hurried to my side and opened the door for me.

"That you're not in love with Stephan?" He stepped back as I jumped out, and I looked up into his big, dazzling blue eyes, which seemed intent on my face at that moment.

"I'm not in love with him." I nodded, almost embarrassed. "I'm not really sure what I was thinking when I agreed to marry him," I said honestly. "Emma never liked him."

"She sounds like a smart girl," he said with a sudden grin. We walked toward the cabin, and I saw Donkey, the goat, sitting outside the door. "He's waiting on Apple. He wants to play."

"He likes to play?" I asked in surprise, gazing at the goat, who had now risen and was staring at me as if he wanted to butt me. I took a few steps back and watched as TJ opened the front door to the cabin. Apple came bounding out, and only after a few seconds did I realize she was racing over to me. I yelped in surprise as she jumped up at me, but then my eyes widened as Donkey came running toward me as well. I shrieked as he came closer and closer.

"Don't worry," TJ said with a bemused expression. "They won't harm you. And if you're going to stay here, you're going to have to get used to these two. They like to think they're human."

"So you don't mind me staying, then?" I asked him, my heart racing as I waited for him to answer. "Or do you still think I should leave?"

"You can stay, Pippa." His voice was soft and thoughtful as he walked over and studied my face.

Our eyes met for a moment, and I could feel myself wanting to melt into the ground from the intensity. "Just know, though, I expect you to help around the ranch."

"Of course." I grinned back at him. "I have a feeling I'm going to be a natural," I said as I gingerly patted Donkey on the head. TJ snorted at my comment, and I made a face at him before we laughed. It felt nice being comfortable around him again. Though, even as I was laughing, a sense of foreboding sat in my stomach. I was starting to face my own truths, yet I still wasn't happy. And I didn't know what would fill that void.

"Good." He nodded. "By the way, we'll head into town in an hour. That way, you can get some clothes," he said as his eyes darkened. I nodded slowly but was desperate to know what he was thinking. I still didn't understand why he'd stopped talking to me or why he'd been so cold when I arrived.

Chapter Twelve

T J

Dear Pippa,

My momma started going to a yoga studio and told me she thinks I should go with her. I was like, no thanks. She said she thinks it will be good for me when I get upset. But I'm not the one that gets upset. I have baseball and my friends.

Did I tell you that my dad forgot my birthday? I thought maybe he'd show up and surprise me here in Florida. I'm not sure what's going on with him. He hasn't called or anything. Mom says she knows he's still alive and is just being his usual selfish, immature *asshat. I guess he took the divorce badly. I kinda miss him.*

I miss you too. I know you wanna ask me that, haha. Sometimes I just wanna get on a plane and see ya, and then we can go and grab a slice of pizza and lay out in the park and pretend we're in Paris, like you always liked to do.

Maybe one day.

Your friend,

TJ

I was surprised to see Pippa with stacks of clothes in her hands as she headed toward the changing room. She had a happy smile on her face as she glanced at me.

"I thought you said you only needed a few things?" I asked as I leaned back against one of the walls. "And you said that you didn't think you'd find anything in this store." I pressed my lips together. Was I going crazy? Hadn't she just said that she didn't think this store was going to work when we'd walked in not five minutes ago?

"I guess I was wrong." She grinned. "I guess I'm not going to be New York chic, but I will fit right in here in Paradise Valley."

"Hmm." I gazed at the plaid shirts, overalls, long johns, and jeans in her hands. "Do you need all of them?"

"I'm not buying all of them, silly. But I need to try everything on to see if it fits and looks good."

"Try everything on?" My eyes widened. "Now?" How

long was that going to take? I'd thought we'd come in, she'd grab a couple of items, and we'd be out within fifteen minutes.

"I don't know." She shrugged. "Maybe ten minutes."

"You can try all that on in ten minutes?" I tilted my head to the side, my eyes challenging her time frame. Was she a speed dresser or something?

"Well, maybe not ten minutes." She bit down on her lower lip and gave me a playful, innocent smile. "Maybe fifteen."

"Uh-huh." I frowned. Was this going to take all day? "Let me call Jack. I was supposed to meet up with him this afternoon about some work stuff, and I'm not sure I'm going to make it."

"You will make it, TJ. This is not my first rodeo. I won't be long." There was challenge in her tone.

"If you say so." I looked around the store, feeling out of place among all the dresses, jewelry, and personal items of clothing. "I'll be outside."

"You don't want to wait around and give me advice on what looks good?" Did she really want my input? I didn't know what looked good from bad, and as far as I was concerned, there wasn't much that would look bad on her with her long legs and curvy body. Though, I wasn't meant to notice that she was now a woman. Or to look at the curve of her lips as she smiled or feel a rush of excitement when she touched me lightly. She'd just ended an engagement. She was here to mend her broken heart. She wasn't here to see if we had a spark of attraction. She wasn't here to see if the chemistry between us was more than friendship.

"Do I have to?" I grabbed my phone and held it up. My fingers held it tightly. I wanted to tease her and tell her that I'd be happy to go into the dressing room with her and tell her how everything fit, but I knew that was totally inappropriate and was liable to get me slapped. Plus, I didn't want Pippa to think I was the sort of guy who was only interested in one thing. I wasn't that sort of guy. I'd never been that guy. And I would never be that guy.

"No, goof." She waved me away. "Go and call Jack and do whatever you have to do. I'll meet you outside."

"Okay, sounds good." I nodded and headed toward the front of the store immediately before she could change her mind. As I walked past a display of necklaces and rings, the sales associate stepped forward.

"Good afternoon. Would you like to surprise your girlfriend with one of our custom pieces?" She smiled sweetly and pointed toward the bracelets. "I can help you choose a piece."

"Oh, she's not my girlfriend," I said quickly. "Or my wife," I joked but soon remembered that she had no idea why that would be funny. "She's a friend of mine that's come to town and just needed to pick up a few things."

"Hmm." The sales associate looked disappointed. "A good friend?"

"I guess so." I nodded slowly. Was this a thing now? Were you supposed to buy friends presents? Or was this girl with the pink-streaked hair just trying to make a commission off of me?

"I know if my best friend surprised me with a necklace or something, I'd be ecstatic." She spoke nonchalantly. "But that's just me."

"Fine, let me see what you have." I looked down at the table, feeling slightly annoyed by her tactics, but as I looked over the pieces, I thought they did look unique and cool, sort of like Pippa. My eyes skipped over the rings. There was no way I was buying her a ring. Men didn't buy rings for women. Not unless it was an engagement ring. The necklaces all looked cute, but I had no idea if Pippa would like any of them.

My eyes flew to the bracelets, and suddenly, I remembered one summer when she'd made us friendship bracelets. She'd made us both the same bracelet, with blue, red, and yellow threads, and it had read, Pippa and TJ, best friends forever and a day. I could still remember her tying it around my wrist, her brown eyes gazing at me in happiness. "No matter what happens, TJ, we will always have each other and our friendship." I'd rolled my eyes, though secretly I'd been happy by the words. Her friendship was something I'd never taken for granted.

I picked up a silver bracelet and showed it to the sales associate. "Can I get this engraved?"

"Yes, sir." She beamed. "I can do that for you. Do you know what you want it to say?"

"Pippa and TJ, best friends forever," I started, but then shook my head. "Actually, no. Let me think."

"Okay. Why don't we go over to the front, where the stamp is."

"Sure." I followed behind her, wondering if I was being too sentimental as I thought about ideas for the engraving. She walked behind the counter, picked up a notepad and pen, and stared at me.

"Any ideas?"

"Yes." I nodded slowly. "Don't fear jumping. I will always be there to catch you," I said softly, and the sales associate looked at me with a light in her eyes.

"That's lovely." She scribbled on her notepad. "She'll love it."

"I hope so," I said, unsure of what I was doing but knowing inherently that I wanted to get her this present. I wanted to let her know that she could count on me, even if I didn't know how to articulate it in words. I pulled my wallet out of my back pocket and searched for my credit card. "How much?" I asked as I pulled it out.

"It comes to one hundred and fifty dollars." She smiled sweetly. "It's real sterling silver."

"I see." I hoped Pippa would like the bracelet. A hundred and fifty dollars wasn't a huge sum, but it was still money that could have been put toward building the cabins down by the river and my larger ranch house. The sales associate swiped my card, handed it back to me with a receipt, and grabbed a pair of glasses.

"Okay, this will take me a little while. I'll wrap it in some tissue paper and a box and give it to you in a bit."

"Sure." I nodded. "But can you just make sure my friend doesn't see if she comes out of the changing room before you're done?"

"Of course. I won't ruin the surprise."

"Thanks." I held up my phone. "I'm just going outside to make a quick call. I'll be back inside in a few minutes."

"Certainly, sir, thank you for your business today." She watched me as I headed out of the door. I looked back over my shoulder and watched as Pippa popped out of the dressing room wearing a pair of tight jeans and a red-and-white-plaid shirt. She'd put her hair in two pigtails, and I wanted to laugh at the image she made from outside the store. She looked like a farm girl on a TV show. Though she was cuter than any of the actresses I'd seen on the screen. I turned away so she couldn't see me watching her and pulled out my phone.

"What's good?" Jack answered the phone in two rings.

"That was fast." I leaned back against the wall. "I'm just here with Pippa as she buys up the entire store."

"Sounds like Jennie." He groaned as he mentioned his younger sister. "I hated it when my folks made me take her shopping. It was like the worst torture."

"Well, I'm happy to say that it's not been torturous just yet." I ran my fingers through my hair. "She said she'll be quick, so hopefully I'll be back on the ranch within the next hour."

"Are you high? You've let a woman out in a clothes store. She'll be there for a good three hours." There was no hiding the enjoyment he was getting out of this situation.

"No, Pippa's not that bad." I peeked over my shoulder and looked back into the store. Pippa had somehow changed into a floral dress and was twirling around, laughing at something the sales associate said. "I have a feeling that sales associate is going to make a huge commission today."

"Oh boy, you're in for a long morning." Jack laughed. "Oh, by the way, Mom and Dad wanted to know if you and Pippa want to come over for lunch on Sunday. Jennie and Josh will be there with the kids, and you know Mom loves to have a full house."

"Aw, thanks." Jack's parents were lovely, friendly, and welcoming people. "I'll ask Pippa if she wants to. I don't even know if she'll still be in town then."

"It's in four days." Jack cleared his throat. "She's in a store shopping her heart out. I have a feeling she's going to be here a while."

"You think?" I asked, though I agreed with him. "I just don't know how this is going to work. My back is already killing me, and I've only been on the couch for one night." I rubbed my lower back and sighed. "I only have one bed, and my couch is not made for sleeping on."

"Have her sleep on it. She's smaller than you."

"She's still bigger than the couch and she's my guest.

She's already got a broken heart. I don't want to give her a broken back."

"There are many ways to break—"

"Don't even go there, Jack," I warned him. Jack wasn't a dirty guy and was generally respectful toward women, but I knew he liked to tease and have fun. I just wouldn't have him talking about or disrespecting Pippa in that way. I wasn't sure why I cared so much, but I wanted everyone to honor her.

"So, what are you going to do?" There was amusement in his tone, though he didn't say anything else.

"Maybe I'll get a blow-up mattress. Not that I really have room for it." I sighed, thinking about the small space in my log cabin. "I could just camp out by the river. Apple would love that. So would Donkey."

"You don't let Donkey into the tent, do you?" Jack sounded shocked.

"Of course not, but he sleeps outside the tent and protects us." I smiled, thinking of my goofy and naughty gray goat. "Maybe I'll even ask Pippa if she wants to go camping. That might be fun."

"A city girl camping?" Jack sounded horrified. "What could possibly go wrong?"

"We used to go to camp together every summer," I reminded him. "She knows what it is to rough it."

"She sure didn't look like she did when I saw her. But I'll take your word for it."

"You just don't like city girls," I retorted. "Not all of them are like the prissy women you—"

"I don't dislike city girls," he protested. "I have nothing against them. In fact, I find Pippa to be quite beautiful. I wouldn't mind taking her on a date to get her mind off her ex. I can show her how a country boy treats their woman."

"I don't think so." My back stiffened at his words. Was he crazy? Did he think I would let him go on a date with my Pippa? "That's the last thing that she needs right now."

"What?" He chuckled. "A fun date with a cowboy?"

"She barely just ended her engagement," I growled. "She doesn't need to be gallivanting around town with anyone right now. She still needs time to heal."

"She said she was over him."

"She's obviously not over him in one day. Seeing your fiancé cheating on you is painful. No matter if he's an idiot or not." As I spoke the words, I realized how true they were. Even though Pippa was laughing and joking and enjoying shopping, there was no way she was feeling whole and okay about everything. She just wasn't talking about it.

Just like I never talked about the pain I felt when my dad abandoned me. No one knew about that pain. No one checked to make sure that I wasn't suffering inside. I was a boy, and my mom and grandparents assumed that because I never spoke about it, I was okay. I didn't tell them about all the letters I wrote to my dad and the calls I made that went unanswered. Or how when I was older, I'd hired a private detective to find him, thinking the reason I hadn't heard from him was because something had happened and my mom hadn't wanted to tell me. Not that anything had happened though. He had gotten remarried and had two more kids. Kids he cared about. Kids he loved.

"Hey, TJ..." Jack cleared his throat. "I was just joking, okay? You coming to trivia tonight?"

"Yeah, we'll be there," I said and took a deep breath. "Hey, I gotta go back into the store and see if Pippa needs any feedback on her outfits. Let's meet up at the ranch tomorrow, okay?" I wanted to be there for Pippa. I wanted to show her that even though she put on a front of being happy, I knew she was hurting inside. I wanted to be there for her. I wanted to show her that I was the sort of man that cared about her.

"Sounds good," he said. "You're a good friend, TJ. I'm glad she has you."

"Thanks," I said as I hung up and walked back into the boutique. Pippa was holding a brown belt with a huge buckle in her hand and just staring at it. As I moved closer to her, I could see that her face was tense and her lips were trembling. Her lashes moved rapidly, and I realized she was having a moment. I rested my hand on her shoulder in support.

"You okay?" I asked her as she turned to look up at me. She immediately plastered a smile on her face and nodded.

"Yup, I was just deciding if I should get this belt or not."

"Why not?" I smiled. "It's cute."

"You think so?" she asked in surprise, holding it up to me. "I thought you would say it was—"

"Hey, if you like it, I like it." I grinned, cutting her off. "How did the outfits go?"

"Good," she said with a grin. "My credit card bill is about to go through the roof."

"Uh-oh. That doesn't sound good. Maybe you should limit the number of items you get."

"It'll be okay, TJ. I'm not going *crazy* crazy." She took a deep breath. "I need some clothes to do stuff in."

"I know." I nodded, debating whether or not I should ask her if she was okay. Normally, I'd go along with her smile and pretend like I hadn't stopped her from nearly bursting into tears. I wasn't good with emotions. I wasn't the sort of person to have deep conversations, yet sometimes I wished I was. "Hey"—I tapped my fingers against my upper thigh—"everything okay?"

"Yeah, of course." She nodded quickly. "I'm great."

"You're not great, Pips." I used my pet name for her. "Talk to me."

"I am talking to you." She made a face. "I am absolutely fine. In fact, I'm fantastic."

"You're a bad liar, Pippa. You have to be heartbroken over Stephan."

"He was a jerk."

"Doesn't mean it can't still hurt." I brushed a loose curl away from her cheek. "Doesn't mean you don't feel the horrible burn of pain from finding out that he wasn't faithful."

"I mean..." She shrugged nonchalantly and played with her loose curls. "It is what it is."

"You forget, I've known you since we were little kids." My heart thudded as I remembered all the days and nights we spent talking about our lives, our futures, and our dreams. "I know your tells. I know you always try to keep a brave face, even when you're hurt."

"I do?" She frowned as if she didn't know what I was talking about. "Really?"

"Yeah." I nodded. "Every time your mom would get on your case and say something that put you down, you'd laugh it off like you didn't care, but I'd see you looking after her with hurt in your eyes."

"You noticed that?"

"Of course." I wanted to tell her there were many things I noticed about her, but I didn't want to sound like a creep. "Your mom was really mean to you. She never listened to what you wanted. She was controlling." I stopped there, as I didn't want to completely go off on her mom and make her resent me. I didn't want to tell her that I thought her mom was one of the most superficial people I'd ever met.

"I didn't know you knew." Her eyes surveyed my face thoughtfully. "We were just kids."

"We were kids, but I still noticed. Plus, I was thirteen when I left. Old enough to know a lot of things." *Like how special you are*, I thought to myself. However, there was no way I was going to tell her that her eyes reminded me of acorns in the fall and that her smile gave me the same feeling a colorful sunrise did.

"Yeah." She sighed. "I guess when you grow up learning to push away your hurt, you kinda push it away and try to forget it's not there." She bit into her lower lip. "It's weird because I've lived my life for so many years following what my mom said and the path she set for me. And I've tried so hard to tell myself that I was happy and that that was what I wanted."

"And it wasn't?" I asked her softly.

"I don't know." Her eyes were wide. "I used to think that all I wanted was to marry a rich man and live on Fifth Avenue and shop to my heart's content. I would keep my job as an assistant and then quit when I got married and had kids." She wrinkled her nose. "It wasn't that I wanted that life, really, it's just that..." She sighed. "Oh, I don't even know anymore."

"You know, I realized I don't even know what you do for a job." I scratched the side of my face. "I don't know anything about your life now, aside from the fact that you just ended your engagement."

"I just realized I don't know much about you either." She shook her head. "We've been out of touch for so long."

"We have." I nodded, feeling sad because I knew that I was the reason why all we did was send Christmas cards every year. "But we can catch up before you go back to the city."

"I'd like that." Her eyes shone bright again. She reached out, squeezed my hand slightly, and moved closer to me. "Thanks, TJ. You always have a way of making me feel better about everything."

"I'm glad," I said, liking how her fingers felt against my skin. I felt a sense of loss once she removed them. She looked back down at the belt in her hand and placed it on the table next to her. "You don't want it anymore?"

"I don't need it. Plus, it was eighty dollars and my American Express balance is already too high."

"Are you sure you don't want it?" I asked her. "I can get it for you if you really want it."

"No, I don't want it. But you're sweet for offering." She grinned at me. "I'm ready to pay, and then we can get home. I bet Apple and Donkey are wondering where you are."

"I'm sure they are." I loved that she mentioned my two pets and was concerned about them. "They both love you already."

"Apple, maybe. Donkey, no. Donkey wants to butt me."

"That may be true," I agreed. "But that doesn't mean he doesn't also love you." We headed toward the cash register, and my eyes widened as the sales associate told her the total was four hundred and fifty-nine dollars. I had no idea women's clothing cost so much. Pippa signed her receipt and grabbed her bags before heading over to look at the sunglasses. When she did, the sales associate pushed a small bag into my hand and grinned.

"Your girlfriend will love it." She winked at me, and I shook my head. Either she hadn't been paying attention to me earlier, or she hadn't believed me. Frankly, I didn't care which one was true. I was glad she'd talked me into buying Pippa a present. I just had to figure out when to give it to her.

Chapter Thirteen

P ippa

Dear TJ,

I have given up meat. Yup, you read it here first. I am now a vegan. So no cheese or milk, even. And you know how hard that is for me because I love ice cream. But I'm doing it for the baby animals. I watched a video yesterday that was heartbreaking. Absolutely heartbreaking. So, I encourage you to think about going green as well.

I tried to sign up for the photography class at school, but Mom didn't think it was a good idea. She said wouldn't I rather be a cheerleader because football players pay more *attention to cute girls in short skirts than nerdy girls with cameras in their faces. I told her I didn't care about football, but then she started laughing and saying that no woman actually likes football. But I know that's not true because Maddie (do you remember her? She was at camp and used to cry every night) actually wants to try out for the football team and keeps telling me all these stats about players and downs. I don't even know what she's talking about half the time.*

I can't wait until I can go off to college. Maybe we'll end up at the same place? How cool would that be?

Your BFF 4 Eva & Eva,
Pippa Chase

"I'm so excited for trivia night." I combed my hair as TJ did up his hiking boots. He looked especially handsome after his shower. He wore a pair of black jeans and a blue shirt that was the same turquoise blue as his eyes. His hair was still slightly damp, and I could smell his smoky cologne in the air.

"It should be fun." He nodded as he looked up at me. "You'll get to meet the entire gang." He grabbed his fluffy white towel and rubbed it against his hair to dry it. It felt so domesticated, sharing this small log cabin with him. It reminded me of when we were young and would have sleepovers.

"I can't wait to meet everyone. Well, I met most of the guys, but I'm excited to meet the other women as well." I stared at him for a few seconds, wanting to ask him if he'd dated any of them but not wanting to be too intrusive. It wasn't my business. For all I knew, he had an arrangement with one or many of them. The thought made my stomach twist, and I knew I'd automatically dislike anyone TJ was hooking up with.

"Yeah, everyone is supercool." He nodded and then paused. "Don't get me wrong, there's a little drama, but nothing bad."

"What do you mean by a little drama?" I put my comb down and headed into the living room area. "Spill the beans, TJ."

"Don't you mean spill the tea?" He chuckled, and I rolled my eyes at his attempt to be young and hip.

"Spill the tea, beans, corn dogs, whatever you wanna call it." I laughed. "Tell me more."

"Well, you already met Mindy from the cupcake store..."

"Yeah." I licked my lips. "You didn't date her, right?"

"No." He recoiled in horror. "Don't get me wrong, she's gorgeous, but she's seriously in everyone's business."

"In a bad way?"

"No, not really." He shrugged. "Anyway, she and Brandon, the bar owner, seem to have this love-hate relationship. They are constantly going back and forth. All of us think they should date, but if you even mention it to either of them, they recoil in horror."

"Oh, weird." I wondered why they were so cagey about

dating. If I were Mindy, I'd date Brandon in a heartbeat. He was gorgeous. "So what about Jack? What's his story?"

"Jack?" TJ frowned. "Why are you asking about Jack? Are you interested in him or something?"

"No!" I said vehemently. "I just ended an engagement. I'm not going to date again for at least a year."

"Oh?" He cocked his head to the side. "A year?"

"Yup!" I said quickly. "I need to figure my life out before I even think about getting into another relationship." I shuddered as I smoothed the front of my dress down. "I need to know me before I even try and get to know someone else."

"Makes sense," he said. "You definitely don't want to rush into anything new."

"Exactly." I poked him in the chest. "So, tell me more about Jack? Is he dating?"

"He goes on dates. He doesn't have a girlfriend if that's what you're asking. I mean, same, like me. I date, but no girlfriend."

"Oh, are you dating anyone that will be at trivia tonight?" I asked him casually, wanting to know but not really wanting to know.

"No." He shook his head. "Haven't been on a date in about a month."

"Oh?"

"Been trying to figure out a plan for the ranch." He shrugged. "Jack and Old Man Roberts are giving me some advice."

"Some advice on what?"

"Where to build the small cabins down by the river." His brows furrowed as he spoke. "I'll take you tomorrow if you want. We can ride the horses."

"That sounds fun!" I grinned at him. "That would be lovely."

"And perhaps we can even camp tomorrow night?" He spoke slowly as if he were unsure how I was going to take his question. "I mean, we don't have to if you're not up to it," he finished quickly. "I know that you're a city girl and might not—"

"We can go camping tomorrow, TJ." I rolled my eyes. "You know I'm not prissy. I love being outdoors." I paused and then added, "Sometimes."

"Perfect." He gave me the biggest grin I'd seen from him in a while. His perfect white teeth shone at me, and his blue eyes sparkled. My heart fluttered as I realized just how handsome he was. And he was my best friend. I felt special being here with him. I felt lucky. I stepped forward without thinking and opened my arms. He looked surprised for a few seconds, opened his arms, and pulled me in for a huge bear hug.

"Thank you for letting me stay," I whispered against his muscular, warm chest. His fingers rubbed my back, and I could hear his heart beating through his chest.

"You know my home is always open to you, Pips," he whispered against my hair, and I closed my eyes. I held him to me tightly. I felt warm and protected in his embrace. I felt safe. I felt cared for. I felt at home. "I've missed you," he whispered, and I felt tears spring to my eyes. I'd missed him even more than I'd thought. I'd missed his voice. His smile. His intimate knowledge of who I was as a person, inside and out. Before I knew what was happening, tears were falling from my eyes and onto his shirt. I felt embarrassed and nervous that I'd make him uncomfortable, but he continued rubbing my back. "Let it out, Pips." His melodic voice warmed my heart. "It's okay. Nothing is so final that it can't be fixed. Well, except for death."

"Since when did you become the philosopher?" I looked up at him with a small smile. "You're a wise man, TJ."

"And don't you forget that." He laughed. "So, tonight we go to Montana Knights for trivia and then tomorrow we'll explore the ranch and camp out?"

"Sounds perfect." I nodded. "And maybe we can make s'mores by the campfire?"

"Was that even a doubt in your mind?" He cocked his head to the side, his warm smile enveloping me in bliss and comfort. I was thankful I'd come here. We'd gotten off to a bumpy start the night before, and I still wasn't sure why. But he was still my TJ, my best friend, my confidant. I knew that if anyone could mend my broken heart and help me figure out what I wanted from life, it would be him.

Chapter Fourteen

T J

Dear Pippa,

I was looking at the sky last night, and I saw a shooting star. Cool, huh? I was wondering if you saw it as well. How cool would it be if we were both looking at the same shooting star? Do you remember that time at camp when we went to stargaze cause you wanted to see Orion? And you turned to me, and you said, "Once in every million years, a star splits into two and sends soul mates into the universe. And that those two souls can spend several lifetimes looking for each other?"

Do you ever wonder if soulmates can be

best friends or if soulmates are just people who will get married? I don't know why I thought about that. I think because no one listens to me or makes me laugh quite like you do.

I don't really miss Brooklyn, but I do miss you. Don't say I never express myself. :P

Your best friend,
TJ Wyatt

Montana Knights was packed when we arrived. Trivia night was always a popular night at the bar, and I waved at Brandon as he served up pints of beer to his patrons. Jack was seated at a table in the far corner of the bar, near one of the many TVs playing various sports games.

"Let's grab a seat, and then I will get us some drinks." I looked back at Pippa, who looked naturally beautiful with her hair tied back and just a touch of pink lipstick on her lips. She'd changed into one of her new shirts and jeans after her crying episode, and I had to acknowledge that even though she looked pretty country, she looked awfully cute. I wanted to tell her she was in Montana and not Texas, but I didn't want her to think I was making fun.

"Sounds good." She nodded, raising her voice so I could hear her over the throng of people chatting. "It's crazy in here."

"We may be a small town, but everyone likes to hang out after the workday is done." As we made our way across the bar, I waved at a few people I knew and winked at Old

Man Roberts as he made a face at me. He was sitting next to his wife and the other older gossips of the town. "Hey there, Jack." We fist-bumped as I took a seat. "How's it going?"

"Good." He grinned. "Mindy is running around like a chicken with its head cut off, having everyone sample some new cupcake recipe she made."

"Where is she? I'll let her know if it's good or not." I looked around the room but didn't see her. "I'm surprised Brandon let her offer people free stuff."

"I don't think he knows." Jack shook his head. "You know, he has a new food menu that includes desserts. No one is going to want to buy dessert if Mindy is offering her baked goods for free."

"Well, hopefully he doesn't find out." I looked over at Pippa, who was rapidly texting something on her phone. "Everything okay?"

"Not sure." She wrinkled her nose. "Emma seems to be having an issue at work."

"Oh?" I raised an eyebrow. "What does she do exactly?"

"She's the vice president of marketing for a tech company." Pippa looked up at me. "It pays well, but she hates it."

"Why does she do it then?" I asked her curiously. I couldn't imagine working somewhere that I hated.

"Because it pays well." Pippa looked at me as if I'd asked a silly question. "I mean, that's why I keep my job too, though it doesn't pay nearly as good as hers does."

"What do you do?" Jack asked her, and I was glad he had because I still wasn't exactly sure what her job consisted of.

"I'm the executive assistant to a movie producer. And it sounds more glamorous than it is. He's a British lord and goes back and forth from the States and England."

"Wow." Jack looked impressed by her job, and I had to

admit, it seemed cool. "Would I know any of the movies?"

"Um...do you watch any British period pieces?"

"Like *Downton Abbey*?" I asked, and she turned to me with a smile and shook her head.

"I wish. The pieces Lord Alistair Montague makes are set back in the days when Romans strolled the streets of England." She played with her hair. "He's also obsessed with The Battle of Hastings and alternative history. His big question is, what would have happened if William the Conqueror hadn't invaded England and won? What if Harold had won?"

"Harold?" I asked her for clarification. I vaguely remembered learning some British history in high school, but I only remembered Henry VIII and all his wives.

"Harold of Hastings," she clarified. "The Norman French army invaded England and essentially when William the Conqueror won, he introduced common law to England. My boss likes to make movies about what England would look like now if common law were never introduced."

"That sounds kinda cool," Jack said. "I took some history classes in college. So, are you really interested in history?"

"Not really." She looked over at me, and we shared a secret smile. "TJ knows I'm not a history buff."

"I always thought you'd be an actress or a playwright." I looked over at Jack. "When we were younger, Pippa used to write all these short plays and we'd act them out in her bedroom or the park." I thought back to us pretending to be kings and queens, dragons and dragon slayers, characters from her favorite books; she'd even written a story about Harry Potter and Hermione falling in love. "They were good as well."

"Thanks for saying that. That was my dream job, but it wasn't practical. The industry is so saturated in New York and I just don't have the talent to make it to the top."

"What?" My jaw dropped. "What are you talking about, Pippa? You're amazing." My head pounded as something she said reminded me of her mom. "Are those your thoughts, or did someone else say that to you?"

"I would say they are a bit of both. My mom may have said these things when I was younger." She shrugged and looked down. "You getting those drinks for us?" She fiddled with a coaster on the dark wooden table, and I realized she was uncomfortable talking about her mom. I hated that her mother had this negative power over her. I hated that her mother made her doubt herself and her abilities and talents. I also knew that this wasn't the time for me to dig deeper to make her feel better about herself.

"What would you like to drink?" I stood up to the sound of Ethan's booming voice as he made his way over to the table with Aiden. They were both dressed alike, in white shirts and blue jeans, and I wanted to laugh. They both needed a woman's touch in their lives.

"What's got you laughing, TJ?" Ethan asked as he took a seat next to Pippa. "Hey, Pippa."

"Hi..." She paused for a second. "Ethan, right?"

"The one and only!" He winked at her, his hazel eyes looking greener tonight. She blushed at his gaze, and I was about to interrupt them when Brielle, Charlotte, and Mindy made their way over to the table. Mindy had a huge grin on her face and an empty plate in her hands. Disappointment flooded through me as I realized all the cupcakes were gone.

"No more cupcakes?" I frowned as I pointed to the empty plate.

"All gone!" Mindy was ecstatic by this fact. "Though don't tell Brandon. I don't want him to kill me."

"Or cancel trivia night." Charlotte glared at her. Charlotte was looking particularly fetching tonight, with her black curly hair straightened. Her blue eyes sparkled as she teased her best friend. I noticed Aiden checking her out as she shuffled some papers in her hand. "Tonight is the only night I get to have fun at the bar and not serve drinks." Charlotte worked at the bar part time and ran the trivia nights. She was also an aspiring comedian and hoped to convince Brandon to have a stand-up night as well.

"He won't cancel trivia night." Mindy rolled her eyes. "This is his busiest night of the week."

"Perhaps," Charlotte said as she placed the answer form on the table. "Think about your team's name. I'm going to go and say hello to everyone and get the questions started in about fifteen minutes, so get your drinks."

"First round's on me." I held my hand up. "Everyone, give me your order and I'll go and get the drinks now."

"I'll help you." Pippa jumped up and headed over to me. Her brown eyes looked happy, and I was glad she was no longer thinking about her mother. "You'll need someone to help you carry the drinks."

"Thanks," I said with a small smile. "I appreciate it."

"I appreciate you," she whispered under her breath before turning to Mindy and asking her something. I loved that Pippa felt comfortable here in Paradise Valley. I loved that she was becoming fast friends with my friends. I also knew that I was going to feel sad when she went back home. I'd missed my best friend. I needed to have her back in my life. Even if that meant having to deal with other demons from my past.

Chapter Fifteen

P ippa

Dear TJ,

Do you remember that time we watched Sleepless in Seattle behind my mom's back, and you pretended you hated the movie, but secretly you loved it (you can't tell me otherwise). Well, I totally just got busted. My mom said I could watch the movie, and I was like, I've already seen it, and she was like, WHAT! HAHA. Oops.

That was a fun night, even if you did get popcorn everywhere. I was thinking, can we establish a set of rules for our pact that we have to obey so we both know! Kinda like a bill of rights, but we will call it a pact of rights. Or The Pippa and TJ Pact of Rights or whatever.

I miss you. I miss sneaking out into the corridor, talking in the stairwell, and pretending we didn't hear Mrs. Bagsby when she shouted at us to go home.

Always and forever!

Your Bff,

Pippa

"I have an idea for our team's name," Mindy shouted to garner the attention of the men who were arguing over who the greatest quarterbacks of all time were. "We can be the winners."

"But we never win." TJ chuckled, and I watched as his eyes moved to me to check that I was okay. I thought it was cute that he'd grown into such a caring man. It shouldn't have been a surprise because he'd always been lovely. I'd forgotten how selfless he was, especially when compared to Stephan, whose only worries revolved around himself and his feelings. I realized that I hadn't thought about Stephan in hours. It wasn't even that I missed him or was sad about the fact the wedding wasn't happening. It was more the fact that I'd dated a man who had obviously never really cared about me for far longer than I should have. And I didn't know if that was because I'd really loved him or if I'd just been so desperate to move into the next phase of my life, goaded on by my mother.

It hurt me that my mother didn't support my path in life. I wanted to make her proud. I really did, but I didn't want to do it at the cost of my happiness.

"Maybe now that I'm here, we will win," I spoke up, and Mindy and Brielle cheered for me. I looked over at Brielle and tried not to be envious of how beautiful she was. She was tall and slender, with long light-brown hair and the most vivid green eyes I'd ever seen in real life. She was best friends with Mindy and Charlotte and worked at the local newspaper running an advice column, which I wanted to hear more about.

"So, you're telling us you're really smart?" Brielle asked, her eyes looking at me warmly as she sipped on her glass of red wine. She was already on her second glass, and we women were on our third bottle collectively. I could feel that I was slightly tipsy myself, but I didn't mind. It had been a while since I'd had a girls' night. Suddenly, I thought of Emma and wished she was also here. She would have loved Mindy, Brielle, and Charlotte. Shoots, she would have enjoyed hanging out with the men as well.

"I wish." I didn't think I was the most stupid woman on the face of the earth, but I was no scientist or academic. "My expertise lies in the entertainment area and literature."

"Oh, are you into books?" Brielle perked up. "I work at the local paper. I thought I'd be writing hard-hitting journalist pieces, but not much happens here in Paradise Valley. So I write the local Dear Aunt Abby column." She giggled. "Sounds boring, but it actually gets quite scandalous."

"Oh, really?" I asked, intrigued, but she pressed her index finger to her lips and shook her head.

"We'll have to grab lunch next week with the girls." She

looked over at Mindy. "Wanna grab lunch next week sometime?"

"Sure," Mindy answered. "I'll see what days Kaye is on the schedule so I don't have to close up shop for a few hours."

"I'd love to grab lunch." I paused and then looked back over at Brielle. "And yes, I love books and especially plays. I used to think I'd be a playwright and make my own plays."

"That sounds so cool." Mindy looked excited. "Are you a filmmaker as well?"

"Well, no..." I shook my head. I enjoyed playing around with a camera and editing, but I wasn't a professional, and I didn't want to give anyone the impression that I was any sort of budding Greta Gerwig, Kathryn Bigelow, or Ava DuVernay. I could shoot a good shot, but nothing I created was Oscar-worthy.

"Oh." Mindy's face crumpled slightly, looking disappointed. "I wanted to make a commercial for the coffee shop and needed someone to shoot it for me."

"I mean, I can help." I smiled warmly at her, surprised she was willing to trust a complete stranger with something so big. "I didn't bring my DSLR camera with me though. It's back home." I wasn't ready to tell them I jumped on a plane in a wedding dress with nothing but my handbag.

"Girls, do we have a name?" Jack spoke up and nodded toward the front of the bar. Charlotte was standing with a mic in one hand and a black pen in the other. There was a whiteboard behind her, which I assumed she was going to use to keep track of the scores.

"TJ's Minions," TJ offered, and we all laughed. Jack held his glass up in admiration of the name, and I was about to say something when a loud screeching carried through the tiny speakers in the corners of the bar.

"Good evening, everybody." Charlotte's tone was cheerful and sweet and it suddenly struck me that she would probably have a nice singing voice. "I hope everyone has chosen the name for their team?"

"Will you choose our name for us?" A blond guy shouted from the table next to us. The group of guys next to him all hollered in agreement, and Charlotte shook her head.

"I don't think so, boys. Sorry," she said sweetly.

"Then, at least let me take you on a date," the blond guy cried out again, and I could see Aiden glaring at him from the corner of the table. Interesting. I noticed that TJ had also noticed Aiden's annoyed look, and we exchanged a secret smile for a few moments. I loved the fact that we both seemed to be on the same page, just like when we were younger.

"Let's get the team names." Charlotte continued without responding, and the group of guys booed before laughing loudly. "Annie, what's your group's name?"

"The Einsteins," Annie Roberts responded, and I tried not to laugh when Mindy whispered, "she wishes," under her breath.

"Cool, cool." Charlotte wrote the team's name on the whiteboard. "Kacie? You guys choose a name?"

I looked over to see a glamorous blonde with superlong hair drinking a glass of champagne. She looked out of place in Paradise Valley. I was even more shocked to see a dumpy-looking Kaye sitting next to her. They looked like exact opposites.

"We're Double *K*," Kaci responded, and Mindy rolled her eyes.

"So original," Mindy whispered under her breath.

"Is Kaci from here?" I asked her curiously.

"Oh yes, she went to high school with all of us. Though she's way more hoity-toity. Her dad is the mayor and her mom owns the bookstore, which is barely ever open because she's always traveling, going to spas and getting plastic surgery." She lowered her voice and leaned toward me. "Word on the street is that she's really into TJ."

"She is?" I tried to keep my face neutral, but my heart was racing. "Is he interested in her?"

"I don't know." She looked over at TJ. "He keeps his cards close to his chest, though I think they've been on a date or two."

"They have?" I tried to ignore the jealous feeling in the pit of my stomach.

"Yeah." Mindy continued, "I think she and Kaye have this dream that they will marry TJ and Jack."

"Kaye likes Jack?" I asked in surprise. He had barely looked at her in the coffee shop.

"Oh, you didn't know?" Mindy said, her brown eyes gleeful. "Jack and Kaye were high school sweethearts."

"They were?" My voice was loud, and I slapped my hand across my mouth. "Sorry," I said. "I had no clue they dated."

"Yup," Mindy said salaciously. "The breakup was the stuff of tabloids as well."

"Oh?" I leaned forward, wanting to know what happened.

"Yeah," Mindy said. "So, Jack—"

"Mindy," Charlotte called out suddenly. "Do y'all have your team's name?"

"TJ's Minions," Mindy shot back, and TJ slammed down his beer cup on the table and cheered. "I never should have said that." Mindy laughed. "He's going to let that go to his head."

"You can say that again," Brielle said. "You girls want any food? I'm going to go up to the bar and order something."

"Ooh, yes." Mindy nodded eagerly. "I could do with some fries." She jumped up and then winked at me. "Conversation to be continued," she said before heading toward the bar with Brielle. I leaned back in my spot in thought. I wanted to know why Jack and Kaye had broken up. It wasn't like I was super invested, but I was curious as to what could have happened that would have been tabloid-worthy.

"Everything okay?" TJ was suddenly next to me, sitting where Mindy had been. "You're not tired or sad or anything?"

"I'm good, thanks." I contemplated asking him if he knew why Jack and Kaye had broken up, but I didn't want him to think I was a huge gossip. I mean, I obviously was a bit of a gossip, but I didn't want him to know that. "I hope we win."

"It's unlikely. We've only won a couple of times."

"Who normally wins?" I asked, looking around the room to see if I could figure it out.

"Usually, tourists in town for the week." He chuckled at my expression. "It's a good excuse for us all to get together though." He looked around the room, and I wasn't sure if I saw his eyes on Kaci or not. She was beautiful, so I wouldn't be surprised if he was into her. I was about to ask him if there was anyone else he wanted to talk to when he leaned forward, grabbed my hand, and pulled me up.

"What are you doing?" My jaw dropped as he swung me around. I could see Jack, Aiden, and Ethan staring at us with bemused expressions as TJ shuffled around and did some sort of two-step. It was then that I noticed the song that was playing. "Billy Ray Cyrus," I blurted out happily. "Don't break my heart."

"I'll try not to," TJ said, and we both laughed at the shared memory. Back when we were at camp, they'd had a dance every summer, and every summer, TJ refused to go. The last summer we were there, I'd sung this song to him when he'd refused to go again and pretended to cry. So then, he'd changed his mind, and we'd danced the night away, laughing, singing, and joking around. At one moment, I almost thought he was going to kiss me, and I'd been so nervous and excited, but he hadn't. I'd been a little disappointed, but I knew that nothing was more important to me than his friendship.

"Very funny." I giggled as he twirled me around. "You can't break my heart anyways because it's already broken, remember?"

"I remember." He nodded solemnly in response as he pulled me into him and looked down into my eyes. "But as your best friend, I am here to ensure it doesn't stay broken for too long. There are far too many—" He paused and twirled me around again. My heart fluttered at his words. Was he saying that he didn't want my heart to stay broken for too long because he wanted to be the one to fix it? Was he letting me know he thought I was cute? I could feel my face warming as I looked at him.

I was attracted to TJ. He was as handsome as they came, and he was funny, sweet, and made me feel good about myself. If I was honest, I did have the tiniest crush on him. However, I didn't want him to think he was the rebound guy. Plus, it wasn't like I was even ready to try to go on a date with anyone else. I had just dumped Stephan and broken our engagement, and even though I knew that the feelings I'd had for Stephan weren't true love, I still needed to process why I'd gotten myself into such a mess in the first place.

TJ Wyatt was my best friend and the very best man I knew, but I was still hurt by the fact that he'd cut me out of his life. Yes, he'd moved, and we'd grown apart, but I had still tried to write and share. I'd even suggested we meet up for spring break and have a reunion, and he'd ignored all of my overtures. It hurt inside that he'd moved on from our friendship, and I didn't even know why.

I was about to ask TJ why he'd stopped writing back to me when Brielle and Mindy headed back.

"There you are, Pippa," Mindy said, grabbing my arm and pulling me toward her. I wondered if she'd done it on purpose or hadn't noticed that TJ and I were dancing. "Brielle and I want your opinion on something?"

"Sure." I smiled and nodded. I looked back at TJ, who winked at me and sat back down with his beer. "What is it?"

"See those two men over there?" She nodded to the bar at two men in cowboy hats. They were dressed in all denim: blue jeans and blue denim shirts. "Do you think the guy with the mullet or the guy with the long beard is cuter?"

"What?" I asked as I watched them, doubled over with laughter. "Is this a serious question?" I looked back over at the two guys. Neither of which were my type.

"You have to choose one." Brielle nodded. "Mullet or beard."

"Hmm." I studied the side profile of the two men before I made my decision. I wasn't into mullets or beards, though I supposed I wouldn't mind a nicely trimmed beard. Not that the man in front of me had a nicely trimmed beard. It looked like it was at least six inches long. "I'm going to say —"

"What are you girls whispering about?" Jack asked as he

and TJ joined us, and we all laughed. TJ stood by my side, his eyes twinkling as he looked down at me.

"Pippa has to choose mullet guy or beard guy?"

"For what?" TJ raised an eyebrow. "Please don't say that she has to kiss one of them. That would be a really immature bet. I think that—"

"Get a grip, TJ." Mindy rolled her eyes. "Your mail-order bride isn't kissing anyone else but you."

"We don't kiss," I said quickly, blushing. "We're just friends..." I looked over at TJ, who had no expression on his face. "And I would choose mullet over beard." I looked back over at the men and tried not to cringe. "Only because I don't want random pieces of food in my mouth if I was with Beard Guy."

"I win." Mindy twirled around. "Uh-oh, Charlotte is glaring at us. I think she just announced that the quiz starts in a minute. Let's all have a seat."

"Sounds good." TJ took my arm and guided me to a seat next to him. I wasn't sure what that meant, but I didn't hate it. "TJ's Minions are ready, Charlotte," he shouted and looked around at us. "Let's go, team."

"We got this!" Mindy responded, but her eyes were looking toward the bar. "Uh-oh, I think Brandon must have heard about the cupcakes I handed out." She made a face, and I looked in the direction she was staring. Brandon had his fist up at her, shaking his head. Then he motioned for her to come up to the bar. She rolled her eyes, stuck out her tongue at him, and then turned back around. "Let's get this party started before Brandon kicks me out of the bar."

"It wouldn't be the first time," TJ said, and I knew I had to ask him more about the story between Mindy and Brandon. Had they dated? Did they like each other? Hate each other?

"And it won't be the last," Jack added as he sat back. I watched as he looked around the room and froze slightly as two women passed by. It was Kaye and Kaci. I wondered if he still liked her. I wondered if she still liked him. I was new to Paradise Valley but was already invested in these people and their lives.

Chapter Sixteen

T J

Dear Pippa,

    I was thinking about the rules for our pact. Feel free to add/change anything you want to include.

    1. We will always be there for each other. No matter what.

    2. We will always be best friends.

    3. We can always tell each other everything.

    4. No matter where life takes us, we will be available to talk, chat, laugh, sing, cry, whatever...

    5. Metallica rocks and NSYNC doesn't. :)

    Gotta go. Grandpops is taking us to Golden

Corral tonight, but we go early so he and
Nanna can get the senior special.
TTYL,
TJ

"You didn't really think we were going to win, did you?" I asked Pippa as she got ready for bed. I watched as she brushed her hair and cried out as she reached a knot in her wavy locks. "I hope you know we had no chance of winning."

"I'm glad we didn't lose because of me." Pippa grinned as she walked to the kitchen in her Snoopy pj's. They looked childish, but she still looked adorable. "I'm going to have some milk and cookies. Want any?"

She looked over at me, and I raised an eyebrow. It was midnight, and she'd just brushed her teeth. "Don't judge me, TJ!"

"Would I do that?" I asked as I started to pull my shirt off. Her eyes were on me, and I stopped as I realized I didn't want to do a strip show for her. "I'm just going to have a quick shower." I dropped my shirt back down and watched as Pippa quickly turned away to open the fridge.

"So that's a no, then?" she asked as she grabbed a glass.

"Did I say that?" I shook my head as I made my way to the bathroom. "I'll have some, but not for five minutes."

"You're going to shower in five minutes?" She looked shocked. "No way."

"I'm a man. I don't need longer than that." I laughed as Apple ran between me and Pippa excitedly. She wasn't used to me having company and was happy to be getting so much attention from another person. "You can give Apple a small chicken strip treat as well."

"Sure." Pippa nodded as she headed toward the couch. "I'm going to turn the TV on. Is that okay?"

"Of course. This is your home for as long as you want it to be. Do whatever you want."

"Thanks, TJ." She sank into the seat, lifting her legs onto the couch under her. She leaned forward, grabbed the remote control, and powered it on. "Do you have anything you want to watch, or can I choose?"

"You can choose," I said. "Okay, I'm showering now." I closed the door behind me and stared in the mirror. My blue eyes shone back at me; they were bright and happy, and I shook my head at my reflection. I pulled my shirt off and dropped it to the ground. I stared at my chest, rib cage, and stomach and ran my fingers across my skin.

"What are you going to do, TJ?" I whispered to myself as I looked down at my body and the tattoo that sat on the right-hand side of my chest. There was a small red heart, and next to it read PC & TJW 4EVA. I groaned at the tattoo I'd gotten at eighteen. It was meant to say Pippa Chase & TJ Wyatt Best Friends 4 EVA, but as soon as the tattoo artist had started, I'd told him to shorten it to initials. And he'd taken that to mean not to add the words best friends. I was embarrassed for Pippa to see the tattoo; I didn't want her to ask questions. I didn't want her to figure out that she'd been my first crush as a teenager and that my feelings for her had lasted long past since I'd moved.

Her letters had been the highlight of my week. When everything around me had gone crashing, she'd been the one to make me smile, to make me happy. I didn't want her to think I'd always been in love with her, though that was true. How did you tell your best friend that you had gotten a tattoo of them on your chest...especially one with a heart? Especially when she'd just gotten out of a relationship.

I reached over and turned on the faucet before pulling my pants off. I stepped into the shower and closed my eyes as the water streamed down my face. I grabbed the body wash instinctively and poured it into my hand. The cherry blossom scent that filled the air made my eyes flow open to look at the bottle I'd grabbed. It was Pippa's body wash. I looked around my usually sparse shower and stared at all the new bottles that had appeared. Body wash, shampoo, conditioner, body scrub, face scrub, and some other bottles whose purposes I couldn't even begin to comprehend. I pressed my lips together at the collection that now graced the bathroom.

It was weird having Pippa here. In fact, if I was honest with myself, it was more nice than it was weird. Only there were so many things she didn't know. So many reasons why I'd halted communication with her. And I didn't know how to approach talking about them. I didn't know if I could ever get over my hurt to make her an integral part of my life again. And I certainly couldn't pursue more. Not when she was heartbroken over another guy. I knew that she was vulnerable. I knew she was trying to figure out what she wanted next in life.

I wanted to help her with that. I wanted her to find herself, be happy and get out of Paradise Valley as soon as possible. Not because I didn't want her there but because I knew the longer she stayed here, the more it would hurt when she left. She fit in well with my friends and me. She was fun and sweet, and I could tell she was already well liked, even by grumpy Aiden and Brielle, who could be quite prickly at times.

I turned the shower off, grabbed a towel, and wrapped it

around my body. It was then that I remembered that I'd forgotten to grab my shorts and T-shirt to sleep in. I wasn't used to taking my clothes into the bathroom with me. I wasn't used to having a guest. Let alone a woman—a woman I was attracted to. My face grew heated as I thought about Pippa and her sweet smile and gorgeous body. I knew I couldn't allow my mind to sink into the gutter. I couldn't cross that line. I respected her far too much for that.

"Ugh," I groaned as I opened the bathroom door. I could hear the TV on and Pippa telling Apple how gorgeous she was. "Hey, Pips," I called out loudly, hoping to grab her attention.

"Yes, Teej?" she called back, her eyes flying to the bathroom door. Her eyes widened as she saw me standing there with only a towel on. Her eyes went up, then down, then up again. I couldn't stop myself from laughing at the shocked expression on her face. "I hope you're not about to ask me for a massage, TJ."

"Get your mind out of the gutter, Pippa." I left the bathroom. "And close your eyes. I forgot my clothes."

"On purpose?" she asked, placing her hands over her eyes, though I could still see a gap between her fingers.

"Oh, totally on purpose. No peeking, Pips."

"Why would I peek?" She giggled and leaned back into the couch. Apple jumped off the couch and came running toward me, her tongue out, while her tail wagged back and forth.

"Apple, stop." I reached down and pushed her back as she grabbed the bottom of the towel and tugged. Apple looked up at me with challenging brown eyes and let out a low growl as she shook her head back and forth, the hem of my towel still in her mouth. "Apple, stop." I pointed my finger at her, and she reluctantly dropped the towel and rolled onto her back. "Good girl, Apple." I leaned down and rubbed her belly for a few seconds.

"Hurry, Teej," Pippa called out. "I'm missing my show."

"One second." I hurried to my chest of drawers and pulled out a pair of black shorts and a gray T-shirt before heading back to the bathroom. I turned back and peeked at Pippa, sitting on my couch, her knees curled up to her chest, her long dark hair hanging past her shoulders. Her hands covered most of her face, and as I stared at her empty wrist, I remembered the surprise present I'd gotten for her. I felt weird about it now. How would she react? Would she like the bracelet? I was no longer sure if I was going to give it to her.

"Are you ready yet?" She dropped her hands and giggled as she saw me standing there. "What?"

"What, what?" I responded, pretending that I hadn't just been staring at her. I held up my clothes, hurried back into the bathroom, and closed the door. I put my clothes on and rubbed the damp towel across my hair to dry it off. I dropped the towel on the floor and then picked it up as I remembered I had a guest and didn't want her to think I was a slob. I hung it over the towel rack and headed back out.

"Okay, I'm ready for my milk and cookies," I said as I headed toward the kitchen. "And what are we watching?"

"*The Ultimatum.*" She jumped up and ran to the kitchen, her bare feet slapping against the floor as she made her way over to me. "Ever seen it before?"

"Never even heard of it." I turned to look at the TV screen. "What's it about?"

"Couples who have been dating for a while and one of them wants to get—"

"You can stop right there; I can already tell I'm not

interested." Her brown eyes glared at me as she made her way closer. "Sounds like a snoozefest."

"It's actually really good." She stopped in front of me.

"Oh, I'm sure it's really thought-provoking." I winked at her. "Is it made by National Geographic or PBS? It has to be, right? If it's so educational."

"I didn't say it was educational." Her lips twitched. "I mean, maybe it is for some men, but..." Her voice trailed off as she wrinkled her nose. "Okay, maybe it's completely trashy, but I love it."

"You always did love trashy shows," I said, grabbing her hair and pulling it like I used to do as a boy.

"I never did," she rebuffed my statement as she pushed me away. "TJ, you take that back."

"Or what?" I grabbed her arm and twisted it behind her back. Not hard enough to hurt, but hard enough for her to not be able to wiggle out of my grip. She was thoughtful for a while, not saying anything, and I reached down and tapped her on the nose. "Don't even think about trying to get out of my strong hold on you."

"Oh yeah?" She bit down on her lip and then ducked low and snatched her arm fast. I was momentarily dazed by the swift movement and dropped her arm. "Got ya." She laughed hard as she reached up on her tiptoes and lightly tapped my nose. "I'm not a goofy little girl anymore, Teej." She did a little dance, lost her balance, and fell against me. I immediately reached out to steady her, and I could feel my heart racing as I held her in my arms. She looked up at me, breathless, and all I wanted to do was kiss her. We stood there for a few moments before she stepped back and grabbed the glasses. "You want chocolate milk or regular?" she asked as she looked back at me, a playful smile on her face, and I just shrugged.

"Surprise me." I ran my fingers through my damp hair and headed to the couch. "And lots of cookies, please." I could see Apple giving me a knowing look as I went to sit down, and I rolled my eyes at her. She was a dog; there was no way she could know that I was starting to want more from my best friend. She'd only been here a short time, but we shared so much history. I mean, I didn't even really know how I felt, so there was no way she could, but if she did, at least she wouldn't be able to tell Pippa.

Chapter Seventeen

P ippa

Dear TJ,

I have this dream of one day living in a small town in Vermont. I will work at a local community theater as a director, and you will be the stagehand, making the sets. And every winter, we will go snowshoeing and build snowmen with carrot noses and red fuzzy scarves. We will live next door to each other, and every evening, I will make you hot chocolate before we act out scenes from plays I write.

Wouldn't that be cool? I wrote this scene today in my new play, Where Did You Go? and the elderly lady has a conversation with her husband who has passed away. I'll share some of it with you because I think it's quite good.

Pamela: Where did you go, Booker? We were meant to dance in street the under the stars in our bare feet.

Gary: Mama, Dad's been gone for thirty years.

Pamela: I had a dream, Gary. He's not gone. He's been with us all these years.

Gary: It was a dream, Mama.

Pamela: It's never just a dream.

It's hard for me to explain the scene without you reading all of it, but I could imagine the set. How cool would that be? I know it's never going to happen. Mom says plays don't pay the bills, but imagine if I were born into a rich family, then I wouldn't have to worry about bills. Hope you're not sweating in Florida.

Your best friend forever,

Pippa

The smell of coffee made me smile as I puttered around the kitchen as quietly as possible. I gazed over at TJ, with his legs sprawled over the side of the couch, and knew that I couldn't allow him to continue sleeping on the too-small and quite uncomfortable seat. I opened the wooden bread bin, pulled out the bread, and popped two slices into the toaster. I went with a simple breakfast this morning: toast and jam with coffee. I could hardly mess that up.

"Something smells good." TJ yawned and stretched as he got off the couch. He tugged his T-shirt down as he headed toward the kitchen. "You're making coffee?"

"And toast." I grinned at him. "I saw you had strawberry jam."

"Sounds great." He stopped next to the countertop and tapped his fingers against a notepad. His eyes surveyed the room, most probably trying to gauge how much of a mess I'd made, and then he picked up a black pen and started scribbling something on the pad.

"Anything important?" I asked as I opened the fridge and grabbed a stick of butter. I'd slept amazingly and woken up with a plan. I was going to help TJ with his tasks on the ranch, and then I was going to create a list of new life goals. I needed to figure out where I wanted my life to go now.

"Just some chores for the ranch." He looked up, his eyes thoughtful. "Mindy suggested I sell some of my produce at the weekend farmers' market. I wasn't interested, but the extra money could help me get closer to my goal of building the cabins by the river."

"Cabins by the river?" I asked him curiously. "For you to live in?"

"For tourists. A peaceful solace for city slickers."

"Like me?" I joked. "Not that I'm really a city slicker. I have always lived in the city, but I'm not one of those banker hard-core types."

"You are an artist through and through." He grabbed the toast I'd just buttered and bit into it. "Yummy."

"TJ, I didn't put the jam on yet."

"You can put it on the next slice." He took another bite. "So, have you written any plays recently?" He cocked his head to the side and observed my face. "I'm surprised you haven't mentioned *Cats*, *The Phantom of The Opera*, or William Shakespeare once since you've been here."

"I do have other interests in my life." I smirked. "Though I did bring *The Complete Works of William Shakespeare* with me on the plane." I didn't tell him there's always a book of that nature in my handbag. "I know it's nerdy, but I love reading his work. He inspires me so much."

"Double, double, toil, and trouble." He pretended to stir a cauldron. "I remember you always wanted us to pretend to be witches."

"I did *Lady Macbeth* back in the day." I laughed as I buttered the next slice of toast and handed it to him. "I think my new favorite is *Richard III*."

"Oh?" He sat on one of the stools and took another bite of toast. There was a small bit of melted butter glistening on his lower lip, and he licked it up eagerly. "Do I know any of the lines?"

"Hmm, let me think." I opened the cupboard and pulled out two mugs. One was green with an I love Paradise Valley logo, and the other one was of a cow that read, "It's Moo Coffee Time." I laughed at the cup. "A horse, a horse, my kingdom for a horse."

"That's Shakespeare?" He looked surprised. "I had no clue."

"Right?" I leaned back into the countertop. "I'd love to write a play that people would quote for years and years."

"Been working on anything recently?"

"Maybe on the side," I admitted. "My mom thought it was a waste of time, and Stephan hated the theater, so I don't get to go to..." My voice trailed off as I realized I'd tempered my passion for theater to please other people. "Anyway, that's not important now." I took a deep breath. "I have a job in film."

"But you're not writing scripts or making films, right?" He blinked at me. "You're just an assistant." He cleared his throat. "I mean to say, you're not actively involved in the production, not that you're not doing much because you're an assistant. There's nothing wrong with being an assistant."

"Don't worry about it. I am an assistant and my job is not engaging at all. I have no active role in any of the projects. Not what I'd choose to do if I was made of money."

"Then why do you do it?" he asked softly. "Why don't you do what you really love?"

"You mean try to get a job on Broadway?" I grabbed some milk and looked at him thoughtfully. "That's an interesting idea, but I don't know if I would be qualified. I've thought about getting an MFA in playwriting; that way, I'd have some credentials, but I don't know about going back to school." I poured the two-percent milk into my cup and tried not to obsess over the fact that I wished it were almond milk. I was drinking far too much cow's milk and eating too many carbs. Not that I really cared. It was just that my mother's voice was always in the back of my head, telling me that I should avoid dairy and all carbs if I wanted to be trim and pretty. "What about you?" I asked him, dismissing my mother's voice from my head. "What do you really love?"

"I love this land." He looked out the window. "I love being here. I love my friends. I want to make it profitable. I want to let other people enjoy the beauty of Montana. I just need to raise enough money to make it happen."

"Was the land very expensive?" I asked, imagining it couldn't have been cheap. Sure, Montana prices weren't NYC prices, but you also don't get your own river in NYC. However, NYC was vibrant and full of life. You could get food at any hour of the day and there was always something going on. I wasn't sure the same was to be said here.

"It took almost all of my savings to buy the land and build this cabin and the barn." He nodded. "I invested money that I inherited in the stock market and made a nice sum. I don't have other income currently, as I want to focus on growing the ranch, so money's a little tight right now. I'm saving every penny that I have."

"That's so cool." In the silence after my comment, I heard a strange noise. I put my cup down and walked around the cabin. "Do you hear that?" My heart raced as I listened to what sounded like a loud grunt followed by a loud thudding. Was this place haunted? If this place was haunted, I was leaving. I would jump in my rental car, drive straight back to the airport, get on a plane, and fly to Hawaii. I bet it would be nice to lie on a beach in Hawaii. A bikini wouldn't hurt my feet like those cowboy boots had done.

"Oh, that's Donkey. He wants to be fed, and he wants to play with Apple. He's used to us coming out early in the morning."

"Oh." I didn't know what to say. I'd never known that goats were so needy. In fact, I didn't know much about goats at all. Strangely, Emma knew more about goats than me. She'd gone on a retreat in Upstate New York with yoga and tried to convince me to join her. But I hadn't gone because it had been so expensive, and I wasn't one for yoga in the first place. An idea blossomed in my brain as I stood there, and I turned around and grabbed TJ by the arms excitedly. "I just thought of a way to help you make money."

"Oh?" He looked bemused as I jumped up and down. "Are you going to tell me this great idea?"

"See if you can guess?" I could hardly contain myself as my excitement grew. "It could be a real money earner."

"You winning a celebrity version of *Jeopardy*?" He grinned. "You seemed to know a lot about celebrity relationships at trivia last night." I couldn't tell if he was impressed or not, but I wasn't going to dwell on it.

"No, silly." I walked toward the front door and opened it. Lo and behold, Donkey was waiting there, with wide eyes and an irritable look on his gray face. "Ta-da." I threw my hands in the air toward Donkey.

"Is this some sort of magic trick?" TJ blinked. "If so, you forgot to say abracadabra."

"It's not a magic trick. Donkey is the answer."

"Donkey the goat?" He raised an eyebrow as he came to the door and looked outside. "Did you bump your head, Pips? What are you talking about?"

"Goat yoga, of course." I grinned at him. "We'll have classes to raise money."

"Goat yoga?" He didn't look impressed. "Um, what?"

"It's a type of calming yoga and people will pay a lot of money. I'll teach the classes. Don't even worry about it." I paused. "You have other goats, right?"

"I was about to buy four more goats from Jack." TJ nodded slowly. "Are you sure you want to do this? I mean, I don't even know how long you're staying."

"Long enough to introduce the people of Paradise Valley to goat yoga and help raise money for your ranch." I paused as I looked at the front of his property. "By the way, what's the name of your ranch?"

"The name?" He stared at me. "I guess TJ's ranch."

"Nope." I shook my head. "That will not do. That's super boring."

"Do you have a better idea?" he asked as he ushered me back inside the room and closed the door. "I'm not creative like you," he said, and I felt myself warming at the compliment. I loved that he acknowledged my creativity and even seemed to like it.

"What about Apple and Donkey?" I suggested as we headed back into the kitchen. "Okay, maybe that's not fun enough."

"No, it's not. Plus, I don't want Apple getting a big head." His eyes gleamed as he gazed at me. "Thanks for getting me excited about my projects again, Pippa. It means a lot that you want to help me."

"It means a lot that you want me to find my way as well," I said softly.

"I guess that's why we've always been best friends." He grinned, and a strange feeling coursed through me. I didn't want to say anything, but I knew I had to. I couldn't go any more days without bringing it up.

"About that, TJ," I said, my lips pressed together. "Why did you stop writing? Why did you stop being my friend?"

He froze as I walked up to him, my hands on my hips, waiting for his answer. I could hear my heart beating rapidly as I waited for him to respond.

"I never stopped wanting to be your friend. I just had a lot of stuff going on that took over." His right foot started tapping against the floor. "I think I told you my dad stopped talking to me, right?"

"Right after the divorce?" I remembered that time. "Because he was sad, right?"

"I guess." He looked away, and I could see a tenseness

on his face. I recalled our childhood letters and realized I had never found out how that had been resolved. Guilt coursed through me at the thought.

"You guys talk now, right?" I asked him softly, my heart sinking as he slowly shook his head. "When's the last time you saw him?" I could barely get the words out.

"I haven't seen him or heard from him since Mom and I left Brooklyn." His voice was void of emotion. "He didn't want to be my dad anymore."

"What do you mean?" I felt guilty for putting him on the spot. "You haven't seen him at all?"

"I wrote him, called..." He took a deep breath. "I even reached out to your mom to see if he was okay."

"You did?" I'd never known that. Neither he nor my mother had told me that. "I think he's okay, right? He's still alive. I mean, I haven't seen him in years, but he was still next door..." I bit down on my lip. I didn't want to mention the young redhead his father had started dating when he'd moved.

"I don't care." He ran his hand through his hair, and I could see a hurt expression on his face that belied his words. "I guess when the divorce went through, he decided he wanted nothing to do with me or my mom."

"But...why?" I whispered as much to myself as to him. "He loved you. He always—"

"Enough, Pippa," TJ growled. "We have a lot to do today and talking about the man who raised me until I was thirteen is not one of them." He headed toward the front door. "I'm going to see if the chickens have laid any eggs and pick some of the veggies for dinner. You want to get ready? When we get back, we can ride the horses around and I'll show you my setup."

"And I can help you pick out your ranch name," I said

softly, not wanting to push the issue. TJ obviously didn't want to talk about his past with his dad. I didn't understand why. More so, I was hurt for him that his dad had just stopped talking to his own son. What a horrific thing to do. But what did my mom have to do with it, and why had he stopped talking to me? I was hurt that he didn't want to share with me. I was hurt that he didn't trust me enough to be vulnerable with me. I reached out, touched the side of his arm, and grabbed his hand. "And anytime you want to talk, day or night, about anything, I'm here for you, Teej. The pact goes both ways, you know."

"I know." He nodded and offered me a brief smile, his hand squeezing mine as we stared at each other. "I'm glad you made me say yes now."

"I didn't make you say yes," I protested and laughed as he winked at me, changing the mood back to light again. "You were practically begging me to sign the pact and say I'd be your best friend forever."

"Really?" He stepped closer to me. "I seem to remember a certain young girl making friendship bracelets and saying we had to wear them always." His blue eyes gazed at me, and my heart started racing. "Where is your friendship bracelet now, Pippa?" He raised an eyebrow and brought his face closer to mine. "Did you lose it?"

"Maybe. Maybe not." I giggled. "I'll never tell." I could see his irises surveying my face as we stood there. His look at my lips was brief but wondrous. This was the second time I'd felt he wanted to kiss me. And I wanted him to. I hated that I wanted him to, but I did. I knew this wasn't the right time though. It would complicate everything. And make things even more awkward between us. We weren't kissing friends. And I didn't even know if he knew I was still "untouched," as Emma liked to say. That certainly wasn't a conversation I wanted to have with him now, either.

"So, let me go and get those eggs." He blinked and stepped back, pulling his hand away from me. I'd forgotten that I was holding it. I was always a tactile and loving person, and TJ and I had always hugged and snuggled when we were young. Though, if I was honest, I couldn't see myself just snuggling with him on the couch now. We were too old for that.

"Sounds good," I said, rubbing my stomach. "Yummy, delicious fresh eggs for the win." I watched as he opened the door and walked outside, and I ran to the bed area to grab my phone. I quickly called Emma. She was the only one I could talk to about this situation.

"Hey, Pippa." She sounded awful, and my heart stopped in worry.

"Oh my gosh, what's wrong, Emma? You don't sound great."

"I got fired yesterday." Her voice was full of disbelief. "David James, my new boss, told me that he wanted me to market their latest product as being the safest savings app in the world, but I found out from one of the engineers that they were actually mining a lot of private data and selling it and I told him that unless he disclosed that fact up front, I would not do any marketing for the product at all." She paused. "And then he said—"

"I don't understand the nitty-gritty tech stuff, Ems, but that sounds awful. Are you okay?"

"Well, yes and no," Emma said. "He said I have principles, which is great, but he doesn't want someone guided by anything other than money working for him. So he laid me off immediately with a three-month severance package."

"Oh my." I gasped. "He sounds horrible."

"He was horrible. The entire company was horrible." She sounded dazed. "I just don't know what I'll do now. I put my life into that job. I didn't travel. I barely took time off. I gave them everything and look where it got me."

"They don't care about you." I sat down on the bed. "I'm so sorry."

"Thanks, Pips. I mean, I have good savings and should be able to find another marketing job easily, but is this what I want to do with my life? Is this who I want to be?"

"I'm starting to ask myself the same questions." I closed my eyes and lay back on the bed. "It's like we had one vision of where we wanted life to take us and maybe we weren't actually headed in the direction we wanted to go in."

"Exactly!" Emma exclaimed. "But what about you? How's it going in cowboy land?"

"It's nice. But a bit weird." I lowered my voice. Even though TJ wasn't in the cabin, I didn't want to speak loudly, just in case. "It's been great reconnecting with TJ. His friends are great. Montana is surprisingly beautiful. The sky is vast and so blue. The mountains are snowcapped, the hills are lush and green."

"You sound like you're that girl from *Little House on the Prairie*." Emma laughed. "Or that show, *The Waltons*. When you go to bed at night, do you say, Good night, John-Boy?"

"Oh yeah, every single night. John-Boy's my favorite."

"Oh Pippa, I miss you so much." Emma laughed. "I'm glad you're there though. You sound so much happier than you were here. Though I attribute that to Stephan."

"What was I thinking, Ems?"

"I have no idea. He was horrible."

"Worse than horrible," I admitted. "He put me down so much." I thought about that for a moment. Stephan had put me down more than I'd even told Emma. I was ashamed of myself for putting up with his behavior. "Emma, do you think that I'm weak?"

"What do you mean, weak? Do I think you'd win a fight against Oscar De La Hoya? No, but—"

"I know I'm not strong. I couldn't even win a fight with a ladybug." Emma laughed at my joke, and I smiled at the sound. She had the most joyous and infectious laugh. "I mean weak-minded. When I think of some of the things Stephan said to me." I cringed for a few moments. "He was really out of line. He'd say negative stuff about my lipstick, my clothes, the books I read, and the fact that I enjoyed TV. I remember he even lectured me once about getting rice with my naan when we went for Indian food. I can't believe I allowed him to talk to me that way."

"You want my honest opinion, Pippa?" Emma asked hesitantly, and I braced myself for what she was going to say.

"Of course. Always," I murmured.

"You wanted to be loved. And Stephan was a good-looking, rich guy, and he chased you." She sighed. "He wasn't all bad at the beginning. I mean, I never liked him, but I saw how he could be charming." She paused, and then she cleared her throat. "Also, I think you never really got over what happened with TJ."

"What do you mean, what happened with TJ? We never dated. He's always just been my friend."

"But he hasn't, though, Pippa. He was your childhood best friend. And you wrote for years, but by the time I met you in college, he'd stopped writing. All he did was send you Christmas cards. And I know you wrote him long letters and sent gifts and stuff." She exhaled a deep sigh. "And I know that hurt you. Because for the first couple of years, all you did was talk about your best friend, TJ. How close you were and how you were going to meet up for spring break and maybe one day you'd live in the same town and be neighbors again." She sounded sad. "And I was so jealous because you became my best friend and I knew that I would never have that friendship with you."

"But, Emma, I love you. You are my best friend."

"I know that. We are like sisters. We always will be. But you know what I realized?"

"What?" I said, feeling a lone tear rolling down my cheek. Emma had unleashed emotions inside me I'd forgotten about. Pain I'd tried to push to the side.

"I regretted being jealous of TJ. Because after the first year of us becoming friends, you stopped talking about him as much. You'd bring him up every now and again, but it wasn't with the same excitement. There was a sadness in you. And I hated that. I wanted to find him and strangle him and tell him that he was a fool for letting your friendship go. That's why I was so nervous you went to Montana. Not because of Stephan or the wedding. Good riddance to him."

"Then why?"

"Because I didn't want TJ to reject your friendship again. I didn't want him to make you feel like you didn't matter or you weren't good enough. A lot of times in life, people think that it's romantic relationships coming to an end that break our hearts and live on inside of us. But it's not. Sure, they can hurt for a while, but we get over them. It's friendships ending that will kill you inside. The what-ifs and the questions of why. Friends are the memory keepers of our souls and lives. Friends are there for us like nobody else will be." Her voice cracked slightly. "TJ broke your heart, Pippa. Not because you loved him as a boyfriend. But because you loved him as more. He was your soul mate."

"I know," I said, thinking back on the years of my friendship with TJ. "I just don't know why he stopped talking to me."

"You need to ask him, Pippa. He owes that to you."

"Maybe it's because I wasn't a good friend. He just shared with me that his dad hasn't seen or talked to him since the divorce. How did I not know that?" The tears were coming faster now. "I remember one letter where he asked if I would spy on his dad, but I thought it was a joke. I didn't know..." I took a deep breath. "I didn't realize..." My voice trailed off.

"Do you know why his dad stopped talking to him?" Emma sounded as confused as I felt. "What sort of parent does that?"

"I don't get it," I agreed, wiping the tears away from my eyes. "I can't even imagine how that made TJ feel."

"Horrible. Heartbroken. Devastated," Emma said softly. "That would break anyone, let alone a kid that's been displaced."

"Emma," I said softly. "There's something else."

"Oh no, what is it?" She paused. "Please tell me you didn't sleep with him."

"No!" I screeched, shocked at her comment. "You know I'm saving myself for marriage."

"So old-fashioned." She laughed. "But I respect you for it."

"Thanks," I said softly. It was a promise I'd made to myself when I was younger, and it meant a lot to me. "I want to give my husband the one thing I've never given to anyone else."

"And I love you for sticking to your guns, Pippa."

Emma's voice was warm. "I hope you know how proud I am of you for staying strong."

"It hasn't been easy," I admitted with a laugh. "Don't hate me, but I kinda think I like TJ and I want him to kiss me, but then I'm not sure if that would completely ruin our friendship, but then sometimes I can't think and..." I ran out of breath before I could finish my sentence.

"Whoa there, Nelly." Emma snickered. "Did you just say you like TJ?"

"Yes," I murmured, not even wanting to admit it to myself. "Am I crazy? He's just so handsome and strong and funny and the way his blue eyes follow me and gaze at me makes me feel like the only woman on the planet."

"Oh boy." Emma sounded thoughtful. "Have you kissed?"

"No," I squeaked out. "But I thought maybe he was going to kiss me last night and then again this morning and I did kinda want it."

"Normally, I would say it's just a kiss, no big deal. I mean, I've kissed plenty of guys, but none of them were men I was living with or good friends of mine."

"So don't kiss him, then?"

"I think right now you have so many other things going on, Pippa." Emma's voice was soft. "I'm not going to say no because I think you have to go with your feelings, but I'm not going to say grab him or anything because I'm not sure this is one of those situations."

"Yeah, I'm definitely not going to do that." I laughed, thinking about how Emma always used to tell me to grab random guys I thought were hot in college to kiss them and how I always chickened out. "I need to figure out my life before complicating it more. But one good thing is that I had an idea for a new play and I'm going to start writing it tonight."

"Oh, yay, I'm so happy for you." Emma sounded wistful. "Wish I was there. Maybe some of that Montana air would inspire me as well." As I listened to her words, a thought struck me, and I could feel my excitement growing.

"What if you came here?"

"What do you mean?" Emma sounded flustered. "Came where?"

"To Paradise Valley." I jumped off the bed. "That would be amazing. You could meet TJ and his really cute friends..."

"Are you trying to hook me up?"

"Would I do that?" I giggled. "But no, I'm serious. Come and visit Montana. You said you wanted an adventure."

"To Australia or Kenya," she said. "I was thinking about seeing kangaroos or lions, not cows."

"What about goats and horses?" I bent down to play with Apple's ears. "And you can meet Apple and Donkey, and oh, Emma, you should come, please come."

"Where would I stay though?"

"You can stay at the cabin with me and TJ. I mean, we'd have to share a bed, but it would be so much fun."

"I suppose it might be a little bit of fun." She was thoughtful. "Maybe ask TJ how he feels and I will check out flights."

"That would be great. I'm sure TJ won't mind, but I will ask him when he shows me around the ranch." I could feel the happiness bubbling inside of me. "Oh, Emma, it would be so awesome if you could come."

"Yes, and I can tell you if I think TJ is worthy of you or not. I don't want you dating another scrub."

"No one uses that term anymore, Emma," I exclaimed, but she was right. I wanted her to give me her opinion of TJ. I felt like he was a good guy. Maybe one of the best men I'd ever met, but it was always nice to have your opinions backed up by someone else. TJ was like a rare piece of art that you loved. Even though you thought it was amazing, you still wanted others to appreciate its beauty as well.

"I still use it," she said defiantly. "But, yeah, my mom was obsessed with TLC, fine me."

"TLC was the bomb." I thought of the old girl band and smiled. "So were NSYNC and Backstreet Boys."

"No one can tell me anything about JC. I was going to marry him."

"I was going to marry Justin. I used to tell TJ that I would be known as Pippa Timberlake and that he should practice calling me that." I laughed at the memory. "I don't know how he put up with me."

"Because you're fun," Emma said, her voice sweet. "Okay, I'm going to get off my butt and head out to the grocery store. We have no food in the fridge."

"Oops, sorry. I was supposed to go this week, wasn't I?" I frowned as I realized I'd left town without doing our weekly shopping as planned.

"No need to apologize. I'll speak to you later." Emma hung up just as TJ walked back into the cabin, his hands laden with fresh, dark-green, leafy vegetables. He headed over to the sink, where he proceeded to wash off the leaves. He was methodical as he cleaned them delicately and then placed them on a paper towel. I walked over to him and looked down at the different veggies: arugula, lettuce, spinach, and Swiss chard. He really did grow a lot.

"Everything okay?" he asked, his eyes gazing at me as I stopped beside him.

"I was just talking with Emma," I said, grabbing a wooden spoon and playing with it. "She lost her job yesterday."

"Oh no." His eyes widened. "Is she okay?" I loved that he was concerned about her, even though he didn't even know her.

"She's fine. She didn't really like the job, but I think she feels lost. She's been in marketing for so long now, but her heart wasn't in it. I guess we're a bit alike in that regard."

"Is she okay financially?" he asked, patting the leaves, drying and opening a drawer.

"Yeah, she made tons of money." I pretended to brush dollar bills into the air. "And she saved most of her salary, so she's good for a bit." I wasn't sure the best way to ask him about my plan. "So I was wondering..." I paused and looked down. "And, of course, you can say no..." I looked up to see TJ's lips twitching, and I licked my lips nervously. "I mean, it's not like this is her only option."

"What is it, Pips?" His blue eyes twinkled like stars in the night sky as he stared at me. "We don't have all day for you to get it out. Much like *Jeopardy*, there is a ticking clock here."

"Whatever, TJ." I stuck my tongue out at him like I used to when we were ten, and he wouldn't share his french fries with me. "Can Emma come to Montana to find herself for a little bit?" I took a deep breath. "And maybe stay here with us?"

"Stay here?" He looked shocked. "But I don't have space for her, Pips." He looked around his small log cabin. "Between you, me, and Apple, we're pretty much packed." He frowned slightly. "And I have to admit, the couch is not going to work out much longer for me either."

"Oh." I pressed my lips together, feeling sad. I'd been

excited for Emma to come to Montana. I wanted her to meet TJ. I had hoped that she would love it as much as I did.

"I mean, she can come and we can figure something out." He looked thoughtful. "Jack has a big house, and he lives there alone. I'm sure he wouldn't mind her staying with him. His parents and sister are also close by, so it wouldn't be just them on the ranch."

"Do you think he would mind?" I asked excitedly, not even pausing to think about what Emma would say. I knew she wouldn't come if I told her she'd be staying with someone else. She hated imposing on people. If I didn't tell her where she was staying until she got here, she'd have no choice.

"Not at all." He chuckled. "He's coming over this afternoon, so we can ask him then."

"Oh, that would be absolutely amazing. Thanks, TJ." I grinned happily. "Okay, I'm seriously going to get ready now. I can't wait to see around your ranch."

"I can't wait to show you my slice of heaven," he said with a small smile. "I've never felt more at home anywhere before in my life." I beamed at his comment, though an inner part of me was sad. Did that include when he'd lived in Brooklyn next door to me? I'd always thought about those years as the best years of my life, but maybe he didn't feel the same way.

Chapter Eighteen

T^J

Dear Pippa,

You know what I was thinking? I was thinking that there's a place in space where we don't ever have to worry about anything. How cool would that be? We would never feel hurt. We would never feel pain. We could eat all the candy and ice cream we wanted to. We'd never question who we are or why people don't like this or even love us.

I guess I'm being philosophical tonight. Have you ever heard of Immanuel Kant? He's a German philosopher. I got a book about him at the library. I've been getting into deep *thoughts these days. Mom says I'm in my head too much, but she doesn't get me, not like you do.*

I guess that's the beauty of having a best friend. They're always there to listen and chat. You've always been that person for me, Pips.

You excited for your graduation in a few weeks?

As Always,
TJ

"Ready to ride, Pippa? I can saddle up the horses now if you want." I looked up from the couch as she walked out of the bathroom, dressed in jeans and a cute top. I jumped up and tried not to focus on how pretty she looked. Why was it that every time I saw her, she seemed to grow more and more beautiful?

"Sure, that sounds good." She nodded and headed toward the front door. "I was thinking that you can take the bed. I didn't think about how uncomfortable the couch must be."

"You're in the bed." I shook my head as we headed outside. I left the door open for Apple to run out and join us. Donkey ran over to her, and the two chased each other back and forth. "I think I'll be fine. We're camping tonight, and then I'll get a blow-up mattress."

"But where will you put it?" She made a face. "That doesn't sound comfortable."

"It'll be fine. I'll figure something out."

"You can sleep in the bed if you want...with me." She blushed.

"With you?" I raised my eyebrows.

"I mean, we'd have a barrier of pillows and stuff down the middle like we sometimes did when we were kids," she said quickly. "Just so you could stretch your legs."

"I appreciate the offer, Pippa, but the bed is all yours." I didn't want to tell her that as much as I would love to share a bed with her, even with a barrier of pillows, I didn't want to tempt fate. "I'll figure something out."

"If you're sure." She looked around. "So we need to think of a ranch name. What's your favorite color?"

"My favorite color?" I pursed my lips and motioned for her to follow me. "Let's go to the stables and talk at the same time. Come on, Apple, Donkey." I motioned to the animals. "Why?"

"Because maybe it can be a part of the name." She followed behind me. I watched as she bent down, picked up a stick, and threw it for Apple to fetch. "Unless your favorite color is chartreuse or something. That would be a weird ranch name."

"You don't remember my favorite color?" I glanced back at her. "You always used to make me do all those quizzes when we were younger. I feel like you know me better than I know myself."

"I wish," she mumbled as she ran up to me. "Sometimes, I feel like I don't know you at all." The words were low, like she didn't want me to hear them. I stopped and stared down at her; she was trying to smile, but I noticed that she was having a hard time maintaining eye contact with me.

"What do you mean by that? You know me better than anyone else on God's green earth." I blinked at her as she gave me a big smile and played with her hair. "Don't give me that fake *everything is all right*, smile. You forget that I watched you grow up, Pippa. I know that *I'm hurt, but I'm going to pretend everything's okay* look."

"I just feel like I don't understand why you stopped talking to me. I feel like you didn't want me in your life. I feel like—" Her breath caught, and her brown eyes appeared moist. "I didn't want to bring it up. I didn't want to bring this day down, but you know I have a hard time keeping things to myself when they're on my mind."

"You think I didn't want you in my life?"

"I think when we turned eighteen, you stopped writing. You never responded to any of my letters. We were supposed to meet up for spring break and summer. We were finally going to be around each other again. We were—"

"My dad isn't my dad," I blurted out, stopping her. Her eyes flew to mine in shock. "I guess he'd always had a suspicion when my mom got pregnant right away that the baby might not be his, but he didn't know for sure until I was twelve."

"Twelve?"

"Remember when I fell off my skateboard and went into the hospital?" I asked her, and she nodded. "He took me to the hospital and when they asked him my blood type, he said the same as him and Mom, B positive. But then it turned out that I was A positive. Eventually it all came out that I wasn't his. He couldn't get over it, so he and my mom divorced. We moved to Florida, and he never spoke to me again."

"Oh my, oh, TJ." Pippa stepped forward and stopped. "I'm so sorry."

"I didn't know. My mom never told me." My shoulders stiffened as I thought back to my teen years. "At first, I thought he was upset with Mom, then I thought maybe he

Jaimie Casey

died, then I was just hurt and confused." I paused, debating telling Pippa everything. I didn't want to burden her with the truth of everything, but I knew I had to be completely honest. "I reached out to your mom right before you were going to graduate. I wanted to surprise you at the ceremony and then take you on a weekend trip. I also asked her if she'd heard anything about my dad because I didn't understand why he'd cut me out."

"I didn't know that." She frowned. "My mom never told me you contacted her. Why didn't you come to the graduation? Why didn't we go on a trip?" I could see that she was perplexed, and I took a deep breath before continuing. My own hurt resurfaced as I thought about the conversation I'd had with her mom.

"She told me not to come. She told me you had plans for the summer. She told me my dad wasn't in my life because I wasn't his and that my mom had lied to him for years. She told me I needed to focus on my new life because we can't go back to the past." My voice cracked, and I stopped. I didn't want to tell Pippa everything her mother had said to me. She'd been cruel and mean and said horrific things about me and my mom. "That's basically it."

"My mom said all that?" Pippa's expression was shocked and angry. "How dare she? I have a mind to call her right now and—"

"Don't." I reached out and grabbed her hand. "She was doing what she thought was best for you. She didn't think I was a good friend for you to have in your life."

"But it wasn't up to her," Pippa shouted. "She can't dictate my friendships. And how dare she tell you about your father. That wasn't her place. She's out of line."

"But she's still your mother, Pips." I squeezed her hand. "I can't lie. What she said to me made me dislike her very

180

much, and that was why I distanced myself from you. You always listened to what she had to say. You studied what she wanted you to study. You bought clothes she wanted you to wear. You even dated guys she thought were good for you. I wasn't that person. And it hurt. Knowing that she didn't want me in your life hurt even more than finding out about my dad."

"I'm sorry." She took a deep breath and rubbed her eyes. I could see she was crying and felt awful for upsetting her. Surprisingly, I was grateful to have told her. It felt like a weight had been lifted off my shoulders.

"I didn't stop writing because I was over you or our friendship. You're the best friend a guy could ever want, Pippa. I stopped writing because I was in a dark place in my life and suddenly, the person who had brought me so much light took me to a bad place."

"I didn't know that." She cast her eyes to the ground. "Do you want me to leave? I don't want to bring up all of these memories for you."

"I was wrong though. You don't take me to a bad place, Pips. You never did. Your mom is not you. And my dad is not you. And that hurt. That pain. It's not on your shoulders. I didn't know if I'd be able to separate everything. But having you here, being around you again. You've brought so much life and laughter back into my home. Back into me." I held her chin between my thumb and forefinger and lifted it so that she could see me when I said, "I was wrong for not writing back to you. I've missed having you in my life."

"You sure?" She offered me a lopsided grin. "You don't have to say that if you don't mean it."

"I mean it." I reached out and pulled on her braid. "I don't say things I don't mean."

"So, did your mom ever tell you who your dad was?" she

asked softly, her eyes surveying mine. A hollow feeling enveloped me as I thought about my biological dad.

"No." I shook my head. "The simple fact of the matter is that she doesn't really know him. She was traveling with some friends, going to national parks. In fact, she was in Montana and Wyoming at Glacier, Yellowstone, and the Grand Tetons for a few months. She met this guy called Lucky. She said it was all good fun. Then they went their separate ways. She went back to New York. She met my dad two weeks after she got back. Then found out she was pregnant a few weeks later." I cocked my head to the side. "She was young. She said she just wanted to believe my dad was the father. She felt ashamed and embarrassed. And I found out Dad was cheating on her and he used me as an excuse to get out of paying support." I took a deep breath. "I was so hurt and angry for so many years. At Mom and Dad. And your mom and you. And just about everyone. Then I got into climbing, I met Jack, and I visited Montana and I fell in love with this place."

"You're so strong, TJ." She opened her arms up and wrapped them around me. "And I'm ashamed that I haven't been there for you. I wish that I would have known. I wish I could have done something to help."

"I know, but I needed to process this myself." I let her squeeze me tight. "I've missed you every single day. I hope you know that."

"I do," she whispered. "I've missed you every single day as well." She rubbed my back and laid her head against my chest. "Sometimes I thought that I'd never see you again."

"I wouldn't have let that happen," I said as I pulled back and looked into her eyes. "You know that, right?"

"I don't know anything anymore." There was a rueful smile on her face. "I'm mad at my mom, TJ. She's tried to run my life for so long. And I'm mad at myself for letting her. And I'm mad at you for cutting me out. And I'm mad at your dad for being a jerk." She took a deep breath, and her eyes were blazing. "I'm just mad at so many wasted years and so many hurt feelings." She bit down on her lip, and I noticed how pink and glossy they were. I remembered when we were teens how she'd loved to try different flavored lip glosses and talked about wanting her lips to be sweet when she had her first kiss. I remembered how jealous I'd felt thinking about her kissing a boy who wasn't me.

"Well, I'm here now," I whispered, wanting to distract myself from kissing her. "And you're here now, too." I grinned. "So no need to be too mad."

"I guess," she said, her eyes roving over my face. I could feel her heart beating faster next to me. Her fingers stopped moving, and she moved her head back before giving me one long, tight hug. "Just know that I'm here whenever you need to talk."

"I know," I said as I ran my fingers through my hair, wondering what she was thinking about.

"And whatever else..." she said, her voice trailing off as her face reddened. What was she thinking about? Her eyes moved back to mine and widened as I continued to stare at her. She was so beautiful. She'd always been cute, but she had blossomed like a butterfly. I moved closer to her, smelling her strawberry scent and smiling. She moved closer to me, her lips parted slightly, breathlessly waiting. My face moved down toward hers, our eyes still locked onto each other. My darling Pippa was here and in the flesh. I was mere inches away from kissing her, and time seemed to stand still. It was like the universe had waited an eternity for this moment and wanted to make sure we enjoyed it.

I took a small breath and leaned down to press my lips

against hers. The anticipation was sweet and exciting. This was our moment.

"Ow," Pippa yelped and stumbled forward. My lips pressed against her cheek for a brief second before she hobbled to the side.

"What the?" I looked around and saw Donkey standing there with narrowed eyes before he bent down to chew some grass.

"Donkey just rammed me in the leg." Pippa rubbed her calf. "Not superhard, but it shocked me."

"Donkey." I glared at my pet goat, and he ignored me. "You act like you own this ranch." I looked over at Pippa and released a sigh. The moment had passed. Gone. I wasn't sure if I was relieved or not. I wanted to kiss her, but not in a moment emotionally filled with so many other things.

"That's it." Pippa turned to me, her eyes excited.

"That's what?" I frowned, wondering what had turned her frown upside down.

"The name of the ranch." A wide smile spread across her face as she clapped. "It's the perfect name."

"Hmm? Are you going to tell me what this brilliant name is?"

"Donkey's Ranch." She looked down at the goat, munching away as if he hadn't just stopped what could have been the single best kiss of my life. "It's cute, fun, and memorable."

"Donkey's Ranch," I repeated and laughed out loud as he looked up at me, a glint in his eyes that told me he thought he was the boss. "I love it," I said. "It's absolutely ridiculous, but I love it. Welcome to Donkey's Ranch, Pippa. I hope you have an enjoyable stay."

"I already am, TJ." She beamed at me. "Now, let's go

ride some horses." There was a pep in her step as she walked away, and I tried not to stare at her pert little butt. She looked over her shoulder at me and made a face. "Just to let you know, I haven't ridden a horse since summer camp, so please put me on the horse that doesn't canter or run. I think I can only handle a very slow trot right now. The last thing I need is to fall into some cow pie or goat poop." She shuddered. "Even though I have a feeling Donkey would love that."

"I got you, Pips." I grinned as Apple ran up to her. I felt light and happy and was looking forward to the day ahead. "And if you want Emma to stay here with us, that's also fine. We can make it work."

"Thanks, Teej." She beamed at me and then did a cartwheel. She spun around, and little wisps of her hair came out of her braid. "The hills are alive with the sound of Pippa," she sang out, her eyes darting across the land. "I just had the best idea for a play." She clapped her hands excitedly. "And we're going to perform it right here on your land."

"What?" I blinked at her. "What are you saying?"

"I'll tell you later. For now, we focus on you."

Chapter Nineteen

P ippa

Dear TJ,

Did you get my last letter? I haven't heard back from you, and I wanted to make sure you were okay. Can you believe we're starting college in the fall? NYU, here I come. Good-looking men of NYC, watch out, Pippa Chase is on the prowl. HAHA.

Do you know what you're going to study yet? I'm thinking theater and screenwriting. I also want to do a semester abroad in England. And go to Stratford-upon-Avon and see a play at The Globe. That would be so cool. Maybe you could visit me. Imagine that? Me in the *hometown of William Shakespeare. Maybe I'll meet a cute English boy. And I'll go around talking about crumpets and tea. Maybe I'll even meet the Queen and that dishy Prince Harry.*

Write back soon. I want to hear all about you and what you're up to. Maybe we can plan on spending Christmas together? My mom has a lot of airline miles, and I could ask her to fly me somewhere.

Your BFF 4 Eva,
Pippa Chase (Soon to be a real playwright)

"This is absolutely beautiful." I gazed at the multicolored rocks at the bottom of the water. The river was set in the middle of the greenest grass, and purple, pink, and yellow wildflowers stretched as far as the eyes could see. In the distance stood a mountain, and birds chirped as they flew back and forth. I felt like I was in the middle of heaven. "No wonder you love it so much here." I looked over at TJ, who was stroking Stella's mane.

"Thank you." He looked at me with a warm smile, and my heart about melted. TJ Wyatt was driving me crazy. I'd been so sure he was going to kiss me right before Donkey butted me and ruined the moment. My heart had been racing so fast that I felt like I wouldn't have been shocked if it had popped out of my chest. "So this is where I thought I'd place two small log cabins." He looked around him.

"Maybe three. I don't want too many people here, just enough to pay the bills."

"I'd stay here for sure." I smiled at him, my heart still aching at the news he'd told me. His dad wasn't his dad; my mom was an evil queen. It was a lot to take in. But it all made sense. I was going to have a go at my mother later. I knew TJ didn't want that, but it was a long time coming. I'd be respectful, but I knew I had to speak up for myself and for TJ. I'd been a wallflower for far too long in all areas of my life. I also wanted to ask my mom what she knew about TJ's dad, who I now hated. The fact that he'd cut his son off for something that wasn't his fault was despicable.

"You wanna head back to the cabin?" TJ asked. "Jack is coming over in a bit and he might be bringing some of the other guys."

"Sure, let's do it," I said with a small nod. "I'm still shocked that all of you are single, by the way."

"Why?" he asked as he put his foot in the stirrups and mounted Stella.

"Because you're all so handsome and fun." I made my way over to Nightstar and patted him on the side before stroking his mane. He looked at me with big, bashful brown eyes. "You're a good horse, Nightstar," I said as I adjusted the reins and then hoisted myself up. The horse's black coat was shiny and soft, and I stroked him again as I adjusted my butt in the saddle and grabbed the reins. TJ looked at me with a small smile, and I was glad I could get back on the horse by myself.

"I do appreciate the compliment." I moved my reins up and down slowly, and Nightstar followed behind TJ and Stella. The horses walked back alongside the river, and I gazed around me in peaceful bliss. "You still down to camp tonight?" he asked as he looked back at me. "I figured we'd get back, relax a bit, wait for Jack and whoever else to come over. Then we'd head back with the tents, and I'd make a fire and grill some steaks."

"Sounds amazing. Do you go camping a lot?"

"A couple of times a week." He halted Stella and waited for me and Nightstar to catch up. "I just love being out here, in nature, staring up at the stars, thinking about the universe...Thinking about life."

"Do you ever think about your real dad?" I asked him as he kicked Stella lightly to get her to move again. I wondered if he'd be upset at my questions. I didn't want to take him to a sad place, but I was curious. I wasn't sure what I'd do if I found out my dad wasn't really my dad.

"All the time. Mom said he didn't know she was pregnant, so it's not like he abandoned me. He didn't know about me. Sometimes, I wonder what would have happened if she'd found out she was pregnant before she left Wyoming. Would he have wanted her to stay? Would he have wanted to marry her?"

"Maybe," I answered, trying to be positive. "Have you ever thought about looking for him?"

"How would I do that?" I could see the sadness in his eyes. "Look online for a man named Lucky who used to hang out in a national park twenty-eight years ago? He could be anywhere now."

"I guess." I sighed. "Your mom didn't have any other information about him?"

"No. If she did, she didn't wanna share it with me."

"I'm sorry." I wondered if my mom knew anything. Our mothers had been quite close when we were younger, which was part of why we'd spent so much time together. If I had a secret like that, I'd want to tell someone. A friend. A neighbor. It was a long shot, but maybe my mom knew something that could help. This wasn't information I was going to share with TJ. It wasn't like he liked my mom, and I understood why. I also didn't want to get his hopes up or have him tell me that he didn't want me to get involved in his business.

"It's not your fault, Pips. So tell me, what's the idea for your play?"

"Oh, the one I wanted to have on your ranch?" I loved how interested he always was in my work. "I thought it could be a story about a nun that found herself working for a widowed dad that—"

"You're describing *The Sound of Music*! Did you think I wouldn't remember the plot of that movie? You made us watch it every year at Christmastime."

"I did, didn't I?" I grinned at him. "When I love something, I guess I really love it."

"Yeah, that's true. You're a loyal one."

"I like to think so. Maybe I'm too loyal." I frowned. "Maybe I need to change it up a bit."

"No such thing as too loyal, Pips." He gave me that look he's been giving me quite often on this ride. "Oh, Jack is already here." He pointed in the distance, and I saw Jack's red truck parked near TJ's. "You ready to canter, or are you not comfortable yet?"

"I'll try," I said, leaning forward to stroke Nightstar's neck before kicking him gently in the side. "We can go faster, Nightstar," I said softly. The horse seemed to understand what I was saying because he immediately picked up his pace. I held on for dear life as his legs stretched to life, and he galloped away.

"Attagirl," TJ shouted as he and Stella galloped past me toward the cabin. His body was lean and easy on the horse as he rode. His dark hair shone in the sunlight, and his tan arms glistened with dark-golden-blond hairs. He rode like a cowboy who was made to tend the land. He was strong, confident, and manly, and a sliver of appreciation shimmied through me as I let Nightstar carry me home.

"Good boy, Nightstar," I murmured as the horse moved sleekly across the field. His mane flew in the cool wind, as did my own hair. I felt like a pioneer discovering and seeing the land for the first time. I wondered if there had been Native Americans on this land previously. I wondered what it had looked like a hundred years ago. The blue sky loomed in front of me with my own picture-perfect panorama. It was beautiful here. It was a place to fall in love and be loved. It was a place to find yourself.

"I think I just might love it here, Nightstar," I called out to the horse. "I think I just might love your papa as well," I sang in a slightly lower voice. "Not that I'm going to tell him that. And I expect you won't either." I giggled at my words. "Not unless you become Mr. Ed, the talking horse, and then I'm in a world of trouble." As Nightstar continued his pace, I realized my shoulders were more relaxed, and my palms were no longer gripping the reins as tightly as they had been. I remembered what it was to ride and be one with the horse, and I loved it. "I'll tell you another secret, Nightstar. When I was younger, I always wanted a horse, but I never told anyone. Because how was that going to be possible in New York City unless you had a rich family with a mansion upstate?" I sat up straight as we approached the log cabin. TJ and Jack watched us as we came in closer, and I lifted my hand in a small wave.

TJ looked proud as he stepped forward and held his hand up to slow Nightstar down. The horse slowed and then came to a stop.

"Hey there, Pippa." Jack looked even more handsome than I remembered as he stepped forward. His dark-blond hair shone like spun gold in the sunlight. "Did you enjoy your ride?"

"I did, thank you." I swung my leg over the saddle and dismounted, feeling slightly disoriented now that I was no longer riding and soaring through the air. "I forgot how much I love to ride."

"We'll make a country girl out of you yet." Jack grinned. "Oh, and before I forget, did you decide about Sunday lunch?" He looked over at TJ. "Mom and Dad want to know if y'all are coming?"

"Sunday lunch?" I asked, questioning him.

"My mom, pops, sister, her husband, and her two kids will be there. Maybe some of the other guys and girls, whoever's free."

"Oh, cool. That's so nice of them."

"Lucas and Wendy are both very welcoming and lovely people." There was a tense look on TJ's face as he gazed at me and then at Jack. "I wanted to ask you, Pippa, before I made a decision."

"I'd love to go." I grinned and looked over at Jack, whose green eyes always seemed to be laughing. "Sounds like a lot of fun. Hey Jack," I asked him before I forgot, "do you have some extra goats we can get for the ranch?"

"Yeah, why?" Jack looked at me and then at TJ, who was groaning.

"Pippa wants to start some yoga class and apparently, Donkey cannot be the only goat in the class."

"How can you have one goat for a group class, TJ??" I rolled my eyes. "We need at least four other goats, I think."

"I can get you hundreds if you want them." He winked at me. "You just let me know."

"Okay, I will." I blushed as he stared at me flirtatiously. I wasn't used to the cowboy charm, and it sure was affecting me. It also didn't hurt that TJ looked ready to bite someone's head off. I was pretty sure he was jealous, which suited me just fine. At least it told me that he cared. Not that I was going to rush into anything with him. I didn't want to make life plans based around a man anymore. I wanted to make life plans based on my dreams and goals. And I knew my biggest dream was to write and direct a play. I just had to figure out how I could make it happen.

"Pippa, are you listening to me?" TJ interrupted my thoughts. "Are you here or on Mars somewhere?"

"If I was on Mars, that would mean you were on Mars as well." I folded my arms. "What did you say?"

"Jack said he and some of the others might wanna come camping with us tonight, and I just wanted to make sure you'd be okay with that." His eyes studied my face. "I know you haven't been camping in a while."

"It'll be fun." I beamed at him and then at Jack. "The more the merrier, I say."

"I wasn't sure if you two wanted some alone time." Jack winked, and I shook my head vehemently. "No, no. We don't need any alone time. In fact, I think that—"

"Invite whoever you want." TJ cut me off and gave me a side-eye look before rolling his eyes. "Pippa, why don't you go back into the cabin while Jack and I discuss business? We might be a while."

"Okay," I said, slightly miffed. I felt like I'd been dismissed, and I didn't like it. "Well, it was good seeing you, Jack."

"You too." He grinned. "I'll tell my mom and dad that y'all will join us on Sunday. We'll be looking forward to it."

"Me too." I smiled and then looked over at TJ. "Anything you need me to do to get ready for tonight?" I asked him as he grabbed Nightstar's reins.

"No, but thanks. You work on your play and relax," he said with a smile. "And maybe think of a logo to go with the ranch name. I wanna get a sign made up soon."

"Oh, I will." I grinned at him. "I'm feeling super inspired." I headed toward the cabin when I remembered Emma. TJ had said that she could stay with us, and while I thought that would be fun, it would also interrupt one-on-one time with me and TJ. And I wanted to see where our relationship was going to go. "Hey, Jack," I called out as he turned toward TJ.

"Yes, Pippa?"

"My best friend Emma wants to come for a visit and TJ doesn't have much space here and I was—"

"She can stay with me." He cut me off and grinned. "TJ already texted and asked." He looked over at TJ. "Any friend of yours is a friend of mine," he said. "I'd be more than happy to have her stay."

"Oh, thank you so much!" I squealed in delight. "She's going to be ecstatic. I'm going to go and call her now and let her know." I debated running over to him to give him a quick hug, but I didn't want TJ starting World War III. Not that I thought he'd attack Jack. Though in some alternate universe of what was appropriate, I would have enjoyed it. It was sad, but a little part of me thought it would be quite thrilling for two men to fight over me. Not that I was interested in Jack whatsoever. Yes, he was handsome. And he had a dazzling smile. But his looks didn't hold a candle to TJ's. Plus, TJ had a heart of gold. When he wasn't being stubborn or holding things in. I was glad he'd told me why he'd stopped talking to me, but I still felt like he was holding stuff in. But I wasn't going to push it. I'd seen the pain in his eyes when he'd talked about his dad. He'd tried to brush it off, but I knew he was still hurting inside. It was understandable.

Anger resurrected itself in me as I made my way into the log cabin. I was upset with my mom. Really upset. And I wasn't quite sure how to approach her. I didn't want to be rude, mean, or cruel, but I wanted her to know that her actions had cost me and had cost TJ. What she'd said to him was not appropriate or kind. And I had a feeling that TJ hadn't even told me the worst things she'd said. He was caring like that. He wouldn't want me to hate my mom. No matter how much he disliked her. I'd have to wait to calm down to call her. Instead, I called Emma. She was always the voice of reason. The one to stop me from being impetuous. I knew that was the real reason I hadn't told her I was going to Montana. I knew she would have stopped me. The phone rang two times before she picked up.

"Hello to my cowgirl best friend. What's going on?"

"I need your advice," I said quickly as I sank into the couch. I needed her opinion on many things in my life, the two most important being TJ and my mom.

Chapter Twenty

T J

Dear Pippa,

Mr. Baker, my history teacher, said I have an aptitude for history that he's not seen in his classes before. He told me he wants me to apply to colleges with strong history programs. I nodded, like I agreed, cause I want an A, but we both know I have to go to college close to home to help take care of Grand-pops and Nanna.

Is NYU still your number one choice? Or is it Columbia now? I'm sure you'll get into both. I have to write my personal statements this weekend. Think I can say, My name is

TJ Wyatt, and I want to go to your school cause I get in-state tuition, and it's cheap? HAHA.

How's it going on the home front? Are you going to homecoming or prom or anything? I wasn't going to go, but some of the other guys on the football team and I are going to go with some of the cheerleaders. There's this one girl, Sadie, who has made it pretty clear she's into me. Hope I can survive the night! Are you dating?

TJ

"Goat yoga, TJ?" Jack bent over with his hands on his knees, barely containing his laughter as soon as Pippa closed the door to the cabin. "What in the heavens above is goat yoga?"

"I have no idea, Jack," I said, joining him in hysterics. "Pippa said it's all the rage in New York and I guess she's some sort of expert. She's going to teach classes or something."

"That woman has you twisted around her little finger already." Jack's eyes surveyed me. "I've never seen you like this before."

"Like what?" I squared my shoulders and grabbed a hoe that was leaning against the barn. "I'm not acting any differently."

"You're grinning and laughing and glaring." Jack rubbed his chin thoughtfully. "I've never seen you like that before, with any woman. And I've seen you around plenty of women."

"Don't put it that way. We both get our flirt on."

"That we do." He paused. "But I thought she was just your friend."

"She is just my friend." He raised an eyebrow in disbelief. "Okay, well, maybe I like her as more than a friend. Maybe I'm falling for her. But she just got out of a relationship and it's not like that between us. We've always just been best friends. We made a pact when we were younger that we would always be there for each other. If we were to date and it didn't work out, what would happen with the pact?"

"But if it did work out, the pact would mean a whole lot more, huh?" Jack's eyes were soft as he stared at me, white-knuckling the hoe. "We've always been bachelors, and I know I'm never getting married, but I guess I never really asked you about your feelings on the subject."

"My feelings on what?" I averted my eyes and stared at the mountains. "We should go climbing next week. We haven't been in a while."

"Yeah, we can go," Jack said and stepped closer to me. "Don't change the subject on me, TJ. Your feelings on marriage."

"I don't have any feelings about marriage." I turned back in his direction and gave him my most nonchalant shrug. "I think it's great for people that want it. And some people, like your parents, have an amazing marriage, but it doesn't always work out that way."

"My parents do have a great marriage now. But it wasn't always that way. When they met, my mom was head over heels in love with him, but Dad was pining over some old love of his."

"Oh really? Sounds like Old Man Roberts and Annie's story. Didn't he say that he was in love with some woman he met from the East Coast?"

"Yup!" Jack nodded. "His summer love that left him to go back home. Then he met and married Annie."

"I'm surprised Annie and your mom don't get jealous, knowing their husbands wanted to marry someone else."

"That's life, though, ain't it?" He leaned against the barn, lifted his cowboy hat off, and picked at an imaginary piece of dust. "We can have all these plans and all these feelings and then somehow none of them ever works out." His voice sounded wistful, and I wondered if he was thinking about Kaye.

"I think everything works out for a reason though. Even if we don't realize it at the time."

"That's what my pops says." Jack nodded. "Ain't no pain or failure that will ever last a lifetime. For everything, there is a season. Love, life, happiness, sadness, joy, anger, envy, jealousy."

"You trying to preach to me, Jack?"

"Ain't nobody ever called me a preacher. My momma would have loved it, but I think I'm good being a farmer." He smiled. "It's a good life we have here. Folks in other places they don't understand the beauty we got here in Paradise Valley, but I think it's pretty much the best place on earth."

"I would agree with that," I said as I surveyed my acres. "Pippa came up with a name for the ranch."

"I didn't even know you were thinking about one."

"Neither did I. She came up with Donkey's Ranch."

"Donkey's Ranch?" Jack looked at me then at Donkey, who was chewing on grass. "She's really got you loving goats now, doesn't she?"

"Maybe she's got me loving her too," I said under my breath, my heart racing at the thought.

"What did you say?" Jack asked, leaning in. "I didn't hear you."

"Oh, I just said we should text everyone and see who wants to camp out tonight," I said quickly. "It's going to be a nice night. Clear sky. Lots of stars." Jack had a knowing look on his face, and I wondered what he was thinking. "So, about the goats?"

"I'll give you five. And I want a free goat yoga class. I can't wait to see how this goes."

"You wanna see the yoga class or Pippa more?" There was a distinct edge to my tone, and I tried to soften it with a smile. I knew I was acting jealous and stupid, but I needed to know if my friend was planning on making moves on her.

"The yoga class," Jack said and wrapped his arm around my shoulder. "You're my best buddy, TJ. I would never make a move on your girl."

"She's not my girl," I protested, glaring at him, though there was a lightness in my heart at his words. "I was just making sure you weren't going to try any funny stuff."

"I would never." Jack threw his hands up in the air. "And she might not be your girl yet, but I have a feeling she will be one day."

"What are you, psychic?" I rolled my eyes.

"Maybe. Better than being called a psycho, which Betsy-Sue from Billings called me when I was fifteen."

"Why did Betsy-Sue, from Billings, call you a psycho?" I enjoyed the lighthearted turn in our conversation as I pulled out my phone to send a group text. "What did you do?"

"I did nothing." Jack mocked being insulted. "Betsy-Sue

got her words confused. I think she meant to say I was the most handsome man that she'd ever seen."

"You're an idiot, and by the way, thanks for saying Emma could stay. I know it means a lot to Pippa."

"Hey, I've got a big house and as long as she's not a busybody or one of those women that thinks only hicks live in the country, then we're fine. Plus, I'll barely see her, what with the work on the ranch and all."

"True." I nodded. "I'm sure she'll be spending most of her time with Pippa. You won't have to worry about her at all."

Chapter Twenty-One

P ippa

Dear TJ,

   I saw Wicked on Broadway last week. I know, I know, I've seen it at least five other times, but this time was different. I could actually feel the characters' emotions. I knew what they were going to say and the things that they should have said instead. It felt so cool having that moment.

   You know what I want to do one day when we're older? I want to have a play in the park or something. Just us and some friends. Goofing off and having fun. And acting out scenes from my head. Wouldn't that be cool? I *wish you were still next door. I couldn't sleep last night because my mind was bursting with ideas. Miss you so much.*

Your one and only best friend in the world,
Pippa

"Pippa, you want a wine cooler?" Mindy headed toward me with two bottles in her hand. I nodded gratefully as she handed me one of the bright-pink-filled glass bottles. "It sure is a pretty night." She gazed around and looked at the row of tents all sitting next to the river. "TJ really does have a nice tract of land here."

"He sure does," I said, opening the top and taking a swig of the cold strawberry wine drink. It tasted more like Kool-Aid than wine, but I wasn't going to complain. "I'm surprised that so many of you could come tonight?"

"We love our group camping nights," she said with a smile, her eyes looking at the men as they set up the fire. TJ, Jack, Brandon, Aiden, and Ethan were all drinking beers and talking about the Broncos, which made no sense to me.

"Why are they talking about the Denver Broncos?" I asked as Brielle and Charlotte approached us with a bag of chips and salsa. "Isn't that a Colorado football team?"

"We don't have any NFL teams here in Montana," Mindy answered. "So most of the boys cheer for the Broncos."

"Old Man Roberts supports the Vikings though," Charlotte interjected. "As he likes to remind me every trivia night when we have a football-related question."

"I'm so glad you girls could make it. This is so much fun."

"We're glad to be here." Brielle nodded toward the chairs. "Shall we go and sit by the fire and talk?"

"Maybe we can play a game as well?" Charlotte asked eagerly, and Mindy groaned. "What?" Charlotte asked innocently. "Games are fun."

"Maybe let me get drunk first." Mindy took a long gulp of the sweet drink. "And eat. And sleep for a few hours."

"Mindy! You're horrible."

"That's why I brought delicious cupcakes for dessert," Mindy said with a smile. "It's the only sweet part of me."

"Ooh, yummy." I sat down on the dark-gray folding chair. It sank into the soil, and I prayed it didn't fall back or collapse. I leaned back gingerly and observed everyone. The guys were chatting and laughing, getting ready to grill steaks; Donkey and Apple were standing close by, hoping to get some free food. The girls were chatting about the bookstore and how it hadn't been open for weeks, but I didn't join the conversation. I pulled out my phone, took a panoramic photo, and sent it to Emma.

Wish you were here. Let me know when you book your ticket.

Oh, that looks fun and who are all those hunky guys? Emma texted back immediately. *I'm booking my ticket tonight. Have so much fun, Pippa. See you soon.*

I smiled at her text and checked my missed calls. Both my mom and Stephan had called me several times and left voice mails. I didn't bother listening to either of them before. I just wanted to forget about them for tonight.

"So, I have a question," I whispered as I leaned forward. "And I know I'm being totally nosy, but it's been killing me."

"What's that?" Mindy asked, grabbing some chips from the bag and chewing on them. She was making me hungry, but I wanted to save my appetite so I could appreciate the steaks and salads I'd made.

"So, remember at trivia night, we were talking about Jack and Kaye," I said, feeling guilty for being such a gossip. "You said they used to date but had broken up and just when you were going to tell me why they broke up, something happened."

Mindy looked at the guys standing about ten feet away. "I guess I didn't get to tell you everything."

"What happened?" I asked breathlessly.

"She cheated on him," Brielle said, her eyes wide as she moved in. "He was the year above her. They'd been dating for two years when he went off to college. They stayed together though."

"Yeah," Charlotte added. "Everyone was shocked because Jack has always been a bit of a flirt, and he's gorgeous."

"He is very cute." I nodded, looking over at him. "So he broke up with her because she cheated."

"You could say that," Mindy said, a scandalized expression on her face. "But it's a bit more complicated."

"What do you mean? She didn't cheat with his brother, did she?" My jaw dropped, but then I remembered that Jack didn't have a brother. I looked over at the guys to make sure they weren't listening.

"No," Mindy shook her head, "Kaye got pregnant two months before graduation and told everyone it was Jack's. He gave her his grandma's ring, but then Ruthie Smith and Katie Matthews told Jack's papa, Luke, that Kaye was further along than she'd said and they did some backdating and figured out that it wasn't Jack's."

"And she totally knew," Brielle interjected. "I mean, she was young, so we can't blame her for being scared, but Jack found out she was lying and they broke up."

"And he ain't never been the same again." Charlotte sighed as she looked over at him. "Which is a pity because he's mighty fine."

"Do you have a thing for him?" I asked, staring at her face.

"For who?" She blushed as she looked back at me.

"Jack."

"Jack? No, not at all. He's a nice guy, but he's not my type." She looked back over at the men. "The men around here are sweet, but they're like boys. None of them are ready for a real relationship."

"Oh?" I asked her, wondering if she was referring to one of the men in particular.

"They're all single, aren't they?"

"I can understand why Brandon is single. He's such a jerk. And he's so full of himself. Sometimes I think that—"

"What are you going on about now, Mindy Messina?" The man in question headed toward us, a cocky grin on his face.

"None of ya business, Brandon Knight." Mindy jumped up, her face red. "I'm going to get another wine cooler. Everyone good?"

"Yeah," I responded and also stood up. I headed toward TJ to see if he needed any help. "Everything going okay?"

"Yeah." He smiled at me. "We're going to put the steaks on in a little bit." He looked me over. "You good?"

"Yes, I was just chatting with the girls." I looked away from him quickly, as I didn't want him to know we'd been talking about them.

"About us guys?" he asked. My eyes flew to his face.

"How did you know?"

"Because women love to talk about men." He winked at me. "And men love to talk about women too."

"Oh? Any women in particular?"

"Well, Ethan loves to talk about Brielle," he said in a low whisper. "And it could just be because they work together, but Jack and I think he's got a thing for her."

"Wow, no way. Really?"

"I mean, I don't know, but if he complained about her any more than he did, he would be the biggest complainer on the planet." He sprinkled salt and pepper on the steaks and looked back at me. "But this is a small town, so it will take years for him to make a move if he ever decides to."

"Is that why all of you guys are single?" I asked him, pretending I wasn't interested in knowing the answer to that question. "Have you ever dated any of the girls?"

"Me?" He pointed to himself as if I'd just asked him for the first twelve digits of pi.

"Yes, you, TJ. Have you ever dated any of them or wanted to?" I knew I was being nosy, but I wanted to know. I needed to know.

"No, Pippa. I have not dated nor wanted to date any of my friends. Female or male." He chuckled and turned the steaks over. "Why did you ask?"

"I was just curious." I shrugged. "Have you never wanted to date any friends then? Are friends off-limits?"

"Hmm." His eyes flew to mine. "Have I ever wanted to date *any* of my friends?"

My heart raced as I waited for his response. This was the question I wanted the answer to. This was something that mattered to me. I ran my fingers through my hair and pretended not to notice how keenly his blue eyes studied me. He hadn't shaved this morning, and I could see his five-o'clock shadow, making him look even hotter.

"Yeah, just curious," I said, swallowing hard. *Be cool, Pippa. Do not act like a desperado.*

"Well, there's—" he started and then stopped abruptly. "Hey guys, everyone stand still," he shouted, and I narrowed my eyes at him. Why wasn't he answering my question? "Jack, Ethan, over by the river," he called out, and I turned to look at what he was pointing at. A tall brown bear was sitting next to one of the tents, and I could feel fear filling me. "Pippa, it's okay, you—"

"Argh," I screamed. "It's a bear," I shouted and ran toward the trucks. TJ grabbed me and held me to him tightly.

"Pippa, stop," he whispered against my hair as he held me to him. "First rule of bear country is that we don't run when we see bears."

"I don't want to see bears." I closed my eyes and pressed my face into his chest. "I don't want to be mauled."

"He's not going to hurt you, Pips. I promise." He rubbed my back. I felt his heart racing against my ear and suddenly realized how warm his body was against mine as he protected me from the bear.

"Thanks," I squeaked out, feeling nervous and panicked. "Are you sure?"

"I'm sure." He rubbed my shoulders. "Look at me... that's just Benjy. He won't hurt you."

"Oh," I mumbled, feeling my heart slowing. "The bear you told me about before?"

"Yes. He's not going to hurt you."

"He's going across the river," Jack said, coming up next

to us, his gaze concerned as he looked down at me. "No need to be scared, Pippa."

"I'm not scared," I said, straightening myself and looking up at TJ. He had an intense look as he gazed down at me. "I was just..." I didn't know what to say to excuse my scream and the fact that I was about to go running like the gun had gone off at the racetrack. "I mean, I was scared a little bit. I'm not Goldilocks, and I don't want to find any bears sleeping in my bed or sleeping bag." I froze. "I'm not sleeping in that tent by myself. There's no way." I shivered.

"It's okay, Pips." He squeezed my shoulders. "Hey, Jack, can you watch the grill for a second? I'm just going to take a walk with Pippa to calm her down."

"I don't..." I mumbled and then smiled at him gratefully. "Okay, maybe a small walk would be helpful."

"I got it," Jack said with a nod, and TJ grabbed my hand and smiled at me.

"Come on, Pips." He led me toward the river, and I pulled on his shirt.

"Where are we going?" I shook my head. "That doesn't sound like a good idea. Didn't the bear just go into the river?"

"He's long gone, Pips," he said as we continued talking. "I promise. I wouldn't put you in danger."

"Not on purpose," I said. "But you don't know if—"

"I know this land pretty well. I promise, no bears will eat you tonight."

"Hmph," I said as he led me to a tall tree. I took a couple of deep breaths and smiled at him. "I'm feeling a little less panicked right now. Thanks, Teej."

"You're welcome." He pulled on my hair gently. "I have something for you."

"What?" I cocked my head to the side; my heart was racing, and I was confused.

"I was going to wait until later, but I think that this is the perfect time." He reached into his back pocket and pulled out a small box. "I hope you like it." He looked shy as he handed it to me.

"What is it?" I took it from him gingerly.

"Open it and see." He nodded toward the box, and I opened it eagerly. Inside the red box was a sterling silver bracelet. I lifted it from the box and read the inscription, "*Don't fear jumping. I will always be there to catch you.*" When I finished, I looked up at his shining eyes.

"That also means don't fear bears. I'll be there to scare them away for you." He grinned. "I got you, Pips."

"This is so nice." I held it carefully. I couldn't believe that TJ had gotten me a piece of jewelry. "You are so sweet." I tried to put the bracelet on but couldn't get the clasp secured properly.

"Let me help you," he said, tightening the bracelet on my wrist. His fingers brushed my skin with a feathery lightness, and I swallowed hard as he let go. "It looks perfect." He smiled, his face moving toward mine.

"Just like me?" I teased him.

"Um..."

"Are you saying I'm not perfect?" I wasn't sure why I was going on and on when the moment was so sweet and perfect.

"I didn't say that," he whispered, grabbing my hands again and pulling me closer.

"So you think I am? You think I'm—"

"Shh, Pippa," he said, his eyes on my lips. I held my breath as his lips came even closer to mine. "You're beautiful, Pips." He smiled warmly, and before anything else could go wrong, he pressed his lips against mine. The world seemed to stand still as he kissed me. I melted against him. Somehow, my fingers found their way into his silky hair, and he kissed me again. I think I heard birds singing, foxes calling out to their friends, and choirs serenading us. The moment was that perfect.

"Wow," I said as TJ stepped back, his eyes dark and full of emotion. There was a grin on his face as he gazed at me.

"Perfection." He winked at me. "Come on, let's head back to the others. Get some food in our stomachs."

"Am I perfection or..." I was not going to ask him if the kiss was as perfect for him as it was for me. I didn't even know what it meant. I didn't even know if he was going to do it again. I wanted him to do it again. I wanted to feel this feeling forever. It was like I wanted to cry and laugh and run through the flowers all at the same time. My heart was filled with joy and happiness. That was the sort of kiss that movies were made about. That was the sort of kiss that made men go to war.

"Come on, you two, we're putting the steaks on," Mindy called out as we got closer to the fire. "Then we're going to play a game of Werewolf to keep Charlotte happy."

"Werewolf?" I stared at TJ. "What's that?"

"Don't worry, Pips. It's just a social deduction game. No real werewolves in the area. This is Paradise Valley, not Forks."

"You know the name of the town from *Twilight*?" This man never ceases to surprise me.

"I remember everything you told me, Pips," he said in a low voice. "You loved that book. You made us watch the movie no less than ten times." He groaned. "How could I forget?"

"I guess." I loved that he'd always been so attentive. It

made me feel even more ashamed of myself for not knowing anything about his dad. I was a bad friend. I was a bad best friend. I had to make it up to him because I wanted to show him I could and would make the best girlfriend if that was where this was going. And I very much wanted it to go there.

Chapter Twenty-Two

T J

Dear Pippa,

I was going to surprise you in New York last week at your high school graduation. My grandpops was going to buy my ticket as a graduation gift. I really wanted to see you. I called your mom, but she told me not to come. I don't know if it's because she doesn't think I'm good enough or what.

I found out my dad wasn't really my dad. That's why he never called or wrote. What kind of man does that to his son? I'm not going to lie, it hurts. I want to punch something, someone, him, but I won't. I don't understand why he'd just cut me out of his life?

I cried last night. For the first time in forever. It was weird. At first, it felt uncomfortable, and then it felt good. Like I was letting it out. I got up at midnight to get some water, and as I walked past my mom's door, I stopped. I listened. She was crying. Like really sobbing. I wanted to push the door open and hug her.

I didn't though. I didn't know what to say. I didn't know if she was sad cos of Dad. Or maybe she was sad cos of me. Maybe she blames me for Dad not wanting us. Sometimes, I feel like I could disappear, and no one would notice. Not even you.

I wish I knew how to tell you I love you. But it would be too weird.

There's no way I'm sending you this letter, by the way. Though I wish I were brave enough.

Your Best Friend,
TJ Wyatt
(Letter stuffed in a copy of To Kill a Mockingbird and never sent)

"I'm so full." Aiden rubbed his stomach and leaned back. "The potato salad was delicious, thanks Pippa."

"You're welcome." She beamed at him happily, her face content and peaceful now that she was no longer scared of a bear attacking her. I stared at the bracelet on her wrist, and a cloak of warmth covered me as I saw her eyes upon it. There was a smile on her face as she ran her fingers across the engraving, and I wondered if she knew how happy it made me to see how happy she was.

It had been weird to hand her the bracelet and then to have our first kiss, but I wouldn't have changed it for anything. However, I wasn't sure how she felt about the kiss. She'd been breathless and kissed me back, but maybe she was trying to get over her pain with Stephan. I didn't want to be the rebound guy. I didn't want to be the bandage on the wound that would be ripped off and thrown away when she felt better again.

"So, are we going to play Werewolf?" Charlotte jumped up, clapping her hands eagerly.

Aiden and Ethan looked at her with bemused expressions on their faces. Her long, black, curly hair was full of life tonight, and her blue eyes were vibrant as she gave each and every one of us a long look.

"Or do I have to pretend to be a werewolf first?" She curled her fingers and howled. "Did I tell you the joke about the werewolf and the moon?" Charlotte asked, grinning. I tried to stifle a groan. Though Jack wasn't so polite. Charlotte ignored him and continued. "They both like to hide when a vampire comes out to play." She giggled, and Mindy attempted a fake laugh. She was her best friend, after all. Pippa looked at me with a confused expression and I winked at her. She'd soon find out that Charlotte's jokes were never great.

Charlotte may have worked at Montana Knights as a bartender and the host of trivia night, but she wanted to be a stand-up comedian. Her jokes weren't funny, but they weren't *not funny* either. Though, I wasn't going to be the one to tell her that. Her jokes were primarily about her family functions and how different they were on her mom and dad's side. Her mom was more country and grew up in Montana, and her dad was African American and from North Carolina. He was kind of country too, but a different kind of country. I loved her parents, and I felt like jokes about them could be funny. She just hadn't found the right ones yet.

"I don't get it." Ethan said what we were all thinking.

"Werewolves like to come out when there is a full moon and—"

"I have an idea." I stood from my chair with force. I knew Charlotte well and didn't want to spend the next twenty minutes listening to her talk about werewolves and vampires. She had enjoyed the *Twilight* series even more than Pippa had. I wasn't sure what it was with women and unavailable men. It seemed to me that the more unavailable the man, the more the woman wanted him. "Charlotte, would you be dreadfully sad if we didn't play the game?"

"What's your suggestion?" She had a slightly peeved look at the interruption, and I felt bad for stopping her from giving her full explanation.

"Pippa is a playwright and hopes to write and direct her own plays one day." I looked down at Pippa. She glared at me, an embarrassed look on her face as she desperately shook her head, telling me to be quiet. "And she's really good," I continued. "I thought it could be cool if we all acted out one of her scenes for fun."

"Ooh, a bit like *A Midsummers Night Dream*," Brielle called out. "I think Ethan should be Puck."

"I vote for Brandon," Mindy said. "He would make a great Puck."

"And you would make a great Bridget Jones, but I didn't say you should be in the movie," he shot back, and she rolled her eyes at him.

"Just because I know how to write and express myself." She paused. "Are you jealous because you don't have basic comprehension skills?"

"Are you upset because you don't have a man?" He winked at her. "Or maybe..." His voice trailed off as he and Jack high-fived and laughed.

"That's not fair," Charlotte spoke up for Mindy. "We all know Mindy could have any man she wanted." She grinned at Mindy. "In fact, I happen to know that there's a certain very eligible bachelor that very much wants to date Mindy... if all the flowers that have been showing up mean anything."

"All what flowers?" Brandon's eyes narrowed as he gazed at Mindy. "Who is sending you flowers?"

Mindy blushed and gave Charlotte a death stare. Charlotte just laughed. "Wouldn't you like to know?" She turned to Pippa. "I love that you write plays. I think it sounds fun. Do you have a script for us to go from?"

"I do not have it in me to memorize a script right now." Jack shook his head and held up his beer. "Sorry, Pippa."

"No need to apologize," she said quickly. "We definitely don't have to act out any of my work. I'm really not that good. TJ is just being polite. He knows I'm trying to figure out my life right now, and I always thought I wanted to work in theater, but I don't know if I'm good enough," she said. "Let's just play the game." She quickly sipped from her wine cooler and looked at the fire. I could tell that she was being self-conscious. I wasn't sure what to do. I could push it because I knew she would love us all to act out her words, or I could let it go until she felt more comfortable around my friends.

"Please, Pippa?" Mindy asked, putting on her best puppy-dog face. "I think it would be so much more fun than Werewolf. Sorry, Charlotte."

"No worries." Charlotte laughed. "I wouldn't mind acting as well. As long as I don't have to kiss anyone." She looked at each guy for a minute and shuddered. "If I have to kiss any of these scoundrels, I will pass."

"No kissing is required," Pippa assured. There was a red hue on her face, and I wondered if she was thinking about our kiss. I wondered if it had meant as much to her as it did to me. Which I knew was absolutely stupid. I needed to be practical and real with myself. Pippa was a sweetheart and my best friend, but nothing had actually changed in my life. I still had no dad. I still had to raise money to build up the ranch. I wanted to show my dad that I didn't need him. That I could succeed without him in my life. I wanted to bring my mom out to Montana. She deserved a nice home. She deserved happiness. I had dreams to make come true, and I couldn't do that if half of my head and all of my heart were focused on Pippa Chase.

She'd already been with one loser. Not that I was anything like her ex, Stephan. I would never speak to her or treat her like crap. But I also wasn't worthy of her. I couldn't afford to give her the life she wanted. I couldn't buy her a penthouse apartment overlooking Central Park. I couldn't give her a monthly clothing allowance to shop on Fifth Avenue. I couldn't fly us to Paris on a whim or spoil her with roses every single day. I wasn't in that position in my life. And the fact of the matter was, her mom would never accept me. She didn't think I was good enough for her daughter, and I wasn't sure if she wasn't right.

"Double, double, toil, and trouble, Pips," I said as I walked over to her. "It'll be fun. You always wanted to act out one of your plays at night, remember?" Her eyes were bright as she nodded slowly. There was a dreamlike expression on her face. I wanted to kiss her again. I wanted to pretend that we were the only two people on the earth and that we didn't have to think about anyone else. But that was a romantic, sappy notion and wasn't reality.

"Okay, everyone. I do have a play I started and you don't have to remember too many lines. I will tell you all your characters and we will just pretend we are them. I want you to think like them and feel like them and talk like them. It will help me discover their character motivations as I start writing." She sounded excited. "If everyone is down, of course."

"Sounds different," Brandon said, sipping on his beer. "But I'm down." He looked thoughtful. "And if you're serious about the theater thing, you might wanna look into The Paradise Valley Theater in town," he said casually.

"Oh, are they hiring?" Pippa asked, an interested expression on her face. "I'd like to help out with their next production."

"The theater's been closed for a while," Mindy said. "So unless you're the one putting on the production, then there's nothing to help with."

"That's what I was going to suggest," Brandon continued. "Bobby Avery, the realtor, was telling me today that the city has lowered the price of the building and there may be a local grant available to help with the purchase if you think you'd be interested."

"Oh, I couldn't buy a theater!" Pippa exclaimed. "One, I'm going back to New York soon, and more importantly, I don't have the money." She looked around the group of people, her eyes settling on me. "This has been a really nice escape from real life, but I can't sleep in TJ's bed for the rest of my life. His couch must be getting really uncomfortable."

"Then don't let him sleep on the couch," Jack called out, and Ethan, Aiden, and Brandon all hollered and whooped. I glared at my friends, though I wasn't loathing the idea. It would be nice sharing a bed with Pippa, though I knew she wasn't that kind of girl.

Chapter Twenty-Three

P ippa

Dear TJ,

Sometimes, I feel like I want to tell my mom to stop trying to dictate my entire life. I want to tell her to let me make my own mistakes. She really annoys me sometimes. And I feel like I can't even breathe.

I told my dad that I was feeling stifled. Like my life wasn't my own. I don't want to disappoint my mom. I want to make her happy. I want to make her proud of me, but I'm scared the real me would never be good enough.

My dad told me that Mom had a lot of disappointment when she was young. He said that her dad, my grandad, was in the war and saw some bad things, and when he came back home, he was never the same. I guess he became an alcoholic and used to shout at my mom and grandma and some other stuff. He said she wants me to have all the things she didn't. He said if she could make me the Queen of England, she would.

I know she loves me. I know she wants the best for me. But I want to live my life, you know?

Your BFF,
Pippa

P.S. I'm not sending this letter because it feels disrespectful to my mom.

"Okay, Mindy, you're going to play Annabel. Your character is really feisty, but inside, she's scared."

"Scared of what?" Mindy asked, trying to focus on me as she chugged on what must have been her tenth wine cooler.

"I don't know. That's for you to decide," I said. "I mean, normally, I would have already figured out all the character's internal struggles, but I've been concentrating more on the story."

"And what's the story about, exactly?" she asked.

"I was going to tell everyone at the same time." I cleared my throat. "Hey, guys." No one paid attention to me. I looked around and bit on my lower lip.

Mindy grinned. "You got to speak a lot louder than that if you want to get everyone's attention, the guys in particular, especially when they're talking about football."

"They really love football, don't they?"

"Of course," she said, looking at me like I was crazy. "Guys love football and baseball and basketball and..."

"Not where I'm from," I said, shaking my head. "Or rather, the men I hung out with. Stephan liked baseball sometimes. But I don't even know if he really liked it or if he just pretended to like it because he had a couple of bosses that liked it."

"Stephan was your ex, right?"

I nodded slowly. "Yeah."

"You were engaged to him?"

"Yeah," I said.

"You don't even seem that sad." She wrinkled her nose. "I hope that's not rude or anything."

"No, it's not rude at all. If I'm quite honest, I'm more annoyed with myself that I dated him and accepted his proposal in the first place."

"Can I ask why you did?" she asked, lowering her voice. "I mean, I know we're meant to be doing this play and all. But you just seem like a cool girl and really fun and strong-willed and I just don't know how you would've ended up with someone like that."

"You know, that's a really good question. I do like to think that I'm strong-willed and I really feel like I have a good set of..." I paused and wrinkled my nose. "I guess, honestly, I just felt like he was the guy that was going to fit in the plan the best." I sighed.

It's kind of complicated. I didn't want to talk about my mom or how TJ had stopped writing to me because then she'd want to know why he'd stopped writing. And now I knew, but I didn't want to talk about TJ's dad issues with anyone else. I didn't know if Mindy knew about them.

"It's okay," she said. "We can talk about it another time." She whistled loudly. "Hey, guys. Be quiet. No one cares about the Vikings or the Broncos right now. Pippa wants to tell us the backstory of this play." I looked over at her, and she grinned. "I can be loud when I want to."

"You can be loud even when we don't want you to be," Brandon said, and she glared at him.

I needed to ask TJ the story behind the two of them. Sometimes, I would catch them looking at each other like they kind of fancied each other. And then, other times, the hate was spitting from their eyes at each other. I knew, though, that love was the opposite of hate. If they really couldn't stand each other, they'd be ignoring each other. There was definitely a story there.

"We're listening," Jack said.

"Come over here, guys," I said. "Let's have a seat around the campfire." I watched as Brandon, Jack, Ethan, Brielle, Charlotte, Mindy and TJ took seats. They all looked at me expectantly. I could feel a frisson of excitement pulsing through my veins. I looked up at the dark night sky. The stars were twinkling. The moon was a quarter, and the trees in the distance stood out.

"So," I said.

"Let me guess how this starts," Ethan said.

"How do you think it starts?" I looked at him.

"It was a dark and stormy night," he said in a low husky voice, and everyone groaned.

"Real original, Ethan," Brielle said.

I stared at her as she laughed. She was really mouthy to Ethan, which surprised me because Ethan was her boss, and there's no way I would've spoken like that to the lord. Well, there was also no way he would accept me talking like that to him, either.

"Everyone, be quiet."

"Mindy."

"What?" Mindy glared at TJ. "I wasn't even talking."

"You were just whispering something to Charlotte."

"I was just asking her to pass me another wine cooler, thank you very much."

"And Charlotte," she called out to her friend, "While you're up, would you grab the cupcakes? Does anyone want a cupcake? These are new caramel and apple cupcakes that I created."

"You didn't invent caramel and apple," Brandon said.

"I invented caramel apple cream cheese and banana pudding, though," she said, glaring at him.

He blinked. "That does sound kind of good."

"They're delicious."

TJ looked around at everyone, and it was silent.

"So, as TJ said, I've always wanted to be a playwright. I'm no William Shakespeare and I'm also no Arthur Miller, even though *Death of a Salesman* is one of my absolute favorite plays."

"We read *Death of a Salesman* in high school," Brielle said. "It was kind of good."

"I think it's brilliant." I was definitely going to have to spend more time with Brielle. I loved that she enjoyed literature and books, and I really liked her. She was fun, open-minded, and sweet, and I didn't have that many girlfriends in New York. I had Emma. She was my best friend, and she was amazing. But most of the other women I knew were just as materialistic as my mom.

My enthusiasm dropped for a few seconds as I thought of my mom. I was going to have to call her tomorrow. I wasn't looking forward to it. There were so many things I had to say to her, so many things I was upset about, and I didn't know how she would take it.

I cleared my throat and looked up. "So my play is about a middle-aged woman who is living in the city. She is happily married with three kids."

"Okay," Ethan said, and I could tell from the look on his face that he was feeling bored.

"But then she finds out—"

"Oh, my God. Don't tell me, an alien from outer space comes and—" Jack starts and quickly closes his mouth when he sees everyone's incredulous expressions. "What? Stuff is always cool when an alien from outer space comes."

"As opposed to where?" Charlotte said.

"I mean if it didn't come from outer space, where else would the alien have come from?"

"I don't know," he said. "Maybe your bedroom?"

"You're so rude, Jack Marley."

"Ooh, am I, Charlotte?" he mocked her. "Sorry, Pippa."

"It's okay. No, an alien from outer space or anyone's bedroom is not in this play. Basically, her high school boyfriend comes back into town and he tells her that he has a secret."

"Oh, my gosh. He's in love with her," Mindy says. "High school boyfriends never get over their high school girlfriends."

226

"That's not true," Jack said.

Everyone looked at him, and a quiet descended on the group. Now that I knew the story, I understood why.

"No, no, no. The secret is that he is dying, and he's been told that he has thirty days to live."

"Oh, that's really sad," Brielle said. "I feel so bad for him."

"It's okay. It's not actually true. He only said that because he realized that as he reached middle age, he had no friends. He'd concentrated all his life on making money and he'd stabbed everyone in the back, and he had only had flirtatious relationships. Nothing serious."

"Kind of like all the guys here?" Mindy said, and all the girls laughed, including me.

"Hey, no fair," TJ said, smiling at me.

"It's not about you, TJ. Don't worry."

"And I didn't think it was about me," he said. "I'm not a middle-aged man, and I haven't struck it rich yet."

There was a sad expression on his face, and I wondered what that was about. I wondered what he was thinking and feeling. He was so hot and cold with me. He'd been so grumpy and distant, and I knew that a part of him still felt mixed emotions about me and my being here.

And I understood why. I hadn't kept up my side of the pact either, even without my mom interfering. I should have reached out more. I should have been the one to say I would come and visit him. Why had he had to be the one to come and visit me?

A despondent feeling overcame me. It wasn't often that I thought of myself as a bad friend. And I knew I wasn't the worst friend in the world, but I also knew that I couldn't hold a match to the sort of friend that TJ was.

I stared at the bracelet on my wrist, sterling silver, beautiful. Even the inscription was heartfelt. TJ was everything a woman could want, and I felt like I was using him. I felt like I had only come here because I was sad. I didn't want to think about it, though.

"Pippa." Mindy tapped me on the shoulder. "I don't want to stop you from thinking about your play and being so imaginative and thoughtful about it, but could you share some of what you're thinking?"

"Huh?" I said, looking around at them. "Oh, sorry. I was thinking about the characters' motivations. Yeah," I mumbled, not sure where I'd left off in my thoughts. "I think that everyone kind of understands where we're coming from, right?"

"Exactly how are we meant to do this?" Aiden asked, looking confused. "I mean, I understand the basic plot, but what character am I, and what are we acting out and saying and..."

"We're just meant to pretend we're those people," I said. "And then I'll write the play and then I'll actually give you guys scripts if you're down." I looked over at Jack. "I'll try not to give you too many words."

"I mean, you can give me some words," he said. "I wouldn't want to disappoint all the females in town."

"You wish," Mindy said. "As if all the females in town are waiting to see you act."

"But you know what could be a really good idea?" Brandon said. "Even if Pippa doesn't buy the theater, maybe we can still put on a play somewhere and help to raise money for the theater. That way, we can make sure no big corporation buys it and builds like a big box store or something in town."

"Yeah, that should be cool." I said.

"Yeah," Mindy said, nodding. "That's actually a good

idea. I've heard that some of the big chains want to come to Paradise Valley and that would really ruin the small-town feel here."

"Yeah, it would," TJ said. "I think that could be a really good idea. What'd you think, Pippa? Could you do it? How long do you think you're going to stay?" he said softly, and I wondered if he was asking that question because he wanted to know how long I was going to stay for the play or how long I was going to stay to figure out what was going on between the two of us.

"Well, Emma told me she's going to book her flight tonight. I know she'll want to be here at least a week."

"A week is not enough time for us to put on a play," Ethan said, shaking his head. "We need at least a month."

"Can you commit to a month, Pips?" TJ said, staring at me, his eyes intense. I could tell that he really wanted to know my answer, but I didn't know if he wanted me to stay or if he wanted me to go.

"If everyone wants me to," I said. "I mean, I have my job, but I can see if I could work from here."

"Or you could just quit," Charlotte said. "I'm sure you could find something around here to do while you figure out what's going on in your life."

"Yeah," Jack said. "I mean, you could become a real mail-order bride. I heard they pay big money for that sort of thing."

"Very funny, Jack," I said sarcastically. "I'm not going to become a mail-order bride, no matter what Old Man Roberts thinks."

"Oh, Old Man Roberts," Mindy said, shaking her head. "He and his wife were in the store today and," she started, then lowered her voice, "turns out they were arguing again."

"Arguing about what?" I asked her.

"Oh, some love of his from before they got married. I don't really know exactly what it was."

"Aw. Is his wife jealous or..."

"I don't know. I mean, they're so happy," she said. "But they never had kids and sometimes I think Old Man Roberts wishes he had a son or a daughter or something."

"I can understand that."

I looked over at TJ, who was pretending not to listen to the conversation. I wondered how he felt not having a dad. I guess it was worse for him because he'd had a dad, but his dad had just stopped talking to him. He'd had someone in his life who loved him and then just dropped him.

My heart broke for him yet again. He'd been through so much and he'd never told me. I'd never been there for him. And now here we were, and I didn't know how I could help him. I didn't know what could fix a broken heart like that.

"Okay, guys. I think I'm ready," TJ said, jumping up. "Why don't you tell us our characters, Pippa, and then we'll just mess around and stuff."

"Mess around?" I questioned. "We're going to act. Act, baby."

"Yay," Mindy said, jumping up and down and clapping her hands. She had definitely had way too many wine coolers. "Let's act our hearts out and then, Pippa, you'll write a play based on these characters and we'll perform it in town. And maybe we'll raise enough money so that someone can take over the theater even if we have to hire them. That way, we don't have to worry about who's going to come over and try to take over the town."

"Sounds like a good idea to me," I said, smiling at them all.

It was weird, but I'd only been in Paradise Valley for

less than a week, but it felt like home. These people were beginning to feel like friends. And as I looked over at TJ, I realized that I was feeling something close to love, which scared me.

Chapter Twenty-Four

T J

Dear Pippa,

It's been five years since I've sent you a letter. I never realized how much I loved receiving those letters. That's not true. I always knew. They were the highlight of my week.

I nearly died today. Nothing crazy. Almost fell off of a mountain. No biggie. I make light of it because if I didn't, I don't think I'd go climbing again. My friend Jack helped me; my rope got tangled, and my harness wasn't attached properly.

You were the first one on my mind when I thought I was going to die. I didn't want to leave this earth without seeing your face one last time. Without hearing you laugh.

Did you know that when we were younger, I kinda had a thing for you?

Or did I just let the cat out of the bag.

I probably won't send this. It's been too many years now.

But if the universe can send out vibes, I hope it lets you know I'm missing you and thinking of you.

And I'm grateful to be alive.

Travis James

"That was fun." I handed Pippa a bottle of water to rinse her mouth as she brushed her teeth. "Everyone really got into it."

"It was so much fun," she gargled out as she continued brushing her teeth. She spat out her toothpaste and said, "Your friends are amazing."

"They think you're all right as well." I couldn't keep my eyes off of her glistening lips. I stretched my arms and exaggerated a long yawn as she gazed at me expectantly. "Okay, time for us to go to bed."

"You mean to sleeping bag?" She wrinkled her nose and looked over to her tent. "This is going to be *so* comfortable."

"At least it's not a couch two sizes too small for your body," I joked, and a guilty look crossed her face. "Don't feel bad though. I gave it up willingly."

"We could share it if you want," she offered again, and I shook my head. She looked as disappointed as I felt, and I laughed, a loud booming sound that carried through the night air. "I don't mean for anything..." Her voice trailed off, and I mentally searched around my brain so I could change the subject.

"So, when are you going to start your goat yoga class?" I asked her as we walked to her tent. We stopped outside, and I looked back toward the campsite. Mindy and Brandon were standing by the fire, arguing. I was starting to think they couldn't be around each other without arguing about something.

"Maybe this weekend?" she said, and it came out as a question more than a statement. "Whenever Jack can deliver the goats. Mindy, Charlotte, and Brielle all said they were down. And Mindy said she will tell Kaye and Kacie." Her eyes peered at me in a weird way, like she was trying to gauge my reaction, but I had no idea what she was trying to find out. "Mindy said she will put a sign up in her store as well, so we can get as many people as possible." She beamed at me. "We'll soon have you building a bigger log cabin and your river cabins."

"You really don't have to do that." I was touched by her gesture. "I will get there at some point."

"With my help." She put her hands on her hips and gave me a stern look. "It might not be thousands of dollars, but it could be hundreds and every little bit counts. We could become the goat yoga capital of the world."

"We could." I pressed my lips together to stop from snorting. I was enjoying the ease with which we could banter. It wasn't that I didn't have faith in her ability to make goat yoga a thing in Paradise Valley, but I couldn't see Donkey cooperating very well. Not that I was going to say anything. I was looking forward to Pippa trying to get Donkey to do yoga. I'd have to make sure to turn my phone camera on during the first class.

"I should create a hashtag and start an Instagram account. Donkey's Ranch Yoga Retreat." Her eyes lit up, and I couldn't stop laughing. "What's so funny?"

"I think we should have our first class before we call CNN and alert them to how hot we are."

"I wasn't thinking CNN, smart-ass. Maybe FOX or *People Magazine*."

"Ooh yes, *People Magazine*. Let's get all those rich Hollywood types out here." I shuddered. "No thanks."

"Don't be a snob, TJ." She giggled and punched me in the shoulder. Her hand was warm and soft and lingered for a few seconds before she pulled away. I could tell she was interested in another kiss, but I knew that if I got my lips on her again, I wouldn't be able to stop.

"I'm not a snob." I shook my head and fake yawned again. "I should head back to my tent."

"Okay." She nodded, but her face fell. "So, do you want to share tents?" She asked softly as I started to walk away.

"What?" I stopped and looked back at her. "Why?" I surveyed her face. "Are you scared?"

"I know you said Benjy is sweet and—"

"I never said he was sweet. He's a bear, Pips. But he won't hurt you." I looked at her tent and then at her. I knew the worst decision I could make would be to get into her one-person tent. I didn't think us being so close would be good for either one of us. And certainly not for our burgeoning friendship, no matter how badly I wanted to forget everything.

"I know he won't hurt me, but I just don't wanna sleep

in the tent alone." Her eyes were wide. "There are other animals out there, right? Elk, moose, sheep."

"Are you really scared of sheep?" I asked her. "You're going to teach goat yoga, but you don't like sheep?"

"I didn't say I don't like them. I just don't think they like me. Just like the cows. If you saw the looks they were giving me when I was waiting for you that first day."

"What looks were they giving you?"

"Like they thought I was a matador holding up a flag and they were just waiting to gore me."

"Those are bulls, Pips. Not cows."

"Same difference." She yawned. "Okay, it's time for me to put on my big-girl pants and get into my sleeping bag." She opened her arms to hug me. "Night, Teej."

"Night, Pips." I enveloped her in my arms, and for some reason, I couldn't let her go. We stood there hugging for what felt like ten hours, but in reality, it must have been two minutes. I released her from my embrace and stepped back. "Sweet dreams."

"You too, Teej." Instead of looking at me, her focus was on the night sky. "I wonder if there are any shooting stars in the sky."

"Just waiting?" I asked her.

"You know what I mean," she said. "Remember when we were at camp and we would search for shooting stars all night, and you said that if we walked far enough, we'd eventually find one?"

"Because I had no clue at ten what I was saying."

"I guess. You were still fun though. Those days were the best."

"They really were," I said, and I realized that we didn't want to stop talking. "Look, if you want, you can bring your sleeping bag to my tent. It's a bigger tent, so we don't have to worry about being stuffed up next to each other."

"Are you sure?" she asked eagerly. "Yes, please." She quickly unzipped her tent, grabbed her sleeping bag, and zipped it back up.

"That was fast."

"I didn't want to give you a chance to change your mind and say you needed to sleep."

"Well, we are going to sleep, Pippa," I said, giving her a look. She wasn't expecting something crazy to happen, was she?

"Get your mind out of the gutter, Teej." She playfully slapped my arm. "I meant we could talk for a bit. You can't be that tired."

"I can't?" I asked her as we made our way over to my tent. We stopped outside, and I leaned down and unzipped it. "Come on, let's get inside and we can figure out which side of the tent you want to sleep on."

"You're sleeping next to the door. That's not even a thought. If Benjy comes by, he knows your smell and he can pass on by. He might smell me and be like she smells like a delicious human steak."

"A delicious human steak?" I grabbed her sleeping bag and put it down on the other side of the tent. She shuffled past me, her hair brushing my face as she moved, and I shifted back slightly. I watched as she lowered herself down onto her sleeping bag. I turned on the LED lantern at the side of my sleeping bag, and light filled the tent. Pippa's brown eyes glowed as she unzipped her bag and got in. She rolled over onto her side and gazed at me.

"So what shall we talk about?" she asked as she shifted in her bag. I was about to pull my shirt off when I remembered that I couldn't sleep in just my boxers in the same tent as her, and I wasn't ready for her to see my tattoo yet.

"What do you want to talk about?" I pulled my boots off and got down on my knees and unzipped my sleeping bag. "Do not say Ben Affleck."

"Why would I want to talk about him? I actually was thinking that we could chat about what we've been up to the last ten years." She grabbed a water bottle from the floor and took a chug. "There are so many years we don't know about."

"I guess." I unzipped my sleeping bag and studied her face. There was something I wanted to ask her. Something that was still on my mind. Something that had made me hate her for years.

"Hey, what is it?" she asked with concern. "Your expression just changed? What are you thinking about? Is it about the kiss? Do you regret kissing me? Is that why you haven't kissed me again? Or is it because of Stephan? Do you think I'm a horrible person to be kissing you when I just ended my engagement? I know it looks bad, but—"

"Pippa, I'm not thinking about the kiss. I don't regret the kiss. I liked the kiss. It's something else." My voice was somber, and I lay on my side and stared at her. "I don't want to ruin the mood."

"You're not going to ruin the mood." Her face froze, and she slapped her palm against her lips and screamed silently.

"What's wrong?" I leaned forward in concern. "Pips?"

"You're dating Kacie?"

"What?" I was confused as to why she would think of something so outrageous. "Where did you get that idea from?"

"I kinda heard that you were dating…" Her voice trailed off, and she blushed. Which was cute, but I was trying to not notice how cute she was right now. I also didn't know how to answer her questions or respond to her comments. Kacie and I had gone to dinner a few times, but there had been no sparks. At least not on my side. I had no interest in Kacie. Whatsoever.

"I'm not dating." I shook my head adamantly. "To be honest, I've been focused on the ranch. Trying to get it up and running. Trying to make something of myself. I need to get this place off the ground. I need to prove to my...to the world that I can be successful with no one else's help."

"You are successful, TJ," she insisted. "This land is amazing."

"It is, but I'm in no position to be a boyfriend, or a husband, or a father." I had to let it all out. I needed to be clear about where I stood. "I can't support a family right now. I don't have the money. I don't have the time. I don't have the mental space... It's not the right time."

"Is that what you wanted to say?" she asked softly. "Because you know I just got out of an engagement, right? I'm not interested in another relationship right now."

"I get it," I said, even though it felt like she'd shoved a knife into my heart. I knew those words should make me feel better about everything, but they made me feel worse. It was like she was shutting me down, and I hadn't even made a move. "I wanted to ask you about something your mother said to me."

"Oh?" Her eyebrows wrinkled, and her lips thinned. "What did she say now?"

"So, back when I wanted to surprise you." I took a deep breath. "She said that you'd wanted to stop writing to me for a while, but you felt sorry for me. She said that you had a kind heart, and you wrote to me so I wouldn't feel like I had no one, but that I was holding you back and your greatest wish was to start college without having to deal with me anymore. That you'd outgrown our childish letters and that I ought to do the same." My head constricted in the same way that it had ten years ago. I'd wanted to die. Literally die. The pain had cut that deep.

"What?" Pippa's eyes almost popped out of her head as her jaw dropped. "My mom did not say that!" She just stared at me. "She said that?" She shook her head vehemently, and I knew in my soul that she wasn't faking it. She'd never said any of those things. It felt like a shackle around my heart falling off. A lightness returned to my shoulders. Happiness returned to my soul. "TJ, I promise you, I've never uttered any words close to that. I promise. I would never say or think those things." She pressed her lips together. "You've thought that all these years?"

"You could say that."

"That's why you were so cold to me when I returned." She nodded as if things were clicking into place. "That's why you didn't want me here. You really thought I would say that?" She sounded distraught and hurt. "We'd been friends for years, TJ. How could you have thought that?"

"Because my dad, who was supposed to love me my entire life, stopped talking to me. I stopped trusting people. I stopped trusting myself. You were my lifeline, Pips. Every week, I waited for my dad to call or come visit, and he never did. But your letters. They were consistent. They made me feel like I wasn't a total waste of space in the universe. And then I wondered if I was bringing the friendship down. You were always so bubbly and fun and I felt like my letters weren't," I explained.

"I never thought you were down." She looked sad. "I guess I should have read between the lines in a lot of your letters."

"I didn't want to be the friend that—"

"Don't you get it, TJ?" she asked me softly. "I wasn't so happy and bubbly. I tried to be that way in my letters, but I missed you so much. You were the only one who ever really listened to me. Who told me I could do and be whatever I wanted. Well, until I met Emma. I was so miserable at home, with my mom constantly telling me what to wear, how to act, what to want. And when I'd get upset, my dad would guilt-trip me about Mom's past." She shook her head and imitated her dad. "'*Your mom just wants the best for you, Pippa. She had a rough childhood. Her dad liked the bottle a bit too much. She had to take care of him. She had to take care of Grandma. She had to give up her dreams.*'" She let out a deep exhale. "I get it, I do. But she's not me and I'm not her. And I hate that I haven't stood up to her. I hate that she ruined our friendship. I hate that I said yes to a man I didn't even love just because he was a guy who offered me everything she said I should want."

"Why did you say yes, Pippa?" I still didn't get it. This was a man she was going to marry. How could she have said yes if she didn't love him?

"Because I didn't believe in true love anymore. Because I stopped believing in myself and who I was." She looked embarrassed. "And I tried to hide my true feelings from myself. I think I gaslit myself. I didn't want to feel the things that caused me pain. I didn't want to acknowledge how hurt I was."

"Stephan hurt you?" I was angry. Maybe I'd have to fly to New York and have a word with this punk.

"No, I was hurt when you stopped writing. I didn't understand why. I thought it was me. I thought it was because I was too goofy. Or my personality was too kooky or different and you were just over me. I thought you didn't want to be best friends anymore. I told myself it was inevitable we would fall apart. Lots of friendships fall apart at college. I'd just never thought that would be us." She rubbed her eyes. "Can I tell you something?"

"Anything?"

"I used my mom's credit card to book a flight to Florida that Christmas. I was going to visit you and make you take us to Disney."

"What? You never said anything." I was shocked by her statement.

"My mom found out and canceled the charge. She told me that I was too young to go flying to some crazy state to be with some boy. She said only women with bad upbringings traveled to be with men."

"What?" This was so crazy. Her mom had a lot to answer for. She had done everything in her power to end our friendship. So many wasted years. "I never knew."

"Isn't life weird?" she said. "There we both were, thinking one thing about life and our friendship. And yet, neither one of us had any clue what had really happened."

"We allowed our inner voices and doubts and hurts to lead us astray. But we were young, Pippa. It's only natural that we wouldn't know which way was up and what was really true."

"Well, we're not teens anymore." Her voice cracked, and she held her pinkie finger out. "Best friends again?"

I held my pinkie out toward her, and we wrapped them around each other's. "Best friends," I said with a small smile. "Though we should get some sleep. Or—"

"Or what?" she said, leaning back and gazing up at the top of the tent. "Will we not get breakfast?"

"Very funny," I said as I leaned over and turned off the light. The tent was filled with darkness now. It was quiet outside the tent as well. Everyone was in bed, snoring away. "So, tell me one good thing that has happened to you in the last ten years," I said into the darkness. She didn't answer right away, and I wondered if she'd fallen asleep. When she didn't respond, I closed my eyes.

"Besides Emma?" she said.

"Yes, aside from her."

"Well, I guess one good thing that has happened would be—" She paused for a moment. "I have enough money saved in a do-not-touch emergency fund for me to go to England and visit Stratford-upon-Avon and I haven't touched it."

"That's amazing," I said. "You've always wanted to go there."

"I have," she said. "It's crazy that I still haven't visited, but Stephan had no interest." I could hear the regret in her voice. "I wanted to go for the honeymoon, but he was like, 'No, we have to go to the beach.'" She sounded annoyed. "I didn't want to go to the beach, but he said that was the perfect destination for me to lose...." She coughed. I froze at her words. What was she talking about? What was she going to lose? I rubbed my forehead, and then my entire body froze as I realized what she was saying. Was Pippa still a virgin?

"He sounds selfish," I said, wanting to ask and clarify but not wanting her to think I wanted to know.

"He was selfish, but he never pretended to be anything else. More fool me." She started humming, and I listened carefully to the familiar tune. I realized she was humming the notes to our camp song. "Is it crazy that I nearly married a man that I detest?"

"Yes," I answered honestly. "I'm glad you're spending this time to find yourself." *Even if that doesn't include me, I* thought to myself. Even though I wasn't ready for a relationship, I still wished there could be something between us. Not that I would tell her that. I didn't want her to go on again about how she was not looking for a relationship. Yes, there was an attraction between us, but Pippa was on the rebound. She was hurt by me and then hurt by her mom and betrayed by Stephan. She needed to find herself and live her life the way she wanted. I didn't want to influence her dreams. I didn't want her to focus on goat yoga and raising money for me. I loved that she was so caring, but I wanted her to focus on herself. She was brilliant and talented beyond measure. She could be on Broadway; I had no doubt about it, and if that was where she wanted to be, I would support her one hundred percent, but I couldn't see myself back in New York.

Not now that I had this solace. This piece of heaven on earth. I felt at peace here. Truly happy and accepted. I had friends who loved me and supported me, and I had a community. I was able to live a life where the past hurts didn't linger.

"TJ," Pippa whispered into the darkness, her voice so familiar and melodic. It reminded me of late-night s'mores, running through the woods, and pretending to be kings and queens.

"Yes, Pips."

"Do you promise that you won't stop talking to me again?" Her voice was light but tinged with hope. "Do you promise that if something makes you doubt me or if you get upset with me, you'll tell me?"

"I promise," I grunted, loving her for caring about me so much that she would make me promise something I'd already intended to do. There was a sweetness that surrounded Pippa. It always had. She was inherently a good person. Maybe that was why I'd fallen in love with her when we were eleven.

"Hey, TJ." She sounded happy now. I could almost picture her face in the darkness, the way her brown eyes crinkled at the corners, the dimple on her right cheek, the freckles across her cheeks and nose, and the way her right ear was slightly bigger than her left ear.

"Yes, Pips?" I asked again. The sound of crickets outside the tent carried in the night, and I wondered if they would make her scream. Would she fear that they were going to attack her?

"What's something good that has happened to you in the last ten years?" she asked softly. "I want to hear about your life."

I lay back and thought for a few moments. "I guess meeting Jack was the best thing that happened to me. I never had a friend like you...until him...we just kinda connected and bonded over climbing and nature, and it's what led me here. And I really do love it here." As I said the words, I realized how happy I was in Paradise Valley. I didn't have a lot of money, I still had questions about my birth father, and I still didn't feel good enough for someone like Pippa. But I was happy.

"I like him," Pippa whispered. "And not in the 'I think he's hot' way, though he is pretty cute. He seems like a nice guy." Her voice sounded down, and I smiled to myself at her transparency. I knew Pippa better than I knew myself sometimes.

"He's like a brother to me." I paused. "But you're the best friend I've ever had, Pippa."

"You're just saying that." There was a hopeful tone in her voice, and I rolled over and grabbed her hand to reassure her.

"I never just say anything." I was breathing heavily now. My heart pumping blood so quickly that I'd be a prime victim for vampires. "You've always been the best friend a guy could have."

"You wanna know something?" Her sleeping bag rustled as she rolled over as well. I could tell she was looking at me, even if I couldn't see her eyes.

"Yeah, always."

"Stephan never loved me," she said matter-of-factly. "In fact, I don't even think he really liked me."

"Why would you say that? He proposed to you. He—"

"He thought I was someone else." Her voice was void of emotion. "He met me at a work event for the lord, and I was dressed up. My job sounds impressive, even though it's really not. He thought I was someone I wasn't. And he never really liked the real me. He thought he could mold me. And maybe a part of me wanted to be molded. But you know what, Teej?"

"What, Pips?"

"I don't want to be molded. I want to be me. Every goofy, weird, crazy, fun-loving inch of me. And I don't wanna work on movies. I want to write plays and direct them. And I don't want to be around people I don't like on a daily basis, pretending to like things I don't care about. Life is too short for that. I don't want to have to work hard to impress someone. I want someone to be impressed simply because I'm me." She spoke with such gusto, and my heart filled with joy at her words. She was coming into her own. She was breaking down the boundaries that had held her in for so long. I knew it was just talk now. I knew she had a difficult journey ahead of her pursuing those dreams. But I was so proud of her. She was acknowledging her hurts and trying to move forward.

"You wanna know something, Pips?"

"Yes," she whispered. Her face was practically on top of mine now. I could feel her breath against my cheek, and I breathed it in.

"I want to find my birth father," I admitted. "I want to find out where I came from. I need closure. I need to let go of the hole in my heart that tells me I'm not good enough to be loved." The words fell out of my mouth before I could stop them. I'd laid my soul bare to her. But then, I'd always been able to be me with Pippa. I'd always been able to be vulnerable.

"You're worthy of every good thing, TJ," she whispered and touched the side of my face. "You are the very—"

I raised my hand, grabbed hers, and pressed it against me before pressing my lips to hers. I didn't care if it was a bad idea. I didn't care if we were two lost people at the beginning of long and very different journeys. None of that mattered to me. Only her. Only the feel of her lips against mine. The scent of her hair beneath my nostrils. Her warm body next to mine, so trusting and brave. I kissed her then for all the kisses I'd ever wanted to give her. I kissed her then for every dream that I'd had that she would one day be mine. I kissed her then for the boy who had gotten a tattoo of her name imprinted on him for life. I kissed her then for the man who was now in love with her, who knew he would have to let her go to find herself. I kissed her because there was no other dream for my life other than to be close to her.

No matter what happened between us, I would always have this moment to fill my mind.

Chapter Twenty-Five

P ippa

Dear TJ,

If you were Romeo and I was Juliet, the story would have ended much differently. You'd know I wasn't ever going to kill myself and I'd know you'd never poison yourself. We know each other that well.

Why am I talking about Romeo and Juliet? We are discussing it in English class and it is just so dramatic. Perfect for me! Ha-ha. Did you read it? Isn't it crazy how that play has lived on for years? I would love people to quote my plays far in the future.

Sometimes I feel like that dream will never

come true. Sometimes I feel like I don't even know how I will be able to pay my bills if I go into theater. At least that is what my mom says to me, every time I mention wanting to study drama in school.

Wish you were here so we could go camping and put on a midnight play.

Your Bard Bff,

Pippa

The warmth of the rising sun hit my back as I lay there in the sleeping bag. I felt blissful and happy, and I whispered TJ's name under my lips as I opened my eyes. I stared at him in the mere inches that separated us. He was still fast asleep, most probably because I'd kept him up half the night talking and reminiscing about our past and thoughts for the future.

TJ and I shared our deepest regrets, biggest challenges, and greatest happiness. We'd connected in a way we hadn't done since we were thirteen, and he was about to leave Brooklyn. My heart soared, thinking about the fact that our friendship was now intact. I didn't know that it would ever be as innocent and sweet as it had been when we were younger, yet it had blossomed into something even more beautiful but even more fragile. I touched my lips lightly, recalling the kiss—or kisses—we shared. They had been magic. And then I thought about Stephan and how he hadn't even crossed my mind when I had kissed TJ or even when I'd woken up. It had been TJ's name on my lips.

I could feel warm tears sliding down my face as I realized what that meant. I knew I was about to start sobbing. I knew I wouldn't be able to control my emotions because I was so overcome with frustration, sadness, and happiness all at the same time. It was weird to believe this was the happiest and saddest moment of my life. The happiest because I was finally reconnected with TJ, someone I had thought about every single day since I was a child. And the saddest because I was finally letting go of the dream that was Stephan. And even though he cheated on me, I knew we had to have a proper conversation. I knew I couldn't just run off like I did. I knew I needed to speak to him, and I needed to speak to my mom. I didn't want to carry this bitterness, this frustration, this anger, this hurt, this sadness. Not if I was going to move on in my life, not if I was going to try to find my true purpose.

I looked over at TJ again. I was already pretty sure I had found my soul mate, but I knew that just because we kissed, it didn't mean that anything between us would be easy. I heard it in his voice and saw it in his eyes. He was trepidatious, nervous, and worried, and he wasn't ready to commit himself to me, which was an absurd thing for me to want, as I just got out of one relationship. I unzipped my sleeping bag carefully so as not to make a noise and then tiptoed around TJ's sleeping bag.

I opened the tent's zipper and started to make my way out when I heard, "Morning." TJ turned over and stretched, his eyes opening. He smiled warmly as his gaze moved up and down and across my body.

"Hey, morning. I'm sorry. I didn't mean to wake you up."

"It's okay," he said, yawning. "Are you hungry, thirsty? Do you want me to..."

"No, I'm okay. I just want to stretch my legs," I said, hoping he couldn't see the remnants of tears in my eyes or on my face.

He licked his lips and ran his fingers through his thick, beautiful, silky hair. "Is there anything you want to talk about?" he asked in a stilted way, and I shook my head, smiling at him.

"I don't regret the kisses, TJ," I said with an impish smile. His eyes blazed with happiness.

"Okay, I was just checking."

"Thanks for checking," I said and then made my way completely out of the tent. "I wanted to look at the mountains and take in the morning air."

"It will feel amazing," he said, smiling. "Enjoy."

"Thanks," I said. I zipped up the tent quickly and hurried toward the river. Panic filled me as I realized that Benjy the bear, or maybe another bear, might come up and find me, but I knew I had to be brave. If I was going to be here in Montana and enjoy it, I couldn't be scared of every little sound and possibility of coming into contact with wildlife.

I had to be smart. In fact, I was going to ask TJ to teach me what to do if I came into contact with a bear, a moose, a bison, or any other animal that could possibly harm me. I was pretty sure he would say stay as far away as possible, but I wanted to know if there was anything I should do if they decided to come at me. I smiled to myself as I made my way down to the river. The sky was already bright, blue, and beautiful, not a cloud in sight.

The river was peaceful and tranquil as I made my way to the bank and sat down. Looking at the grandeur surrounding me, I understood why they called it Paradise Valley. I grabbed my phone from my pocket and debated between calling my mom or Stephan first. I wanted to call Emma, but I knew it was still early, and I knew I was only trying to avoid the very real conversations I needed to have. I took a deep breath and called Stephan. He answered on the second ring, which surprised me because he almost always made me go to voice mail.

"Pippa, where are you? What is going on?" he snapped into the phone, with no care or concern in his voice. I pressed my lips together. This was how he treated me, but then, if I were in his shoes, maybe I wouldn't have those emotions either if my fiancée had left me the week before the wedding.

"I told you I'm in Montana, Stephan. I just thought I should call so we could clear the air."

"Are you coming back? Are you going to be here before the wedding? I have so many people from the company coming to this wedding. I've already received gifts. I..."

"Stephan, you don't want to marry me just like I don't want to marry you," I said gently, not wanting to be mean.

"What are you talking about? I proposed to you."

"And you also cheated on me." I didn't want to be angry, and I didn't want to make him defensive.

"Look, it was a one-time thing, Pippa, okay? I have needs, and well, you're not sleeping with me."

"I told you I was saving myself for marriage. I told you —"

"I know," he said, cutting me off. "You were saving yourself for the one person that you loved or whatever, so you could show them that you really love them so you could give them the only thing you'd never given anyone else. But I have needs. I'm a man. I'm not a virgin, Pippa, and if a woman is going to take care of my—"

"Stephan, you just don't get it, do you?"

"Get what? It was just satisfying a physical need, Pippa. I didn't think you would care."

"Why would I not care? That's a huge thing. It's the most intimate act you can do with another person. It's meant to be special, Stephan."

He let out a long sigh. "You need to stop reading romance books, Pippa. You need to get your head out of the clouds. You need to..."

"I need to what?" I was almost shouting now.

"You need to stop believing in daydreams. This is real life. People have sex. Men have needs, and you know what? It's not always with their soul mates. I don't even think there are soul mates in the world. I don't think you have to be in love to do it. Yeah, I said it."

I knew then that Stephan and I would never come to a meeting of the minds. I knew then that we'd never be able to have a conversation about what had gone on and about our relationship where we saw eye to eye. And I would have to be okay with that. I think we were just coming from two very different places.

"You hurt me, Stephan, and I think I hurt myself."

"What do you mean you hurt yourself? What is this, some new age crap?"

"No, I think we both know that we're not in love with each other."

"Let me get this straight. *You* don't love *me*?"

"I think I loved who I thought you were in my life. I loved that you wanted to marry me. I loved that you gave me so much attention in the beginning at a time when I..."

"Yeah, you were in a bad place. You were feeling like crap, la-di-da-di-da, so what? Now you're in a better place because you're in Montana, and all of a sudden, you don't need me," he said with contempt.

"It's not about that. It's about the fact that you slept with someone else. It's about the fact that you don't love me, Stephan. Tell me, do you love me? Do you really and truly love me? Do you want me to be the mother of your children? Do you?"

"I don't even want children, Pippa."

"What?" This was news to me. "We talked about having at least three kids."

"No," he said. "You talked about it, and I just listened. You wanted me to be a better listener, remember?"

"So you never wanted kids?"

"No, and I didn't really think it was going to be a problem because it wasn't like we slept together."

"But we were getting married, we would have on the honeymoon."

"Yeah, well, I guess there were a lot of conversations that we didn't really have."

"But we did have them, Stephan."

"Look, Pippa, it's really early and I have things to do."

I heard a noise in the background, and I froze.

"What's that?" I asked. The noise grew louder. It sounded like someone giggling. "Are you with someone, Stephan?"

"Look, I gotta go now. I don't know how much money I'm going to get back on these deposits and if I don't get back all of it, I would like…"

"Stephan, you know I don't have any money and you know you cheated on me. You're not getting back anything from me."

"Come back to bed," the feminine voice said.

"You're with someone?" Was this guy for real?

"Well, you broke off the engagement, Pippa. What did you—"

"Have a nice life, Stephan. Go gaslight someone else," I said, hanging up the phone.

I lay back down in the grass. The wet dew penetrated through my clothes and dampened the back of my head, sending a chill through me. I didn't know whether to laugh or cry. That conversation had been worthless. He didn't get it. He would never get it. It would always be my fault. And if that was the way it had to be, I didn't care. He wasn't the man for me. He would never be the man for me.

And I wasn't going to feel guilty about the fact that I'd broken off the engagement. I wasn't going to feel guilty about the fact that I realized that I'd never really loved him.

I knew I needed to acknowledge the fact that I was still hurt. My heart wasn't broken because I loved him. My heart was broken because the possibilities of what that love meant to me were gone. And then TJ came into my mind again—his boyish smile. I looked over at my wrist and the bracelet he'd given me. He was the sort of man that you wanted to give your heart to. He was the sort of man that if he told you he loved you and proposed to you, it meant something. My heart ached, wishing that I could be that woman for him, wishing that he wanted me to be that woman for him, wishing that he was in a place in his life where he wanted that. But then I thought about all his hurt, pain, and the fact that his father had abandoned him.

The fact that he didn't know who his birth father was and how he wanted to know that. I grabbed my phone and called my mom. This was another conversation I was not looking forward to.

"Pippa Chase, where are you?" My mother answered the phone on the first ring. This was not unusual.

"You already know I'm in Montana, Mom."

"On that boy's ranch," she said, sounding scandalized.

"His name is TJ Wyatt, Mom. You've known him since he was a little boy. You know he was my best friend."

"You haven't had any contact with him in years. I thought that was over."

"You tried to make it over, Mom," I said in a low voice. There was silence on the other end. "I know what you did, Mom."

"What did I do now, Pippa? What are you going to be upset and mad about at me for now?" I hated the fact that she was already on the defensive, that she was already upset and annoyed.

Why did I have so many narcissistic gaslighters in my life?

"Mom, TJ told me that he wanted to surprise me for high school graduation and that he had planned to take me on a trip. And you told him not to come. You told him that I never really valued his friendship and that he was bringing me down."

"He was bringing you down, Pippa. You wouldn't even really date. All you were doing was writing those letters to that boy."

"He was my best friend, Mom. I missed him."

"And he was in Florida. The friendship was over." She sounded shrill. "That's not real life, Pippa. You're not going to carry on some dalliance by letters for some kid that you knew when you were a kid."

I took a deep breath. "You knew that his dad wasn't his biological dad."

She sighed. "That's not my business, and it's not your business either."

"He came to you, Mom. He came to you because his dad had stopped talking to him and you were mean and you were cold, and you don't speak that way to people, let alone a young boy."

"He wasn't a young boy at that time."

"He wasn't a man, Mom. He'd just turned eighteen."

"What'd you want me to say, Pippa? Do I regret how I spoke to him? Yes. Sometimes, I feel like I was a little harsh, but I did what I thought was best for you. I was looking out for you and your future. My mom didn't do that for me. I was a protector of her for my dad. I didn't get to lead the life, I—"

"That was your life, Mom. And I'm sorry that grandpa was an alcoholic and I'm sorry that he had PTSD from the war and he took it out on you and your mom, and I'm sorry that you didn't get to be the socialite that you wanted to be. I'm sorry you didn't get to buy expensive clothes and live in a fancy penthouse and hobnob with the rich and famous. That's not the life that I want, Mom. I don't want to marry someone from money. I don't want a job where I'm not happy every single day just so I can tell people I work for a British lord, or so I can say I'm married and live in a penthouse apartment that's cold and—"

She cut me off. "So you just hate everything about me then and everything I've done for you. Your entire life has been for nothing."

"I don't hate you, Mom, but it kind of broke my heart. You hurt my best friend in the world. You almost ruined our friendship."

"I'm sorry, Pippa. I just did what I thought was best."

"Mom, do you know anything else about TJ's dad?"

"What do you mean do I know anything else? How would I know—"

"Mom, I know you and his mom were friends, and you used to have drinks together every now and then. She must have confided something to you. You must have known something. Mom, please. TJ needs to figure this out. There's a hole in his heart. His dad abandoned him. Do you have any idea how that affected him? He was thirteen years old, his parents were going through a divorce, and his dad never spoke to him again. He called, he emailed, he sent letters, and he got nothing back. How would you feel if I stopped talking to you now, and you called and messaged, and I never spoke to you again, and you didn't understand why? And then someone just popped up and said, 'Oh, wow, she wasn't your real daughter. She didn't love you. Move on with your life.'"

"You wouldn't stop talking to me, would you?" She sounded panicked, and I sighed.

"I wouldn't do that to you, Mom, because I love you and I know we all make mistakes in life. I'm not happy with you right now and I don't forgive you yet because what you did was bad, really bad. But I do love you and I know one day we'll get to a place where we can put this behind us, but today isn't that day. We can get closer to that day if you tell me everything you know about TJ's parents."

"I just know that his dad found out that he wasn't his biological father."

"I know that already, Mom."

"Okay, I'll tell you what I know if I can remember it correctly. His mom met his dad in a small town in the Pacific Northwest."

"In the Pacific Northwest like Seattle or Oregon or..."

"No," she said. "Maybe I got that wrong. I think she was visiting Yellowstone, so somewhere near there."

"Yellowstone. So she was in Wyoming or Montana."

She sighed. "I can't remember all the details. It was some guy she met up there and they were together for a couple of months. He had one of those really common names."

"What do you mean, really common names?"

"I don't know..."

"But I thought she only knew him as Lucky."

"That was his nickname. She knew his real name. Come on now, Pippa. She dated the guy for months."

"True," I said. "There was no way that his mom didn't know his real name, or maybe he'd given her a fake name." I was thinking out loud. "Can you please try and remember the name?"

"I don't know. She called him Lucky."

"But you said it was a common name. She must have mentioned it once or something for you to remember that part."

"Let me think. John, Mark, David, Robert, or Gary."

"Robert?" I questioned.

"Yeah, might've been Robert."

"Hmm." I thought back to what I'd heard about Old Man Roberts and the fact that he'd been in love with someone before. Could he be TJ's dad? They did vaguely look alike. But what would the chances be that TJ's dad was Old Man Roberts? That just would be crazy.

"Are you positive it was Robert, Mom?"

"I don't know if it was Robert. I just remember thinking to myself, well, that's a really common name. No wonder she wasn't able to find him and tell him that she was pregnant."

"Mom!"

"Or I don't know," she said, "maybe it was Peter or Luke or Raymond or..."

"Okay, Mom. And there's absolutely nothing else?"

"Well, there was one thing," she said, "but I don't know how helpful it will be."

"Tell me, Mom, every little thing is helpful."

"Well, I know that he lived on a ranch."

"Mom, in Wyoming or Montana? Yeah, that's not helpful. Pretty much every guy in those states lives on a ranch."

"I told you I didn't think it would be helpful."

"There's nothing else that you know? Please, Mom, this is important for me and for TJ. And if you want me to not hold this against you for decades, you're going to have to try to remember something."

"Hold on, let me think," she said. I waited in silence for her to think and try to bring up a memory. I knew that if she couldn't think of anything else, I was going to have to call TJ's mom. But if she wouldn't tell TJ anything, I doubt she was going to tell me.

"So, I remember, she told me that he swept her off her feet and he liked line dancing and that...Oh, he came from this really hippie-sounding town."

"What do you mean by hippie-sounding town?"

"I don't know, it was some town that sounded like it would be on a TV show like *Little House on the Prairie* or *Leave It to Beaver*."

"I don't know what you mean, Mom, please."

"You know something like Heaven's Paradise or a Lovely Paradise or..."

"Paradise Valley," I whispered, my heart racing.

"Yeah, that was it. I remember when she told me, I was thinking to myself, Paradise Valley because it's so beautiful, or because a lot of crazy dirty stuff goes on there, you know what I mean?"

"Mom!"

"I'm just saying."

"Paradise Valley, Mom, that's where I am right now. That's where TJ lives."

"You're in Paradise Valley?" she said.

"And there's a guy who's older, and his name is Robert, Old Man Roberts, they call him."

"Well, I don't remember his mom saying she was dating a guy called Old Man Roberts."

"Well, he wouldn't have been an old man twenty-nine years ago, Mom. He would've just been regular Robert."

"Well, they called him Lucky," she said.

"Hmm. I need to find out if Old Man Roberts's nickname is Lucky." My heart was racing. Was Robert TJ's dad? "Is there anything else you can remember, Mom?"

"Well, there was one thing I recall now that we're talking about him."

"What?"

"She said that Lucky had horseshoes everywhere."

"Okay..."

"No, I mean everywhere. He had a belt that had a horseshoe on it. He had a cowboy hat that had a horseshoe on it. He was really into horseshoes. I think that's why he went by Lucky or something like that. It was some weird story to do with horses or horseshoes and how he was addicted to them. That's all I can recall. I remember, now, thinking to myself, that is so country. And she was so *not country*."

"By the way, there's nothing wrong with the country. In fact, it's really beautiful here. It's—"

"What are you trying to say, Pippa? Are you trying to say that you're staying in Montana because you're that upset at me? You're going to give up your life and throw it away to live in some hick—"

"It's not some hick anything, Mom. It's beautiful. It's

the most beautiful place I've ever been in my life and I love it here. And I'm not saying that I'm going to be here forever. Because, guess what? I am going to work on Broadway or off-Broadway or in a theater. Wherever I can get a job. I'm not going back to work for the lord. I'm following my dreams."

"But—"

"But nothing, Mom. I love you and I understand that you wanted to guide me in the direction you thought was best, but I need to live my life for me now. I need to meet someone that I will really and truly love, who will really and truly love me for who I am. And I need to work at a job that makes me want to get up in the mornings, that makes me happy, that fulfills me."

"You're going to make no money. Who makes money in theater? Who do you think you are, Idina Menzel?"

"I didn't say I want to act, Mom."

"Well, that's a good thing because—"

"Mom."

"Sorry," she said. "I just wanted to be the best mom to you, I wanted—"

"I know, and you've been a great mom, but I need to live my own life now."

"You sound different," she said.

"How so? I'm still the same person."

"You sound like you've matured." She took a deep sigh. "You know part of the reason I always used to offer you my opinions?"

"No, why?"

"Because you always wanted them, Pippa. You always wanted me to tell you what you should do, where you should go, and I guess I kind of ran with it."

"I wanted your feedback and your advice because I

didn't want to make a bad decision," I said. "I was afraid to make the wrong decision, and I've made a lot of really bad decisions because I was scared to go with what was in my heart. I was scared to follow my dreams. I was scared to acknowledge that I wasn't happy and I don't know why I've been like that."

"I want you to be happy, Pippa. You're my daughter, my only child. I love you. All I want is for your happiness. You know that, right?"

"I know, Mom. Thank you."

"You're welcome," she said. "Pippa, before you go."

"Yes, Mom."

"Tell TJ I said I'm sorry." Her voice was sad. "I shouldn't have said those things to him. I know it doesn't sound like a lot now, but I've had sleepless nights about what I said and what I did when I saw how much pain you were in. When I saw how much you missed your best friend, I didn't mean to ruin that. I know you guys had something special."

"Thank you for acknowledging that."

"You're welcome. Am I going to see you soon?"

"I don't know, Mom," I said. "But I'll let you know when I'm in New York." I hung up the phone and placed it on the grass next to me. I closed my eyes and ran my fingers across the dew. I was at peace with my conversation with my mom. She sounded like she regretted what she'd done. It didn't make anything better, but it was a start. A frisson of excitement flooded through me as I thought about the new information that I had. TJ's birth father had a common-sounding name, possibly Robert. His nickname was Lucky, and he loved horseshoes. It wasn't a lot to go on, but it was something.

Especially now that I was almost positive that he lived

in Paradise Valley as well. I knew it was a huge coincidence, but I also knew that God worked in miraculous ways. TJ had met Jack for a reason. TJ had fallen in love with Paradise Valley for a reason, and I had a feeling that was because that's where his father was, and I was going to help him find him. I'd broken TJ's heart when we were eighteen, even though I hadn't known it, and I wanted to help put it back together. I was going to make it my mission to be the friend to him that he'd needed all those years. We'd made a pact to always be there for each other. And I had come here and called upon him because I needed him, and I knew in my heart that he needed me as well, and I wasn't going to let him down.

Chapter Twenty-Six

T J

Hola Pippa,

I am trying to learn Spanish. I only know three sentences though. Not enough to move to Mexico or Ecuador or anything. Have you ever thought about living somewhere else?

I wonder what it would be like to just start over in life. I told Gramps that I'd love to take his old boat and live on an island. He told me that sounded like a great plan. He's great. He's the best part of living Florida. Yes, he's even better than Disney. I said it.

Do you think that you could ever live on an island? I don't want to be isolated, but if you *were there, and my gramps and nanna. And my mom can come too. I guess I should start learning how to make a fire. Maybe when I'm older I can be on Survivor. That would be cool.*

Adios,

TJ

"Who's hungry?" Mindy called out to everyone at the campsite. I stretched my arms, got out of the tent, and walked toward the table I had set up.

"I'm hungry. Why? Are you making something?" I asked her with a wide grin.

"No, but I was going to tell everyone to come back to my shop and I'll make coffee and breakfast. I think Kay is there, so everything should be up and running."

"Okay," Jack said, making a face. I felt bad for him. He and Kay weren't the best of friends, and I knew he didn't hate her, but I knew he had a hard time having to be around her so frequently. Mindy didn't particularly love Kay either but had given her the job when she'd found out that Kay didn't have enough money to support herself and her son. Mindy Messina was a great person, even though she was nosy.

"Hey, what's going on?" Pippa said as she made her way back over to the group.

"Mindy just offered to make us breakfast," Charlotte said happily. "I know, for one, I want one of your mochas, and I want a breakfast sandwich," she said.

"Oh, I'm hungry too," Pippa said with a smile. She

looked over at me. "Are you hungry, TJ?"

"I could eat." I nodded.

"Shall we all get ready and then we can head over?"

"Sounds good."

Mindy looked down at her phone. "Okay. I am going to go now, but try to get there within twenty minutes, guys, okay?"

"Yes, boss," Brandon said, and we all laughed. Mindy gave him a look, and I wondered if she was going to retort something back, but she didn't say anything.

"Did you have a nice walk?" I asked Pippa as I headed over to her.

"It was nice. Actually, I went down by the river and I just lay out." She smiled at me. "And I spoke to my mom and Stephan."

"Oh?" I asked, hoping she'd elaborate. "And how did those calls go?"

"They were helpful," she said. "I mean, they were weird, but they needed to happen."

"Weird in what way?" I asked. I wondered how in-depth the conversations had been, if she missed him, or if she felt guilty about kissing me. There were so many things I wanted to ask, but I didn't want to pry.

"Well, I told my mom off. I let her know that I was not happy and she wanted to apologize to you. Supposedly, she's been regretting what she said."

"Okay," I said, nodding, not knowing how to respond to that. Her mom obviously hadn't regretted it that much because she'd never contacted me to apologize or to put me and Pippa back in contact.

"I know," she said, touching the side of my arm, "her apology doesn't mean much at this point, but she knows that you're an important part of my life and that if she pulls something like that again, I don't know if there will ever be any coming back from it."

I stared at her for a couple of seconds and nodded. I understood what she was saying. Her mom had almost decimated our relationship, which I was going to find hard to forgive, let alone what she'd said to me about my dad and my mother's situation.

"And Stephan?" I asked, staring into her brown eyes, wondering if she missed him. If she wanted to get back together with him, and if he'd been able to get her to forgive him.

"He's an asshole," she said and slapped her fingers across her mouth. "Sorry, I didn't mean to say that word."

"No worries, it seems you're only speaking the truth." I winked.

"I tried to explain to him how he hurt me and how he betrayed me, and he basically tried to blame me."

"What? No way." This guy seemed like a piece of work.

"Yeah. Basically, he said because I was..." She paused and blushed. "Well, you know."

"I think I know," I said. Because she was a virgin was what I believed she was saying.

"Yeah. Well, because I'm pure, or whatever, he felt like I wouldn't care and that he could get it from someone else."

"And what, he thought you wouldn't mind?" I said, grimacing. "He is such a jerk, and he's not a good guy at all."

"I know," she said. "And I told him what I told you. He didn't love me and he didn't even like me."

"What did he say?" I asked her, wondering if she was going to break down.

"He tried to deny it, but it was lackluster." She shrugged. "It doesn't matter anymore. It's my past, and as weird as it may seem, I'm ready to be over that entire situation. I'm ready to be over him. I'm ready to forget that part of my life."

"You can't just forget, though, Pippa," I said softly. "That's not how life works. I know right now you feel like you didn't love him and that he wasn't a good guy and he cheated on you, but there was obviously something there at some point for you to have gotten that far into a relationship with him. There must've been some positive things."

"There were," she said. "He liked movies, though now I feel like he just liked the fact that he knew a lot of important people that made them."

"But that was something you enjoyed together, right?"

"Yeah. He liked to read a lot of literary fiction." She laughed. "He thought what I liked to read was trash, but..."

"Maybe I should stop you," I said with a smile. "It seems like you can't think of anything positive about him."

"Why do you want me to think about something positive?" Her eyebrows drew in in thought. "Do you want me to get back together with him? Do you think I should give him another chance? Do you..."

"No," I said. "But I don't want you to beat yourself up for being with him. Right now, I feel like you're remembering all the bad things and then you're judging yourself too harshly because you're thinking to yourself, why was I ever with him when everything was so bad? And it wasn't always bad. It couldn't have been. And maybe it wasn't the most amazing, but there must've been some things that drew you to him. I just don't want you to be too harsh on yourself."

"You're a good person, TJ," she said.

"Thanks," I said, not wanting to tell her that I wanted her to process and get over Stephan so I could have a chance. I stared at her lips, so pink and plump, and I wanted to pull her into my arms and kiss her. I wanted to walk down by the river and tell her that I'd always had a thing for her, that I had always imagined the two of us watching the sunrise in the morning and the sunset in the evening and whispering sweet nothings into each other's ears. But it wasn't the right time. It wasn't the right place. It wasn't our time.

"I'm going to apply for some theater jobs, both on Broadway and off-Broadway, for whatever I think I can help and qualify for," she said. "I really want to do this, TJ. I really want to pursue my love of theater."

"That's great," I said. "When do you think you're going to start applying?"

"Tomorrow," she said. "The sooner, the better, right? There's no time like the present." She squared her shoulders. "I can make it in the theater world. I just have to try. I just have to get my foot in the door."

"Yeah," I said. "That is very true." I felt deflated inside. I didn't want to think about her going to New York again. I didn't want to think about her leaving Montana.

"Oh, and Emma texted me. She got a flight for Monday. So I said we could pick her up at the airport if that's okay."

"Of course," I said. "Sounds great."

"Hey, Jack?" I called out.

"Yeah?" He looked over at me.

"Pippa's best friend Emma will be here next week."

"Oh, what day? I'm going into Billings on Monday."

"Oh, she arrives on Monday," Pippa said, her face crestfallen. "Should I tell her to change her flight if she's staying with you?"

"I don't know," he said.

"No," I said quickly. "She can stay with us, and then the next day, she can go over to Jack's."

"Okay," Pippa said. "That works, if you don't mind, TJ."

"I don't mind," I said, shaking my head. "In fact, I look forward to having her. I know Apple and Donkey will be very happy."

"Apple will be happy and Donkey will not be happy," Pippa said gaily.

"True," I said. "Donkey is starting to feel like my ranch is being invaded."

"Hey, when are we going to have the goat yoga class?" Brielle asked, and Jack rolled his eyes.

"I was thinking Saturday or Sunday morning," Pippa said, "What works for everyone?"

"Sunday morning works best for me," Mindy said.

"Me too," Charlotte said.

"Me three," Brielle said.

"I guess it's Sunday then," I said.

"Don't forget you guys are coming over for Sunday lunch," Jack added. "I already told my parents."

"Sounds cool," I said with a smile.

"So that sounds like a plan. Sunday morning, we'll have our goat yoga. Then we'll head over to Jack's and grab lunch, and then Sunday evening, we can do something fun?" Pippa said, her eager eyes imploring.

"And what's something fun to you?"

"I have an idea," Charlotte interjected, and we all looked at her.

"What's your idea, Charlotte?" I asked, slightly upset that she'd ruined the moment between Pippa and myself.

"I think that we should all go to Old Man Roberts's and pick strawberries."

"In the evening?" Mindy said, raising an eyebrow.

"I think that would be absolutely fantastic," Pippa said, nodding eagerly. "I would love to go to Old Man Roberts's ranch. I would love to spend more time with him and ask him about his past. Didn't someone say he was in love with someone before he got married? I love a good scandal or love story."

"Yeah," Mindy said. "He's always going on about his summer love with some lady from the East Coast."

Pippa's face grew excited. "I would love to learn more about that. I know that the first time I met him, I thought to myself, wow, this is an interesting dude, and you seem to get on so well with him, don't you?"

"I guess." I shrugged. Why was she talking so fast? Why was she going on about Old Man Roberts? "You seem quite interested in him, Pips. Something I should know?" I asked, and she stared at me for a couple of seconds and burst out laughing.

"Of course not. He's married, an old man, and I'm not interested in anyone right now," she said and then blushed.

"Oh?" I wondered if that included me.

"Well, you know what I mean. I'm finding myself."

"I know." I wondered how long it was going to take her to find herself and how patient I could be.

"Come on, guys. I'm leaving now," Mindy said as she headed toward her truck. "And you know that the bacon-and-egg sandwiches are not going to last long."

"I'm on my way," Jack called out.

"Sounds good. Come on, Pippa," I said as we headed toward my truck, "let's go and get breakfast."

"Okay," she said. "We'll see you at the store."

Pippa and I walked companionably toward my truck. I opened the door for her; she jumped into the passenger seat, and then I closed it. I headed to my side, got in, and turned on the ignition. "Did you have fun last night?" I asked her.

She smiled. "I had the best night ever."

Chapter Twenty-Seven

P^{ippa}

Dearest TJ,

I miss you. I miss you. I miss you.

Sorry that I haven't written in two weeks. Life has been crazy. I got the flu and it was awful. I couldn't sleep. I couldn't eat. I thought I was outside of my body. It was so weird.

I wonder if that is what aliens feel like, if they exist. Sometimes I feel like an alien. Like people see one thing, but I feel a different way inside. I wonder if people ever really see us the way we see ourselves.

I think that you're the only person that has

ever seen me as I am. I wonder if you would recognize me, if you saw me now. I want us to live close together soon. I know I keep saying that, but it's true. I've never had a friend like you before.

Your Best Friend For All Time,
Pippa

Mindy's cupcake and coffee store smelled of banana bread and freshly brewed coffee when we entered, and I could hear my stomach growling in sweet anticipation. TJ's lips twitched as we entered the store, and I could tell from the look on his face that he was looking forward to eating as much as I was.

"Over here, TJ and Pippa," Jack hollered to us from a booth in the corner of the shop, and we headed toward his table. Ethan, Aiden, and Brandon were all seated with him. I noticed that Brielle and Charlotte were standing next to the counter at the front of the store. I was about to head over to see what they were talking about when I noticed Old Man Roberts and his wife, Annie, sitting at a table with a couple I didn't recognize. I studied Old Man Roberts's face and then looked over at TJ to see if I could see a resemblance. My heart raced as I realized they both had blue eyes and a strong jawline. It wasn't exactly DNA, but I felt like this was a strong coincidence, given all the information I already had.

"Morning." I waved at Annie, and she gave me a small smile before tapping her husband on the shoulder. He looked over, gave me a big wink, and then a wave; I waved back at him.

"Old Man Roberts really does seem like a cool man, doesn't he?" I said to TJ as we continued walking.

"I guess." He shrugged and grabbed a chair. "You can take a seat in the booth, Pips. It's more comfortable."

"Thanks," I said, turning back around to look at Old Man Roberts to see if I could pick up any other clues. What I really wanted to do was chat with him one on one and see if I could ask him what he'd been up to twenty-nine years ago. I'd have to do it out of earshot of his wife though.

"Hey, TJ, did I tell you that my dad got two new horses?" Jack said, his voice eager. "The mare was sired by Country House, who won the Kentucky Derby four years ago."

"Wow, that's awesome," TJ said and then looked at me. "Jack's dad has a couple of racehorses that he enters into derbies. He used to want to be a jockey when he was younger."

"But he was too big." Jack laughed. "Poor Dad. Sometimes, I think he wishes that he still could ride in a race, but I think he's just happy that he has a stable full of horses."

"If you ever think you want to get a horse, we'll have Luke pick one out for you. He has a sixth sense about the connection between horses and their humans," TJ told me.

"Really?" I asked, wanting to concentrate on the conversation but also wanting to go over to Old Man Roberts and do some detective work. "That sounds fun," I mumbled as I tried to think of a way to get up.

"What sounds fun?" TJ frowned. "Are you listening to me, Pippa?"

"Uh, yes... Sorry, I was just hoping to ask Annie some questions about the theater and playhouse and see if there was anything I could do to help before it got shut down for good."

"Oh, sure." His frown cleared, and he tapped his fingers against the clean white tabletop. "She's over there. Why don't you go and ask her and I'll grab some menus."

"Perfect." I jumped up eagerly. "Thanks, Teej." I beamed at him and then looked over at the other three guys. "What?" I asked them as they all grinned at me.

"Are you certain you aren't a mail-order bride or something?" Brandon asked, winking at me. "TJ sure seems to wait on you hand and foot."

"No, he doesn't. Don't be stupid." I pressed my lips together. "I'll be right back." I sauntered over to Annie and Old Man Roberts as if I didn't have a care in the world. "Oh, excuse me," I said with a small smile. "I didn't mean to interrupt you, but I wanted to say hello."

"Good to see you again," Old Man Roberts said, his eyes twinkling. "Just think, you thought I was your beau for a few moments."

"I didn't really." I laughed and shook my head.

"I must have a thing for women from New York," he said, and my jaw almost fell to the ground. This had to be an admission of his relationship with TJ's mom. Maybe he even knew TJ was his son. I didn't know how he would know, but this was starting to feel like fate.

"And I bet they have a thing for you as well." I grinned, and I could see Annie glaring at me. Oops! I'd gotten a bit carried away. "Annie, I wanted to talk to you about the playhouse. I'm not sure if you remember, but I'm very interested in theater, and Brandon mentioned they were trying to sell the old playhouse, and I thought maybe I could help you and the other townsfolk so that we could save it."

"But how can we save it? Who's going to take it over?

We have a lot of actors in this town, but we don't get any directors and I can't see us finding any anytime soon."

"I mean, I could direct the first play," I mumbled, not exactly sure what I was saying. "Until you find someone else. I love directing and I don't mind. Really, I don't. But we'd have to find a way for the town to raise enough money to save the theater."

"You'd be interested in directing one of the plays?" she asked, her eyes lighting up.

"Sure, plus, it would look great on my résumé for Broadway shows," I said quickly. I didn't want anyone to think I was planning to stay in Paradise Valley. I didn't want TJ freaking out, thinking that I was some sort of psycho and that I'd changed my entire life plan because of a kiss. Or rather, a couple of kisses. No matter how sweet and steamy they'd been.

"Well, I will have to tell Ruthie and Katie." Annie beamed. "Maybe we can meet in the town square later today or maybe tomorrow and chat about it."

"I'll have to ask TJ about it, but I'm sure that would work." I looked over at Old Man Roberts. "Did you know that his mom came through here before he was born?" I was trying to sound casual but knew I sounded anything but. "In fact, I think she dated a guy local to here. How cool, huh?"

"I guess so." He shrugged and grabbed his coffee mug. "Plenty of people come through Paradise Valley."

"I guess that's true." I bit on my lip. "Maybe I'll be *lucky* enough to..." My voice trailed off to see if there was any reaction to my use of the word lucky. "Hey, do any of you guys ever feel lucky?"

"I don't know." Old Man Roberts grabbed a biscuit off his plate and took a bite. Annie pulled out her phone and handed it to me.

"Why don't you put your number in here?" she said with a small smile. "Then I'll call you and let you know what time we can meet up this afternoon and then we'll figure out when we can hold auditions."

"Auditions?" I frowned. "What auditions? We don't even have the theater. And we haven't chosen a play."

"Well, you can do that." She tapped my hand so that I'd enter my number. "You are the expert, after all."

"I wouldn't say I was an expert by any means." I stared at her graying hair as I typed my phone number in. "I mean, I've written a few plays and my dream is to have them performed, but I haven't even applied to any jobs on Broadway or anything. Partially due to my mom and—"

"What's your momma got to do with anything?" Annie said, cutting me off. "And why does it have to be on Broadway? A theater is a theater, right? And we got a theater here in town that needs ownership and someone that loves it."

"I mean, it does, but I live in New York, and I don't have money to buy a theater." My face was warm, and I looked at TJ, who was heading back to the booth with two menus. "Here you go." I handed her the phone. "Call or text, and I'll see what I can do to help." I looked over at Old Man Roberts. "You keep staying lucky."

"Huh, I'll try," he said, giving me a wink and whispering to his wife, "I told you she was a funny one." I pretended I didn't hear and made my way back over to TJ. I needed to tell him what I'd found out. I needed to tell him that I was pretty sure that Old Man Roberts was his biological dad. I wasn't sure how he'd feel about that. I knew that it would be a lot to emotionally untangle. I wondered how Annie would feel knowing that TJ was her husband's son. I hoped she would love him and treat him like family. I wanted that for TJ. I needed them both to embrace him with open arms.

"So you got to speak to Annie?" TJ asked as we took a seat back at the booth. He handed me the menu, and I looked it over for a few seconds before telling him what she'd said.

"She thinks I should direct a play here," I said casually. I could feel all the men staring at me. "We did say we should try to put on a performance to raise money, so this is almost the same thing."

"You staying in Paradise Valley then?" Jack asked, his eyes fixed on me as I looked down at the menu and studied it hard. I didn't know why this question was coming up from so many people.

"No," I said quickly. "I have nowhere to stay. TJ can't keep sleeping on the couch. Plus, I don't have the money to buy a theater or anything like that. And I don't know if the new owner would hire me anyway. Plus, I have to go back to New York soon, and well, you know..." I could feel TJ's eyes on me. "What?" I mumbled.

"You can stay for as long as you want," he said. "Don't let my bad back make you leave." I could feel my heart racing at his words. I didn't know what to say. Did he want me to stay? Did he like me as much as I liked him? There were so many questions I wanted to ask him, but there was no way I was going to bring them up in front of Jack, Ethan, and Aiden. We'd have to wait until we got back to the ranch. And then I didn't even know what I would say. I didn't want to presume that just because we shared a couple of kisses that he was interested in more with me. He wasn't that sort of guy. I knew that. I knew that he still thought I was trying to get over Stephan. I also knew that I didn't want him to think he was a rebound for me.

"Thanks, that means a lot," I said, smiling at him.

"We don't mind you staying either," Brandon said as he

got up. "Okay, let me go and talk to Mindy and see what is taking her so long. My latte is still not on the table."

"Go and give her a piece of your mind," Jack said, and Brandon glared at him.

"Do they have something?" I whispered as Brandon walked away and stomped toward the front of the restaurant. It seemed to me that Mindy and Brandon were constantly arguing. And when two people spent that much time arguing, it made me feel like there was some sort of chemistry or history there or at least some sort of magnetic attraction between the two of them.

"They're both just stubborn." TJ shook his head. "There's nothing romantic there. Mindy can't stand him."

"And Brandon is always complaining about Mindy," Jack added. "Like always." Were they really that dense? Did they not see why it was obvious to me? There was a thin line between love and hate, and Mindy and Brandon were definitely skirting along that line. I wouldn't be surprised if they got together eventually. But I wasn't going to say anything. I had my own issues to deal with.

"I see," I said as I sat back in the booth.

TJ leaned forward and whispered into my ear, "You wanna go swimming later?"

"In a pool?" I asked him and then answered my own question. "You mean in the river, right?"

"Yeah." He grinned. "Maybe we could go fishing as well?"

"If you want," I said with a small nod. "Annie might want to meet up later to discuss the theater, but aside from that, I'm free like a bird." I smiled, and suddenly, I felt self-conscious. How did I already have other plans in the town? I'd barely just arrived, but already, it was starting to feel like more of a home than New York City did.

"I do want," he said, a thoughtful expression on his face. "There's something I want to show you."

"Oh? What is it?" I asked him eagerly. A part of me wondered if it was a kiss. I could feel myself warming at the thought. Swimming in the cool, tranquil waters on his land and then having him hold me in his arms so that he could kiss me would be so romantic. That would mean he had deep feelings for me. Because I knew I had deep feelings for him. I knew that I loved him. I knew that he was the only man I ever wanted. And I would wait however long it took for him to believe that. As I sat there, I thought to myself that I was completely over the top. I was hoping and dreaming of things that didn't seem realistic. How could I reunite with my best friend and then fall in love with him in a matter of days? It didn't make sense, though I was starting to realize that in life, it didn't matter if things made sense, so long as it didn't negatively affect myself or anyone else I cared about.

Chapter Twenty-Eight

T J

Dear Pippa,

I read a book yesterday that you recommended to me. Bridge to Terabithia. I know you read it when you were young, but I never read it until recently. And yes, I read it because I remembered how much you wanted me to read it, and it made me feel close to you. Guess I was missing you. Did I make your day?

Also, spoiler alert: how did you not tell me about that ending? I think I may have cried. I didn't think they had those sorts of endings in kids' books. Talk about devastated. It got *me thinking about what I would do if you weren't in my life anymore. I don't know if I could ever survive that.*

I'm so glad we're best friends. On my lowest day, I can think of you, and that will put a smile on my face.

Any more book recommendations?

TJ

There are times when I feel like I don't make the best decisions, and this was one of them. My eyes didn't know where to look as I stood there waiting for Pippa to disrobe. I shouldn't feel this nervous. It's not like anything was going to happen, but there was a sweet thrill of anticipation in the air. The electricity between Pippa and me was undeniable. Even if both of us wanted to deny it.

Pippa was standing there in a pair of shorts and an over-sized plaid shirt, but I knew she was about to take them off. And that meant I was going to have to take off my shirt as well. Taking off my shirt meant she'd see my tattoo and then would come the questions and the answers that I was still not ready to give her. I could see Pippa sneaking furtive glances in my direction, and I couldn't stop myself from moving closer to her.

"What is it?" I asked her as she lifted her shirt up slightly. I could see a glimpse of her pale stomach beneath the material, and my stomach stirred. "Pips, are you scared of going in the river? I promise there are no bears swimming."

"What about piranhas?" she mumbled, her face turning a rosy pink. Was she being serious? Did she really think we had piranhas?

"What are you talking about? We don't have—"

"I know." She cut me off, her voice high-pitched. "It's just that I don't think this bathing suit fits me properly. I do thank you for stopping at the General store so I could pick something up, but I think it might be a bit small for me."

"Oh, is that why you're looking so worried?" I couldn't believe she was self-conscious about her body. "Pips, I've seen you in a bathing suit before. We practically spent every summer swimming together."

"But we were kids then." She hesitantly lifted her shirt again. "I just—"

"I'll turn around," I said with a grin as I spun to face away from her. "Take off your clothes and just jump in the river. That way, I won't see anything I shouldn't see." I did as I said, even as my mind told me off for being so polite.

"There's nothing you would have seen, TJ," she exclaimed. "The bathing suit is not that inappropriate. I just feel like it might be a little tight." I heard the sounds of her clothes hitting the ground. "Okay, keep facing that way and close your eyes. I'm running into the water now." I closed my eyes obligatorily and then reopened them as I heard the sounds of splashing in the water. I slowly took off my shirt and pants and headed to the river. Pippa was swimming lazily, and I tried not to stare at her body as she moved gracefully through the water.

I jumped in and swam around a bit to get my skin accustomed to the cold. I swam back and forth for a few minutes before coming to a stop. I treaded water for a few more and then looked around to locate Pippa. She was about five feet to my right, standing close to the riverbank, staring at me, a languid expression on her face. About half of her body was out of the water, and I understood the comment she'd made about the bathing suit now. Her bikini top clung to her like a second skin, and the contrast between the bright red against her creamy skin was stark. I smiled as my eyes moved up, but I ensured I didn't look at any body part for too long. I didn't want to make her uncomfortable.

I swam over to her and stopped, my feet coming down onto the muddy riverbed. I looked back up at her, my gaze lingering on her lips as she tilted her head to the sun.

"This feels amazing," she said before looking back at me. "I can see why you want to build some cabins at this location. People would pay big money to stay down here."

"You think?" I asked, her words filling me with warmth and hope. I had to make the ranch a success. It was going to be the way I supported myself and my family. My plan was to turn this into an eco-friendly resort. If I couldn't get the cabins built in the next year or so, then my dream was likely dead. I couldn't survive on my depleting savings for much longer without getting a real job.

"I know so." She grinned. "If I had the money, I would spend it on a vacation here."

"Well, I hope your words come to fruition." I splashed water onto her stomach. "I need to start building the first cabins as soon as possible. Ideally, I'd like to be in business next summer."

"Oh, wow, that's awesome." She splashed me back, the water crashing into my chest and my face. "When do you start building the first cabin?"

"Not sure yet." I took a deep breath. "I'm waiting on approval for a commercial construction loan, but I need a certain amount of money before they will loan me the rest and I don't have it yet. I mean, I could use the land as collateral, but I don't want to do that."

"Oh." She looked despondent. "How much money do you need? If you don't mind me asking?"

"I have to come up with a hundred grand for the loan to go through," I shared with her. I didn't have secrets from Pippa—well, not a lot. "I've got about eighty grand in the bank. So I need to raise another twenty." I smiled as her eyes widened. "Yeah, it's not a small chunk of change."

"Well, I have a couple of grand in savings. It's all yours."

"I don't think so. But thank you for the offer. I'm not taking your savings, Pippa." I held my hand up as she protested. "I'm grateful, trust me, but it wouldn't feel right. I'll get there."

"Can your mom help?" she asked softly, her face falling as I shook my head.

"She would if she could. She didn't get much in the divorce and she's taking care of my grandparents. And she needs to save for her own retirement." I looked down at the dark river water and flicked ripples with my fingernails. "One of my dreams is to be able to take care of all of them. If I can just make enough money to buy them a bigger house and get a caretaker in to help my mom with her parents, I would feel so much better about everyone's situation." I looked up at her. "I wanted them to come here, but they're used to the constant sun now in Florida. Mom says she could never go back to a cold climate."

"Aw, but has she been here?" She looked around, licked her lips nervously, and gazed back at me. "Has she ever been to Paradise Valley?"

"No." I pressed my lips together. It was one of the biggest hurts in my life that my mom wouldn't come out here. She said it would bring up painful memories. I didn't press her. I knew she'd met my biological dad somewhere in the vicinity of Yellowstone, and I didn't want to trudge up anything that would bring back the pain of that time in her life. I knew she was still devastated at my father's rejection and the fact that he had a new family out there.

"Oh..." Pippa's tone changed. She turned away from me, and I frowned.

"What is it, Pips?"

"Nothing," she said quickly, shaking her head vehemently while looking at her fingers under the water. "I was just wondering how she was doing and stuff." She looked up at me through lowered lashes. "Did she say if your dad was older than her?"

"Huh?" I blinked at the sudden change of subject. "You mean my birth dad?"

"Yeah." She nodded slowly. "I was just wondering if he was around her age or perhaps a little bit older?"

"I don't know. Why?"

"Just in case we wanted to search for him, I wanted to find out what age range we'd be looking for."

"We're not going to be able to find him." I shook my head. "All I know is that he was from Wyoming or Montana and that he goes by Lucky. Not a lot to go on, Detective Pippa."

"I know that's not a lot," she said as she stepped closer to me. "Wanna race across the river?"

"I will beat you." I chuckled. "Easy."

"I know." She stopped next to me, her eyes moving from my face to my chest. I could see she was breathing a little heavier now. She gasped suddenly, and her eyes flew to mine. "TJ?"

"Yes, Pippa," I said, knowing what she was about to say.

"What's that?" she asked, touching the tattoo lightly

and withdrawing her fingers like they were on fire. "When did..." Her voice trailed off, and I grabbed her fingers and pressed them to the tattoo.

"PC and TJW 4 eva," I said slowly. "Pippa Chase and Travis James Wyatt forever." I cocked my head to the side. "It was meant to say best friends forever, but the tattoo artist misheard me and this is what he wound up doing."

"You tattooed our names," she said breathlessly. "On your body."

"Better than on my tongue, am I right?" I realized I was still holding her hand but didn't want to let it go.

"You never said." Her fingers ran along my skin again, this time of their own volition. "When did you get it?"

"The month before your graduation. I wanted to surprise you. You always used to get on me for not saying it." I laughed. "You always wanted me to say it more. I wanted to show you once and for all that you were my best friend. You were my everything."

"You never showed me." She shook her head and water droplets from her hair sprinkled onto my chest.

"I didn't get to surprise you, remember?"

"I can't believe my mom did that. But I also shouldn't have just let it go. I should have pushed you harder when you stopped writing. I should have demanded you speak to me. I should have flown out to you. I should have read between the lines of your letters when you talked about your dad and missing me and, well, just everything," I rambled on and on.

"You don't think my tattoo is creepy?" I ran my fingers through my hair. "I was scared for you to see it."

"I think it's the sweetest thing I've ever seen in my life." She took a step closer to me. "You're a sweet one, TJ Wyatt."

"I don't think anyone has ever called me sweet before," I said in a husky tone. I stared down into her wide brown eyes and swallowed hard. "I'm not feeling so sweet right now."

"Oh?" she questioned, licking her lips as she ran her fingers down my chest and then pulled them away. "That's a pity."

"And why is that?" I asked as we just stared at each other. I wasn't sure what this moment was. There was a frisson of electricity between us that was undeniable. This was growing more and more complicated. I loved Pippa. I was attracted to her. She made my heart race. She made me want to be the best man I could be so I could be good enough for her, but the timing was just not right.

"I can see your mind racing. Don't overthink it. Just kiss me, TJ," she whispered, a pink tinge on her cheeks as she gazed at my lips.

"Who says I was thinking about it?" I said with a wide smile before swooping her into my arms and dipping her to the side. I pressed my lips down onto hers, and she melted against me as she wrapped her arms around my neck. The kiss seemed to last forever, which was perfect for me. I never wanted it to end. In fact, I never wanted this day to end. It was perfect. We were happy in each other's company and were drifting back into each other's lives seamlessly. At this moment, I could forget all the complications of the future. We'd dealt with the misunderstandings and hurts from the past, but the future was murky. I was in no position to have a serious girlfriend. She was in no position to have a new boyfriend. And we didn't have time to get there.

She was going to leave and go back to New York to look for a job on Broadway. She needed to be in theater; that was her dream. She loved making up stories and wanted to bring them to life. I couldn't ask her or expect her to give that up. And the fact of the matter was that the mayor was going to sell the playhouse, even if Annie, Ruthie, Katie, and even my friends wanted to save it. They needed a real buyer to take it over.

My heart stopped as an idea crossed my mind. There was one way to get Pippa to stay in Paradise Valley. It was a crazy idea, but as I looked down into her trusting, beautiful face, I knew it was the best idea I'd ever had. I just needed to find out if Pippa had any interest in staying. I didn't want to push it because I didn't want to put that pressure on her, but I'd have to think of another way. Because if she did, I'd move the heavens above to make it happen.

Chapter Twenty-Nine

P ippa

Dear TJ,

Do you want to get a dog or a cat when you have your own place? I was thinking that it might be really cool to have a pet pig or something. They are so cute. Though they might be a bit smelly for an apartment.

Also, I don't know if a Co-op would approve of a pet pig. Could you imagine if Mrs. Seger came face to face with a pig in the stairwell? She'd post notices on every empty wall she could find complaining about me.

Could you imagine me walking my pet pig

down the street? And taking it to Mr. Singh's bodega on the corner? That would be so funny.

Not that that will ever happen. You can't have a pig in the City.

Will you move back to New York once you're done with school?

Miss you,

Pippa

TJ and I walked back to his cabin side by side. My heart was full, and I was in a state of bliss, so I hardly noticed when Apple and Donkey came running, their little legs carrying them quickly as they greeted us. I was a little nervous that Donkey would headbutt me again, but he stopped about a foot away from us and looked me up and down. Progress. Apple jumped at my legs, her tongue out and tail wagging, wanting to be picked up. When I lifted her in my arms, she licked my face eagerly.

"She loves you." TJ gazed at his dog lovingly and called Donkey over to him. The grumpy goat stared at him before sauntering over. TJ rubbed him briefly, and then the goat walked away. "Are you hungry?" he asked me as we continued walking. I put a squirming Apple back down onto the grass and nodded.

"I could eat a horse—Oops!" I slapped my hand across my mouth. "Don't tell Stella or Nightstar that I said that."

"I won't," he said, his face stern as he wagged his finger at me. "Let's hope Donkey doesn't say anything."

"I think Donkey and I are friends now." I waited as TJ opened the cabin door. "I hope he enjoys goat yoga."

"We'll see." TJ ushered me inside, and I smiled at his manners. It was so nice being around a real gentleman.

"I'm going to charge twenty-five dollars a class," I said eagerly. "That will help to raise money for you to get the loan."

"The money will be helpful to get my new life started." I wasn't sure what he meant by his *new life* or why he'd had a stern look on his face, but I wasn't going to dwell on it.

He headed toward the living room area and turned the TV on. I watched as he flicked through the channels and stopped on a football game.

I supposed it would have been too unrealistic to expect him to put it on *Love is Blind* or *Hart of Dixie*. Still, I wouldn't begrudge him his football games. "You want burgers tonight?" he asked as he walked to the kitchen.

"That sounds good, as long as they're cheeseburgers."

"Is there any other way?" He grinned as he opened the fridge. "Why don't you go and shower and I'll get everything started. And then when you're done, you can make a salad and I'll grab a shower."

"Sounds like a plan to me," I said as I went to the bathroom. It felt nice being so domesticated with TJ, even if it didn't mean anything. In the bathroom, I gazed at myself in the mirror and gingerly touched my lips. The way he'd kissed me in the river had made me swoon. We'd kissed three times now. I didn't know what it meant, but I did know that I didn't want them to stop anytime soon.

I'd almost told him about my suspicion that Old Man Roberts was his dad, but my questioning hadn't triggered anything in him, so I'd decided to keep my mouth shut.

I pulled my damp clothes off and thought about TJ's tattoo. I couldn't wait to tell Emma everything about it and today in the water and the earth-shattering kiss. I hoped she liked TJ, and I wondered if she'd like any of the other guys. I had a feeling that she would think that Brandon was hot, but I didn't know his deal with Mindy. I turned the faucet on and stepped into the shower with so many thoughts in my head.

"La la, the sun is shining," I sang as the warm water cascaded down my back, "and I am driving my car down the road of love." I giggled at my made-up song. "My beau is handsome; his blue eyes sparkle, and he's all I need." I grabbed the body wash, giddiness taking over.

"Oooh," I exclaimed as a new idea hit me, and I began to flesh out my idea to the showerhead. "A story focused on a middle-aged blue-eyed cowboy, who's been waiting on his first love to find him again." My entire body was shaking as the ideas came crashing through my brain. "Shane," I said excitedly. "I'm going to call the lead character Shane." This was going to be amazing. I hadn't been this excited to write something in ages.

A banging on the door made me freeze.

"What is it?" I called out.

"Annie just rang me," TJ shouted through the door. "She wants to know if you still want to meet later this evening in the town square. I told her I'd ask and let her know."

I wanted to meet up with the ladies but didn't want to go out again. I wanted to spend a nice, cozy evening inside with TJ. "Maybe invite her and the other ladies to goat yoga," I called out as I grabbed the bottle of shampoo and poured it into the palm of my hands. "Tell them we can discuss everything after the class." I rubbed the shampoo into my scalp and scrubbed.

"Okay, sounds good."

I washed and conditioned my hair before I decided to

shave my legs. I planned on inviting TJ to share a bed with me in the evening so he didn't have to sleep on the couch again. I would make a wall of pillows between us, but just in case our legs touched, I wanted to make sure mine weren't stubbly. I would let him know that we wouldn't even be allowed to kiss in bed, though I wasn't sure how much I'd be able to enforce that. I very much wanted to kiss him. I very much wanted to fall asleep in his arms with my head on his chest. But I didn't want to cross those blurry lines. Plus, I had a feeling I'd be up half the night putting my new ideas down. I needed to ask TJ if I could borrow his computer. Maybe he would even read some of the scenes with me so I could hear how they sounded. That would be cool.

I stepped out of the shower, grabbed one of the thick, fluffy white towels, and wrapped it around my body.

I quickly dried my body, pulled on my pj's, wrapped the towel around my head, and exited the bathroom. TJ was sitting on the couch, rubbing Apple's stomach, and shouting at the TV. I'd never understand why guys shouted at the TV while watching sports; it's not like the players can hear you.

"Good shower?" he asked, shifting over on the couch to make room for me. Apple looked up to see who had taken her daddy's attention away from her, and I was pleased to see her tail wagging as I approached.

"Yes, thanks." I smiled at him shyly. "I'm so hungry. Do you want me to make fries with the burgers and salad?"

"You around all that oil?" He chuckled and shook his head. "I think not."

"I won't burn down your cabin, Teej. I promise."

"I only have the one cabin. I don't want none," he said, leaning back, his eyes crinkled. "But if you want fries, I can make them."

"I'll even peel the potatoes." I ran the towel back and forth against my hair to dry it. "Oh, and I was thinking that you should sleep in the bed tonight. We'll build a barricade down the middle so we both stay on our own sides."

"You don't trust me to stay on my side?" His voice was husky and filled with humor, and I looked up at him through lowered lashes. Was he teasing me, or was he upset? As soon as I saw the look on his face, I knew he was teasing. That was the thing about TJ; he was always good-hearted and made me laugh.

"No, I don't." I wagged my finger at him while giving him my best stern face. These were my favorite moments with TJ: joking around, laughing, and being goofy. "In fact, I think I've half a mind to call your mother and tell her."

"Oh no, not my mother." He mock shuddered and jumped off the couch. He fell to his knees and pleaded with me. "Please don't call my mama. She couldn't deal with another conversation about me being a naughty boy."

"You're such a naughty boy." Laughter filled the air as we both enjoyed the lightness of the moment. TJ jumped back up and headed to the kitchen, Apple following behind him eagerly. I followed suit and draped the towel around my shoulders. The scent of burger meat wafted through the air, and I licked my lips as I sat at the island counter.

"Would you like cheddar, American, or brie on your burger?"

"Brie? Fancy!" I jumped off the stool and headed behind the counter. "Do you have fig jam?" I opened one of the cupboard doors to look inside.

"Fig jam?" He looked confused. "Is that a thing?"

"Yes, it goes well with brie." I grinned at him. "Normally, I have it on a crusty baguette, but I bet it's amazing on a burger as well."

"Oh, hmm." He looked thoughtful for a few moments and opened another cupboard drawer. He pulled out two bottles and handed them to me. One was Smucker's strawberry preserves, and the other was orange marmalade. I stared at him, wondering if this was a joke.

"What's this?" I asked as I took the bottles.

"Jams." He shrugged. "I don't have fig jam, but these should work, right?"

"Well, no. Strawberry jam is not the same as fig jam." I giggled as I looked around the kitchen. "Anything I can help with?" I noticed Apple was hanging out next to the dishwasher, her brown eyes on our every movement. "No, Apple, no special treats today. But maybe your daddy will let you have a small treat," I whispered to her.

"She's going to start to look like a treat if I keep giving them to her." He mock growled and then opened another cupboard. He took out a small bully stick and handed it to me. "Here, you can give this to her, but only because her little nose is most probably going crazy with the smell of the beef."

"Aw, who spoils their dog?" I winked at him as I bent down to pet a now eager Apple. I motioned for her to sit before handing her the bully stick. She grabbed it from me, ran into the living room area, and lay on the rug. She held the stick in her two front paws and started chewing on it.

"I may or may not spoil my dog." He opened a bread box and pulled out some burger buns. "You want them toasted?" He stared over at me. "And do you want brie?"

"I will have American, please. Toasted, yes. Do you have mustard, mayonnaise, and ketchup?"

"Is my name Travis James Wyatt?" he asked, and I laughed.

"You sound like a country music star." I lowered my

voice and pretended to strum a guitar. "My name is Travis, da da da dum. I like to sing and play the drum," I sang. "I like the country. I have a goat. I'm a single man. But I don't own a boat." I rapped my fingers against the countertop, and he laughed.

"That sounds like a blues song," TJ said, grinning. "If I were a country music star, I'd be singing something more like this: Took my Ford pickup with my dog in the back, went to find my lady, we're going to the track. She's so purrt-tyyy. She's so kind. These lovely nights in Georgia are always on my mind." His voice was low and gravelly, and I stared at him in shock. Since when did TJ have a nice singing voice?

"That was so good. Have you been holding out on me?" I narrowed my eyes and tried to ignore the flutter in my heart as he stared at me. "Since when can you sing like that? And those lyrics were pretty cool, too. You should move to Nashville. You've got the voice, the looks, the—"

"I've got the looks?" His eyes gazed into mine teasingly. "Are you saying I'm good-looking, Pippa?"

"I mean, I'm not saying that you're not?" I teased him right back. "You're not the Hunchback of Notre Dame."

"Well, I'm glad to hear that." He opened the oven, grabbed an oven mitt, and placed the buns on a tray. "I'll put that on my Tinder app profile: My best friend says I'm not as bad as the Hunchback of Notre Dame."

"Ha ha. Very funny." I shook my head, my brain whizzing with questions about what he'd said. "Are you on any dating apps?"

"No." He looked at me. "Are you?"

"Huh?"

"Oh, yeah..." He groaned. "I almost forgot about your failed engagement."

"Don't call it that. That sounds awful."

"What shall I call it then? A winning engagement?" He cocked his head to the side and darted out of the way as I went to punch him in the shoulder.

"No way." I glared at him. "Is it horrible that I'm so glad that I caught him cheating on me?" I waited to see if TJ had any reaction to what I said. "Not that it didn't hurt, but it was like someone threw a bucket of cold water over me and woke me up. It was like I'd been in a fugue state and wasn't aware of my true reality. Does that make sense?"

"Yes, perfect sense."

"Trust me when I say that Stephan Snothead is the man I will always be thankful got away." I silently thanked my lucky stars that I escaped marrying that man. "Can you imagine if I became Pippa Snothead?"

"No, I never would have been able to stop teasing you, Mrs. Snothead."

"Ugh. I wonder if we ever would have become friends again if I hadn't shown up?" I bit down on my lip. I didn't want to get emotional, but it was still on my mind that TJ had cut me off (granted, he had a good reason), and I couldn't stop thinking about the fact that we may never have made up if I hadn't made my way to Montana.

"I know you think that I wouldn't have reached out," He said, casting his eyes toward me. "And I can't say that I would have reached out soon. Maybe not even next year, but I would have reached out, Pips. You've always been on my mind. You're literally on me." He chuckled. "You're the only person in the world that knows everything about me."

"Really?" I shook my head in disbelief.

"You're the only one that knows about my dad. I haven't told anyone here about the fact that my dad isn't my real dad and that my biological dad could be in this state somewhere."

"Not even Jack?" I stared at him in shock. Jack was his best friend. They were so close, and I knew that they had a friendship I'd never be able to have with him. The bromance was something that a man and a woman could never really have.

"Not even Jack." He shook his head. "He is my best friend here. He's changed my life. But we don't talk about those things. I guess, as men, there are certain things we don't talk about."

"Like Kaye pretending to be pregnant with his baby?"

"You know about that?" He looked surprised. "But yes, we've never discussed Kaye. Just like I never discussed our broken friendship. Or anyone we date. Or my dad." His lips thinned. "Maybe that's not healthy. Maybe we should be able to talk about things like that. But that's just not our friendship. Jack is a real cowboy. He's fun and open in so many ways, but he is a man who is one with his ranch. His father basically let him take over the running of the ranch when he turned twenty-one."

"Oh? Is his dad old?"

"No. Luke is really into racing horses and wants to spend more time going to races and focusing on that stuff, so Jack has taken over the day-to-day."

"So he doesn't date at all?" My eyes widened. Jack was gorgeous, and from what I could tell, he was a bit of a flirt. Was it possible he didn't date at all?

"Why do you care?" TJ's voice was grumpy all of a sudden. "Are you asking because you want to—"

"Oh, TJ, no, I'm not interested in dating any of your friends. I think that's kinda obvious, don't you?"

"Why do you say that?"

"Because we just kissed earlier today." I put my hands on my hips, even as my face burned. "Really?"

"So you kinda like me?"

"Maybe." I stuck my tongue out at him. "What's so funny?"

"You are." He grabbed my hands, pulled me toward him and gave me a quick kiss on the lips. "I maybe kinda like you too. Now scoot, go and watch TV, and let me focus on the food. Dinner will be served in about twenty minutes." He nudged me out of his way.

"Can I change the channel?" I asked as I made my way to the couch. "I'm not into football."

"Not that ultimatum show again."

"We can do *Love is Blind* or *Too Hot To Handle* instead if you want."

He groaned in response as I changed the TV channel. "I'll take that as a response that I can watch what I want." I sat back, got comfortable, and patted the cushion next to me for Apple to join me. She grabbed her bully stick, jumped up, and snuggled in. Even though I had *Too Hot To Handle* on the screen, all I wanted to do was look at TJ as he puttered around the kitchen. He was so cute and fun and seemed like he was a good chef as well. I grabbed my phone to text Emma, realizing that if I just sat there staring at TJ, I was going to look like a creeper.

Pippa: What are you doing?

Emma: Packing for this trip. I cannot believe I'm going to Montana.

Pippa: I'm so excited to see you. You will love it.

Emma: I hope so. It's not like it's Hawaii.

Pippa: True, but it's just as beautiful.

Emma: Suuurreee. Hey, I was thinking we could take a trip to England when we're done in Montana. Now that I'm not working, I have time. We can go rowing on the Avon, and you can pretend that you're the ghost of William Shake-speare, and we can watch some plays and eat bangers and mash and spotty dick.

Pippa: And toad in the hole.

Emma: And black pudding.

Pippa: And haggis.

Emma: We're going to be fat at the end of the trip.

Pippa: HAHA. Just a little bit. I miss you. Can't wait to see you.

"What's so funny?" TJ interrupted my thoughts as I laughed loudly at Emma's texts.

"Oh, I was just texting with Emma and she was saying we should visit England after our time in Paradise Valley. Now that she has no job, she has time to travel, and we were just listing all the different foods we would eat."

"You're going to go to England?" The smile he was giving me was forced and not genuine happiness.

"Yeah, you know I've always wanted to visit Stratford-upon-Avon. Who knows, maybe I'll even find a job in theater in the UK?" My stomach churned at the thought. Once upon a time, the possibility of getting a job in England would have been the dream, but now, I didn't want to move there. I wanted to visit, of course, but I didn't want to be away from TJ. Not that far away. Not that I would tell him that. I didn't want him to think I was a stage-five clinger.

OMG! I could imagine what everyone in Paradise Valley would say. "Did you hear about that Pippa Chase? She ran away from her fiancé in New York, showed up at TJ Wyatt's ranch in a wedding dress, begging him to marry her. They shared a couple kisses, and now she won't leave." I shuddered at the thought. How embarrassing would that be?

"You'd move to England?" TJ grabbed two plates and slammed them down on the counter. "I mean, I guess you might get a job with Andrew Lloyd Webber."

"Yeah, that would be so cool. Maybe he'll think I'm super talented." I wanted to roll my eyes. Andrew Lloyd Webber wouldn't even hire me for free. I wasn't that good. Not yet, at least.

"That's because you are." TJ's voice was gruff. "I mean, I want you to follow your dreams. When are you guys going?"

"Going?" I stared at him. "You mean to London?"

"Yeah." He nodded. "Just trying to figure out if I should get the blow-up mattress or if I'll have my bed back soon."

"I already said you can share the other side of the bed with me." My voice was stilted. "But if you want me to find somewhere else to stay, I can. I don't want to be an inconvenience." Well, that was a new record. We'd gone from laughing and flirting to tension in the air within ten minutes.

"That's not what I said." He sighed. "I was just saying that I think you will really flourish in London and that—"

"I didn't say I'm going tomorrow, TJ. I don't even know if the trip will happen. And that's all it would be, a trip." I rubbed Apple's belly. "I was just saying that Emma is coming, and she suggested that we visit London at some point."

"Guess you're over Paradise Valley already, huh?"

"No, I'm not." I got off the couch and walked over to TJ in the kitchen so we could be face to face. "I love being in Paradise Valley. It's beautiful and special, and I love being here with you. This town is amazing. Shoots, if I had the money, I'd buy the local theater and set up shop here. But I don't have the money. So that's not a possibility. But just know, TJ, that I love Paradise Valley."

"You love it?" he asked, his eyes twinkling as I stopped a few feet from him. There was so much innuendo laced into his question it was almost as if he had asked if I loved him, which I knew he hadn't, of course, because that would be crazy.

"Yeah." I cocked my head to the side. "I really do." And even though we were talking about the town, I was also talking about him. He'd always been the one for me. He'd always been the one to look out for me. To care for me. To make me want to follow my dreams. He backed me up, even when I'd been crazy, goofy, or maybe not making the best decisions. He was the sort of man that everyone deserved to have in their corner. He was my best friend. But I also knew I wanted more. I wanted to spend the rest of my life with this man.

I thought about the letter in my handbag. The letter no one knew about. The letter I'd never given. The letter that had been one of the most honest I'd ever written. I needed to share it with TJ. I needed him to see who I was and the thoughts in my brain. Though, I wasn't going to do it tonight.

Tonight, I just wanted to relax and enjoy burgers. Tonight, I just wanted us to be us.

Chapter Thirty

T J

Dear Pippa,

It has been nine hundred and fifty-five days since I last saw you. Isn't that crazy? It's also been that long since I saw my dad as well. He's really taken the divorce badly. Mom says we just need to give him time. I miss him. I was hoping he would come and take me to a baseball game, and we'd talk about how he never made a home run, even though he played baseball for seven years. How is that even possible?

How are your mom and dad? Did I tell you about the time I caught your parents *kissing in the kitchen? It was so gross, but I suppose that means they still love each other, so that's good. They won't be getting divorced, and you won't have to deal with your dad being depressed over his marriage ending.*

I really hope to see you soon.

TJ

"Just be cool, TJ," I mumbled under my breath as I stood inside the bathroom next to the door. I was overthinking everything that was going on with Pippa. I'd almost bitten her head off when she'd mentioned visiting England with her friend Emma. When she'd told me about the trip, all I'd been able to think about was her leaving me. Her not being here. Her not rubbing Apple's belly and looking at her with such a doting expression. I didn't want her to go. And now it was bedtime, and we were sharing the bed, and I had to be a gentleman. Well, that wasn't true. I didn't have to be one. I wanted to be one. Because I knew that Pippa was special. And I knew that she deserved respect. I didn't want to push her to do anything she wasn't ready for.

I didn't want to push the physical, the mental, or the emotional. Not until she was over Stephan completely, and I knew that could take time. She'd been upset that I hadn't come to find her and repair our relationship, but I had questions as well. What if she hadn't caught Stephan cheating? Would she have gone ahead with the wedding? Would she have vowed to love him forever? Given herself to him on their wedding night? The thought made me sick.

I slowly opened the door and stepped out. Pippa was sitting back against the headboard, a book in her lap, Apple was on her lap sleeping, and there was a stack of cushions down the middle of the bed. I tried not to laugh at the sight. She looked up from the book and met my eyes.

"Good shower?"

"Yup." I walked toward the bed and stopped. "I'm going to grab a glass of water. Do you want anything?"

"No, thanks." She shook her head. "I was just going to read a couple more chapters, but if the light bothers you, I can stop."

"Not at all." I grabbed a glass and filled it before heading back to the bed and crawling onto my side. Apple opened one eye lazily, glanced at me, and then closed it. She didn't even attempt to move onto my side. "What are you reading?" I asked her as I took a sip of the water. Her hair was hanging down her back, and she was wearing a loose white shirt with a huge raccoon on it. I was surprised she'd added that top to her collection when we went shopping.

"*The Inheritance Games*." She held the book cover up. "I saw a Bookstagram post about how good it was, so I decided to give it a try."

"A Bookstagram post?" I shook my head. "No idea what that is."

"You've heard of Instagram, right?" She smiled as she laid the book to the side. I tried not to notice how bright her eyes were or how pink and luscious her lips looked.

"Of course." I rolled my eyes. "Where women go to show off their best twerks."

"TJ! That's not all that's on Instagram. There are many of us, including myself, who go on to talk about books that we've read and enjoyed. In fact, it was Emma that really got me into it. There are thousands of people that spend their time making really cute videos and posts of books they've reviewed and stuff."

"Cool. Cool." I nodded, finally getting it. "And I take it you like the books you've seen reviewed?"

"I've found some really amazing books, and I take it you still don't love reading?"

"I don't mind reading." I pulled the sheets down and got under them. "But no, I don't do it for fun."

"You don't know what you're missing."

"You could say that about many things." I shifted back into the pillow. "Um, can we move this big cushion from in front of my face? I can't even see you to talk to you."

"That's fine," she said, plucking the cushion up and throwing it to the end of the bed. "Is that better?"

"Much better." I smiled. I could smell her strawberry scent again and tried to ignore it. "So, what do we have planned for the next few days?"

"Goat yoga and lunch with Jack's family on Sunday, and then Emma comes," she said excitedly. "I think you're going to love her."

"Hopefully, she will love me as well." Pippa shifted her body so she lay back in the bed as well. She rolled onto her side so we were eye to eye. I wondered what she was thinking about. I wondered how often she still thought about our idyllic childhood friendship. I knew she thought about it sometimes, but I wondered if the memories were as vivid and special to her. I hoped so.

"She will," she answered with a yawn. "What do you know about Old Man Roberts?"

"Old Man Roberts?" I asked her, surprised that she'd brought him up again. "Not a lot. I mean, he's a local rancher. He used to work at Jack's dad's ranch for years. He's really close to the Marleys. I see him around town and he'll do work around here every now and then. He's a good teacher. He's shown me a lot."

"Aw, that's awesome." Pippa's eyes were gleaming now. "I'm so glad you two are close."

"I wouldn't say we were close. He's just a man-around-town kind of guy. I don't know him that well."

"Does he have children?" she asked. "Or are they not in town?"

"I don't think he has any kids. Why the obsession with him? Don't tell me you have one of your crushes on him?"

"What do you mean one of my crushes? I don't have crushes on every man I meet. Especially old men."

"You used to be in love with George Clooney."

"Old Man Roberts is not George Clooney, TJ. If he was, then yes, maybe I'd have a crush on him. But seeing as he isn't, then no, I do not have a crush."

"Just checking. I know you have weird taste." I winked at her, and she reached over and hit me on the shoulder. I grabbed her wrist and pushed her back, and we both laughed. "You do have weird taste." I reached my hand down so I could tickle her.

"TJ! No, don't tickle me."

"Admit you have weird taste," I said as she giggled uncontrollably, her body shifting back and forth.

"Never!" she screamed. Apple let out a large sigh and jumped off the bed, not wanting to be a part of our antics, I assumed.

I grabbed Pippa's other wrist and pinned her to the bed. I looked down into her face, and my heart expanded as I stared at her beauty.

"TJ, stop." She stuck her tongue out at me. "I will never admit anything."

"Okay then," I said, letting go of her wrists and then

gathering her into my arms. Her face was mere inches from mine now. "I don't want to talk about other men anyway. In fact, I don't want to talk at all." My lips hovered over hers, and I closed the inches between us and pressed them against hers gingerly, waiting to see how she would react. Her eyes danced with glee as she moved her hands around my neck and deepened the kiss.

Chapter Thirty-One

P ippa

Dear TJ,

Suzi and I went into Manhattan to audition for a commercial. We thought we were going to hit it big on TV, but it was so sketch. It was in this old building with these older-looking men. And one of them told Suzi to put on a bikini and pose on a couch. My Spidey senses told me something was off, so I grabbed her, and we ran down the stairs and out of the building.

Suzi said I ruined her chance of making thousands of dollars. I said I saved her from becoming a statistic. Then she told me that *some guy approached her at Popeye's, and that's how she found out about the audition. I will never listen to Suzi again. She always has these crazy ideas that she thinks are going to make us famous or rich, and they never do.*

She laughed when I told her she needs to be sensible like me. RUDE.

Anyway, do you remember when we had that lemonade stand in Prospect Park and I juggled for money, but then I couldn't juggle any of the balls, and we made no money. That was a fun day but sad.

Hope Florida is great.

Pippa

XOXO

TJ and I settled into a pattern over the next couple of days. He tended to his ranch, and I worked on my play. He'd cook dinner, and I'd do the dishes. We'd watch some TV and play a board game, and then, at bedtime, we'd go to our respective sides. We'd kiss for a few minutes, then he'd roll back onto his side and fall asleep. In the morning, TJ would be out of bed before I even awoke. Every day, he'd have coffee ready, and when he took a break from his duties on the ranch, we'd go on a walk with Apple and Donkey. It was a nice routine, and I was starting to love it.

The only thing that irked me slightly was that TJ stayed on his side of the bed every night. I wanted him to hug me and hold me tight. I wanted to fall asleep in his arms and kiss all night long, but I knew that was unrealistic. Emma told me she was shocked that he hadn't attempted more. She said that every other guy she knew would have been begging for it to go further, which I knew was true. I'd dated enough men to know that they usually weren't satisfied with just kissing.

I didn't know what it meant, though. I didn't know if TJ wanted more or if he was respecting my wishes. Or if he didn't want to push it because he didn't want me to get the wrong impression of our relationship. Maybe he was scared I'd become too attached if things were to go further.

"Morning, sleepyhead." TJ headed toward me in a gray shirt and black shorts. "Ready for goat yoga this morning?"

"Yes!" I sat up in the bed and took the mug from him gratefully. "Thank you so much."

"You're welcome." He sat on the edge of the bed. "I have some toast for you as well. You need to eat something before you work out this morning."

"You didn't have to make me food. I could make toast." I sipped on the coffee and stretched out my limbs. "How was your morning walk with Apple and Donkey?"

"They missed you. Donkey is also wondering who all his new friends are. Have you come up with names yet?"

"I figured we could see what their personalities were like today and then name them." I grinned and searched around for my phone. I needed to google goat yoga again. I'd forgotten exactly what to do, and seeing as I was teaching the class, I would have to figure it out. "I'm so excited for the class today. Seems like a lot of people are going to be here. You sure you don't mind us having it outside of the barn?"

"Not at all. You're doing this to help me and the ranch."

"I just want it to be a success," I said. "I want people to

come from far and wide for these classes." My panic set in as I realized I was actually going to have to teach this class. What was I thinking? Was I capable of teaching a goat yoga class that people would enjoy so much that they would tell their friends? I wasn't even good at yoga, let alone goat yoga. However, I was good at creating experiences. I would create an experience that people would be talking about for years to come. It would be amazing. It had to be.

"It will be great," TJ said and stood up. "I mean, you're the yoga queen. People will love it."

"Yeah." My throat felt dry. "Now was not the time to tell TJ that not only was I not the yoga queen, I wasn't even the princess—I wasn't even in the royal court. If anything, I was the villain. I was the one they wanted to banish. But maybe I was being unfair to myself. I'd taken many yoga classes in New York; maybe I was more balanced now. Maybe...

"Okay, I'm going to go and finish setting up the mats outside. Jack just texted and he will be here in a few minutes to help me set up."

"Oh, that's so sweet of him." I swung my legs out from under the covers and stood up. "Is he going to join us?"

"No, but he's going to take some photos for our Instagram account."

"What Instagram account?"

"I'm joking." He laughed. "But he is going to take photos to send to his sister. She'll send them to her friends, and who knows, maybe we'll have even more people at the class next week."

"Uh, yeah, sounds great." I nodded and headed to the bathroom. "Let me have a shower and get ready, and I'll come out and help you guys in a bit."

"Sounds good." He smiled at me. "And don't forget to eat your toast."

"I won't." I entered the bathroom, closed the door behind me, and locked it. I leaned back against the wood and closed my eyes. My heart was racing, and I was starting to feel panicked. What had I done? I knew I had good intentions, and it was a good idea. I just wasn't the one to be carrying through the idea. How on earth was I going to teach goat yoga? Especially to so many people.

"Okay, who's coming?" I mumbled to myself and counted on my fingers. "Mindy, Charlotte, Brielle, Kaci, Kaye, Annie, Ruthie, Katie. Oh my days, Pippa, that's eight people." I wish I could say the sweating I was doing was from the steam of the hot shower, but I'd yet to turn it on. I took a couple of deep breaths and reassured myself, "It'll be fine. It will be fine." I unlocked my phone, and my fingers scrambled across the screen. I went to search and entered *goat yoga*. A bunch of cute photos popped up with stunning women in fashionable athletic gear posing with goats, and I smiled at the photos until I realized that I was not going to look like that when I did yoga. My hair was going to frizz in seconds, and I wasn't the sort of woman that glowed when working out. I was a woman that sweated.

"Okay, okay, look up some poses," I said, my mind going blank as I thought about yoga poses. I couldn't even remember the basic poses. How was I going to pull this off? It seemed impossible. Everyone was going to think I was a fraud. And TJ had put so much into this. He'd gotten goats. Mats. Snacks. Water bottles. He'd gone all out to help me make this a success.

"Pippa, you can do this," I lectured myself as I called Emma. I needed a pep talk from her and perhaps some tips as well. Emma loved yoga. She would be able to tell me what to do. The phone rang five times before she answered.

"Hey, Pips, what's going on? I'm just running around getting some last things for the trip." She sounded like she was out of breath. "Did you know how much cowboy boots cost?"

"You're buying cowboy boots?" I laughed. "No wonder we're best friends. I bought some as well and let me tell you, they are so uncomfortable. I wouldn't waste your money."

"Then how do all these cowboys wear them all the time?"

"Because they are actually cowboys and break them in quickly, and their feet are used to them. I mean, get some if you want, but I don't think it's worth it, seeing as you won't even be here that long."

"True, true, so to what do I owe this call?"

"I need your help. I'm in big trouble," I whispered. I knew TJ was no longer in the cabin, but I didn't want him to hear anything, just in case he came back.

"Oh no, what happened now, Pippa? You didn't tell Stephan you'd get back with him, did you?"

"No way," I screeched. "Are you out of your mind?"

"Just checking. So what is it?"

"I'm teaching a goat yoga class today."

"You're what? I thought I heard you say you were teaching a yoga class today." She laughed.

"I am."

"What? Are you out of your mind? Pippa, you can barely walk a straight line sober, let alone teach a yoga class."

"I'm doing it to help TJ. We're trying to raise money for him to build his cabins. He needs a hundred grand to be able to qualify for the loan and he doesn't have enough."

"Oh boy." Emma was quiet for a few moments. "Couldn't you have put on a play instead?"

"I mean, yes, but he has this cute goat, Donkey, and I remembered how you were into goat yoga and paid so much money and I thought that would be a great idea, but I didn't really think about me actually teaching it." I groaned. "And everyone is going to be here in an hour and I don't know anything."

"Oh, Pippa, just explain to everyone that you don't really know yoga and apologize and—"

"Are you out of your mind?" I cut her off. "There is no way I'm letting TJ know that I can't do this. He has gone out of his way to help me get this off the ground. I don't want him to know that I suck."

"Pippa, I think that—"

"Emma, are you going to give me some tips, or do I need to hang up and look online again?"

"Oh, Pippa, I cannot believe you are dragging me into this. Can you remember any of the moves?"

"Um, maybe downward dog?"

"Okay, so start with some breathing techniques and meditation," she said thoughtfully. "Then chant."

"Chant? Do they do that in yoga?"

"Not really, it's meant to be peaceful, but I have been in some yoga classes where the teacher has us chant to find our inner warrior." She paused. "That wasn't really my favorite class because I went to find my zen, but it was an interesting experience. And I guess you can do that for a bit. You do like to chat."

"I like to talk about books and trashy TV shows and Shakespeare, not ooey-gooey earth stuff. I don't know that stuff. That's not me."

"Look, just say something like, 'Everyone, close your

eyes and picture yourself on an island or in a field or what-ever. You're naked and free and one with the earth. The earth is flowing through you and...'" She paused. "Well, you can add whatever you want. People eat that up."

"Okay, I can do that, and then I'll do downward dog." I paused. "But when do I add the goats?"

"I'd wait until the end," she said. "To be honest, I don't even know how that works. Like, are the goats trained beforehand?"

"Oh, man, I didn't even think about that." I froze. "They don't poop, do they?"

"Of course, they poop. Every living animal poops, or they die."

"I don't mean generally, Emma." I sighed. "I meant while they are doing yoga. They know not to poop then, right?"

"Hold on, let me call one of my goat friends and ask them." She laughed. "I have no clue, Pippa. I really wish that I did, but I honestly have no clue."

"This is going to be a hot mess, isn't it?" I said it as much to myself as it was to her. "What on earth was I thinking?"

"Just tell TJ that you made a mistake. Just tell him that —"

"I gotta go, Emma," I said quickly. "I'll see you in a couple of days." I hung up and went back to Google. I made my way to the toilet and sat down. I needed to teach myself to become a yoga teacher in forty-five minutes. And I needed to be so good that it would convince everyone to tell their friends and invite them to the next session.

I was dead meat. And I didn't know how I was going to pull this off. The only positive that could come out of the session would be a conversation with Annie. If I could get her to confirm that her husband was known as Lucky or that he collected horseshoes, I would all but confirm that TJ was his son. And that would be major. TJ would have his biological dad, he could start healing, and that was all I wanted for him. I wanted him to feel whole.

I failed him as a friend when we were younger, not realizing what had gone on. I wasn't going to fail him as a friend again.

Chapter Thirty-Two

T ᴶ

Dear Pippa,
Watch The Godfather. It is epic.
That is all.
TJ

"Good morning, everyone." Pippa beamed at the group as she stood on the black mat and looked around. Her long hair was tied back, and she was wearing black yoga pants and a hot-pink top that clung to her. She looked gorgeous, and I was almost tempted to join the class myself.

"Morning, Pippa," Annie spoke up from her mat at the

front. "Thank you for inviting us. I've never done yoga before."

"Well, you will love it," Pippa said as she put her hands together in a prayer gesture and then stood on one leg. She attempted to place the other leg against her stationary leg but stumbled slightly and put it back down. She blushed slightly and fluffed her hair. Hmm, I wasn't sure what that was about.

"I heard you made two hundred dollars this morning," Jack said from his seat next to me. "This goat yoga is a nice little money earner."

"It will be once I pay myself back for the mats and towels." I nodded. "Thanks for the goats."

"Any time." He grinned. "What's mine is yours and all that."

"We're not married." I laughed. "I think that only applies in marriages."

"It applies in families as well." He hit me on the shoulder. "You know you're like a brother to me."

"Same, bro." I sat back and looked at him. "Is it weird having Kaye here?" I nodded toward his ex. I never brought her up, and now I realized it was weird that he and I had been friends for so long and had never touched on deeper subjects.

"Honestly, no." He looked at the women on the mats. "It's been so long now. I was hurt back then. The lies were a lot to swallow, but she was young. I don't hold it against her." He shrugged. "We all make mistakes in life."

"I suppose that's true," I agreed. "I've made some in my life." I looked back at Pippa and watched as she told everyone to take a seat. She had such a kind, gentle aura around her. She always had. Never once in our friendship had I ever questioned who she was or how she felt about me as a friend. Even when we argued, she was never mean. I never should have believed what her mom had said. I never should have cut Pippa off. Yes, I'd been broken by my dad, but that wasn't Pippa's fault. I should have been straight up with her. I should have told her what her mom had said. I should have confided in her what I was thinking and feeling. I should have been direct. I'd wasted so many years not having her in my life because of that mistake.

"We all have." Jack looked at me thoughtfully. "What's got you looking so pensive?"

"Pensive?" I raised an eyebrow. "I didn't know I was looking pensive."

"You seem different this morning." He tapped his boot against the ground. "Everything okay with Pippa?"

"Great actually," I said softly. "She's amazing. We've —"

"Been knocking boots?" He winked at me, and I shook my head.

"Not at all. Pippa, well, Pippa is waiting for marriage. For her true love."

"Admirable." He looked at the class again. "I bet that couldn't have been easy for her relationships."

"Yeah, I guess not." I lowered my voice and ran my hands through my hair. "I love her," I said as I looked into Jack's green eyes. He blinked as he stared back at me, his eyes light with humor, his lips twitching. It was funny looking at Jack. Sometimes, I noticed some of my own mannerisms in him. I supposed that came from being friends with someone for so long.

"You're only just realizing that?"

"You knew?" I frowned. "But how?" I asked, truly in awe that he picked up on my feelings before I had.

"I saw the look you gave her as soon as we pulled up to

the ranch that day," he said. "Before she even said who she was. You knew."

"I mean, I kinda guessed. She still looked the same," I admitted with a nod. "I knew."

"Your eyes lit up, and you smiled, and I saw the look on your face. It wasn't there for long, but I saw it. The longing. The love. The pain." He shrugged. "She's your one."

"Poor timing though." I sighed. I was about to continue when an odd noise made me look back to Pippa. She was on her knees with her hands in front of her, and she was humming. But it was no ordinary sort of humming. It almost sounded like she was being strangled.

"What's happening?" Jack looked confused, and we stood up and moved closer to the barn.

"Ohhmmmmmmmmmm. We are one with the earth. We are children of the sky. We are dirt in human form. Ohmm-mmmm," Pippa sang out, and Jack and I exchanged glances. I shook my head, as I had no idea what was going on. I saw Mindy's eyes pop open as she looked around at the other women. So far, all the other women were still kneeling with their eyes closed.

"Lift up your right leg and stretch it out," Pippa said loudly as she lifted her right leg. Her entire body started shaking as she stretched it. "Ohhmmmmmm, we are here today to embrace our true beings, our inner child, our quests for love and life, ohmmmmmmmmm," she sang as her leg started shaking again.

"This is not like any yoga I've ever seen in my life before," Jack said. "But I guess it's different with goat yoga."

"Yeah, I guess so." I blinked as my brain scrambled, and I started thinking about our childhood. How Pippa had always fallen off of skateboards, how she'd never been able to do pull-ups, how she hadn't been able to walk across a balance beam without falling off. My heart thudded as I stared at her. It didn't seem to me that her equilibrium was any better today than when we were younger.

"When are the goats going to be added?" Kaci shouted at Pippa and looked back at me with a flirtatious smile.

"Soon," Pippa answered quickly. "Just as soon as we are one with the universe."

"I don't want to be one with the universe," Kaye said. "I want a goat on my back helping me to get rid of my—"

"Listen to the teacher, Kaye," Annie chastised her. "You're making me lose my zen."

"I never had any zen," Kaci shot back. Pippa's face flushed as her eyes opened. She looked up at me, and I saw her face was already red. Was she already out of breath? They hadn't even done much yet.

"We will be working with the goats soon." Pippa stood up. "Everyone stand up. We are now going to do a mountain pose, which is appropriate because we are in this beautiful setting with the mountains in the background. It reminds me of this—"

"No one cares," Kaci mumbled, and Mindy, Charlotte, and Brielle all gave her a dirty look.

"This is going to go down." Jack chuckled. "How many more minutes do you think before Kaci starts shouting?"

"Let's get the goats," I said quickly, and we headed for the barn as Pippa started chanting again. I grabbed Donkey and some of the other goats while Jack grabbed the ropes around the other ones. We headed back to the women, and Pippa was twirling her arms in the air, doing some sort of snakelike movement.

"Is she a certified yoga instructor?" Jack asked as he stopped behind me. I could hear the humor in his voice and see the sparkle in his eyes. He wasn't looking for an answer.

I pressed my lips together and tried not to laugh. "I hope I can return those mats and get my money back."

"Shall we put them all out of their misery?" he asked, and I shook my head deviously.

"No." There was a glint in my eyes as I winked at him. "Let's see how it goes once we introduce the goats." I cleared my throat. "Pippa, the goats are ready now," I spoke up, and she looked over at me with a weak smile. "Ready for them?"

"Sure." She nodded as she stared at the goats. "It's baa-baa time."

"Sheep say *baa*," Kaci shouted, and I looked over at Jack and nodded. We both let go of the goats simultaneously, which may have been a mistake. All the goats, except for Donkey, went running toward the women. I heard screeches, screams, and laughing. Pippa continued to sing as if chaos wasn't going on around her.

"Everyone, grab your goat."

"This goat is trying to kill me," Ruthie said as a goat brushed past her. She hobbled away from the mat, screaming, "Attack of the killer goats!"

"That would be a good movie." Jack grinned as we stood there. Then his jaw dropped as Pippa started yodeling. "Is she crazy?" Jack shook her head. "What is that noise?"

"Just Pippa being Pippa." I laughed and whistled loudly to get everyone's attention. "Ladies, the goats don't seem to be ready for the class, I'm afraid. And they have ruined Pippa's moment. I'm so sorry, Pippa." I could see the women looking at me like I was crazy. We all knew that the class had been ruined long before the goats had joined in, but no one was going to contradict me. "Jack, take the ladies to the cabin and I will make everyone some coffee."

"I need Irish whiskey in mine," Charlotte mumbled, and Brielle nodded in agreement.

"Take them inside, Jack, and I'll gather the goats with Pippa."

"Sounds like a plan." He nodded. "See you in a bit." He waved to the ladies. "Come on, follow me," he said as he headed toward the cabin. The goats walked away and chewed on grass and Pippa stood there with a deflated expression.

"Are you mad?" She looked down at the ground, her face beet red. "I messed up."

"I'm not mad." I grabbed her hand. "More confused as to why you'd offer to teach a goat yoga class when you obviously don't even know how to do yoga."

"I forgot I suck, then I remembered this morning, and it was too late."

"It could have been worse." I offered her a wide smile.

"Oh?"

"They could have pooped on everyone." I squeezed her hand, and she giggled. "Though I have a feeling you wouldn't have minded if Kaci had been one of those people."

"She's not exactly the nicest woman. Though I suppose this wasn't the best yoga class ever."

"Maybe not." I touched the side of her face and then kissed her cheek. "But I appreciate the sentiment. I know you were doing it to help me."

"I just want to make your dreams come true, TJ."

"You are, Pippa," I whispered under my breath. "Just you being here has made my life so much better."

Chapter Thirty-Three

P ippa

Dear TJ,

You know I have no interest in watching The Godfather. However, I will make a deal with you. I will watch it, if you watch How To Lose A Man In Ten Days.

Deal?

Pippa

Embarrassment and shame filled me as I walked back to the cabin with TJ. He'd been lovely about the class, but I knew he'd been laughing at me. I'd seen the looks he and Jack had given each other. What a mess it had all been. I'd been so nervous that I hadn't even been able to stand on one foot. What sort of yoga teacher had no balance? And then, when I could tell everyone was getting restless, I'd yodeled.

Who did I think I was, Maria from *The Sound of Music*? How cringey the whole thing had been, and now I had to face everyone. I wanted to tell TJ to send them all home, but I still hadn't had a conversation with Annie yet. I still hadn't confirmed that Old Man Roberts was TJ's dad. That would be the only thing that would make this all okay.

"It'll be fine, Pips." TJ's voice was filled with mirth as we got to the cabin, and all I could do was hang my head, still ashamed of myself for the mess of a class I'd tried to teach. I raised my head and walked into the cabin, even though I had my proverbial tail between my legs. Everyone was crowded in the kitchen and living room area, drinking coffee and eating the cinnamon rolls that Mindy had brought. They all turned to look at me as we entered, and I was about to apologize to everyone when Annie stepped forward.

"Jack explained to us how you were stressed out about the goats and that everything was his fault," she said, her face full of sympathy. "He said he didn't bring the right goats."

"He did?" I looked over at him, and he winked at me. "I mean, the goats were stressing me out a bit."

"Oh, I can just imagine," Annie said. "The next class will be better."

"Oh, yeah, indeed it will." *I won't be teaching it though,* I thought to myself as I smiled at Annie. "I hope you still had a good time."

"Oh, it's always nice coming out here to TJ's ranch. My husband and I love what he's done here."

"Oh?" I asked her. "You know this piece of land?"

"Do we know it?" Annie threw her head back and roared with laughter. "My husband and I sold the land to TJ. He's like the son we never had."

"Really?" I licked my lips. This was going perfectly. It was almost like a movie. I couldn't have written it better myself. "So, there's something I have to tell you," I said, looking at TJ. He was chatting with Charlotte and laughing, and I felt my heart swelling.

"What's that, dear?" Annie asked me as she took another bite of her pastry.

"So, it's about TJ and your husband," I whispered.

"Yes? What about them?"

"Does your husband consider himself lucky?" I asked her, my eyes boring into her. "Did he ever have the nickname Lucky?"

"Didn't you already ask me this?" She frowned as she shook her head. "I wouldn't say that he's particularly lucky, no."

"Does he like horseshoes?" I rubbed my forehead. Maybe she didn't know his old nickname. Maybe he stopped using it after he lost TJ's mom.

"Horseshoes?" she repeated after me, confused. "In what way?"

"Like, do you have a lot of them in your house?"

"I wouldn't say that, no." She shook her head. "In the stables, yes, but not in the house."

"Okay." I took a deep breath. I was going to have to come out with it. She was obviously not going to make this easy on me. "Have you ever considered the fact that your husband may have children that he created before you both got together?" I really hoped he hadn't been cheating on her when he met TJ's mom.

"Robert?" She stopped eating, her eyes widening. "My Robert?"

"Yes," I said softly. "I don't mean to spring this on you, but I think that—"

"My Robert can't have children." She cut me off as she shook her head. "He had an accident as a child. I won't go into details, but it meant he could never be a father. I knew that before I married him. His girlfriend before me, she left him when she found out, you see. So he was sensitive about it. He told me on our second date." She paused. "Was there a reason why you were asking me this?"

"No." My stomach sank at her words. "No reason at all." I was glad I hadn't gotten his hopes up. I was glad that I hadn't told him my suspicions. I wasn't sure who I thought I was. I was certainly no *Harriet the Spy* or *Miss Marple*. There I was, thinking I'd solved the case and hadn't even been close.

Chapter Thirty-Four

T^J

Dear Pippa,

I wanted to say thank you. I know I'm not one of those emotional guys, but having you in my life all these years has been the one constant I've always known I could count on.

Never change, Pips.

It's surreal that we've been friends for all these years, even though we haven't seen each other in ages.

Now back to your regular scheduled programming.

TJ

. . .

"We don't have to stay at Jack's parents' place for long." I looked over at Pippa, who looked despondent in my passenger seat. She'd been down ever since the failed goat yoga event. I'd tried to tell her it wasn't a big deal, but she seemed to be taking it poorly.

"No, we should stay for as long as you want." She offered me a small smile. "It was very nice of them to invite me over."

"I'm sure we'll have fun and you'll get to meet his entire family. They're lovely people."

"I'm glad," she said, her eyes widening as we approached Marley's ranch. She seemed taken by the upside-down horseshoe sign as we drove through the open gate. "This place is huge," she said.

"Yeah, the Marley's are quite well-off." I laughed at her awestruck expression. "Welcome to Horseshoe Ranch."

"Horseshoe Ranch?" she questioned, an excited and surprised look on her face. "As in horseshoes?"

"Yes, as in horseshoes, the shoes horses wear on their hooves." I wondered if she had hit her head during her failed attempt at goat yoga. "I think I told you, Luke, Jack's dad, is really into horse racing. He wanted to concentrate on that. That's why he stepped back from the day-to-day stuff." I pulled up outside the main house and jumped out of the truck. I was headed around to open Pippa's door when she jumped out and ran to the wrap-around porch.

"There are horseshoes everywhere." She looked left and right so quickly I was afraid she'd give herself whiplash. "Is Jack's dad really into horse*shoes*?"

"I don't know." I shrugged.

"I mean, does he have a lot of horseshoes in the house and stuff?"

"I guess he does." I was starting to be concerned for Pippa's well-being, wondering why she was asking all these questions. "I guess he considers them good omens."

"He thinks they're good luck, huh?" She was grinning now, and I was still confused.

"I guess. Come on, let's go inside." I held my hand out for her, and she practically skipped as we made our way to the front door. "You're not still upset about the goat yoga, are you?"

"No, no one was mad at me. Jack saved the day." She smiled. "That was really nice of him."

"Yeah, he's a good guy," I said as I lifted the horseshoe knocker and knocked on the door.

"TJ, there you are." Mrs. Marley answered the door, a warm smile on her face as she gave me a quick hug. She looked over at Pippa and reached out to hug her as well. "You must be TJ's friend Pippa. I've heard so much about you. I'm Wendy Marley, Jack's mom."

"Hi, it's nice to meet you." Pippa looked around the house as we stepped inside. "You have a beautiful home."

"Thanks, it has been in my husband's family for generations."

"Wow." Pippa looked at me with wide eyes. "That's cool."

"Let's head into the family room where everyone is," Mrs. Marley said as we followed her. Pippa looked around the old homestead in awe, oohing and aahing at everything she saw. Before getting to the family room, we entered the kitchen, where Jack and his dad were sitting at the table, playing dominoes. "Jennie and her husband, Josh, took the kids to the park but will be back soon."

"Would you like something to drink, Pippa?" Mrs. Marley asked. "We have alcoholic and nonalcoholic options."

"Just some water, please," Pippa said as Mrs. Marley turned her attention to me.

"TJ, why don't you introduce Pippa to everyone, and I'll get her some water and you a beer."

"Sounds good. Thanks." I brought Pippa to the table and introduced her. "Mr. Marley, I'd like you to meet Pippa." He stood up, held his hand out, and grinned.

"Nice to meet you, Pippa. I'm Lucas Marley. My friends call me Luke."

"Nice to meet you too." Pippa smiled eagerly. "Did you ever go by any other name or nickname?" she asked him, and I was surprised at her directness toward this man she didn't know.

"Nickname? Not in years, I haven't."

"Oh, okay." Pippa looked disappointed but quickly changed her expression as she saw me looking at her. Mrs. Marley brought our drinks over and handed them to us. She looked at her husband with a loving expression, then back at Pippa.

"They used to call him Lucky Luke Marley back when he was younger because everything he bet on always won."

"They did?" Excitement crossed her face again, and she gave me a look. I had no idea what she was trying to communicate to me. "Did you hear that, TJ? They used to call Mr. Marley *Lucky*?" She stressed the last word, and it was then that I understood what she was intimating. My heart stopped for a second, and then I dismissed the idea. There was no way that Mr. Marley was my dad. There was no way. He was married. He had two kids. Two grandkids.

Jack was my age. I shook my head at Pippa to get her to stop it, but she ignored me.

"So, Mr. Marley, how long have you and Mrs. Marley been together?" she asked him, and I tried not to roll my eyes.

"I think it's been thirty-five years now," he said with a small smile. "She's the love of my life."

"Oh." Disappointment crossed Pippa's face, and I realized she'd really thought she'd found my dad.

"We did have a little break though." Mrs. Marley looked at her husband. "About six months apart, right before we got married."

"Oh?" Pippa's eyebrows rose. "When was that?"

"Right before I was born, right, Mama?" Jack laughed at her scandalized expression.

"Yes, your dad and I fell pregnant pretty soon after we got back together." She looked at Mr. Marley and smiled. "Your father had to decide whether horses and other women meant more to him than me."

"And I chose you, my dear." Mr. Marley walked over and kissed her on the cheek.

"And when he chose me, we were both pretty happy." She squeezed his hand and they shared a warm smile.

"And we've lived happily ever after." There was a doting expression on his face.

"We have." She smiled and looked over at Jack. Jack's expression changed, and I watched as he tapped his fingers nervously against the tabletop. He took a deep breath and stood up.

"You dated someone during that time, didn't you, Dad?"

"I did have a summer romance. Your mom knows all about it, and it's water under the bridge." Mr. Marley nodded. "She was a pretty young thing, from New York, in fact. She was traveling through the national parks and I showed her around. She left and your mother and I got back together."

"And I don't have any regrets that he took that time to himself. We both needed that time," Mrs. Marley said, her eyes on Pippa. "It is time, I think." She directed that statement at Jack.

"Time for what?" Mr. Marley asked, looking into the kitchen. "Is the roast done?"

"Not yet, dear." She shook her head. "Jack, I think you should explain."

"Okay, Mama." He looked at his dad and then at me. "So years ago, I thought I was going to become a doctor and I was thinking about going into genetics."

"I remember," Mr. Marley said. "When you were in college."

"Yes." Jack nodded. "Anyway, long story short, that led to me doing a DNA test to see my ancestry."

"What did you find out? You never mentioned any of this before," his dad said.

"I found out there was a match for a possible half-sib."

"What?" Mr. Marley frowned. "What do you mean? Wendy—" His mouth formed the shape of the letter *o*. "This doesn't make any sense. I would've known if Wendy were pregnant before we got married."

"It wasn't Mrs. Marley," Pippa interrupted. "It was you, Mr. Marley."

"Excuse me, what are you saying?" He looked as shocked as I felt. I looked over at Jack, who nodded, and I felt a barrage of emotions enveloping me.

"My mom's name is Tina." I looked at Mr. Marley. "She traveled to Yellowstone and Glacier twenty-nine years ago. She was from Brooklyn."

"Tina," he said her name softly, his eyes on me, sizing me up. "Your mom is Tina from Brooklyn?"

I nodded.

"But why didn't she contact me? Why didn't she let me know? I would have been there for her. For you." He shook his head. "I don't know what to say."

"She only knew you as Lucky," I explained. "She didn't know how to contact you."

"Aw, yes," He sighed. "We knew it would only be a summer thing. I was Lucky from Paradise Valley, and she was Tina from Brooklyn. We didn't even share our ages." His face was ashen, and his hair seemed grayer as he looked me up and down. "You're my son."

I didn't know what to say. The whole thing seemed surreal. I was in complete shock. Then I looked over at Jack and Mrs. Marley, and they didn't seem so shocked. "You knew?" I asked him, my eyes narrowed. He nodded slowly.

"I did a lot of research. Hired private investigators. It was surprisingly easy to find out more information about your mom," he said. "I questioned my dad one summer, and he remembered a lot."

"I didn't even know." Mr. Marley shook his head. "I had no clue."

"I didn't know what to think or feel," Jack said. "I wanted to find my half brother and see how I felt. And then I met you. And I knew the first time that we met that you were my brother. And I also knew you were in a lot of pain. So I decided to just be your friend. I wanted to tell you. I planned on telling you when you told me about your dad. I know it sounds weird now, but I was going to be like, well, about that...when you opened up. But then you never brought him up." He sighed. "So I told my mom because I knew this could destroy her marriage. And I asked her if I should tell Dad."

"And I said no," Mrs. Marley spoke up. "I said don't tell him until we know you would want to know. Luke is like a bull. I knew that as soon as he found out, he would want to contact you, and I didn't know if that was what you needed at that moment. You were so broken, so hurt, so angry. I wanted us to be there for you. And then, when you were ready, I wanted to tell you." She sighed. "Maybe it wasn't the right decision. Maybe it wasn't our decision to make." She looked over at Jack, and he gave her a quick hug. "I just wanted the news to be something that would bring you closer to us...to Luke...and not further away."

"I understand." I nodded. And I did. I looked over at Mr. Marley. At his familiar face, his warm smile. And then I looked at Jack. He looked worried and tense. I could see it in his face. Then I looked at Pippa. The hope. The excitement. The joy. Joy for me. She'd wanted this for me. She'd understood how badly I needed to know where I came from. She knew how much this meant to me. I didn't know what else to say. I was so overcome with emotion.

She walked over to me, grabbed my hand, and squeezed. She looked up at me and gave me the biggest, most loving smile I'd ever seen. "Don't fear jumping, TJ," she whispered, "I'll always be there to catch you." She gave my words back to me, and my heart filled with love for her. I took a deep breath and stared back at my new family. My head was pounding, my body was shaking, but happiness filled me.

"I can't lie. This is a lot. But it's a good lot." I nodded slowly. "And I don't blame anyone for what happened or for when I found out. I'm just glad to know. This is so surreal." I licked my lips. "I need to process it all. I did one of those

DNA tests to help me find my birth father, but with so little information on him, it didn't give me much to go on. It must've been before Jack did his test because there were no findings of a half-sib at that time in the database, but I guess it added my information to their database for you to find out you had a half brother, Jack."

"You take all the time you need to process this, bro." Jack stepped forward and gave me a hug. I looked into his eyes—the eyes of the person that had changed my life. The friend who had taken me under his wing and brought happiness back into my life. He'd always been there for me and taken care of me since I'd known him. He'd been the best brother ever and had kept it all a secret.

"We'll have to start catching up." Mr. Marley still looked dazed. I had a feeling it would take him longer to process everything. "But when you're ready, please feel free to call me Dad because I certainly want to tell the world about my new son."

"Just what Paradise Valley needs: more gossip," Pippa said sarcastically. Her words were light and innocent, but they broke the tension in the room. She was right, of course. First, I had a mail-order bride showing up at my ranch, and now I'd found a long-lost father. I sure hoped that the rumor mill would be off of me soon.

Chapter Thirty-Five

P ippa

Dear TJ,

I was telling my friend, Lisa about our pact and she said that she's never heard of friends making a pact like that. She said she's only heard of marriage pacts. I told her that what we had was most certainly not a marriage pact.

Could you imagine if we ever got married? Wouldn't that be so weird? Do you think you could live with someone like me? Actually, don't answer that. It was a weird question.

Lisa also said she thinks we're so close because we're only children. I think we're so *close because we've always been there for each other through every step of our lives. Just know I will always be here for you.*

And if you want a marriage pact for when we're forty-five, let me know! :P

Pippa

"I cannot believe that Jack is your real brother." I sat on the couch with Apple on my lap as TJ made popcorn in the kitchen. "Isn't life crazy?"

"It can be really crazy," he said as he drank his beer. "I did something crazy last night as well."

"Oh?" I paused the TV so I could pay full attention to him. "What did you do?"

"You have to promise not to be mad." The microwave beeped, and he took the bag of popcorn out. "You want butter?"

"Of course," I said. "And some red wine."

"Oh, yes, tonight we drink." He pulled a wine bottle up out of nowhere. I watched as he grabbed a corkscrew and twisted the cork. He pulled out two glasses from the cabinet above his head and poured us each a glass. "Here's to me finding my biological dad, figuring out I have a brother and a sister, and a niece and nephew, and just to you being here."

"Are you going to tell your mom?" I asked as he brought me over a large glass of wine. "Thanks," I said as I took it from him.

"I will have to give her a call later this week."

"Awesome," I said, grinning at him. "How do you think she will take it?"

"I have no idea, but I want to handle it delicately. She's been through a lot. And I know she's still hurting from what my dad...my other dad..." He frowned. "Well, what that man did to her."

"And to you, TJ." I reached up and took his hand. "You may be in contact with your biological dad now, but that's not going to make the pain of abandonment from your other dad go away." I sighed. "That's a pain that will hurt forever. I just don't want it to hold you back from anything in life. I just don't—"

"I love how you care for me, Pippa." He sat beside me on the couch and pressed his finger to my lips. "I love how you care so deeply about me and my feelings. You've always been that person in my life. You've always made me feel special." He looked nervous. "Not having you in my life for all those years was the worst thing that has ever happened to me."

"Me too." I said. "It was so rough."

"I can't lose you again, so I did a thing. It might sound crazy. It might seem weird, but I need you in my life. I know that you have to process your last relationship and your feelings, and I don't want to rush you into anything. I didn't do this to force you to be with me. I know that we can't rush things, but—"

"What's going on, TJ?" I cut him off. "What are you talking about?"

"You said that you loved Paradise Valley. You said that if you could stay, you would." He paused. "I know you love theater and it's your dream to write and direct plays. And I think you would be fantastic at it. I think that the world needs to hear your voice and see your plays."

"Thanks, TJ. That means a lot." I beamed at him. "Those words mean everything to me."

"I bought the Paradise Valley Playhouse," he blurted out. "Well, technically, I put in an offer, but it was accepted and I'm under contract, but yeah, it's yours. You have your own theater. You can produce your own plays."

"What?" I screamed in shock. "TJ, what are you talking about? You can't buy me a theater. You can't—"

"No strings attached, Pippa. I don't want anything from you. I don't need anything from you; I just can't lose you. I don't want you to move back to New York or to England and I know that's selfish of me, but you said you loved it and I just thought..."

"That's not why I'm upset, TJ." I shook my head. "You don't have the money to buy the playhouse. How did you put in an offer?"

"I used the eighty grand I have as the deposit," he said, looking sheepish. "It's—"

"TJ Wyatt, you cannot spend your hard-earned money on me. You cannot buy me a theater." I glared at him. "That money is for your ranch. That money is for you to build your cabins. I will not let—"

"Don't you get it, Pippa? I love you." He ran his hands through his hair. "I love you more than I've ever loved anyone in my life. I've loved you since we were kids. You are everything to me. Your dreams are my dreams. I can raise more money. I can figure something else out. We didn't have long to raise money for the theater, and I know you will do the most amazing job running it. You can start living your dreams, Pippa. Don't you know that is all I want for you? That's all I want for me. Seeing you happy makes me happy. That's what it is to love someone." He grabbed my hand. "And I know this is a lot to put on you, but I can't lose you. Even if you just want to be friends. I don't care. That is enough for me."

"Oh, TJ." Tears sprung into my eyes, and I jumped up and headed toward my handbag. I opened it up, pulled out a white envelope, and walked back to the couch. "Read this," I said as I handed him the letter. He frowned as he saw Stephan's name on the envelope. "Open it, please," I said softly.

"Why?" He looked upset and confused.

"Stephan and I were supposed to go to Shakespeare in the Park and I was going to give it to him right at the end of the night."

"And you want me to read it?" He blinked in confusion. "Now?"

"Yes." I nodded, my heart racing. "No one knows this letter exists besides you and me. I didn't even tell Emma. Obviously, I never gave it to Stephan."

"Okay then, here goes." He ripped the envelope open and pulled out the yellow paper I'd written the letter on. "Shall I read it out loud?"

"Sure." I sat back, closed my eyes, and listened to him reading it.

"Dear Stephan, do you know that my salutation in this letter was the first signal something was wrong? It should say to my love or to my dearest, but those words wouldn't be true. I hate to do this by letter, but I find that I express myself best with words.

"Stephan, I have to call off the wedding. I know that this is short notice, and I apologize for that. You may be angry with me, even pissed off. You may want to scream and shout. But one thing I know is that you will not be heartbroken.

"I know this because neither of us is in this with our

hearts. Not you, and certainly not me. I don't love you and know you don't love me. We were convenient in each other's lives. It sounds weird writing that, but it is true.

"Years ago, I had a best friend. A boy called TJ. He was my best friend, and I loved him. I loved him as only an innocent child can love another. He was, I think, my soul mate. My heart has never been the same since he's been out of my life. I miss him more than I've even acknowledged to myself. The last ten years of my life have felt like I'd lost a part of myself.

"And you didn't fill that hole. In fact, you made that hole feel bigger. You made me doubt myself. You made me feel ugly. You made me feel worthless. Stupid. Like I couldn't do better. And I almost believed you.

"But then I remembered what TJ always used to tell me when we were younger: Never doubt yourself, Pippa. Even if I'm not there, I got you.

"And you know what? I'm not doubting myself, and even though TJ is no longer in my life, I've got myself. I'm going to be okay.

"I hope your ego and your pride aren't hurt too much by this letter. But we were never meant to be. Not in a million years.

"I'm walking away for you and for me.

"From the girl who finally found her voice,

"Pippa.

"You were going to leave him?"

"Yes, I was going to call it off anyway. I suppose seeing him cheating was just another slap in the face of how much of an idiot I'd been."

"But you showed up here in your wedding dress…" He frowned. "You'd been crying."

"I wanted to wear it one last time." I made a face. "I

spent a lot of money on that dress. It was a nice dress. And I was crying because I was nervous and sad and mad at myself. I'd known that relationship was dead for a long time. I didn't care. The only person constantly on my mind was you."

"Is that true?" His eyes were alight as he shifted closer to me. "Does that mean?" he asked hesitantly, and I nodded slowly.

"It means I love you, TJ. It means I've always loved you. It means that fifteen years ago, we made a pact to always be there for each other and those words are still the most important in my life."

"They're the most important in mine too, Pips," he said, pulling me onto his lap and gazing into my eyes. "Fifteen years ago, we made a pact that said we will forever be there for each other whenever we needed the other one." He ran his fingers through my hair. "Now I want to make a new forever pact," he said. "I want to promise you that I will love you forever because I cannot imagine my life without you in it. I love you, Pippa. I don't want to let you go. I want our forevers to be forever."

"I love you too, TJ." I leaned forward and ran my fingers through his hair. "I want to make a new forever pact as well because we are destined for each other. We always have been, for now and forever."

"For now and forever and ever," he said, grabbing my face and pressing his lips against mine. He kissed me as if he'd never kissed me before. He kissed me as if he would never kiss me again. He kissed me as if this were the last kiss we'd ever have. I kissed him back just as passionately. This wasn't just a forever pact. This was a love pact, and I knew we would be in love until we were old and gray. TJ was my person. My love. My everything. TJ and I made a forever pact that would continue for the rest of our lives.

* * *

"Pippa, I have something for you." TJ stood next to the couch, a stack of letters in his hands. There was a lopsided smile on his handsome face as he held them out to me. My heart raced as he sat down on the couch next to me and pressed his thigh against mine.

"What are those?" I took the letters from him and stared at the brownish envelope on the top. I read my name and studied the familiar scrawl of his handwriting. "Letters for me?"

"Ones I never sent." He nodded as he reached his arm around my shoulder and played with my hair. "In full transparency, some of them may sound hurt and slightly mean. I think I went through a passive-aggressive phase when your mom told me off and I was trying to process my feelings."

"Oh, TJ." I turned toward him and pressed my empty hand against the side of his face. "Are you sure you want me to read these?"

"As sure as I want you to be my wife one day." He nodded slowly, grabbed my hand and kissed my palm. "As sure as Donkey is that he doesn't want to be surrounded by all those other goats."

"As sure as Apple is that she wants every piece of fallen bacon she can find?" I continued and we both burst out laughing as Apple came running over to us. Her ears perked up due to hearing her name and bacon in the same sentence. "I love her." I leaned down and rubbed her ears. "She's so cute."

347

"You're so cute." TJ kissed the side of my face. "And I love you. And I love that you love my dog."

"How could I not? I love everything about this place." I placed the letters on the coffee table and kissed him on the lips. I loved the feel of his lips on mine. So warm, strong, and magical. I stroked his silky hair back behind his ears and stared into his warm blue eyes. "How did you get to be so handsome?"

"I don't know." His eyes danced as he kissed the tip of my nose. "How did you get to be so beautiful?"

"I'm not that beautiful." I giggled as he traced his finger along my cheekbone to my chin. "What are you doing?"

"Studying your face." His voice was serious as his eyes moved along every centimeter and imperfection on my face. "I want to memorize every inch of you. Your eyes, nose, lips, eyebrows, every freckle, every mole, every loose tendril of hair." He whispered as his fingers traced the freckles under my eyes like they were in a line, and he was connecting the dots. "I want to know that when I'm old and gray, even if I can't remember myself, I will always remember you."

I blinked rapidly at his words. I didn't want to cry. Even though they would be happy tears. I wasn't sure how or when it had happened. But my life was everything I'd ever hoped it could be. TJ was the perfect mate for me. He wasn't perfect, just like I wasn't perfect, but we were perfect for each other. I'd never really thought I'd meet someone like him. I never thought I'd be lucky enough to fall in love with my best friend and have him love me back.

"Promise me that when we're old and gray, we will always spend the time to just look at each other." I grabbed his hand and squeezed it. "I mean, really look at each other and feel each other's presence."

"I promise." He grabbed my face and pulled me in

closer to him. "I promise that when you talk, I will listen. When you cry, I will dry your tears. When you laugh, I will feel your joy, and when you have nothing to say, I will just hold you. And love you. And protect you. And care for you. And do everything I can to make your world perfect. Because all I want is to be the man you can depend on. I will support your dreams and always put your needs before mine."

"No, you can't do that. You have to—"

"Your needs are my needs, Pips. I love you to the end of time."

"I love you to the end of time, plus a day."

"I love you to the end of time, plus infinity." He grinned. "We're about to embark on a new phase in our lives and I wouldn't want anyone else by my side. Only you, Pips."

"I love you, TJ. This love..." I paused as he kissed me on the lips and then pulled back.

"This love is forever." He winked at me. "And that's what they call a pact."

Epilogue

Pippa

"Donkey, come here," I called out to the goat as he followed TJ toward the barn, "I got you a ball."

"He doesn't play with balls, Pippa. He's not a dog."

"I know he's not a dog, but I thought maybe he would play fetch. Apple grabs the ball, but she never brings it back."

"That's because she doesn't share well," he shouted, and then I watched as he came running back to me.

"What are you doing?" I asked him. "I thought you had to grab something from the barn?"

"I can grab it in a moment." He picked me up and swung me around. I wrapped my arms around his neck and giggled before he finally put me down. "I won't be able to do this once Emma arrives."

"Yes, you will." I squeezed his upper arms and looked at my watch. "She should be here soon." I could hear the excitement in my voice. "I can't believe she didn't want me to pick her up."

"You said she didn't know when she was going to arrive,

right?" He frowned. "Didn't she take a later flight in exchange for a big airline credit?"

"Yup, and they are flying her first class. But she didn't know when she would get on a flight." I sighed. "I just can't wait for you to meet her. I think you'll love her and she will love you too."

"As much as you love me?" He winked at me, and I shook my head.

"I don't think that's possible, Teej." I stared at him for a few seconds. "What did Mr. Marley say when he called?"

"He wants to go to lunch next week. He apologized again. Said he would love to reconnect with my mom." He looked thoughtful. "I have to speak to her and see how she feels. It's weird, Pips. All my life, I never really felt like I belonged in my family, and now, with Jack and the Marleys, they already feel like home."

"That's because they love you." I hugged him to me. "They see how wonderful you are."

"You have to say that. You're my girlfriend." He held me close and rubbed my back. "Did you tell Emma she's staying with Jack?"

"No, I was going to wait until she arrived. I mean, she's staying at the log cabin tonight. And then we'll meet Jack at Mindy's for breakfast and then she will see he's great. And I'll just be like, 'Oh, by the way, he has a big house and he's offered to let you stay.'"

"That's going to work?" he asked me, skepticism in his tone. "Maybe tell her tonight. I don't want to just spring this on her. I don't want her to think that I don't want her here. I want to win her over."

"She will love you." I grinned at him. "Trust me, you are so much better than Stephan. She will adore you."

Ring, ring.

I grabbed my phone from my pocket. Both TJ and I stared at the screen. It was my mom.

"Answer it, Pippa," he urged me. "She's your mom. She's worried about you."

"But—"

"But nothing, forgive her. We need to move on. We need to focus on us."

"Fine," I said as I answered the phone. "Hello?"

"Darling, I wanted to see how you were doing." My mom sounded like she thought we hadn't just had it out a few days previously. "And how is your friend?"

"TJ is great, Mom. And he's my boyfriend now. We've declared our love for each other, and I'm not leaving Montana," I blurted out. TJ pressed his lips together, and I saw him giving me a disapproving look. He was the one that convinced me to answer the phone.

"What?" My mom's voice sounded strained, and I was surprised she hadn't completely lost it. Maybe she was growing after all.

"I said—"

"But your job with the lord," she protested. "You have to be in New York for all the—"

"TJ bought me a theater. Because he knows how much I love being able to write and direct and he has faith that I can do this for a career."

"I thought he had no money." My mother sounded shocked. "How can he afford to buy you anything?"

"Because he used the money he was saving for his ranch to buy me a theater." The thought still made me sick to my stomach, but I didn't want to tell TJ that. He'd made the move out of love, which was the sweetest and most grand gesture anyone had ever done for me. He was an absolutely amazing man, and I wasn't sure how I would ever repay him. I looked over at him and I could see the pride on his face. The love in his eyes warmed me, and he made me feel like the luckiest woman in the world.

"You can't let him do that, Pippa. That doesn't sound like a good idea."

"He already did it, Mom. He's in contract." I tried not to sound nervous. I wasn't even sure how to run my own theater, but I didn't want to panic in front of TJ.

I was waiting for Emma to arrive. I knew she'd be able to give me good advice. There was silence on the phone as my mom processed what I'd told her.

"He loves you," she said simply as if I hadn't just told her that a few minutes ago.

"And I love him." I didn't care if it sounded weird to my mom after Stephan. I didn't care what she thought after she'd tried to ruin our friendship.

"You were both really attached to each other." She sounded like she was in a dreamlike state. "I thought it was because you were young. It was clear to see you had a connection. I thought it would die. I was wrong. I am so sorry, Pippa. I know it doesn't sound like much now."

"It really doesn't, Mom." I didn't want to be mean, but I needed to stay firm.

"I know my words don't mean much." My mom was silent again. "I want to gift you a hundred and fifty thousand dollars."

"What?" I shouted. "What are you talking about? You don't have that sort of money."

"Dad and I were going to gift it to you at the wedding. I never told you about the small inheritance Dad and I had in stocks. We were saving it for a rainy day."

"Mom, I don't—."

"I thought you were happy. I thought Stephan was

what you wanted. I was wrong, and I realize that now. Use the money to help TJ with his ranch."

"Are you sure, Mom?"

"I'm sure. He's the one for you. He loves you and you love him. You have to support him because he has supported you. And I love that for you. He's been there for you when I haven't. I will forever be indebted to him for that."

"Thank you, Mom." I grabbed TJ's hand, trying to stop myself from jumping up and down. "You don't know how much this means to me."

"I can hear it in your voice. You sound happy. Really happy. I've missed that in your voice." She sounded like she was crying. "I'm sorry, darling. So very sorry."

"Don't be sorry, Mom. Maybe you and Dad can come out and visit one day."

"I'd love that." She blew her nose. "Please give TJ my love. I can't wait to see you both."

"Okay, Mom." I paused. "Love you." I hung up the phone and looked at TJ, whose expression was full of questions.

"What's going on?" he asked me. "You sounded angry and then dazed. Does she still hate me?"

"No, she sends her love. She wants to come visit."

"She does?" He looked shocked. "Not quite ready for that yet."

"Me either." I laughed. "But maybe one day."

"She can come to our engagement party." He grinned at me, and I could feel my heart racing. He leaned down and kissed me, and I melted into him. "I love you, Pippa. In fact, I think I love you more than..." His voice trailed off as we both looked up. A black car was speeding down his driveway and came screeching to a halt. He stepped back, and we headed toward the car.

"It's Emma," I screamed excitedly as I watched her barreling out of the car, her short blond bob bouncing as she made her way to us. "Emma." I ran toward her so I could hug her. We hugged tightly for what felt like hours. "You made it."

"I made it." She pushed me an arm's length away, looking me over. "You look happy." Then she looked at our surroundings. "This really is the middle of nowhere, isn't it?"

"I would hope not." TJ came up behind me and held his hand out to her. "Hi, I'm TJ."

"So you're the infamous TJ." Emma gave him a once-over and grinned. "I see why Pippa fell for you."

"Emma!"

"I need to catch my breath," she said. "Some jacka—" She looked at TJ. "Some bad driver pulled out onto the road as I was headed here. Nearly made me crash."

"Oh no. Are you okay?"

"I'm fine. I still have my life, even though I did drive off the road for a couple of seconds, and some cowboy honked and laughed at me as he drove past in a big red Ford pickup truck. Like how country can you be?"

"This is the country," TJ said with a laugh. "I'm sure it wasn't done on purpose."

"I think it was." Emma scowled. "Stupid cowboy in his stupid truck. He should lose his license." She gasped as she pointed to the main road. "That's him. Oh my word, he's following me."

"He is? Should we call the police?" I looked over at TJ, who had a bemused expression on his face. "What's so funny, TJ?"

"Look who it is," he said, pointing to the truck as it came up the driveway. My stomach sank as I saw who it was. This was not good. This was not good at all.

"Call the police now. That...that wannabe cowboy is following me," she screamed, but then she marched over to the truck, held her hand up, and pointed at Jack as he got out of the truck. Contradicting how scared she said she felt. "What are you doing here?" She glared at him. "You nearly killed me."

"Oh no," I groaned as I looked at a grinning TJ. "What's so funny?"

"You wanna tell her that she's going to be living with that wannabe cowboy, or should I?"

Thank you for reading The Forever Pact, the first book in The Bachelors of Paradise Valley series. I hope you loved it. If you would like to read a BONUS CHAPTER from the book, you can find it here.

The next book in the series is The Last Single Cowboy, featuring Emma and Jack. You can preorder the book here.

Acknowledgments

They say no man is an island and this book would not have been completed without the support of many. First and foremost, I would like to thank God for allowing me to write for a living. I am blessed to be able to follow my dream of writing and do not take it for granted.

Secondly, I would like to thank the readers who have picked up my book and given it a chance. There are so many books for readers to choose from and I'm thankful you gave my book a chance. Even more so, if you're reading this right now.

I would also like to thank my editor Marla and proofreader Rosa for diligently going through my words and fixing the errors I missed.

I would be remiss not to thank my alpha and beta readers for going through draft #1 and providing me feedback so that I could perfect the book to the best of my ability. Thank you to Kayla Powell, Ashley Grindstaff, Waseema Chaudhri, Tiffany Price, Crystal Hahnstadt, Teddy, Vanessa Mata, Trina, Heather Haughton, Katelyn Kongable, M Killian, Megan Lubinski, Amber Voelz, Brittney Norton, Monica Cooper, Kerri Long, Deana Black, Pamela Nunn, Marabeth King, Randi Goff, Christine Catarino, April Thomas, Antonia Mancinelli, and Amanda Diaguila Stephens. If I have forgotten to include you, please accept my sincerest apologies.

Love,
Jaimie
XOXO

Also by Jaimie Casey

The Bachelors of Paradise Valley Series
The Forever Pact
The Last Single Cowboy
The Secret Diary of Mindy Messina
The Plus-Ones of Wedding Season
The Anonymous Love Confessions

www.ingramcontent.com/pod-product-compliance
Lightning Source LLC
Chambersburg PA
CBHW051324250626
47155CB00007B/2442